WEEKS AND DAYS

WEEKS AND DAYS

S.E. PHINNEY

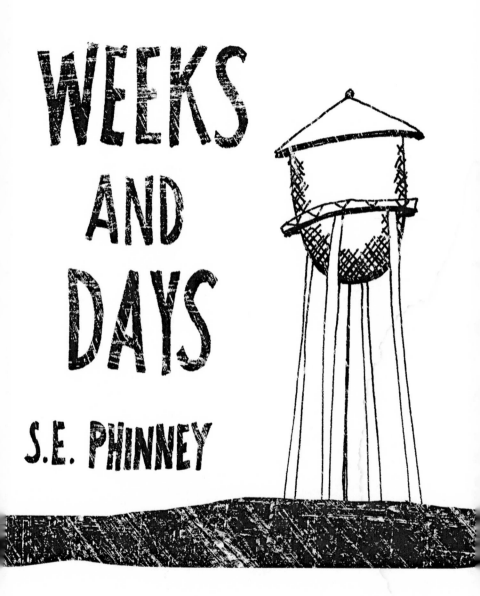

GOSSON PRESS PORTLAND, OR

Weeks and Days
Copyright © 2016 by S. E. Phinney
Published in the United States by Gosson Press

www.gossonpress.com

Library of Congress Control Number: 2015920079

ISBN 978-0-9970489-0-2 (hardcover)
ISBN 978-0-9970489-2-6 (ebook)

First U.S. Edition: April 2016

10 9 8 7 6 5 4 3 2 1

"Sorry," Stephen said, without sounding sorry at all. "You're not on this list." He paused. "You are, however, on my list."

I blinked. I was standing in front of the mostly empty candygram table, after school on Valentine's Day. I should have explained that I knew I wasn't on the list—that I hadn't received an over-decorated memo telling me I had hearts to pick up, that I hadn't even expected to receive such a memo, and that, in fact, I was only hoping I might be able to buy a leftover box for my younger sister. Tammy, at eleven, was just old enough to love Valentine's Day approximately ten million times more than any other day, but I suspected she hadn't received anything significant at school, either.

I should have been telling Stephen all of this from the start, before he even asked my name. But I guess I was just too surprised.

Even knowing he was on student council (which in itself was perplexing), Stephen wasn't the type of person anyone expects to see running a booth for valentines. That said, he was perhaps the only boy in our school who could sit alone behind a table festooned with pink crepe paper and piled with boxes of candy hearts and look neither smug nor uncomfortable. I, meanwhile, was becoming less and less comfortable with every second that passed.

I blinked again. "What?" I said.

Stephen looked up from his second clipboard. "You're not on the list for a candygram," he said. "But I made a list of all the girls who weren't getting one and you're on there. I bought a couple extra boxes, and I was going to give everybody one heart."

I stared at him.

"But then I decided that was unwise," he went on. "It's probably unsanitary, and it also has the potential to be taken disastrously the wrong way. The boxes have mixed messages, but individually… If I give someone a single heart that says 'be mine,' they're a lot more likely to think I actually mean it than if they get a whole box, where the 'be mine' is mixed in amongst seven other phrases. So I decided to do boxes instead, but my budget wouldn't support one for every girl.

"But," he said again, "you're the first girl off my list to turn up, so you get one. Here," he said, and, without a modicum of ceremony, picked up a box and held it out toward me. "Happy Valentine's Day."

After a pause that was slightly longer than I wish it had been, I took the box and thanked him. "Good," I said, and, trying to keep some dignity intact, explained about Tammy. "Now I can just give her this one."

"No you can't give it away," Stephen said, affronted. "It's a present from me."

"It's a pity gift," I said flatly.

"Well, when you put it that way."

"I don't really want a pity gift," I said. "And also, I'm fairly sure none of the other girls on your list will, either. It's not about the candy, it's about getting to think that someone likes you." Which made my idea of getting something for Tammy seem pretty useless, but then, being eleven, she'd actually eat the candy, which none of my classmates ever did. It was more the idea of it we were after. "You should have just sent them as secret admirers," I told Stephen.

"There are sixty-two girls on my list," he said. "I don't have sixty-two dollars for that kind of thing. It had to be first come, first served."

"Then you should have just picked at random. Honestly," I said, "I think most of us would rather get nothing. Can you imagine the humiliation of deciding, hoping against hope, to come up here, just in case your memo maybe got lost, squaring your shoulders and smiling brightly and asking, and then having to be told, by a normal, decent-looking boy, no less, that you're not on the list, but you are on this other list of losers that he's made, so here, you get this consolation box of cheap candy."

Again, Stephen looked affronted. "I paid higher than market value for this," he said. "These boxes are seventy-five cents each at the grocery store."

"You didn't understand the sentiment at all, did you?" I said. "That's not what I meant by cheap."

"I did," he said, then took four more boxes off the pile and held them out to me. "Here. I won't do any more."

I was surprised, and so said something asinine. "I don't really want five boxes of candy hearts."

"Give them to your sister, then," Stephen said, and raised his arm a little higher. "These four."

"But not this one," I said, giving the first box a small shake. I wanted to, but somehow couldn't quite roll my eyes. "It's special, from you, for me."

"Right," he said. "Although, if it makes her feel better,

you can tell her that these are also special, from me."

"I doubt that'll make her feel better," I said.

"It'd be rather unsettling if it did," said Stephen. "Especially as I don't know any eleven-year-olds. It might say some things about your sister that none of us wished to know."

I wasn't sure how to respond to that. I thought he was joking, but wasn't totally sure. "Well, can I at least pay you back?" I asked.

"No, just take them," he said. "Or hadn't it occurred to you that perhaps boys like giving things on Valentine's Day just as much as girls like receiving them?" He paused. "Besides, what else would I do with them? Probably no one else was going to come anyway, and I don't want five boxes of candy hearts, either."

"All right," I said, and took them. "Thanks."

"Eh," Stephen said, and shrugged.

When I got home, Tammy was face-down on her bunk bed, sobbing, which she continued to do for the rest of the day, even after I placed all five boxes of hearts on her shelf. I rubbed her back and told her that boys, and especially sixth grade boys, were idiots, and it would all get better in a couple of years.

I didn't tell her that the reason it had gotten better was that I'd finally managed to stop caring about such things; that wouldn't have helped. And I certainly didn't tell her that I hadn't properly gotten a single Valentine's token. That wouldn't have helped, either.

Tammy ate the hearts over the weekend; by Monday, all traces of red and pink had been removed from the school, and I thought that was the end of it. In fact, I'd already all but forgotten about Stephen when, a week and a half later, he came up to me in the hall. We didn't have any shared classes, and I'd rarely seen him around. I found out later that he'd abused his student council privileges to look up my schedule and find out where my locker was located.

He fell into step beside me and for several moments I thought perhaps we were just coincidentally walking in the same direction at the same speed. Then he cleared his throat and straightened his hat. "Emily, right? About what you said—that I was a normal, decent-looking boy. What did you mean by that?"

"I…" I may have stammered a bit. "I meant what it means, I guess."

"Oh," he said. "I don't suppose when you used the word decent, you used it the way some people do to actually mean, like, mad awesome." He didn't really make air quotes, but the way he said "mad awesome" made me hear it like he had. His diction was so precise; with the rounded vowels and clipped consonants, he sounded like a British radio announcer from World War II. Even though the likelihood of a British radio announcer from World War II ever having used a phrase like "mad awesome" is extremely unlikely.

"No," I told him. "I didn't."

Stephen wasn't mad awesome-looking. That doesn't mean he was ugly or unattractive, either. But there's a lot of room between unattractive and mad awesome, at least in my book. He was just normal, like I'd said.

"Well," he said, seeming unperturbed. "I didn't suppose you had. But I figured there was no harm asking."

"Oh," I said carefully. I didn't feel that way at all. I hadn't actually shot him down, but if our places had been reversed, I'd have felt like he had.

Stephen shrugged, and then said, like he knew, "We're

different, you and me. But I don't intend to waste any more time being shy. Let me be honest. It's not you, it's me. Two weeks ago, I didn't know your name to your face. I know everyone in my class—side effect of being on student council for six years—but you're not in my class."

His watch beeped then, four sharp little beeps before Stephen tapped the face, silencing it. Without breaking stride, he dug one hand into his pocket, pulled out a little case and extracted two small, white tablets, put them in his mouth at once, and swallowed. He did this all so matter-of-factly that I almost thought I'd imagined it.

"Until the, er, candygram incident, I didn't know anything about you," he went on, as if nothing unusual had happened. "I still don't know anything about you, other than your name, that nobody sent you anything for Valentine's, that you have an equally undesired younger sister, and that you think I'm normal."

For some reason, I latched onto the last part, rather than taking offense at what he'd said about Tammy and, with only negligible misdirection, implied about me. "Normal-*looking*," I said, even though I remembered that wasn't exactly what I'd told him.

Stephen shrugged again. "I'll take that."

I wasn't at all sure what was happening. And, while he may have looked all right, I also wasn't at all sure any more that normal was an appropriate adjective to apply to Stephen.

He glanced at the numbers on the doorway we were passing. "I can't accompany you any further in this direction," he told me. "I'll be late for seventh period. But we'll speak again later, all right?" He was still using the English accent.

"Are you for real?" I asked. I couldn't help it.

He'd already started heading back the way we'd come, but for a few steps he turned, walking backward to look at me. He smiled; it was just the slightest bit crooked. "For now," he said.

He showed up at my locker after school a few days later. "What are you doing this weekend?" he asked.

"Why?" I responded.

"Would you like to do something?" he said. And then, when I didn't immediately reply, "I didn't have anything in particular in mind. What do you like?"

I didn't really have a lot of experience with teenage boys. I had an older brother, but he was much older, already twenty-three. I'd been too young to pay much attention when he was a teenager, and even if I had, it'd been so long ago that most of it probably wouldn't have been relevant any more.

So if there'd been nothing special about Stephen, I wouldn't have known. But I liked how direct he was. In my mind, there were two types of teenage boys. Type one: fictional, boys who were amazing and implausible and, like Stephen, direct—the kind of boy who would decide he liked a girl (usually an odd girl), walk up and declare his intentions, and summarily sweep her off her feet—in other words, perfect boys who, in real life, didn't actually exist.

And type two: the regular ones, whose numbers were made up by, among others, all of my male classmates, who were basically ordinary, who liked sports and belching and girls with bigger breasts than I'd ever have, and none of whom would ever unexpectedly approach a girl in the manner described above—unless he were one of those unfortunate, unintentionally creepy persons who goes through life without ever learning acceptable ways of behaving socially, and in that case, there would be no sweeping off of feet.

Despite behavior that meant he either belonged in the unintentionally creepy camp or was a fictional character, Stephen didn't come across as too socially off, and he'd assured me the other day that he was, in fact, real.

I was forced to revise, quickly, my previous assumptions about males between the ages of roughly twelve and twenty-five. I knew that Stephen didn't play sports (though he may well have watched them) and he probably burped after eating or drinking, and probably did spend a fair amount of time making eye contact with girls' chests—but it was also true that, on this occasion and on our previous two encounters, he hadn't behaved in any of the prescribed regular teenage boy ways. In fact, he was doing a pretty good impression of a fictional character—just, without the fictional part.

"I don't know," I said. I meant more along the lines of "I don't know if I want to do something with you," because at that point I was still kind of thinking he had to be too good to be true. There was bound to be some fatal flaw—or worse, an elaborate joke—because if any girl in the school was going to get a fictional character come to life asking her to hang out, the very last girl it would be would be me.

Not because I wasn't a little odd, like those girls usually are. But I always found it a bit hard to believe in books where some perfect boy would inexplicably fall in love with this radically, deliberately unusual girl who he'd never even spoken to before. Also, I wasn't that odd—not radically, and certainly not deliberately. (That, rather, would be my friend Mari.) I was more just on the periphery.

In other words, I didn't want to get my hopes up.

Even though I also kind of did, because every girl's dream, no matter how impractical she knows it is, is that a contemporary young adult fictional romance will happen to her.

Stephen's response demonstrated that he had interpreted my "I don't know" as in regard to his query about what I liked, not doubt about, well, him. "Not even one thing?" he said. "I get that at this stage in life, most of us are still figuring ourselves out. That's reasonable to expect. But you must know at least one thing you like, even if it turns out to be something you later can't stand and you're mortified to look back and reflect that you spent time on such a pursuit."

He was right—about the first part. I didn't know what I liked, nor who I was. I was, I suppose you could say, in between identities. I stayed at home, and read a lot. Reading a book isn't really something you can do this weekend with another person, so instead, I asked Stephen what he liked.

He didn't answer me. "Tell you what," he said. "Do you like helicopters?"

As a matter of fact, I did not like helicopters, and I told him so.

"I have a fear of heights myself," he said. "But I'm getting over it." He paused. "I didn't mean going up in it. Apparently there's some kind of historical airshow this weekend. My neighbor's a mechanic," he added, as if this would explain why he knew such a thing. "But what about hiking?" he suggested, switching without preamble. "How do you feel about hiking?"

"It's still calendar winter," I said. Yes, spring was starting to show, but we had three more weeks before the equinox, and it wasn't all that unusual to get moderate to heavy snowfalls as late as mid-March.

"Yes, the twenty-first," he agreed. "That's too long to

wait. So, if you're expecting snow, there's skiing."

He was joking. At least, I think he was joking. For some reason, this unsettled me. "I'm sorry," I said. "I'm going to miss my bus."

It didn't occur to me until later that he must have known I was lying, because it had been at least fifteen minutes after the bell when I'd finally left him at the candygram table the first time we'd talked.

"I'll drive you," he said anyway.

I shut my locker slowly and put my backpack on only halfway. It was awkward with just one strap, but it was my way of demonstrating that I still wasn't sure if I wanted to go with him. He seemed aware of it, and didn't say anything until we were in the parking lot.

He had a fairly nondescript car, sort of an older, less offensive forerunner of a sport utility vehicle, rougher around the edges, too angular to be boxy. If I'd been guessing, I would've said it was a decade or more older than we were. Probably a manual transmission.

We stood side by side in front of the hood, and Stephen looked over at me. "We call it the wagon," he said, like a name. "It was my grandfather's until he got too old to drive; then he kept it in storage until I was old enough. He gave it to me on my birthday, against my parents' express wishes. He said it'd be a good starter car, because you can get into crashes in it, and afterwards, nobody'll be able to tell the difference."

"Have you?" I asked.

"Crashed? No. But I suspect he'll have." He fished his keys out of his pocket and looked at me again. "Do you have your license?" he asked; I nodded. "You can drive, if you want. I'm not always the most... reliable driver."

This, in combination with the revelation that he'd been

given the vehicle at least in part because of its ability to hide evidence of previous damage, was not entirely reassuring. I stood on my toes and leaned forward to look through the windshield, then fell back. "I can't drive stick shift," I said.

"We can remedy that in future," he told me. Then he spun the keyring around his finger and walked to the driver's door. "Come on," he said. "I'm not that unreliable."

Stephen's driving was fine. In fact, compared to that of the average high school student, it was probably very good— good enough that I even started to relax. We were halfway through town before I realized he hadn't asked me any directions. I opened my mouth, then stopped, and decided not to say anything. Not because I believed he would somehow know where I lived. Just to see what would happen.

What happened was a cul-de-sac at the edge of town, in an older development that no one had ever gotten around to building anything beyond. Stephen's house was slightly left of center at the end of the loop, with a two-car garage and an empty double-wide driveway, and a third spot in gravel to the left of the other two. Stephen parked in the gravel, and turned to look at me as he unbuckled his seatbelt. "Here we are, then," he said brightly.

"I thought you meant you were going to drive me home," I said. "Like, to *my* home."

"Oops," he said. "Sorry."

"Did you do this on purpose?" I said.

Stephen didn't look away, or seem chagrined or embarrassed, or even lie, like I'd thought he might. He looked right at me, shrugged one shoulder, and smiled. "Possibly," he said.

We went in through the garage door, which led through the laundry room, up two steps, and then into the kitchen. The dining room was small and cluttered. One of the four places at the table was covered with a near-solid layer of papers and envelopes, a small calculator, and various household detritus. I guessed Stephen was an only child.

The left side of the dining room was open to the living room, where a gleaming picture window looked out on the backyard. Stephen led me straight past it and into a long hall. "Bathroom," he said, knocking lightly on the first door we passed; then, as we reached the end of the hall and he nudged the last door open, "and me.

"Rather small, isn't it?" he said conversationally. "But then, the whole house is. And it was much better when I still had a twin bed. But when my parents upgraded theirs, they decided I ought to have the old one. It is a nice bed," he admitted. "Just, a bit like trying to fit a porpoise into a fish tank." He paused. "That said, since I got it, I've never had the slightest difficulty playing lava in here."

I could easily see how that might be true.

"Do you like lava?" Stephen asked, then clarified, "The game, not the substance."

I hadn't played lava in years, of course, but I remembered it being fun. However, I could also see how choosing to play a two-person game of lava in a teenage boy's bedroom could quickly lead to having to make the sort of decisions that I was not, at that point in my life, eager or prepared to make. "Does anyone like lava, the substance?" I asked instead.

"I'd like to touch it," he said. "The substance, not the floor." He'd sat down on the corner of the bed and, I'd noticed, placed his hands under his thighs, holding the bottoms of his feet just a hair up from the ground. After standing awkwardly for another moment, I sidestepped and sat facing him, on the edge of a hard-backed chair just inside the door. I tucked my feet up on the bottom rung, in the spirit of things.

"Theoretically, of course," he told me. "I mean, there is a reason we aren't touching it. Maybe I'd just like to see it, for real. It's on my list."

"Really?" I said. "You have a list?"

"Well, not really. I just want to do as much as I can, while I still can. But if I did have one, that would be on it. And now I'll ask you again: what would you like to do?"

I shifted slightly on the chair, because I really didn't know.

"Anything," Stephen said. "Anything you want. It doesn't have to be realistic. You can walk on the moon. Become a celebrity. Break the Guinness record for world's longest fingernails."

I looked down at my hands, where the nails were bitten down so far that my fingertips resembled the deformed digits of someone afflicted with elephantiasis. "Maybe not that one," I said, then looked up at Stephen. "Were you one of those boys who was continually checking out the illustrated version of the *Guinness Book of World Records* from the library in fourth grade?"

"You're very good at changing the subject," he said. "To answer your question, no, I was not. But everybody's seen those crazy curling fingernail pictures." He shuddered a bit. "And it doesn't have to be special, either," he said, as if there had been no horrible-fingernail-induced interruption. "Maybe you just want to eat a really good ham and cheese sandwich. No? Join a marimba band?" he suggested. "Learn to drive stick? Do a cartwheel in the rain?"

"A cartwheel in the rain?" I repeated. I know a lot of people have fantasies about doing things in the rain (obviously they're imagining a different, warmer and gentler, rain than the sort we get), but I think those fantasies are usually more along the lines of kissing than acrobatics. "Really? Do *you* want to do a cartwheel in the rain?" I asked him.

Stephen shook his head. "Been there, done that. Got my hands very muddy. If you attempt it, I'd suggest you do so right after it commences raining. Don't wait for the ground to get saturated."

I couldn't imagine Stephen doing a cartwheel, in any kind of weather, but this wasn't the kind of story you made up.

"It wasn't a very good cartwheel. I almost fell over because one of my hands got sucked in. Of course, it likely wouldn't have been a very good cartwheel even without that," he said. "And I'd advise you to use someone else's yard," he added. "My mum was very upset about the mess I made in the lawn. I had to tell her a burrowing animal must've done it." He smiled, and I did too. "But I doubt she'd've believed me if I'd told the truth, either, so there is that."

"Why a cartwheel in the rain?" I asked him.

He was quiet for a moment. Then, "Because I could," he said. "Think about it. You're sixteen, am I right? You're young, and healthy, and there are a lot of things you can do now that, physically, you won't be able to do fifty years from now, or thirty, or ten, or perhaps even fewer. Perhaps there're even things you were once able to do but even now find you can't.

"Sometimes," he said, "on family visits, I'll sit and watch my little cousins play. They can run and run and run and never get tired. I firmly believe you could enter any average, untrained six-year-old in a marathon, and he'd finish near the top of the pack. And we all used to be able to do that, you know. Or at least the vast majority. But I couldn't do that now. Could you?"

He didn't wait for me to answer, but I supposed the

answer was obvious. I could no more run a marathon than I could walk on the moon. "That's why," he said. "There's only so much time. There're only so many chances." He paused. "I don't mean to sound so much like a pretentious motivational ass."

"That's just your voice."

Stephen laughed, which was what I'd hoped would happen. It was true that, now I'd heard a bit more, he didn't always sound like he was speaking the Queen's own English, but he did still sound a lot more posh than anyone I'd ever met.

"Yes, well," he said. "It's a bit of a funny story. When I was in fifth grade, our neighbors hosted a foreign exchange student for a year—Juan Martín. He was great; I idolized him. My parents paid him to come over on the weekends and teach me Spanish, but I think he would've come over sometimes, anyway. He called me Thtephen, even when we were speaking English. Apparently everyone in Spain has a lisp. It's what first got me interested in accents."

"Hm," I said. "I hope you don't expect me to believe you've been speaking with a Spanish accent all this time."

"No, of course not," Stephen said. "Don't think I'm being disloyal to Juan Martín, but I decided I didn't fancy affecting a speech impediment. We watched a David Attenborough documentary at the beginning of seventh grade science, though, and that, I'll admit, had more appeal. So I went through puberty," he said, very proper. "And when I emerged, my voice had broken into Received Pronunciation."

Stephen took me home early, before either of my parents returned from work. He didn't walk me to the door, but he did wait at the curb, engine idling, until I'd made it inside. Before

I got out, he leaned over and said, very seriously, "Emily. I want you to think of something."

"What?" I asked. That could mean anything.

"Something you like. Something you want to do," he told me. "I understand you're a private person, but I'd really like to know. Even if it's something that winds up meaning nothing."

I was flustered. This was the same boy who'd talked about tearing up the lawn, doing cartwheels in a rainstorm. Who, as we'd left, had stood up on the bed and jumped from its corner to the hall, crashing halfway into the door-frame as he did so, to avoid the imagined lava I'd already forgotten about. And now he seemed so very serious. "I—okay," I said.

"Good," said Stephen.

I managed to fumble out of my seatbelt, and fled before he could say anything else.

That weekend, I was distracted. Mari was retaking the SAT the following Saturday, and cramming like a woman possessed. She responded to my calls by letting me go to voicemail, then texting "STOP!!!" and finally just turning her phone off. It wasn't really unreasonable, but it almost made me wish I'd decided on a retake, too.

Homework was no help, either; I finished everything easily—more easily than I would've hoped, in fact, as studying would've been a welcome focal point. Once everything was done, I drifted through the house in a mild daze, thinking about Stephen.

This sounds like a crush, the behavior of a suddenly lovesick teenage girl. But it wasn't a crush; I wasn't thinking of him that way. I didn't obsess over his many fine qualities (actual or exaggerated), or imagine scenarios in which he might declare his love for me.

Instead, I was trying to unravel him, analyzing his behavior combined with everything that he'd said. He didn't come out like any other person I'd ever known, and not just because of his manner of speaking. Chiefly, there were two things that bothered me, two things I couldn't figure out.

One was his directness. He'd been so open, so unafraid. These were characteristics I associated, quite intimately, with confidence, which itself was something I typically associated with someone at the very top of his game. I'd known who he was, but nothing more; Stephen, while not actively disliked, also wasn't exactly a paragon of popularity.

I supposed he could have been behaving as he did because he was at the opposite end of the spectrum, absolute rock bottom, and had nothing to lose, but that didn't strike me as right, either; such circumstances didn't usually inspire confidence. Besides, he'd hidden nothing, except—and this was thing number two—the reason for his interest in me.

It couldn't, I told myself, be something so simple as the fact that I'd said, in a moment of preoccupation, that he was decent-looking. I supposed I'd been pretty bold going up to him at the candygram table the way I had—and then, to top it off, taking him to task for planning (however unintentionally) to break girls' hearts even more than they were already broken. Maybe he was attracted to that.

Or maybe he supposed he'd broken my heart, too, and was trying to make up for it. Pity friendship.

That wasn't a flattering thought.

I tried not to think about any of it. And I tried to tell myself I didn't owe Stephen anything. Yes, he'd asked me to think of an answer and I'd told him I would, but he hadn't extracted an actual promise. The more I thought about it, though, the more I realized I wanted to know, myself. It isn't always fun being sixteen, even in the best of circumstances. And it's even less fun when you know you're not happy, but have no idea what you want to be doing instead.

I wasn't sure how things with Stephen were supposed to work. We both knew where one another's houses were located, and obviously he'd managed to find my locker, but we hadn't traded phone numbers or added each other on anything. We didn't have any classes together. I didn't even know if we were on the same schedule for lunch. And I didn't have any way of finding out. Which was just as well; I wasn't sure, either, that I wanted to be the one to approach him in the first place.

I didn't think I'd bored Stephen completely to tears Friday, and he was, allegedly, waiting on an answer from me. But I couldn't bring myself to believe that that might be in any way urgent or important to him. I guess I expected he'd find me eventually.

Of all the possibilities for eventually that I imagined, Monday morning was not one of them. When I left for school at seven fifteen, Stephen was parked squarely at the end of the walkway leading to our front door. He'd turned the engine off and I could see through the window that he was simply sitting, still and patient, hat pulled down and collar turned up. He wasn't even watching the house.

I walked around the back of the wagon and knocked, rather hard, on the front window. Stephen jumped; he must not have noticed me before. We stared at each other for several moments, and then he started to roll the window down. "What are you doing?" I demanded, when he'd gotten it about halfway.

He finished rolling. "Giving you a ride to school," he said.

I continued to stare at him. The air inside the cab, I noticed, was only marginally warmer than outside. "How long have you been here?" I asked.

"Ten minutes, maybe," he said, without looking at his watch. "Fifteen, tops. I wasn't sure when you'd leave. I didn't want to miss you."

"Why?" I asked.

"Why?" he repeated, looking a bit confused. "Well, I'd feel rather stupid sitting here all morning if you'd already gone off and gotten there yourself."

I shook my head. "No, why are you giving me a ride?"

"Oh," Stephen said, and sort of shrugged. "I didn't think you'd mind."

It was obvious to me that I would accept. I didn't think he was the type to follow me at a crawl the entire trip to the bus stop, so it wasn't that I didn't want to take that chance. It just seemed silly to insist on the bus when someone was already waiting with a car, hoping to take me right there. Still, I hesitated.

"You might want to get in on the other side," Stephen said. "Unless," he added, a bit carefully, "you wanted to sit in the back. The seat pops forward," he explained. "Although ideally not with me in it."

I walked to the passenger side, around the front this time. Stephen rolled up his window fast, then reached over and popped the latch to my door so it opened, however minimally, just before I got there. I supposed it was his attempt at being chivalrous. I got in (staying in the front seat), and he turned the key in the ignition. The heat came on immediately, full blast.

"You must get to school early," he said, a few blocks away.

I said something imprecise about my bus's circuitous route.

"Oh," Stephen said.

"And you?" I asked after another block, even though this was shaping up to be one of the most banal conversations I'd ever had. But "oh" seemed like too odd a place to leave it.

"No," he said. "Well, occasionally if Kyle"—that was Kyle Santiago, the senior class president—"wants to have a meeting and can't get Mrs. Chalmers"—that was the class advisor—"to approve us all missing class, we'll meet early. But otherwise, no, I generally tend to make it in right before the bell rings."

"Oh," I said (which, as far as finding a decent place to leave the conversation, did nothing to help).

"Would you like me to buy you a coffee?" he said after a while.

"Oh," I said (yet again). "I don't actually…"

"Drink coffee?" he finished, smiling. "That's all right. I don't, myself. That's always the problem. Sometimes I wonder what trying to go on dates is like for adults who don't drink alcohol, either. Not that I was suggesting a date," he added quickly. "Nobody goes on a date at seven in the morning on their way to school."

"It's more like seven twenty-five," I said, and immediately, inwardly, cringed.

"Well," said Stephen. We were stopped at a light, the first car at the intersection. He drummed his fingers against the top of the steering wheel, though not loudly enough to be audible, and looked over at me. "What about juice? Can I buy you a juice?"

"It's okay," I said. "Really, I'm okay."

"Because I think I'd really like some juice right now," he said anyway. At the next intersection, he turned left instead of right, and a few blocks later pulled up to a natural foods store. He put the parking brake into place and looked at me. "Please don't stay out here," he said.

I'd been inside a few times before—my dad liked the bulk bins—but not frequently enough, nor recently enough, to know where things were kept. Stephen, on the other hand, led me directly to refrigeration. "Are you sure—" he started.

"I can buy my own juice," I said. Perhaps I snapped it. Mornings, I will readily admit, are not my favorite time of day.

"All right, all right," he said, taking an exaggerated step back and holding up his hands (the effect was slightly spoiled by the plastic bottle in one). While we waited for the cashier, he looked at me sideways. "At least you're being decisive," he said, "for once."

"Do you want to try my kind?" he asked, when we were back in the wagon. I couldn't tell if he was being worryingly solicitous or just concerned about my apparent unwillingness to try new things. I had a bottle of orange juice, pulp free. He had blueberry-pomegranate.

"No," I said. "It's okay."

"Okay," he repeated. He pulled back out of the parking lot.

"I'm sorry," I said finally; I couldn't stand the silence. There was the engine, and the sound of the heater, and, periodically, at red lights and some stop signs, the sound of Stephen swallowing another mouthful of juice that appeared to have roughly the same consistency as Greek yogurt.

"What?" he said. He looked at me so suddenly we swerved a little bit.

I swallowed. "Morning's not really my best time," I told him.

"Oh," Stephen said, shrugged and smiled. "Well. That."

He parked at the edge of the student lot, though it was still only half full. "So," he said. I stopped trying to unfasten my seatbelt and looked up at him. "Did you have something to tell me?"

Mentally, I froze. For a moment I almost hoped he was expecting some sort of extended apology. Then I realized what he must have meant: the thing he'd asked about last week. The answer he was waiting for. And I had actually thought of something—or rather, remembered something—but I didn't respond.

"It's okay," he said finally, lightly. "You don't have to if you don't want. But I'd like it if you did." He took another sip of juice—a half sip, compared to the previous. Maybe he had better control when he wasn't driving.

I looked down. "It's stupid," I said.

"Really," Stephen said, in a very flat tone that did an excellent job of indicating disbelief.

"You'll think it's stupid," I amended.

"I won't think it's stupid," he said. "Really. Are you not remembering the things I said?"

"I want to learn to develop film," I said in a rush, before I could talk myself out of it.

Stephen didn't say anything for a moment. For me, it was an almost impossibly long moment. Then, "All right," he said.

"All right?" I repeated. I may have slightly panicked. "All right what? All right it is stupid?"

"Of course not, no," Stephen said. "All right, we can do that, then."

I blinked.

"The community college has a darkroom," he went on. "I assume they let it by the hour; they do with everything else. Or, you're old enough, you could probably take an actual class. They have a lot of evening classes. Spring term probably starts soon."

"Oh," I said. "Well, but, I don't actually want to take pictures. Just develop the film. And make the prints, I guess. But not the camera part. If I just wanted to take pictures, I could use my phone." I paused. "I think what I want is the physical, tactile part. Taking a reel full of transparent tape and exposing it to certain liquids for a certain time and turning it into tiny little images, and then projecting those images onto a blank piece of paper with a certain kind of light, and certain other chemicals, and when you're all done, it's worked, and you've made something out of nothing."

"Arguably," said Stephen, "there are a lot of ways you could make something out of nothing."

"But it's not the same. Even a drawing isn't the same, because you go through all the steps gradually, you fill in the details, you do the sketching. Every single detail is down to you—your ability, and your choice. Film is different. It's more like…"

"Magic," Stephen said.

I nodded. "Magic."

"And I suppose," he said, "if someone else takes the actual, original pictures for you, then it's even more so."

I hadn't thought of that. "Yes," I said, "but that's not why. Pictures don't mean as much any more. We all have thousands now; anybody can point and click. Honestly, I'm slightly surprised you even knew what film and darkrooms are."

"You wound me," Stephen said. "Film isn't that archaic."

"Sorry," I said. "I didn't mean—I just meant that—"

Stephen shrugged. "People forget."

"Or they learn too much more. There's not a lot left now that's still magic."

"Precious little," he said. "Well, I'll be your photographer, if you want. I suppose I can point and click as well as anyone."

"Oh." I blinked. I don't know what I'd expected for his response, but I'm sure it wasn't that.

"Why did you think I would think it was stupid?" Stephen asked.

"I—well. Because people who want to do photography are supposed to want to take pictures. But I don't care about the pictures in the end. I mean, not really. I just care about making them. Also, it *is* archaic."

"Fair enough," he said. "Although I still don't. Think it's stupid, that is. Anything you legitimately want to do, that makes you happy doing, shouldn't be laughed at. Nor need to be rationalized."

"Well," I said. "Thanks."

Stephen drank some more juice, holding the bottle in his left hand. His right hovered over the belt release. "We should probably go," he said. "It must be near eight."

He was right. The lot had filled considerably. He pulled his bag from the back seat, and we got out at the same time. His door was closer to the building, and he stood at the corner of the hood and waited for me.

"I'll see you after school, then," he said as we walked, threading between the unevenly-parked cars. I didn't say anything. "I hope I've not been too forward," he said.

"No," I said, surprising myself a bit. "It's okay. Well, no, I mean, you kind of have. But it's okay."

It was cloudy, but Stephen looked at me and smiled like the sun was in his eyes.

Stephen was waiting at my locker at the end of the day; his last class must have been very nearby. "You didn't exactly say yes or no. But I thought to save you the circuitous bus ride..." he said, and held up his key. I thought about it for a moment. Then I shrugged.

"Do you have homework?" he asked as we walked. "Or are you bored?"

"Uh," I said.

"That was supposed to be my subtle way of asking if you want me to take you directly home. Having homework," he said, with air quotes in his voice, "was supposed to be your excuse for bowing out graciously, without me having to hear, so indiscreetly, that you'd rather not spend any more time in my presence."

I blinked at him. "That was..."

"Convoluted?" he suggested.

"I don't know," I said. "I mean, it made sense, but just... the way you said it."

"Oh." He nodded like he knew what I meant. "Sometimes I forget I'm not a journal article?"

"Er," I said.

"I said it, you didn't," he reminded me. "No offense taken. I only hope you don't mind."

"No," I admitted.

"Good," he said. "So then, do you have homework or not?"

"I always have homework," I said.

He gave me a huge, and obviously fake, smile. "Oh. Okay."

"But I didn't mean it like you meant it," I rushed to say. "I just meant—it's junior year; don't they say that's the hardest? So of course I always have homework. Didn't you, last year?"

"Oh, right," he said. "Let me rephrase, then: do you have a lot of homework? Or any that needs to be seen to with expedience?"

I raised my eyebrows. It wasn't just the accent that set his speech apart, I was realizing, it was the vocabulary. "None with... expedience," I said.

"You're in luck, then." He walked around and unlocked the passenger door for me before walking back to his own side and getting in. "Someone just spent his utterly useless leadership period on the phone with the registrar at Hayworth."

Hayworth was the local community college. Of course.

I decided, for the moment, to be more interested in leadership. "Really?" I said. "Utterly useless?"

Stephen looked over at me and smiled halfway. "Do I really seem like a leader to you?" He waited a moment, then reversed out of the spot. "Good choice, not answering," he said. "But it's true. It's a required class, because I'm in the student council, but there are two periods of leadership, and they put Kyle and Bonham in one, and Shelly and me in the other. Kyle's good, but he can't do anything without Shelly because he really, really needs her to keep him on task, and Shelly knows everything about everything, but can't come up with anything new on her own. Bonham and I don't really do much."

Bonham was the senior class vice president. He played football, but he was the kind of person who'd never bothered with wearing a letterman jacket, because everybody already knew who he was, and not just from sports. He had one of those personalities. Shelly was the secretary, but she was more reserved. I didn't know her at all.

"To be honest," Stephen said, "mostly I just sit there and watch people paint banners.

"Today, I told Mr. Clemens we were thinking of doing a sort of 'options for post-secondary education' pamphlet for people who didn't apply to four-year colleges, and needed to talk to someone at Hayworth. Probably unnecessary bother; I doubt he would've cared if I'd just walked over and started using the phone. He doesn't actually teach us anything; he uses leadership as prep for his other classes. They just need an adult to be in the room.

"Anyway," he said, drawing the word out, "they've got intro to black and white photography Tuesday evenings from six to eight forty-five. Term starts tenth of March, or, well, Tuesday, so the eleventh. You can take it dual credit, non-credit, or college credit only, prices vary. Oddly enough, dual credit seemed the best value, so I put you down for that."

"Wait," I said. "Put me—you didn't actually sign me up for this, did you?"

"It starts next week," he said. "Now's not the time to be waiting around. But no, I didn't. I had all the other information, but the counseling office's printed records only show the last four digits of your social, and believe it or not, the computers require an administrative password to see the rest."

He said this in a completely neutral voice, while navigating a left-hand turn, uphill from a stop, across two lanes of traffic. I think I ought to be forgiven for not immediately being able to tell he was making a joke. I simply stared at him instead.

"Relax," Stephen said, once the road was more

manageable. "I never. They don't print out your social, any part of it—or at least, if they have, it's not kept any place I can get to. All I know is your name and schedule and locker assignment. Which I'll admit may seem slightly invasive, but everyone can see that. You know the paper they give you on the first day of school, with your schedule in all capitals and a bunch of weird numbers printed in Courier New? They print two copies of it. You get one; the other goes in a binder. One for each year, alphabetical order. They're on a little table in the back of the counseling office. Anybody could walk in and see."

"Anybody?" I repeated. I found this somewhat difficult to believe. The printouts had not only locker numbers, but also combinations, on them.

"All right, I'll admit that at this point, the counseling staff probably assume I'm visiting on student governmental business when I drop by," he said. "If a non-elected official were to try, they might be challenged."

"Oh," I said. This made more sense. "No offense," I told him, "but I really can't believe you're an elected student government official."

"No," said Stephen. "Neither can I."

Stephen took me through to his room quickly; I still hadn't had the chance to really look around the house. I had expected we'd keep to the living room, but, as on Friday, neither of his parents were there, so perhaps he was capitalizing on their absence. It made sense.

The year before, I had been partnered for an English assignment with a boy named Jeremy, who, in terms of romantic prospects, had significant negative value. Nevertheless, I valued my grade (if not necessarily the time required to be spent with Jeremy), so I brought him home after school one day to study. I had planned to use the desk in my bedroom, but was surprised, upon entering, to find my father sitting there. He had taken the afternoon off work and been waiting for the past hour. He marched Jeremy and me back to the dining table, then spent the next three hours "reorganizing" the kitchen cabinets so he could keep an eye on our every move.

On that point, however, perhaps my dad—having just finished raising a teenage boy, and prior to that, been one himself—was being a bit overprotective. I was his daughter and Jeremy was an unknown quantity. An unknown quantity who, it turned out, could hardly have been less suave if he'd been a mollusk, but Dad couldn't have known that.

I wasn't sure yet where Stephen fit on the suave scale. In honesty, suave didn't seem like the right sort of word for him at all. On the other hand, though, I was fairly impressed, in spite of myself, with how much he'd already been able to coax me into doing.

I sat in the chair by the door again. Stephen sat where he'd sat before, too, cross-legged, then reached across and picked up the laptop that sat on the little desk beside his bed. "We can sign up now," he said, placing it on the bed next to him, sideways so I could see the screen. "The woman I spoke to said it's actually much easier now to enroll online than on paper, even for a first-time student."

"We?" I said. I didn't know if it was some sort of inverted royal we (which seemed the most likely), or if he meant more along the lines of "you'll sign up, and I'll help you," or if he really did mean we as in "you and me, both of us, together."

"Yes," he said. "You need me for the pointing and click-ing, so I assume I ought to be there for at least some of the class bit, and I doubt they'll let me sit in for free."

"Oh," I said. "Are you sure?" This was all happening very quickly.

"Sure. But I'll just be a community member, I think. Here we are, then." He'd already pulled up the course catalog on the college website. "Unless you think your parents wouldn't approve," he said quickly, looking up. "Is eight forty-five too late for you to be out on a school night?"

It was so ridiculous I didn't know how to answer. I didn't even have a curfew; I'd never needed one. Then again, my father tended to get a bit less permissive in situations where members of the opposite sex were involved. If he found out I was taking the photography class with Stephen, rather than alone, it was not outside the realm of possibility that eight forty-five might indeed be too late.

"Of course not," I said. The promise of dual credit, I figured, would be enough to convince my dad. The fact that I had taken the initiative and already signed up might help, too. I leaned forward, elbows on my knees. "How do I do this?"

"Here." Stephen didn't actually pat the bed, just laid his left hand down next to him for a moment.

I hesitated, then decided that even if worse came to worst, at the very least there would be a fairly sturdy-looking laptop between us. And also that it would be a lot easier to type from over there than it would if I maintained my current position. Actually, not much at all was tenable about my current position. Still, when I moved to the bed, I sat on the other corner.

Stephen immediately moved two feet closer, then picked up the computer and planted it in my lap, leaning over to move the cursor around, showing me where to click. The outside of his thumb, resting against the edge of the frame, brushed my leg for a moment. Then he seemed to realize and lifted it back up, holding it in the air awkwardly, the same way he'd held his feet off the carpet before. He kept talking to me as if there had been no change.

"Well, that's that, then," he said when we were both done (save the payment of fees, which my parents—Mom, perhaps, rather than Dad—would have to take care of). He closed the laptop and moved it back to the desk, and looked at me.

"Thanks," I said.

Stephen shrugged.

"What do you want to do?" I asked, then, so he would know I was speaking more hypothetically than asking about that moment, added, "Aside from touching lava, I mean."

"Everything," Stephen said.

I frowned. "That's not very specific," I told him. I was sure that if I'd simply said "everything" when he had first asked me, he wouldn't have deemed it an acceptable answer.

"I have a few things in mind," he said after a moment. "Can I get back to you?"

"All right," I said. Fair was fair.

"Do you—" he said, then hesitated. "Is there anything you'd like to do in the shorter term?"

"You mean like right now?" I asked.

"Yes," he said, smiling. "I mean like right now."

"Um," I said.

Stephen leaned back a little and stretched, then leaned forward again and stood. "Right now," he said, looking down at me, "I'd like a really good ham and cheese sandwich. Later I'll need to do math homework. In the interim, would you like to go for a walk?"

"I could go for a walk," I said. I assumed he meant with him.

"Good," said Stephen. In the kitchen, he put me at the far end, with him between me and all the appliances except the microwave, which was so large it appeared almost threatening. "You can sit on the counter if you want," he said, nodding to the clear spot behind me. "Mum's not home."

I pulled myself up and watched him move along the kitchen, opening and closing drawers and cupboards and the fridge. "Do you want anything?" he asked. "I make really good sandwiches."

I told him I'd be okay.

"What kind of bread should I use?" he asked. He'd covered almost an entire section of counter with an array of sandwich fixings, and was holding up three loaves of bread, none of which were pre-sliced. "Pumpernickel, spelt and white, or this new one with Asiago cheese blended in and"— he set down the other two and held the bag close to his face, squinting through the plastic window—"that looks like caraway? Well?"

My dad, no doubt, would've had a great answer for him. I didn't. We always had whole-grain bread at home, but I was still used to the kind that was cut into half-inch slices and came in a full-plastic bag (not a mostly paper one) with a twisty on the end. I shrugged helplessly.

"Asiago, then," Stephen decided. "You can never have too much cheese."

I let myself become absorbed in watching him prepare the sandwich. First, he put away almost everything he'd gotten out; apparently the fixings he chose were largely reliant on the type of bread. He poked at the middle of each thick slice—to test the texture, I guessed—and set them at angles to one another on a plate. In between, he layered two different kinds of ham into an oval shape, topped with a thin slice of sharp cheddar and a sprinkling of shredded Parmigiano-Reggiano (because there was no Asiago in the fridge). "Normally," he told me, while waiting for the plate to turn its fifteen seconds inside the microwave, "I'd use a less offensive appliance for this purpose, but we're in a bit of a hurry, aren't we?"

The microwave finished and began beeping in an undeniably offensive way, although I had a feeling that wasn't what Stephen had meant.

Back in his work area, he arranged a bed of torn pieces of dark red lettuce and what looked like ribboned kale on one of the bread slices. The ham and cheese pile went on top of that. Then he pulled out a mandoline, sliced two tiny radishes into perfect coins and pressed them into the melted cheese, and finally, the second slice of bread went on top.

The remaining lettuce went back in the crisper, ham in a parallel drawer, cheese in the refrigerator door (it had its own shelf). "Mum insisted on the mandoline," Stephen said, as he carried it and the Microplane over to the sink to rinse off. "She's convinced I'll slip and slice off a finger if I use knives. Of course, she wasn't much happier when she saw how sharp the blades are here, but at least now, unless I work very hard at it, I can only remove half a finger at best." He had to shout to be heard over the water, and I noticed his accent didn't change.

"But I suppose all parents are a bit like that when it comes to their children and sharp objects," he added, then shut the tap off with his elbow. "She doesn't care much for the grater, either."

Despite what he'd just been discussing, Stephen then

took a heavy serrated knife out of a drawer, cut the sandwich diagonally, and arranged the knife to appear as though it had carelessly been left out on the counter. He took one sandwich triangle and offered me the other half.

I shook my head.

He took a bite, swallowed, then said, "Are you just not very hungry, or are you repulsed by one of the ingredients? Or," he added, "is it because I've touched all of them?"

It certainly wasn't the latter. And, while I had never been the greatest fan of radishes, repulsed wasn't the right word for what I felt about them, either. "Just not that hungry, I guess."

Stephen seemed to accept this. He shrugged and wrapped the second half in cling film and tucked it in the fridge. "Should we go?" he asked. "I don't mind eating while we walk."

"All right," I said.

There were no sidewalks, so we walked up the right side of the street, hugging the curb, then turned onto a larger street, running the opposite direction from the way we'd come in. Stephen finished the last of his sandwich and brushed the crumbs off against his jeans.

"I don't like eating where other people can watch me eat," I said suddenly, surprising even myself.

"Really?" Stephen said. "Why?"

"I don't know," I said, which was true. "I just… don't. It's stupid, I know. I…"

"It's not stupid," he said. "I'm sure there's a reason for it, somewhere. That said, you should perhaps try to change. You're probably going to have to eat in public eventually, and it's nothing to be embarrassed about. Everyone eats, don't they?"

"It's not that," I said, but then shook my head. I'd never been able to clarify it.

"We can practice if you'd like," he said. "Would it help to have someone there, but I'll promise not to look at you?"

"I don't know," I told him, frustrated. "It'll probably be better once I know you, anyway."

"Wait," said Stephen. He turned around so he was walking backward, facing me from a few steps ahead. "What do you mean, once you know me? You already know me. Don't you?"

"I've only just met you," I told him. "Like, less than a week ago." I reflected on what I'd thought about for most of the class period following the first time Stephen had spoken to me in the hall. How, until then, I'd never really heard him speak before. He was on the student council, but the treasurer wasn't expected to ever read the morning announcements or get up with a microphone at assemblies and give a play-by-play of the sophomore-versus-senior hot dog eating contest. I supposed he'd given campaign speeches at the ends of the previous years, but I couldn't remember them.

Of course, there had been our previous conversation, at the candygram table. It hadn't helped, though; I'd been so flustered, and righteously offended, that I hadn't paid much attention to what his voice sounded like.

It was important because knowing what someone's voice sounded like—and not just their accent (or lack of) but also their rhythm, word choice, manner of speaking—was, for me, an integral part of actually knowing the person. Being able to read something or to hear someone else say some-thing, and imagine, clear as a bell, *my* person saying that same thing in my head. Maybe it's not so important now, with so much conversation happening via email, or text, or even app, but people in old movies used to say things like "I'd know that voice anywhere," and I knew exactly what they meant. It didn't just mean recognizing a voice when you heard it, it meant being able, even years after you'd heard it last, to call it up in your mind. That, to me, was a special kind of familiarity.

Stephen's voice was easy because he'd made it unique. But a week earlier, I hadn't even known it was unique. I recognized it now (or at least I thought I would). But I hadn't heard him speak enough yet that I could hear it without hearing him. "I barely even know what your voice is like," I said.

"I can talk more—I can talk a great deal more—if you'd like," he said. "Though I suppose you're right. I did say not too long ago that I knew almost nothing about you—including, until very recently, your name. I like to think I know a bit more now." He stopped walking for a moment and tilted his head to one side, looking carefully at me. "I'm not saying I've reached the upper limit for things I'd like to know about you—certainly not—but I also wouldn't put us at strangers."

"I didn't mean we were exactly strangers," I said.

"No," said Stephen. "But perhaps you and I have… different standards of acquaintance."

"Perhaps," I agreed. It took me a long time to get used to people, but Stephen's was a nicer way of putting it.

"So," he said. We reached another corner, at the top of a slight incline, and he turned around finally, walking beside me again. "What do you want to know? Or, perhaps, what do I need to know? Should we do the thirty-six incredibly personal questions designed to make strangers fall in love with each other?"

"What? No!" I exclaimed, then swallowed; it had come out a bit more vehemently than was probably polite. "I mean, no."

"Of course not," Stephen said. He paused, then: "It was a legitimate sociological experiment, from the mid-nineties. Recently it's seen a bit of coverage in the news media. I found it interesting—I find the way the human brain works very interesting. I read a lot of articles." He paused again. "But let's not talk about what we like to read."

"What?" I said again. This was rather limiting. I didn't have a lot of other activities.

"No books," he said, "and no music. If we talk about books and music, it'll end up making us like each other less."

"Okay," I said, because it's true—there's always going to be something somebody absolutely loves that another person absolutely doesn't.

Of course, though, we did eventually wind up talking about books, but mostly unspecifically, focusing on reasons we disliked them (but, nevertheless, wound up reading them anyway—Stephen, it seemed, read just as much as I did). We talked about how the characters—main, supporting, and minor, all—were nearly always unrealistic and annoying, and how everyone had either incredibly staid and outdated or improbably exotic names.

Although in the interest of fairness, I had to admit to Stephen that I did have an exotically-named older brother: Lasse. Mom was going through her Scandinavian phase when he was born. Fortunately that phase had passed by the time she had me, since our last name, McGowan-Reed is ridiculous enough on its own, even without a first name that often prompts people first meeting my brother to just look at him funny for a while, then finally give in and ask what the hell country he's from. Lasse doesn't seem to mind, but I'd be mortified. Constantly.

"So," Stephen said, giving me the look first-timers usually give Lasse, "let me get this straight. "Your brother is called Lasse McGowan-Reed?"

"Yes," I told him.

"Wow," he said, shaking his head. "That does sound like bad fiction."

I rolled my eyes. "I'll pass on the compliment."

"Right," said Stephen. We were walking back toward his house by then. He was kicking a pebble. "I feel a bit bad taking the piss, though," he said after a while. "It must be hard, writing a novel. You have to tread a very fine line between making your characters and the things they do realistic and relatable and not making them incredible bores."

"I've thought that, too," I said. "But I don't know. Even when they're supposed to be regular, normal people who just have something exceptional happen to them, they're not really normal. I mean, even if you think you're normal until you turn sixteen, if you suddenly discover that you're actually an adopted changeling, and your real father is the Unseelie king, that obviously isn't normal. Or even if you are a totally normal human, but the Unseelie king, significantly younger this time, randomly chooses you to be his mortal bride, well, you're really not 'just an average girl' any more."

Stephen gave me another strange look. "Just what kinds of books are you reading?" he asked. This, I supposed, was why he'd initially suggested we not talk about what we liked to read.

"Girly ones," I told him. "Bad ones, sometimes. Sometimes," I admitted, "I'll read them even if I can tell from the cover flap that they're going to be terrible. It depends on how I'm feeling."

"Well," he said, "at least you're honest."

"I hide them, though," I said. "Either I use an e-reader, or, if I'm at the library, I put them in between two responsible-looking books to check out, and then if I ever read in public, I put a fake cover on."

"Well," he said again, "that's very industrious of you. May I ask what your fake is?"

"*The Hound of the Baskervilles*," I told him. "I wanted to choose something that would be reasonable enough to be reading, but that wouldn't be popular enough that anyone would get excited seeing it and want to talk. No one's ever asked me about it, which is a good thing since, I mean, I know what happens, but I haven't actually read the book."

Stephen grinned. "I read the abridged version when I was nine or ten," he said. "I was obsessed with phosphorus for at least a month afterward. Not my parents' favorite phase. Although," he added after a moment, "probably not their least favorite, either."

He kicked the pebble again. I was amazed that he hadn't lost it already, although perhaps it was a different one.

"If I find it," he said, "I can lend you my copy. I feel like making book recommendations normally would violate the terms of agreeing not to talk about books, but this one has illustrations."

"I miss books with illustrations," I said.

"I miss children's books, full stop," Stephen said. "They're so straightforward. But they're never boring, they're just all action. They get things done." He paused. "Can I tell you something? Why books targeted to our age group never seem to be stories that could really happen? It goes back to the line

I was talking about earlier, between relatable and boring. The problem is that there's no middle ground. We're too jaded, and it's harder for us to suspend our sense of disbelief. And when we could be having adventures, we waste time instead having feelings and doing things like imagining we're falling in love.

"So books for teenagers have to have that, because that's what teenagers want, even though I think most of us don't actually get to fall in love. So, of course, when the characters do—when the characters do, really, anything that we'd like to, but haven't or can't—it seems unrealistic. And there's no middle ground because reading about a completely normal life is too relatable, and becomes, by default, boring. Look at it this way: you're fairly normal, wouldn't you say?"

"I guess," I said. "Fairly." I certainly wasn't outstanding.

"Okay," said Stephen. "So you're normal, you're realistic. And now I don't mean to offend you, and I don't mean you're boring, and I definitely don't mean to say you're destined to be a book where nothing happens, but would you really be interested enough to want to read a book about your life thus far?"

"Well," I said, "no." Because it was true—there was nothing really special about me—at least, nothing special enough that people would want to read about. The most interesting thing that had happened in my life was Stephen's sudden, inexplicable interest in me, and as far as I could tell, there was nothing particularly interesting about Stephen, either (aside from his sudden, inexplicable interest in me, perhaps).

"Only thus far, though," he said, and gave me a little smile. "That's how I think most of us are. I don't think I'd even want to read a story about Bonham or Kyle, and they're both fairly compelling, as far as normal people go."

I nodded. Even Lasse, with his fiction-ready name, to boot, wouldn't have made the most interesting subject for a book. "So what's the solution?" I asked.

"I don't know," he replied. "I think sometimes people try to balance it, sort of—they just have one really wild, out-there character, and then everybody else is normal and relatable enough, and they're made interesting not in and of themselves but by being swept up by that one person. But"—he shrugged—"it still doesn't quite work. I always wind up thinking, 'yeah, right,' and wondering, 'why don't any of my friends have a motorcycle?' " He grinned. "Or even riotously curly red hair and a nose ring."

I smiled, too. "I hope you're not hoping I'll say a nose ring can be arranged."

"No," he said. "Then I'd think you were trying too hard. It's exasperating."

I nodded again. It was true.

"So," Stephen said; we were almost back to the house. "Do you feel like you know me yet?"

"Um." I still didn't, not totally, but the way he'd phrased the question, it would've felt rude to say no. "Better."

"I'll take that." He shrugged, like that was the answer he'd been expecting. "But we can do this again. I mean, we could do this again, regardless. Walk. It's nice. Although if you'd rather not... I just thought, if you're still at a point where you feel the need to keep your distance, as activities go it is fairly innocuous."

"Okay," I said.

"Okay yes?" Stephen asked. "As in yes, we can continue to walk?"

"Yes," I said.

"Good."

We went inside just long enough to get my things from his room; then he drove me home. "You know," he said, when he stopped at our front walkway, "something else about books. I sometimes wonder why, when I look at girls' eyes and they're brown, I don't immediately think of food and beverages to describe the color. Because in books they always seem to be... chocolate. Cinnamon. Coffee-colored."

I nodded. I'd seen this convention applied to hair, too. But usually only in certain kinds of books. We'd managed not to mention any specific titles, other than *Hounds*, but I suspected that, secretly, Stephen was reading some of the same almost irredeemably bad books I was. "Don't forget honey brown," I told him.

"Right," he said. "Although, etymologically, you might be surprised to find that honey, the food, actually comes from honey the color, not the other way 'round." He paused. Then, "What color are yours, by the way?"

I stiffened. "You're trying to get me to look at you, aren't you?"

Stephen shrugged. "What if I am?"

"I'm not going to melt under your gaze and fall into you," I said. "We're not going to look into each other's eyes and suddenly click, or see into our souls and feel the clichéd zing of an instant connection. We're not going to kiss."

"Of course not," Stephen said, very matter-of-factly. "I just want to see what color your eyes are."

My eyes, like the rest of me, are fairly uninteresting. But I figured there was no real reason for Stephen not to get a look. I raised my head and stared at him.

He leaned forward—for a moment I thought he was going to put his hand on my chin—and peered at me intently. Finally, after what seemed like an eternity, he leaned back to his own seat and nodded once. "A.1. steak sauce, I'd say."

I couldn't help it; I had to smile. I shook my head at him and let myself out.

"I'll see you tomorrow," he called. And then he waited until I'd opened the front door before driving away.

On Tuesday, Stephen asked me to tell him about the worst vacation I'd ever been on. "Because," he said, "ultimately, good vacations are all the same. You had a great time, blah blah, here are your jealousy-inducing pictures, blah blah, you can't wait to go back, blah blah the end. Maybe it's different if it's something really amazing. But for the most part, it's the disasters that make things memorable."

"All right," I said. I didn't have to think very long. I told him about the time Mom made us go camping at a lake, which turned out to be more of a swamp, resulting in me (and, somehow, only me) winding up with twenty-seven very large, very itchy mosquito bites, mostly on my face. Dad was so worried about food safety that everything we ate that week was cooked until it resembled a charcoal briquette, my air mattress had a leak, and to top it all off, Tammy, who was just past being a baby, woke me up every night crying.

I probably cried even more than Tammy. I'd had a terrible time, but I'd also been pretty insufferable myself. Lasse still made fun of me for it from time to time, calling me "the morose alien-toad thing," which, to be fair, was about what I did look like in most of the photos from that trip.

Stephen nodded sympathetically in all the right places, but then, he laughed at me, too. "So," he said, "your brother. What's he like, really? I'm an only child, remember, so I can't quite tell if you've been describing a run-of-the-mill semi-antagonistic sibling relationship or if he's actually an asshole."

"Oh!" I said. "No. Lasse's cool." I paused, considering that word choice. "I don't mean cool like you'd say 'that's cool' to mean something's okay, or acceptable to you. I mean, he is that too. But what I mean is that he's actually cool. Like cool cool. Like people like him."

"You know, this doesn't preclude being an asshole," Stephen said.

"He's not," I said, and it was true. "He's nice. I mean, you can't pin everything on him making fun of me for one thing. That's what siblings do. They tease each other."

I looked at Stephen and couldn't quite place his expression—melancholy, perhaps? "I wish I'd had a sibling," he said.

He didn't say why, and I didn't ask. There are some things, I figure, that you just know, and don't ever really articulate.

"If I asked you now to tell me about your best vacation," Stephen asked after a while, "would you be able to think of one?"

I shook my head. "Nothing really stands out," I admitted.

"Not now," he said. "Even if you could make it up, would you know what you wanted?"

"You mean a hypothetical future vacation?" I said.

He nodded. "If you could go anywhere, what would you do?"

It was the kind of question that I think people probably do sometimes ask when they just want to know your answer. But I think it's also the kind of question people don't usually ask unless they already have their own figured out. I didn't have an answer, any more than I ever had. But I took the bait and asked Stephen instead.

"Oh," he said, slowly, long and drawn out. "Now? I

think—I'd like to take a train trip through Europe. I wouldn't even need to stop or get out. Just get on, get a window, and go."

I frowned. It had always annoyed me when people claimed they'd been to certain places, and later it was revealed that the extent of their visit consisted of an hour-long layover during which they hadn't set foot outside the airport. "I don't know," I said. "Not getting out even a little? Is that even really an experience?"

"It's enough," he said. "It's enough an experience for me. It's just a different kind of experience. Everyone wants to visit the Eiffel Tower, or this or that museum, or historical site, or what have you. And nothing wrong with that, if that's your cup of tea. But really, is there anything intrinsically more special about the Eiffel Tower than, say, an uninhabited stretch of Polish countryside? Arguably, yes, there certainly is, but also, arguably, there isn't.

"I suppose there's the view—but with me, I wouldn't really appreciate that. So I suppose it's the novelty; if I went to the Eiffel Tower, it would just be for the sake of being able to say I'd been to the Eiffel Tower. But I'd just as soon be able to say I'd been somewhere unpronounceable in Poland.

"It's kind of like you, with photography," he said. "You don't want to take pictures just to have pictures; you want the process of creating them. The Eiffel Tower is a destination; it's a result. I'd rather have a journey. Or a process. A lot of very small experiences that, together, mean something, rather than one big thing that, ultimately, may or may not."

He sighed. "Ultimately, the process may not, either. But, at least, I think it has more potential."

"So," said Stephen. He was waiting at my locker again after school.

"I have to tell you something," I said, before he could say anything further. "Wednesdays after school I volunteer at the library."

"Okay," he said, which wasn't what I was expecting. "I like the library."

"You can't come with me," I told him. "I mean, they don't pay me, but it's basically like a job. I can't just have people hanging around."

I shut my locker, and he started walking next to me. "It's okay," he said. "I won't bother you. At least let me give you a ride; you know it's on the way."

I sighed. "All right," I agreed.

Stephen parked in the lot and came inside with me, but by the time I'd returned from the staff room with my volunteer lanyard and a truck of books to shelve, he'd disappeared. I didn't know if he'd left the building or not; there were a lot of places in the library for someone to disappear to.

Later I found him in the stacks. He had one arm up above his head and was leaning against the wooden support at the end of the row, scanning titles on the second shelf. "You don't have to stay," I told him, and he jumped. "My mom picks me up after work, on her way home."

He straightened and nodded, but didn't prepare to go. "I like it here," he said. "How long have you been volunteering?"

"Since the start of freshman year," I said.

He nodded again, appreciatively. "It's funny I've never seen you."

"I mostly just shelve things," I said.

"Right," he said and glanced over toward my still partially

full truck. "I won't bother you any more. I'll see you tomorrow, okay?"

"Okay," I said.

And we did.

The following Tuesday, after Stephen brought me home, I slipped into the "random room" in the basement and picked out one of my mom's cameras. During one of her phases, she had collected them. None were particularly expensive or special, and even if they had been, once her phases were past, she tended to become rather apathetic to the objects representing them (Lasse, fortunately, being the notable exception). Mom thought her job was incredibly boring, or, if not that, incredibly uncreative. Consequently, she went through a lot of phases.

Currently, she and her friend Shirley were trying to teach themselves pottery and failing wildly.

I figured this would be another point in my favor when I told my parents I was taking an actual organized class. I don't know if it really would have helped (I never brought it up). Regardless, they were convinced—I think mostly by the fact that I was getting dual credits, and for a lower price than the college tuition alone would have cost.

I also told my parents that one of my high school classmates had signed up, and, to save them the bother of taking me back and forth every week, had offered to drive. I tried to avoid using gender-specific pronouns as I said this, but failed. Dad must have decided, though, that a boy who chose to spend his evenings taking community college classes for personal enrichment didn't present much threat to my safety or virtue. (Lasse, it must be said, had never taken community college classes.)

We were the youngest people in the class. Aside from Stephen, the only person enrolled non-credit was a middle-aged man named Robin, who, he said, had had his children late in life and wanted to learn to take pictures of them in a way that mattered.

When it was Stephen's turn to introduce himself to the class, he said he was there "being a supportive friend."

On my turn, I mumbled something incoherent and probably inaudible about darkroom chemistry while staring fixedly at my hands. Stephen reached across, behind our shared table, and put his hand on the back of my chair. I couldn't feel it—he wasn't actually touching me—but I knew it was there. I managed to look up and tell our classmates that I'd always preferred to be behind the camera rather than the center of attention. People actually laughed. In a good way, I think. Stephen's knuckles brushed the back of my shoulder.

Later, the professor—"Sylvia," she'd said, "nothing fancy"—passed out a short syllabus and a longer list of materials and equipment. She told us that there would be no scheduled homework assignments or tests, and that we would instead be graded based on the quality of photographs we produced. She would expect ten prints, each to meet certain criteria, and on the last class of term, we would assemble them into a small show in the room, for our peers to enjoy and for her to judge. This, she explained, was how photography would be evaluated in the real world. In the real world, it didn't matter how well we memorized F-stops or exposure times, or how well we wrote about theory. It would matter what the photos looked like.

I swallowed. This was not exactly the approach I'd had in mind, and I wasn't sure how well I'd be able to make this method work.

Sylvia had also told us, however, that for the rest of the term, we could come in during any of the college's open hours, unlock the darkroom using the keycode printed on our syllabi, and use it on our own time. That was more along my lines.

After the preliminaries, Sylvia went over the very basics of camera use—how to load film, how to adjust focus if your camera didn't do it for you, and then how to override the presets and do it yourself if it did. Stephen pulled out a miniature notebook with a spiral binding along the top, creased into a long, soft curve from wherever he'd been carrying it, and took messy, miniscule notes. I tried to read them later and found that, aside from a few places where he'd written in extra-large block print, apparently to emphasize, I couldn't.

No one had film to develop on the first day, so after a brief overview of the developing process, and an even briefer tour of the darkroom itself, class ended early. Before letting us out, though, Sylvia gave everyone a white plastic reel and a long strip of old, already developed film to practice loading. We had to do it three times looking, and then again with our eyes closed, since when it came time to do so with actual film, we'd be in pitch dark.

Stephen was better at it than I was, and he seemed so pleased—to be able to do it, at all—that I couldn't be annoyed with him. We stayed after everyone else had gone; Sylvia had zipped her briefcase and was loading the leftover reels back into a cardboard box. "Sylvia, hi," Stephen said, approaching her. "I wanted to ask—I'm not taking the class for credit—would it be okay if I just take the pictures, and Emily develops them and does the prints?"

Sylvia gave him a considering look. "Honestly," she said,

"if you're not doing credit, there's no reason not to let you. I'm very relaxed. You can do whatever you want, as long as it doesn't interfere with anyone else." I got the impression that she didn't mean that just in reference to Stephen, but that she didn't really care what anyone in the class did, as long as it didn't interfere with anyone else. I can see how some people might think this was a bad thing, a sign of apathy. It wasn't.

Then she looked at me. "If you're being graded, you'll have to do your own stuff, though." She pursed her lips. "Unless I watch you all the time, which I obviously can't, and wouldn't want to, either, there's no way I can know what you're doing with the processing, so I'll make you a deal. You come in at least twice during class sessions, develop a roll of film and make a couple of prints while he sits in the hall, and I'll assume you've done all of what you turn in."

I blinked. This was somewhat different than what I'd been expecting.

"Oh," Stephen said, seeming equally surprised, "if that's the concern, honestly, I'm trying to limit my exposure to chemicals and radiation. I want as little as possible to do with the darkroom—I'm really just here to point and click."

I think Sylvia and I both looked from Stephen's face to his hands at the same time. He was still idly rolling his strip of film on and off the reel. He hadn't even wrinkled the ends—not even a little bit. It would be easy to assume he'd done this before.

Sylvia shrugged. "In that case," she said, "I want him to be in all your final photos."

"Even the landscape one?" I asked.

Sylvia shrugged. "You'll still focus on the landscape. Just place him somewhere near the edge, in the middle ground. I don't need to see details of his face; just enough to know that it's you taking the picture, not him."

I nodded, and refrained from mentioning that theoretically, Stephen could still set the whole thing up with me standing in as a dummy, then hand the camera off and walk back into the frame, leaving me to do nothing more than push the shutter. But, of course, Sylvia would've been aware of this. She must have just decided, for whatever reason, to trust us.

"Okay," I said. I looked at Stephen. "Okay?"

"All right," he said.

Sylvia smiled. "I'll look forward to seeing your work. Was there anything else you wanted to discuss?" Stephen shrugged, and I shook my head. "I'll see you next week, then. Have a good night and"—she glanced at her watch—"enjoy your extra hour."

"Oh," Stephen said, and looked sideways at me, "I'm sure we will."

Thursday after school, I ate half a sandwich that Stephen made for me. It was pumpernickel with dill Havarti and Black Forest ham and watercress, all grilled together in the toaster oven. He said it was a good starter sandwich, and I should expect them to be progressively more adventurous in the future.

Normally I would've thought that a sandwich made on non-wheat bread, with fancy lettuce and imported cheese, was fairly adventurous already. However, in comparison to previous sandwiches I'd seen Stephen make, it was, in fact, quite tame. He liked to narrate the sandwiches he was building; otherwise I wouldn't have known what half the ingredients even were.

Stephen put my half of the sandwich on a salad plate, and jumped up to sit on the counter next to me. "Good?" he said.

It was, surprisingly so. Well, perhaps surprising wasn't the right word; I didn't expect it to be bad. But it was good in a different way than I'd expected.

"It's the heat," he informed me. "A good sandwich is almost always elevated with heat. It brings all the flavors together, just a bit more—so what you're eating becomes one cohesive thing: a sandwich, rather than one bite of meat, one bite of cheese, et cetera."

"I see," I said.

"When I was little," he said, "all I would eat was grilled cheese—specifically, cheddar on white—and I had to have the crusts cut off. But at least it was grilled."

He finished before I did, but not that much before. I was taking small bites, still conscious of the fact that, even though he was doing a fairly good job of not looking my direction, there wasn't a lot else for him to look at, either—it was still very close to having another person watch me eat.

He waited next to me until I was done, then took both our plates, rinsed them, and put them in the dishwasher before turning back. "So," he said. He looked straight at me. "Do you want to walk again for a bit? Or would you rather go back to my room and make out?"

I stared at him for several seconds, sure I was imagining things. The clock above the door to the laundry room ticked. It sounded slow.

"What?" I finally asked.

"I said before that I don't intend to waste any more time," he said. "And at this point, I think it's inevitable." He took another step toward me and leaned against the counter, folding his arms. It was the smoothest thing, probably, I'd seen him do, but somehow I got the impression that he was actually imitating, in rather a mocking way, someone else being smooth, not trying to pull anything off himself. "Do you agree?"

I swallowed. My mouth felt very dry, for reasons that had nothing to do with the sandwich.

Stephen smiled, and pushed off the counter again. "I'm just saying," he said easily. "I'd actually be very shocked if it happened today. I just thought I'd put the thought out there: I do think it'll happen. Do you agree?"

I bit my lip and looked away. I would've gladly shoved an entire sandwich into my mouth and chewed it in front of him (and a bunch of other people, besides, had they been there), if it'd meant I didn't have to respond.

I thought about all I'd thought about Stephen over the past two weeks, even though I didn't really have to think about it at all. I'd already come to the same conclusion he had. I guess I just hadn't admitted it yet.

I looked back up at him. His expression wasn't achingly hopeful. His eyes weren't blazing; he didn't look nervous or tense. He looked like he always looked—standing, slightly limp, with his arms at his sides, his lips slightly parted in neither a smile nor a frown.

"Probably," I said.

We went outside and walked toward the mouth of the cul-de-sac. Stephen had his hands in his pockets. He'd found another rock to kick.

"It's a bit awkward," I said after a bit.

"Perhaps," he agreed. "But ultimately, I think, less awkward than pussyfooting around it for however long, trying to work out if we like each other, but being too scared we don't to actually do anything."

I said nothing to that. Pussyfooting around issues was all kinds of my business.

"I won't apologize," he said, and I nodded. "And you did agree with me," he said.

"I said probably," I told him.

"All right," he admitted. "But I still tend to think of that as more positive than negative. It's not as if you said flat-out no."

Again, I said nothing.

"You know," he said, after a while, "what if there are only so many chances? I hope I didn't—I don't want to fuck this up."

"You won't," I said.

"Yeah?" He looked at me and grinned. "So, on a scale of one to ten, how well would you say you know me now?"

"Six and a half," I said. I was feeling generous. "Maybe a seven."

"And how well," he asked, "would you need to know me to hold hands?"

I looked at his hand on the side next to me—or rather, because I couldn't see it, I looked where I knew his hand was, hidden inside his coat pocket. Mine were the same, with mittens on. "It's too cold for that," I said. It was an answer, but not the kind of answer he wanted. But the truth was that on a scale of one to ten, I didn't know.

We sat cross-legged on Stephen's bed. My back was to the window; my front was facing the door, facing him, a good foot and a half of bedspread between us. Outside it was pouring rain.

I was practicing loading film onto the developing tank reel, but I still wasn't very good at it. The most frustrating part was that I knew it should be easy. After another failed attempt, I held the reel and semi-mangled film mess out to Stephen. "Could you maybe do this part?" I asked.

He was fiddling with one of Mom's older cameras and didn't take it. "I won't always be around to do it for you," he said, then shrugged. "Sylvia said you had to do at least two on your own, anyway, for the grade. And I thought you wanted to learn all the developing stuff." He nodded at the reel. "That's part of it."

I sighed. "Could I at least watch you do it once?"

Stephen put the camera down and held out his hands. "You have to be gentle. I think you're trying too hard," he said. "The film wants to go on here; it wants to curl up again. All you have to do is feed it in; it'll do the rest. Just ease it along."

His voice was slow and calm, almost hypnotizing. "You're pushing too hard at the beginning, and then sometimes you start the second part too soon." He stopped winding and pulled the film out again, handed it back to me. "Just relax."

I imagined my hands were Stephen's hands. He never seemed to move fast—at least, he never seemed to move too fast—and his movements looked natural. When he turned the reel, it looked like a long, smooth glide, rather than what it actually was: a ratchet. Looking at him, and then at myself, it was like comparing the movements of an air traffic controller and a child shaking a snow globe.

"Good," Stephen told me. "Good. That's so much better. Look, you didn't wrinkle the end this time at all."

He had me wind and unwind the whole roll again, and then again. "Now try it with your eyes closed," he said. He took the film and reel from me and put them on the bed. "It's just like you've been doing," he told me. "It's easy. Relax."

I fumbled around for a while but eventually got it. It

was harder in the dark, but not that much. "That's good," Stephen said, his voice low. "It looks great. Keep going." I finished. "Again."

I pulled the film off and fed it back on, turned the right side of the reel back and forth in my hand to continue the film's advance down toward the center post. "Still good," Stephen said.

I felt him shift on the bed and his weight moved forward. Then I felt his lips against mine, dry, slightly uneven in texture, but not that different from normal skin. They were the only parts of our bodies that were touching.

For a second, I froze. Then, my eyes still closed, I kept turning the reel.

I stopped when the film ran out, and then Stephen leaned back. I opened my eyes. He looked away for a moment, then looked back, smiled a little. I looked down at my hands in my lap. The reel was perfect.

"Do you want to keep going?" Stephen said.

I wasn't sure if he meant kissing or practicing with the film. I didn't say anything.

He reached to his side and picked up the camera again, removed the lens and started cleaning it. "Have you shot anything yet?" he asked. "I can have a roll ready for tomorrow if you want, but if you have your own you'd rather use…"

I didn't. I'd spent a fair part of the weekend pretending to take pictures of my sister (who, like all eleven-year-olds, was an aspiring model, and elated to learn that I was enrolled in a photography class) but I didn't want to waste film. Tammy had grown up digital and didn't understand that film was finite—but she also didn't understand how manual cameras worked, so I'd just made a clicking sound with my tongue to represent the shutter, and she was satisfied.

After a while, I'd started to feel guilty, so then I took a bunch of actual pictures for her, with the camera on my phone. Later that evening, she spent an hour going through and making an album of her favorites. I took my phone out and showed Stephen the one I liked best.

"What?" he said, which was reasonable. I'd responded to his perfectly normal question by doing something that didn't make sense at all.

"That's my sister," I told him before putting the phone away. "Tammy. I pretended to take enough pictures of her to fill at least three rolls of film, and then I took a bunch more phone ones because I felt bad for lying. But I didn't actually take anything for, well." I made a vague sweeping gesture that Stephen, I hoped, understood.

"All right, then," he said.

"You kissed me," I added.

"I did," he said, without looking up. He paused, then did look at me. "I told you I was going to."

"You did not," I said.

"All right, perhaps not in those exact words," he admitted. "But you knew it was going to happen."

"I wasn't really prepared," I said. "I…" I didn't finish that sentence. I didn't really know anything I would've done to be more prepared.

"Eh," said Stephen. "I know it was a bit, well. But your eyes were closed. To be fair to me, Sylvia did say to practice with your eyes shut. It was not all my nefarious intent. If it was all nefarious intent," he said, "the lights would've been off."

Then he sighed, pushed the front of his hat up slightly and brought it down again. "Look. I know it wasn't the smoothest, or the most romantic. But it was… all right, right?"

"It was all right," I said quietly. "Although it's not like I really have anything to compare it to."

"Oh, good." He seemed relieved. "You had me worried for a moment there. I mean, I know I mentioned it before, and you didn't disagree, but I thought—" He stopped suddenly. "Wait, you don't mean that was your first kiss?"

I looked away and sort of shrugged.

"I'm sorry," Stephen said.

I looked up at him sharply. He'd sounded sincere.

"I didn't know," he said.

"If you had known, what? Then you wouldn't have done it?" I asked.

"Well, no. I mean no, I wouldn't have *not*," he clarified. "But, I don't know. I could've made it more special."

"Some things are better when you're not trying too hard," I said, and held up the reel. I'd done it again.

Stephen blew his breath out and leaned back a bit. "Still." He shook his head. "I've never been anybody's first kiss."

"So you've…" I said.

"You're the sixth person," he said. "Fourth girl."

I raised my eyebrows. The way he'd said it, it was the kind of thing you couldn't not raise your eyebrows to.

Stephen smiled. He was going to make me ask.

"Who have you kissed?" I said.

"Well," he said. "For one, Shelly."

"Shelly Kennedy?" I asked. "The secretary?"

He nodded. "The president, too."

"Too?" I said. "As in—really, you've made out with Kyle, too?"

"Well," said Stephen, "I think saying we made out would be pushing it a little. It was under five seconds. Definitely no tongue."

"Can I ask?" I said.

"Fair enough," he answered. "It started with Shelly. Start of freshman year. We all kissed her, to celebrate being elected as high school student body officers. Although that actually happened at the end of eighth grade, so maybe it was in honor of our inauguration.

"So we all kissed her, well enough, but then she got annoyed and said we were being sexist, and wanted us all to kiss each other, too. And Bonham said he didn't care—mouths were all the same—and Kyle didn't really seem to mind, either. And really, fair's fair. So I've also kissed Kyle and Bonham."

For some reason it was easier to imagine Bonham kissing Stephen than the other way around. Actually, it was a lot easier to imagine Bonham kissing a lot of different people than to imagine Stephen. Probably because I'd actually seen Bonham kissing a lot of different people. Well, not a lot, but more than Stephen, anyway.

"I have made out with Deb Patterson, though," he said. "She was also my first kiss. We dated for a while in eighth grade."

"Oh," I said, nodded. I knew Deb, albeit vaguely. We'd played soccer together.

"And the last," he said, "was Cilla Connor."

I blinked.

"I know, right?" Stephen shook his head. "It was a fluke, though. We didn't date. Well, I was her date for sophomore homecoming—her freshman, my sophomore. I kissed her goodnight after, and she didn't stop me, but then on Monday, she told me she thought we were better just being friends.

"I never really talked to her besides that night, though. We weren't friends. It was a double date with Bonham. He was trying to date one of her friends, and I think she was probably expecting, like, a wide receiver, at least, and instead she wound up with me."

Normally in this sort of situation, I would've said something along the lines of "you're not so bad," but I understood what Stephen meant.

Cilla Connor was beautiful. When our class voted on senior awards, she would win both best hair and best smile. (Lasse had won best laugh, which he'd told our parents about, and also (I'd gathered, based on messages in his yearbook) most likely to get a sleeve tattoo, which he hadn't mentioned.) I didn't even get nominated for those things.

Frankly, it was more than surprising that Cilla had gone to homecoming with Stephen, even as a freshman. She must have really been counting on Bonham to pull through for her. With, like, the quarterback.

I swallowed. "I'm no Cilla Connor," I said. I hadn't even gone to freshman homecoming.

Stephen shrugged. "Cilla Connor doesn't matter now," he told me. "Cilla Connor," he said, "has never been in my bedroom."

The college had two actual darkrooms—that is, the tiny light-tight rooms off the main one, used just for developing—and, after making us chant, in unison, the process we'd learned the previous week, Sylvia sent us in in pairs. I expected Stephen to go with me, even though we only had one roll of film between us, but he volunteered to stay back in the classroom the entire time. I guessed he hadn't been joking when he'd said he wasn't really interested in the developing and printing side of things.

The tanks were made to hold two rolls at a time, so I

partnered instead with Robin, the middle-aged man who wanted to photograph his daughters. He was nervous; in the dark, I could hear the churchkey slide off the edge of his film canister four times before he got it open. He was a good partner, though—he didn't expect me to do everything, nor did he insist on doing everything himself.

He did let me do all the pouring, but I understood why. After we finished the fix and turned a low light back on, I could see his hands, just slightly, shaking.

I added water to the tank for the final wash, while Robin stared at it longingly; after a few more moments, we went out into the hall, letting the next pair in as we waited. Robin paced up and down, just beyond the light lock. He was too anxious to return to the classroom—too on-edge to focus—sure he'd retain nothing Sylvia might say during the twenty-minute wait.

"I don't want to mess it up," he said. "It's silly, I know. Here I am, a man with two thousand pictures on my phone and even more on my computer. And I know that when I go home tonight, my girls'll still be there. If I mess it up—if I've already messed it up—I can just shoot another roll. But it's not quite the same, you know?"

I didn't know what was on my roll—or rather, on Stephen's roll that I was developing; he'd taken none of the pictures in my presence. Earlier that day, he'd casually tossed the exposed roll to me, saying nothing. I wondered if it was helping me to relax, not knowing. I hadn't shot a potentially prize-winning (or, as in Robin's case, above-the-mantel-frame-worthy) picture that I had to worry about losing. For all I knew, I could've been processing a dummy roll.

When the twenty minutes finally passed and we returned to the darkroom, emptying the tank and unwinding the film, I saw that the roll was not, in fact, blank. Robin and I squeegeed the strips through our fingers and hung them up, clothespinning the ends so they'd pull straight as they dried. Both, as far as I could tell, looked normally exposed. Robin was so relieved his hands started to sweat.

Back at the classroom, Robin sank into his seat, but I stood in the doorway for a minute, watching Stephen. His jacket was draped over the back of the chair and he'd hunched forward, both arms wrapped around his notebook at angles. Under the table, his leg was uncontrollably twitching.

When I sat down, he looked over and gave me a thumbs up. "You smell like chemicals," he whispered.

"I know," I whispered back.

"It's okay," he told me. "It's not the bad kind."

He smiled, then turned back to Sylvia. I did, too.

Thursday, we went to the college straight after school. Stephen came into the light lock with me, then gave a little sideways nod and rotated back into the hall again.

In the mild reddish glow of the darkroom's safelights, I blinked until my eyes adjusted. There was only one other person there—one of the younger students, Aisha, I thought. We mumbled greetings and then went about our business.

I found my film and cut it into five-negative-long strips, sliding them carefully into a plastic sheet as Sylvia'd shown us. All I really wanted to do that day was make a contact print.

I set the enlarger height and the beam intensity. Then I laid down a sheet of paper and smoothed out the film, and then turned on the light. Eight seconds on, then back off. Then the developer, the stop, the fix, finally the water bath.

I kept the paper face-down the entire time, even though

I'd told Stephen that what I was most excited about was watching an image suddenly bloom into being, where a moment ago there hadn't been a thing. I hadn't been nervous before, developing the film in the pitch black with Robin. But now I was scared.

When I finally took the print out of the water, I glanced at it just long enough to see that there really was something there, that my blacks and whites were crisp enough, that the images were clear. Then I pinned it up to dry, put my things away, and left without looking at it.

Stephen was waiting, and stood when I came out. "Well?"

"I couldn't look," I told him.

"Okay," he said, which wasn't what I'd expected. He nudged my shoulder and smiled. "Next time, then."

"I was thinking," he said Friday. "Next class, you should just stay over here after school, in between. Not that I mind driving back and forth, but you're only home for like forty minutes anyway before I go back and get you. It just seems a bit unnecessary, doesn't it?"

I swallowed; I wasn't sure how to phrase it. "My parents," I said. "My parents would want to know."

"So?"

"My parents don't actually know that I know you, apart from class," I told him. Of course I had my reasons for not telling them—Dad was overbearing and Mom was… embarrassing—but it was still a bit awkward to admit to Stephen. "They think I met you because of taking the class, not… taking the class because I met you."

"Your parents don't, er, know about me?" he said.

I shook my head. "They haven't even noticed you give me a ride to school," I said. "Or in the afternoons. I mean,

I'm home when they get there, and I'm still getting all my homework done. I haven't really given them any reason to think I might be doing something else. They know you're my ride for photography, but that's it." I paused. "I think they think you're exemplary. Anyone who takes college classes in his spare time, I guess. Otherwise I probably wouldn't be allowed."

"They're really that strict?" Stephen said.

"Not really. No. I haven't given them any reason to be. But theoretically. And any time the opposite sex is involved," I said, remembering—again—Jeremy. "I think Lasse may have left them with a slightly inaccurate idea of what the average adolescent boy is like. Although, to be fair, whatever they think probably isn't entirely off the mark. I mean, look where I am now—at a boy's house, in his bedroom, lying on the bed, with no adults home. Should I go home tonight and tell them that?"

"All right, fair enough," said Stephen. "I suppose that isn't something I'd include pre-introduction."

"What about your parents?" I asked. "Do they know about me?" It felt weird saying that, like I was the other woman Stephen was hiding in some dirty, secret affair.

"No," he said, rather blandly.

"No?" I repeated. It wasn't really that I'd expected him to say yes; I think it was just the way he said it.

"It hasn't come up," he said. "When I talk to my parents, we talk about other things."

"What're they like?" I asked. "Your parents, I mean."

Stephen shrugged and put his hands up behind his head. "Oh, they're just normal parents, I suppose. Nice enough, but they work too hard, worry too much, the lot. I suppose."

"What do they do?" I asked.

"Oh," Stephen said. He seemed mildly surprised, like he hadn't realized he hadn't already told me. "Mum's a radiologist," he said. "It's been… useful.

"And Dad's in community corrections. He works with the people who're bad enough to need monitoring, but not so bad they deserve prison. I think it's always been a slight disappointment to him that I never brought anyone home who looked like they needed profiling.

"Not that I think he'd want me to be friends with any of his clients," he added quickly. "I think he just misses not being able to screen people who might get close to me. Being able to say 'Aha!' and sweep in and save me from a future life of crime."

"Ah," I said. "So would they like me more or less if my screen came out in the negative?"

"Oh, undoubtedly less," Stephen said. "Why? Anything you want to tell me?"

"Hardly," I said.

"Yeah," he agreed. "Sometimes I wish I'd met Bonham later in life than I did. At least with him, Dad could reasonably expect that he might find something. You, Emily, you're so wholesome."

"This you say while I'm lying in your bed."

"Lying *on* my bed," he said. "There's a difference."

"Right now, if I was really wholesome, I'd be playing spring soccer with Mari and I wouldn't even know where you live," I said. "Right now, this feels about as wholesome as curdled milk."

"Well then," said Stephen. He propped himself up on one elbow and grinned at me. "I hope you like yogurt."

———————

Stephen gave me a new roll of exposed film after school Tuesday. "So," he said as we buckled ourselves in, "are you staying over?"

"I haven't told my parents," I said.

"You could call one of them, in a while," he said. "Leave a message that I've picked you up early. Considering that I have picked you up, albeit directly from school, it's not technically lying."

That wasn't really the problem. I'd lied to my parents before. Nothing major, but I was sixteen; anyone who reaches that age without ever having told their parents anything slightly untrue must be physically incapable of speech. There's no other explanation.

The problem was that I didn't want to lie to my parents. I wanted to tell them about Stephen. I didn't want to deal with their reactions, but I wanted them to know—because they were important to me, and Stephen, I realized, had become important to me, too.

The problem was that I still didn't know what to say.

"Would it help if they just met me?" he asked.

I thought it actually might. But, "I'll have to think about that," I said.

"You can meet mine," he said. "Tonight," he added, as if it was meant to be tempting. The idea, though, was the utter opposite.

"I have to go home," I said finally.

"All right," Stephen said.

We passed an intersection and he changed lanes. After a few more blocks, I realized he'd actually changed direction, looping back toward my house instead. "I didn't mean now," I told him.

"It's okay," he said, quietly. He didn't turn back. "I

understand it. You don't want to see me all the time. And you're already going to see me again tonight. I can back off."

"It isn't that," I said. I'd spent half the weekend just wondering what Stephen was doing.

"It's okay," he said again. "It's probably good that we don't…" He turned onto the hill leading up to my street. "I'll see you at five thirty."

"All right," I said, because I didn't know what else to say. I let myself in through the gate and latched it behind me. Halfway up the walk, I turned and looked back. Stephen had ducked down in his seat so he could see me through the passenger window. He gave a little wave. I gave him the best smile I could, which, under the circumstances, wasn't very good, and went into the house. I felt as though I'd just been broken up with, although I'd never been broken up with and didn't know what it actually felt like. I wondered if that was, somehow, what had happened.

I also wondered if Stephen would show up at five thirty like he'd said he would.

He did. In fact, he was three minutes early.

"Sorry," he said as soon as I got in.

"What?" If anything, I would've thought I was the one who needed to apologize.

"I was a bit of a dick." He sighed. "Sometimes I just… Look. I've been scared. And I don't want you to be scared. And that's what makes me forget—but I don't want you to ever feel like I've forced you, or pressured you, to do anything. I don't mean to—I don't want to make decisions for you. But I suppose I've come on a bit strong, haven't I?"

"I'll meet your parents," I said.

"What?" If we'd been driving—fortunately we weren't— we probably would've crashed.

"I'll meet your parents," I said again.

"All right." Stephen licked his lips slowly, swallowed. "But I don't want you to do it because I asked you to."

"Of course I'm doing it because you asked me to," I said.

"But you shouldn't—"

"I want to," I said. "So far, ultimately, I've mostly enjoyed all the things you've asked me to do."

"You have?" Stephen asked. "I mean, I know I've kind of forced your hand."

"You haven't held a gun to my head," I said. "Anything you got me to do, I still had to decide to let you get me to do it, right? And I don't mind meeting your parents. They're obviously important to you, and also I've eaten so many of their sandwich fixings over the last two weeks."

"They'll just think that's me," Stephen said dismissively. Then his voice changed. "I am sorry, though. That isn't what I expected you to say."

"What did you expect?" I asked.

"I dunno." He shrugged, and finally put the wagon into gear. "Not that, anyway. Maybe something more along the lines of agreeing that I've been a dick."

"I don't think that's true," I said. "You just know what you want."

Stephen laughed, a short bark of a laugh. "In a vague sort of sense, I suppose that's true," he said. "Details? I wish."

We went into class, and Robin came over and talked excitedly about a print he'd made of his youngest daughter over the weekend. When he went back to his own table, I turned to Stephen. "Why don't we ever do anything on the weekend?"

"You always wait for me outside," he said. "I didn't think you'd want me to just show up unannounced."

"We could've made plans," I said. It occurred to me then that, aside from the very first time he'd asked me to hang out, Stephen had never suggested any kind of weekend activity. Of course, I hadn't either, but by that point it was fairly clear that Stephen was the driving force in our relationship.

He shrugged. "I'm not very good with making plans," he said.

"Have you read about the experiments they did with little kids, where they get to eat either one marshmallow now or wait ten minutes and get two? So you'd be the one marshmallow now type?"

He frowned until he realized what I was getting at, then smiled. "I'd be the outlier in that experiment," he said. "I wouldn't want to eat any marshmallows at all. But offered a different reward, no, I wouldn't say it's impulse control that's my problem."

"You don't want to do everything, now?" I said.

"I do," Stephen agreed. "But in moderation. It's not that I can't compel myself to wait, it's that I don't think, later, I'll be able to.

"You know, in another iteration of that experiment, the experimenters lied to half the children before they did the test. The other half, they made a promise and kept it. The children with the broken promise were far more likely to eat the marshmallow right away rather than wait. It's not just poor impulse control and the need for instant gratification. It's whether or not you believe the thing you want will still be there."

"I'm not going anywhere," I said.

"Well, that's a bit presumptuous, don't you think?" he said. But then he smiled again, and moved his hand over so his pinky touched mine. "It's nice of you to say that. But it's not just you." He paused. "Do you ever feel like you're running out of time? I do."

Sylvia strode to the board and started class then, and our discussion was involuntarily tabled.

After the lecture, we walked down the hall to the darkroom, foregoing the fifteen-minute break in the hope of beating the rush as everyone else in class also headed that way. Stephen stayed in the hall while I went in through the light lock. A moment later, I came out, shaking my head. Apparently half the class, at least, had had the same idea. "It's packed," I told him. "There's no chance."

I took the film he'd given me from my pocket and held it out, but he didn't take it. "Go get your contact," he said. I swallowed; he looked at me fixedly. "Go get it," he repeated.

When I came back out with the contact print, Stephen took it in both hands. The images were tiny, no larger than the film itself. The tones were crisp, but the sheet was mostly black—all the areas of film that had been clear, plus all the areas where there hadn't been any film at all. Stephen squinted and leaned forward a bit. I did, too.

We were quiet. Our heads almost touched.

"I think this one might have turned out," he said after a while, pointing to a frame about a third of the way down. "You don't have to print it. I didn't really know—I was mostly just trying to figure out how the camera worked. I don't expect any of these to be anything."

I didn't quite agree. Sure, there were a few shots that, even in such small scale, were obviously out of focus or blurred or even, perhaps, accidental. But there were also several that didn't look bad at all.

"Did you really not look at these?" Stephen said.

"No," I told him.

"Can't say I blame you," he said, amiably. He didn't seem disheartened at all. "Or that one, either," he added, nodding in the direction of my pocket. "I'll try to do something a little more interesting next time."

"They're not so bad," I said. "And they're so tiny on here, anyway. You can hardly even tell."

Stephen nodded. "All right," he said after another moment, and touched an image near the bottom. "Will you print this one for me?"

It was a circle, silvery grey, with four rays coming from the sides, thinner near the middle and thickening as they approached the edges. They were, I thought at first, off center, and I wondered if I'd be able to arrange my paper and zoom enough to straighten them in the print.

Then I realized they looked better that way, starting at neither due north nor an ordinal, but rather, approximately, north-northeast. The top and bottom were still perfectly balanced with each other, as were the left and right—just in reverse. It made the image more interesting—art, instead of an uninspired, too-careful snapshot.

"What is it?" I asked Stephen, because I couldn't figure it out.

His finger brushed over the image, just barely. "It's the bottom of the water tower," he said. "Standing right below it, looking up."

"I didn't know that," I said. "I mean, I didn't know you could get right up under it."

Stephen just shrugged. "You can," he said. Then, "Will you print it?"

I said all right.

There were still too many people inside. Since we'd been there, no one had come out, and three more had gone in.

There were only seven enlargers, and I wondered what they could all possibly be doing. "Do you want to wait?" I asked.

He shrugged again, ran his finger up and down the edge of the sheet. I focused on his strokes. They weren't quite even. "Do you want to go?" he said. "I wouldn't guess anyone else is leaving. But I don't mind waiting," he added. "You can put your head on my shoulder."

"I'd probably better not," I said.

We walked back to the wagon, and Stephen unlocked my door before going around to his own. "So what do you want to do for the rest of class?" he asked. "You aren't expected home for at least another hour, am I right?"

He was, but I hadn't thought yet of what that meant. I stood on the pavement for a long moment, until finally Stephen leaned over, looking up through the open door at me. "Well?" he asked.

"Show me the water tower," I said.

In a way, I was surprised I'd said it, but in a way it made sense. The college was in the old part of town, and the water tower was nearby, on top of the hill above Main Street. It had always been the less prestigious side, the wrong side of the metaphorical tracks, where, despite the lower prices, no one wanted to build their business or home. So the water tower, which had been on the outskirts when it was built, was on the outskirts still. Actually, the area was almost deserted. Which, I suppose, was convenient for Stephen's purpose, of being there when he probably wasn't supposed to.

He turned up an impossibly steep street with a few houses at the bottom and then nothing. Just after levelling out at the top of the hill, the road turned to gravel.

The tower loomed ahead of us; it was even larger than I'd realized, up close. The sweep of Stephen's headlights showed a few old metal fence posts, the chain link between them long since fallen down or removed. Off to one side was a small cinderblock building with a corrugated roof that I guessed housed some sort of pump or purification system. There was a huge padlock on the door and a faded sign—"Danger," it read, in all caps, "do not enter—authorized personnel only."

We certainly weren't authorized personnel. But then, if they'd really wanted to keep people away, there would've at the very least been a road gate.

We got out and I stood in front of the wagon, put my hands on my hips and tilted my head back to look up. Stephen leaned against the hood. "Well?" he said.

"It's bigger than I thought," I said.

"I thought so, too, the first time I was here," Stephen said. "Up close. We only ever see it from far away; there's no reason to be here, or even near here. Everything else is so far away." He said all of this without looking at me. Standing behind him and to the side—and in the dark—I could see just a sliver of his face. "It's all a matter of perspective, I suppose."

"Why did you come up here?" I asked him. Somehow I had the feeling it hadn't been just to take a photograph. If that had even been his first trip.

"Why not?" he said. He turned and looked at me then. "You know, I figured out that if you park precisely, there's not so much room between the top of the wagon and the bottom of the ladder than you couldn't reasonably climb it. Or you could just bring an actual ladder, I suppose, but somehow that's not as compelling."

He reached across the hood and took my hand, pulling me up to stand next to him. We both turned back to face the tower again. "What do you think?"

I wasn't entirely sure what he was asking. "About… climbing the tower?" I said.

He glanced at me sideways and shrugged one shoulder, smiled with only one corner of his mouth. It was obvious enough what he meant.

"I thought you were afraid of heights," I said.

"I'm working on it," he told me.

When we got back in the wagon, he turned the headlights on, then rubbed his hands together for a moment like he was cold. "All right?" he said to me.

"Fine," I said. "You?"

"All all right," he said. He shifted into first, then second, and we crept out of the turnaround, past the edge of the gravel, down the hill. On Court, he put on the blinker and changed lanes, then turned. "We're going to yours?" I said.

"Unless you'd rather I take you home now." There was still plenty of time to change direction.

I tapped my fingers up and down along the window ledge and didn't answer.

We went in through the garage, laundry room, kitchen, as usual. "Stephen?" a woman's voice called, which wasn't usual. For a second I froze. Logically, I knew that Stephen's parents would be home by now. But knowing wasn't the same as being confronted with the reality. "We didn't expect you this early," the woman continued. She had to be his mother.

"Everything all right?" came a man's voice. That would be his dad; aside from the lack of an English accent, he and Stephen sounded almost exactly alike.

"Everything's great," Stephen shouted back. He stopped midway along the kitchen and opened one of the cupboard doors, then leaned in and let his weight push it shut again. "Do you want a sandwich?" he asked.

"I'm okay," I said, or rather, whispered.

"What?" his dad called. Stephen didn't answer. A moment passed, and I heard rustling coming from the direction of the living room. "Did you say something?"

"Stephen?" His mother asked again. She sounded closer.

A moment later she appeared around the corner of the fridge, Stephen's father next to her. Stephen turned to face them. "Mum, Dad," he said, "this is Emily."

I smiled. Hopefully not too awkwardly.

His parents exchanged a look. It seemed mildly disapproving, though I couldn't think why that would be. I hadn't gotten the impression, from either décor or Stephen's indications, that they were overly conservative, the type of parents that might be too protective of their only child. And Stephen, I knew, hadn't mentioned me to them before (or at least he hadn't four days ago), so they couldn't have known anything about me other than what they could see. Thus, I was puzzled. It wasn't as though I had a face tattoo.

"She's normal. No need for check-ups," Stephen said. I could tell he was gritting his teeth. "We go to school together. Emily's a year younger."

If anything, his parents' looks of disapproval intensified (although, weirdly, they seemed directed more at Stephen than at me). This wasn't what I'd expected at all. I wanted to cower behind Stephen, or at the very least cling to his hand. I did neither. "It's very nice to meet you," I said instead. "Dr. Stuart, Mr. Stuart."

"Pleasure to meet you, too, Emily," Stephen's dad said finally.

"Yes," said his mom. She smiled, tightly.

"We have to review some things for class," Stephen said. "We'll be in my room." He brushed by his father, and I had no choice but to follow. I sat on the chair by the dresser like I had the first day. Given the circumstances, it seemed safer.

Stephen seemed to understand. He sat on the end of the bed, but leaned toward me until he was almost as close as he would've been if I'd chosen the bed, too—perhaps closer.

"That was a bit strange," I said.

"Don't worry about it," Stephen murmured. We were both talking more quietly than usual. His parents hadn't followed us, but we knew they were out there. "They're more startled than anything, really." He grimaced a bit. "Perhaps I should've prepared them."

"Is it okay for me to be here?" I asked.

"I'm certain it is," he said. "As far as parents are concerned, I think you'll have it easy, Emily. I'm supposed to be the predator, remember? I'm supposed to be worried that when you introduce me to your parents, the first thing your dad'll do is offer to show me his gun collection." He paused. "Er. Does your dad have a gun collection?"

I told him no and he seemed genuinely relieved. "Does your dad?" I asked.

Stephen shook his head once. "He's not the one you have to worry about."

I'd kind of gotten that impression, and chose not to pursue it. "Does he, though?" I asked.

Stephen sighed. "He has one very tiny pistol he keeps for work purposes, as a safety precaution, in case one of his clients unexpectedly gets crazy or belligerent. Or, more likely, one of his clients' housemates. And no, he's never fired. Last time I asked, he said he'd only had to flash it once. Never even drawn. In other words, don't feel unsafe."

"Okay," I said, then hesitated. "What about your mom?" Stephen laughed. "I didn't mean it like that!" he said. "Mum with a gun… well, ray guns, maybe. But no. I just meant, well, she's a mum, you know. She worries. Isn't that what they do?"

"Oh." In my case, it was my father who did the bulk of the worrying, or at least seemed to. But maybe it was a gender thing. I tried to remember whether Mom had worried over Lasse when he was my and Stephen's age, then stopped trying to remember because I realized she still worried over him, incessantly. "Right."

"But if you're happy, then I'm happy," Stephen said, "and that's all that matters."

"That you're happy?" I snorted, even though I knew that wasn't what he'd meant.

"Well, yes, that, too," he said. "But if you'll recall, I first said if you're happy. Are you?"

I pulled back then, brought one knee up to my chin, my foot on the seat, hands wrapped around my ankle. I looked at Stephen. I won't say he looked earnest; that isn't the right word. Hopeful isn't either. He just looked like he'd asked me something important and genuinely wanted to know the answer. "Yes," I finally said. I didn't know if it was entirely true, but at least it was more true than not.

"Yes," Stephen said back. He smiled.

"Your parents?" I asked.

"Happy?" He shrugged. "But as I said, don't worry. They'll come 'round."

"What do you think they're doing right now?" I said.

"Mm. Straining their ears, most likely. But otherwise… Mum's pleased, in spite of herself, that you knew to call her doctor, and Dad's feeling simultaneously proud of Mum and slightly inferior, the way he does every time he's reminded that she's got a doctorate and he only has a Masters. Mum, especially, will want to not like you. But they can probably tell you're a decent sort, or I'd not have brought you home. That said, I suspect someone should be along to check on us momentarily. So. Have you taken any photos yet?"

"Not really," I told him. "I have an idea for what I want to do for the motion one, but nothing else."

"Yes?" Stephen said.

"Water." I'd always been slightly fascinated by those photos of waterfalls, or rapids in a stream, where the water isn't recognizable at all as liquid, but instead appears as a white floating mist. "You know how sometimes, with a long exposure"—this, I now knew, was the actual cause of such photographs, not any sort of change in the water—"where it looks like fog?"

Stephen nodded slowly. "You like things," he said, "don't you, that aren't what they seem."

I shrugged. I supposed I did.

"You're deeper than I originally mistook you for," he said. "No offense."

"Why would that offend me?" I asked.

"Well, not now," he said. "Previously."

"So, what?" I said. "Previously you thought I was a witless idiot who took everything at face value and only liked things that were pretty and obvious?"

"I wouldn't say that," Stephen said. "Previously I didn't have an opinion about you. And I don't mean previously as in a few hours or even days ago. Longer than that. Weeks. Has it been months?" He answered himself. "It hasn't. But more than a month, anyway. From the first time I spoke to you—you constantly surprise me."

Out in the hallway, one of the floorboards creaked.

"Anyway," Stephen said loudly, "next time we have the

weather for it, I thought I'd try a red filter; it's supposed to make the clouds pop. Think I could borrow yours?"

"Er," I said, taking a moment to catch on. Stephen nodded encouragingly. "Okay," I said. "Yeah, I'll try to remember to bring it next time. But would you also take some without it? I want to see if I can add it in post, if I use a different filter during printing."

"Yeah," said Stephen. He leaned across to his desk. "Let me write that down."

A moment passed and Stephen's mother's head appeared around the edge of the doorframe. "Oh, hi," she said, as if she was surprised to see us there.

Stephen stared up at her, his eyebrows raised. I smiled.

"Emily, can I offer you anything to drink?" Dr. Stuart asked. "Some water?" She hesitated slightly. "Or soda?"

"Mum, really," Stephen said. "The least you could do is offer her some juice."

"That's okay," I said. "I'm fine, thank you. Dr. Stuart," I added.

"Oh, well, then," said Dr. Stuart. She seemed disappointed, but in a different way from when she'd first seen me. I wondered if it was because the excuse of bringing me back a beverage would've given her another opportunity to eavesdrop on Stephen's and my conversation. "If you do need anything, please don't hesitate to ask. And Stephen, please remember this is a school night. If you need to give your friend a ride home, your father and I still expect you back by nine thirty."

"Yep," Stephen said. Then he turned back to me and carried on with our faux conversation. "What about a polarizer? Have you got one of those? Bye, Mum."

His mother lingered for a bit longer, then, apparently

accepting defeat, retreated back down the hall.

Stephen threw the notebook he was holding back to his desk. "As I said, she's a mum. She'll be better once you know one another. But getting back to what I was saying. You're not just some shy, passive thing."

But I was pretty much a shy, passive thing. "I—"

"I'm not saying you're not at all shy, or not at all passive. Which has been a fortunate thing for me," he said. "But I mean you don't just spend all your time hiding in a corner, getting walked on."

"I don't think hidden corners typically get that much foot traffic," I said.

Stephen rolled his eyes. "And you argue with me," he said. "I meant to say this earlier. You're... not a challenge, but... The first time I drove you over here, for example. I mean, I basically kidnapped you. At some point, you had to have known I wasn't taking you home. But you let it happen. You never said anything, until we got here, and then you called me on it.

"It's been a bit like that with everything. You put up with my shit, but somehow you find a way to let me know that you're not just going along because it's easier to go along, that you know exactly what I'm after, and everything you've agreed to do, you're making a conscious decision. I feel like you mostly let me do whatever I want, but only because what I want also happens to suit you. And when it doesn't suit you, well, you've definitely let me know."

In a way, this was true. Still, I couldn't think of the last time I'd definitely made up my mind about something and stuck to it.

"Your problem," Stephen said, "isn't that you're a push-over—which, you have to admit, is rather the impression you give off. It's that you don't know what you want. So you don't really see the point in disagreeing. Am I right?"

"Mostly," I said. There weren't a lot of things that felt really definite, really important to me any more. When I was six, I knew, with certainty, that I wanted the magic glitter writing set, with the llama packaging, not the unicorn. (Lasse had disabused me of the notion of unicorns, as well as a number of other fantastical creatures and tales, at an unkindly early age.) Being sixteen was different.

"I'm going to keep asking you what you want," Stephen said.

"Why?" I asked. "I mean, I get that it's important to make choices and have opinions."

"You do make choices and have opinions," he said, frowning. "Just, I think you only really do when someone pushes you to. Of course agreeing is still technically making a choice. But not a really thoughtful one. You float through a lot, don't you?'

I looked away. I'd never thought of it like that before.

"Don't feel bad," he said. "So did I, until a few years ago; in some ways, so do I still. You only need practice."

"Okay," I said, then, again, "but why? Why me?"

"You're here," Stephen said. Then, "Oh, come on, I didn't mean it like that." He paused. "You like me," he said. "At least a bit? More than a bit?"

I shrugged.

"Don't agree just because you don't want to offend me," he said. "I mean, I am your ride home, but I'm sure you could find alternate transportation if it were a total pinch."

I just smiled; I didn't agree or disagree. I think Stephen knew exactly how much I liked him—quite possibly more than I knew myself.

"More than a bit, then." He smiled, too. "As for myself, I think I've made my feelings abundantly clear. And I think it's our responsibility as individuals to live as well as we can, and I think that for two people in a situation such as ours, it's also part of our responsibility to help each other in that task. I'm not going for the whole 'do unto others' thing—I mean, yes, ideally you'd do those things as well—I'm saying that when you encounter another person who personally matters, you don't just milk them solely for your benefit."

I licked my lips and swallowed. "You said earlier, as long as you're happy, then I'm happy."

"Yes," he said, nodded. "That."

We went back to the college after school Thursday. Aisha was there again, and Stephen stayed in the hall. I developed the roll of film he'd given me, then printed the water tower while it rinsed. It was even more compelling in large scale. I pinned it to a clothesline at the end of the room and stared up at it as it dripped, until I worried Aisha might be watching.

Then I hurried back to my enlarger. I'd chosen four other negatives; when I was finally satisfied with the prints, I lined them all up side by side. The water tower was the best—and not just because two nights earlier, Stephen and I had stood under it together in the dark—but the others weren't bad, either. Everything was clear, the balance was correct, the subjects were arranged exactly one-third in from an edge of the frame. Technically, they were perfect.

But lots of photos are technically perfect. Stephen's were also good. They were interesting, and not just because he'd held the camera at an angle. All the subjects were inanimate, but somehow, he'd managed to put life—or at least, a sense of life—into them.

I wondered if he knew. I wondered if he had, in fact, done this before.

Aisha wandered over and looked past my shoulder at them. "This is nice," she said, tapping her fingernail against the corner of the one I'd placed in the middle, full of light and shadows and sharp angles. Even at eight by ten inches, I wasn't sure what it was.

"It's—they're—Stephen's," I said.

"Oh," she said coolly.

I couldn't tell if she was less impressed or just annoyed that I was printing pictures I hadn't taken. "It's just for fun," I said.

"Well, yeah," she said.

On the other side of the room, a timer dinged, and Aisha left me to move sheets from one bath to the next. I was relieved. I wasn't sure what I was supposed to say to that.

I moved the prints to a drying shelf, pushing them all the way to the back so they wouldn't interfere with anyone else's later on, then checked the new roll of film. I'd fished it out of the tank and hung it to dry in between the third and fourth prints, but it was still too damp to handle. I said goodbye to Aisha and let myself out.

Stephen stood up, brushing his hands on his jeans. "Well?" he said.

"Is there anything you want to tell me?" I asked.

He looked at me carefully. "That I'd like to put my arm around your waist?" he suggested.

"That's not exactly what I was going for," I said.

"No?" He sounded coy, though, not disappointed. I supposed that was how he'd expected I'd react.

"That's not how I meant it, though," I said. "I meant—"

I didn't finish. Stephen raised his eyebrows and held out

one arm. I took a step over; he reached around my shoulder and pulled me in to his side. I looked up at him, and for a second I thought he was going to kiss me. He didn't. Instead, he squeezed my arm, then dropped his hand down until it rested on top of my hipbone, curled all the way around to the front. His fingers would have fit perfectly inside my pants pocket. "How's that?" he said.

We were standing incredibly close. In addition to his arm across my back, I could feel his whole side pressed against mine. We weren't doing anything that was even the slightest bit socially unacceptable, but I was terrified that Aisha—or, really, anyone—would come out and see us. It felt so very intimate.

If we'd been in a novel, Stephen would have turned my body so it was more closely facing his, rather than abutting. I would've started to say something and spluttered; he would've whispered shhh and pressed his index finger against my lips.

If that had happened in real life, I would have started laughing, probably.

Of course it didn't happen. "Don't I smell like chemicals?" I asked.

"Yes," he said (without leaning down to breathe in the scent of my hair, another thing his fictional counterpart would've done). "But it's all right. I don't mind this kind."

I will not lie; I wanted him to kiss me right then.

He didn't.

"Aisha liked one of your photos," I told him.

He seemed faintly surprised. "They're yours, too," he said.

"I think they're mostly yours," I said. "I mean, if you took the negatives to the PhotoMat, they could do the same things I do, and you wouldn't say they were half the Photo-Mat guy's."

"It's different," he said.

"How?"

"I took them for you," he told me. "Except the water tower, possibly. I mean, of course I took that one for you as well, but I also took it for me."

"It came out," I said. "They're all still drying. I did some others." I was inviting him, in a way, to go back in with me to look, even though I knew he wouldn't. "The new roll's still drying, too."

"We can come back later," Stephen said. "Tonight?"

"Maybe," I said.

"So, are you enjoying it as much as you thought you would?" he asked. We'd started walking back toward the exit, which necessitated moving apart slightly, but he was still holding me. I wondered if the movement of my hip under his fingers felt strange, or if he liked it, or was indifferent entirely. To me, it felt a bit odd, but, I realized, I liked the sensation of being held onto.

Then I realized that Stephen had been referring to my work in the darkroom when he'd asked about enjoyment. "I am," I said. Although I suspected I'd enjoy it even more if I had the entire place to myself, without Aisha there. But I wouldn't have minded having Stephen in with me instead. That might've even been an improvement over being alone.

I don't think I'd realized, until just then, how comfortable I felt with Stephen. He hadn't asked me again where I'd place him on the one-to-ten scale. Maybe he knew that assigning a number between one and ten wouldn't be appropriate any more.

"Are you?" I asked. "Enjoying it?" Maybe I was just asking about the photography class; maybe I was also asking about, generally speaking, me.

"I am," he said, and smiled, just a little bit. We were back to the wagon. "Where to?" he asked.

I knew it was too late to do anything but have him take me home. Thus far, I'd always managed to be back, alone in my room, by five fifteen, when my parents arrived from work. I didn't want this to be the day I got home late and they realized I hadn't been coming straight in after school like they thought I had.

It wasn't that I didn't want them to find out, ever, but I was still clinging to the idea that there had to be a better way.

Stephen seemed to know that home was, for the moment, the only option. "What about tonight?" he said. "How strict are your parents, really?"

I smiled. "Are you asking me to do something tonight?"

He shrugged. "Anything you want," he said. "What else do you like?"

Which wasn't exactly what I was hoping for. "What else do *you* like?" I asked him. "It's still your turn." I remembered asking him, weeks ago, what he wanted to do. He'd put off answering, and never gotten back to it. "I hadn't realized we were taking it in turns," he said.

"We're not, necessarily," I said. "I just mean... sometimes I feel like we're so unequal. You're so—you've done so many things for me, and sometimes I wonder—what do you get out of it?" Numerically, I suppose, my tally wasn't that large, but I was thinking, specifically then, of him sitting on the floor in the hall while I developed and printed film that he'd shot for me. It wasn't insignificant.

"You don't mean that, really," Stephen said. "What do I get out of it?" He rolled his eyes. "Who else would tell me about horrible camping trips? Who else would eat all my ridiculous sandwiches?"

"I thought they were 'really good ham and cheese sandwiches,'" I said.

"They are, at that." He smiled. "But what I mean, I suppose—I could count all of them. I could count the slices of ham and the number of different greens. I could be very precise. But some things aren't quantifiable. We've discussed this before," he said. "We discussed this on Tuesday, in fact."

We had, I knew, if not in the same words. "I know," I said. "I understand. But sometimes I feel like—what about the things you want to do?"

Stephen shrugged. "I hope you don't think I'm setting you up to owe me," he said. "Everything we've done have been things I wanted to do, too."

"You wanted to take me straight home on Tuesday?"

"With minor exceptions, then," he admitted. "But there are always minor exceptions. That's what people do: they compromise."

"I know," I said. "And I'm not saying we don't both do that. I just think, maybe, I'd like to do something you choose. Something specific."

"Do you?" said Stephen, and almost immediately I regretted saying it. Some of the things Stephen had previously mentioned wanting to do, I remembered, involved helicopters and lava. But I nodded, if perhaps a bit stiffly.

"All right," he said. "It's not all about specifics and big things, though. That said, I'll try to come up with a—an event."

We were nearing my house. "So," he said again. "Tonight?"

"You have an event already for tonight?" I said.

"I don't have anything at all planned for tonight," he said bluntly. "But I'd like it very much if you'd come out with me."

I hesitated. There were only a few blocks left. If I'd been in Stephen's place, I probably would've been tempted to drive slower, but I don't think he was.

"What time?" I said. I was faintly surprised.

I could tell Stephen was, too. He took a moment to respond. "Five forty," he said. "Bring your coat."

"Okay," I said. He stopped at the last stop sign, then a little further on, in front of our gate. "See you then," I told him. I let myself out and started to shut the door.

"Hey, Emily," he said, just before I did, and I caught it and leaned back in.

"Hm?" I said.

"Thanks."

Eventually, after a lot of aimless driving around, we wound up at a park, one of the only cars in the lot. "So, spring break next week," Stephen said. "Any plans?"

I shook my head. "Last year we went to Yellowstone and Glacier, so the vacation fund is still exhausted. Mom took a couple days off, and Tammy's trying to wrangle a trip to the mall, so if my parents give in, we'll probably all make a day of it, but nothing else. You?"

"I don't make plans," Stephen said.

"Oh." I remembered.

"It's nice to know you'll be around," he said. "Tuesday class and all."

The college was, of course, on a different schedule from the high school. And, while Sylvia had said on the first day that attendance was in no way mandatory, I was still pleased that I'd be able to be there. Not that I didn't (usually) like our family vacations. But I also liked the fact that I was actually doing something I enjoyed, solely for the reason that I enjoyed it. And I guess I also enjoyed that Stephen was there, too.

"Maybe I'll see you." He smiled. I wasn't sure if it was because it was funny that the extent of our interactions over the next week and a half might just be if he happened to run into me, or because he was actually joking.

"Maybe," I agreed.

His watch beeped, a tiny sound almost entirely muted by his jacket sleeve; almost before I'd realized what it was, he'd brushed it off again. His left hand moved down, into his pocket, and then back upward. He grimaced slightly, swallowed. "Let's walk to those trees," he said. He started to reach for the door, and I almost did, too, but then I stopped, and looked back at him.

It was all so polished. If I hadn't been paying attention, I might not have even noticed a thing. I wanted not to notice anything. But it was too polished to ignore.

I'd seen him go through the routine before, every week, toward the end of Sylvia's lecture—he always tried to muffle the watch's beep, but never quite succeeded, and I always wondered, for the few moments until I forgot, why he couldn't just turn the alarm off. He never turned it off. And it wasn't only then, during the photography lectures; it was every time, I realized, that, like tonight, I'd been around him in the evening.

And then, one other time, too, I remembered—almost the first time we'd ever spoken. But that had been different, at school, in the middle of the afternoon. I couldn't decide if that meant anything, or, if it did, if the repetition or the difference in times made it worse or better.

Everybody, I reasoned, took aspirin from time to time. And lots of people had allergies, or needed antibiotics, or took medications for various reasons. The only thing that struck me as unusual was that Stephen always took his immediately after his watch beeped. Scheduled maintenance, that meant, rather than as-needed.

I had learned from my grandmother, who died when I was nine, that people either loved or hated to talk about medicine. The ones who enjoyed it were usually miserable and wanted to brag about how ill they were. The ones who avoided it weren't necessarily ashamed, but they also weren't proud, and they wanted to pretend as best they could that they didn't need to take anything. Stephen hadn't been particularly discreet, on any occasion, but he also didn't strike me as particularly miserable.

I really didn't want to bring it up. But I thought maybe I'd better.

"Stephen?" I said.

"Yeah?" He glanced over, his hand still on the door.

"What was that?" I asked.

He swallowed, and then he let go of the handle and brought his hands back, folding them together in his lap, looking down, away from me. "I've had a headache," he said, "for a year and a half."

I think he expected me to question it. No one has a headache, continuously, for a year and a half. Especially not otherwise-healthy teenage boys, who never even seem like they're in pain, really.

But when I was nine, one of my grandmother's bridge friends, a balding, middle-aged man named Elias, had had hiccups for twenty-nine days. I remember this because I'd never had hiccups for more than a minute or two at a time. I thought it was preposterous. But Grandma didn't make things like that up.

And, frankly, an eighteen-month-long headache still seemed a lot more reasonable to me than a month-long case of hiccups.

There was no reason, either, for Stephen to lie. I didn't think he was. If he wanted to explain it further, I wouldn't stop him, but I didn't feel any need to press.

So he had chronic headaches, so he had to take pills—there was nothing wrong with that. It wasn't like he was dropping E. "Okay," I said. I reached over and put my hand on top of his.

He looked at me for a second, then back down at our hands, together there. "Yeah?"

I ran my fingers up between his, from nail to knuckle, feeling the little hairs there standing on end, feeling each finger slowly relax as he let me unlace them. He turned his right hand over and wrapped it around mine; inside my grip, his hand faintly tremored. "Yeah," I told him.

He swallowed. "Let's walk to those trees," he said again.

His hand slipped away from mine, and when we met again in front of the wagon, he didn't take it back. It was almost okay, but not quite. We walked through the grass silent, not touching, and I almost wished I hadn't said anything, after all. A few hours earlier, we'd been so close I was nearly on top of him, but now, he didn't even seem to want to hold my hand.

Maybe, I told myself, it wasn't just me; maybe it was the timing, the temperature. Maybe things were different alone in the fading dusk. Maybe it had actually been easier under the fluorescent hall lights of the community college.

"If it weren't dark," Stephen said after a while, "I could teach you to drive."

"I already know how to drive," I reminded him.

"I know," he said, then nodded backward in the direction of the wagon. "I meant stick."

I remembered that he'd said he'd teach me. Well, perhaps implied it. "Maybe next week," I suggested.

Stephen didn't say yes or no, still reluctant to make any concrete plans, I guess. "Do you want to learn?" he asked.

"Do you want to teach me?" I asked back. Even though I was scared that he'd say no.

Stephen stopped walking suddenly and faced me. "I've never taught anyone anything," he said.

"I'm sure that's not true," I told him.

"No, really," he said. "I don't have a little sibling like you do. And at school, I'm smart enough, but I'm not smart in a way that I was ever the one people'd come to when they needed more help explaining things. And my parents are startlingly tech-savvy for adults. Dad knows more about my phone than I do."

"Well," I said, "then you can teach me. How to drive stick."

"What if I can't?"

"You can," I said. "Just tell me what you do. You know, talk me through it, until I'm able to replicate it as if you'd done it yourself. If I can't get it, it'll be my fault for being clumsy and uncoordinated, not yours. You'll be fine. You taught me how to wind film onto the developer reel," I remembered.

"No, I didn't," he said. "Sylvia did. I just repeated things in a calm voice until you finally got it on your own."

"Maybe that's all you have to do, then," I said. "Make sure I know, theoretically, what to do, and then just keep me calm until the rest of me figures it out."

"I suppose maintaining calm would be beneficial," he

agreed. "If you're anything like I was, learning, there's an awful lot of lurching involved."

He turned around, then, and started walking back toward the parking lot. I hesitated. I'd never before seen him act quite like this. He looked over his shoulder. "You're thinking about the trees, aren't you?" he asked.

"Er," I said.

"I'm sorry," he told me. "But I'm not going to walk you over there so we can make out in a little grove of trees in the park. That's a terrible cliché. Besides," he added, "there's probably another couple already doing that."

I hadn't actually been thinking of that. In fact, that possibility was, perhaps, the furthest thing from my mind right then. "I—are you mad at me?" I said.

"What?" From what little I could tell, he seemed genuinely confused. "Why would I be mad at you?"

"Because I asked..." I hesitated, not wanting to bring it up again.

Stephen sighed, and I knew he knew what I meant. "It's not my favorite thing to think about," he said, "but it's not a big secret, Emily. And honestly, the amount of time you spend around me, I think it'd almost be worse if you didn't ask." He sighed again. "I'm not mad. Not at you, anyway. Annoyed at myself, if anything."

I wanted to put my hand on his arm, or shoulder, or something, but didn't know what to do. It occurred to me suddenly that maybe I'd been reading him all wrong. That his sudden distance wasn't because I'd bothered him asking about the pills he kept taking; that he was already bothered by me, in general, or at least by me pushing him too hard. Maybe all he wanted was to be friends, if even that much. Maybe the trees had never been a consideration at all.

Because Stephen didn't like clichés, I knew. But he also didn't strike me as the sort of person who required a romantic setting in order to make a move. I don't mean to say he was overly aggressive, but if he'd wanted to kiss someone, he seemed like he'd just go ahead and do it.

It occurred to me Stephen hadn't kissed me again, not since the first time. It hadn't been that long—a week and a half—but it felt like it'd been long enough that if it was going to happen, it should have. It occurred to me that it might not. Ever.

There were a lot of mixed signals, things that I thought meant something when I was being optimistic, but (when feeling less certain) may have also, and just as easily, meant only that we were becoming closer friends: all the times I thought he was going to kiss me, but didn't. The hands. The physical closeness. The dropping of references to us making out into casual conversation. But he hadn't ever made any real indication that he might actually do something. He'd never actually moved his mouth nearer to mine.

Another thing that occurred to me was that I could kiss him. But I didn't want to. It wasn't because I didn't want to be kissing him, but because I was afraid of how he might respond. I was afraid of seeming too desperate. There was a large difference between kissing a boy because it was the twenty-first century and girls could initiate things, too, and kissing a boy because he didn't want to initiate it because he didn't want anything initiated.

I agreed with him on the point he'd made, a while ago, that if we liked each other romantically, it was silly to pretend we didn't in case our counterpart didn't agree. But that was easier said than done—especially in light of what had happened: Stephen had told me it was inevitable that we'd kiss.

Then he'd kissed me. Then he'd never done it again.

What if that meant that, when we'd kissed, he'd realized I wasn't, in fact, the girl for him? Sometimes you try things that you think you'll like—maybe you even, consciously, try very hard to like—and they just don't work out. What if that one time was it, and now he was just trying to let me down easy?

"Maybe I should go," I said. I had my phone; I could call someone to pick me up. Mari wouldn't ask questions if it was obvious I couldn't stand her to.

"Shit," said Stephen. "No. Don't. I mean, don't even think about that." He paused. "Look, I'm not making out with you in the trees back there for the same reason I won't make out with you back in the parking lot. Another cliché there. And I know you haven't had the pleasure of the wagon's back seat, but I can assure you, it's less than ideal in terms of comfort."

I wished I had something witty to say in response. As it was, I just felt more confused. High school kids making out in the back of a car probably is one of the biggest clichés in the world, but it's still not a cliché you enact with just anyone. I didn't know if I quite believed him—that this was all just because he didn't want to be like everybody else—but the only other explanation, now, was that he was making fun of me, and that, especially after all this time, was too awful to even consider.

Stephen reached over and his knuckles brushed against the upper part of my arm. "This is coming out really wrong," he said. "It's not you, it's the location."

I may have breathed an audible sigh of relief. Well, it was more than just audible. I think I almost started to hiccup. "Really?" I said.

"Rest assured," he told me, "I am serious about this. And

I would like very much to put my tongue in your mouth."
He paused again. "I know part of the point is to do normal
high school things, which means parks and parking lots, but
I just can't convince myself it's an appropriate venue."

"I…" I said. "I'm noticing some logical disconnect
between those two sentences."

"How so?" said Stephen.

"Are you trying to be romantic?" I asked. If he was, he
was doing a very poor job.

But, "Oh, no," he said. "I'm about as unromantic as they
come. Have you forgotten Valentine's Day?"

"No," I said. "And that's the impression I got from the
first part. But if that's the case, then you shouldn't have a
problem with the utter lack of romance in kissing someone
in the back seat of a car."

"You're right, I shouldn't. But it's not that," he said.
"And frankly, the back seat of a car could be very romantic, I think, if done correctly. It just seems so, I don't know,
cheesy, at least in this instance. Like, wow, could you have
been any more predictable, bro?"

"I guess," I said. It did make sense. And it meant that he
didn't despise me. That was good, too.

"To be clear, I'm not diametrically opposed to cars and
parks," he said. "At some point. I just feel like those situations should be coincidental, not contrived. This feels too
contrived. When we kiss again, it'll be interesting."

"When?" I repeated, still tentative.

Stephen stopped suddenly. "What do you mean,
when?"

"I don't mean—" I said. "I just sort of—I've kind of
gotten the impression that it maybe wasn't going to happen.
That you maybe… weren't." If interesting was all he was

concerned about, well, there'd been plenty of opportunities for interesting over the past week and a half.

"Shit," Stephen said again. He pushed at his hat for a second, looking down, before turning back to me. "I hope I haven't completely fucked this up. I got the impression from you that I ought to take things slow. You didn't have the most favorable reaction the first time I tried."

"I didn't know," I said. "What was I supposed to..."

"Maybe not show me a picture of your little sister?" he said.

"Well, maybe you could've not told me the last person you'd kissed was Cilla Connor," I replied.

"You asked," he said. "Did you want me to lie to you?"

"Well, no," I told him. "But, maybe? I mean, look, maybe I didn't have the most favorable reaction because within five minutes of the first time I kissed another person, ever, I'm being compared to Cilla Connor."

"Cilla Connor has a reputation for being pretty," Stephen said. "Not being good at kissing. And I don't see why she matters anyway. And I did not compare you."

"Maybe you didn't mean to," I told him, "but you did. You compare an already-insecure girl to Cilla Connor, how do you think that's going to make her feel?"

Stephen sighed. "I'm sorry," he said. "However, please keep in mind that, as I told you before, I do not give a shit about Cilla Connor. The only person I want to kiss is you. Okay? I want to kiss you. And it seems you're of the same mind regarding me, so would you please quit shooting me down?"

"Shooting you down?" I asked.

"This afternoon, for example," he said. "You asked me if you smelled like chemicals."

"Wait," I said. "You really were going to kiss me?"

"About ninety percent of the time when I'm not driving, and an extremely unsafe percentage when I am," Stephen said, "I might be going to kiss you. Okay?"

"Okay," I said, a bit shakily.

"And I am going to take you home now, because as tempting as the back seat is, we are better than that. Are you down?"

"With the back seat?" I asked, for some reason.

Stephen started laughing. "No, I meant with me taking you home now," he said. "I know it's still early."

"Oh," I said. "That. No, I'll just tell my parents there were too many people in the darkroom to do much work. It's fine."

"Why did you ask about the back seat?" Stephen asked a little later, while we waited at the exit of the parking lot for an oncoming car to go by.

"It was just an automatic reaction," I told him. "It was the last thing you said."

"Oh. So, would you be down with it?" He pulled forward, shifted gears. "Look. I know this is easier said than done, but please don't feel insecure. Obviously I've been being a dick again, and you—you're pretty decent, okay? And I mean that in the mad awesome sense."

I bit down a smile and looked out the window.

"Yeah?" he said. I could hear him smiling, too. "So, you won't worry? And," he added, "you're good for making out back there? I'm going to take the lack of an immediate, indignant no as a yeah."

"All right," I said, even though I was also rolling my eyes.

"Good answer," Stephen said.

After a while, I looked over at him, properly. The street-lights cut in through the windows, shining more, and then less, as we approached and passed each one, and his profile was constantly cast in and out of shadow. The only thing really concrete was the line of his jaw, lit from below by the dashboard light.

I'd looked at Stephen a lot before then, both before we'd kissed the first time and since. But it was the first time I'd looked at him and really realized that this was a boy whose mouth would touch my mouth, whose tongue would touch my tongue. More than that, maybe.

Ahead of us, a yellow light changed to red and Stephen slowed to a stop. "Are we all right, Emily?" he asked. "Really?"

I wanted to tell him that all right wasn't the right phrase for what we were. But I couldn't think of any words that would be better, and I didn't want to push things too quickly, either. "Yeah. We're all right," I said.

The light changed.

"Good," he told me.

"Did you have a good spring break?" Stephen asked Monday morning.

I shrugged. "It was what it was."

The truth was that I'd missed him. He'd taught me to drive, but that had only taken two days, a few hours each, and that time had mostly involved me being so focused on moving my feet in opposition to each other that we'd barely talked. Our scheduled photography class had been similarly brief in terms of conversation; we hadn't spoken during the lecture, for obvious reasons, and then Stephen had waited in the hall while I'd developed a roll of film for Sylvia to watch. Then he'd taken me home early.

We might've done something on Thursday, but sure enough, that was the day Tammy finagled herself a family outing, and on Friday, I was too exhausted from said outing to even want to do anything.

I hadn't seen Stephen since he'd dropped me off at the library Wednesday afternoon; I had no idea how he'd spent the rest of the week. "You?" I asked.

Stephen shrugged, too. "I missed seeing you," he said, and I felt myself brighten.

"Really?"

"It's generally not my wont to tell direct lies," he said. "How late can you stay tonight? Past five? Five thirty? Six?"

"I could probably manage that," I said. I was pleasantly surprised—I hadn't thought he'd notice my absence that much.

But I guess he had. "Brilliant," he said.

We never really talked much in the mornings, and that day was no exception. Especially after nine days of sleeping in, we were both still groggy.

Stephen was more alert when he met me in the parking lot that afternoon. "So I know I asked for six," he said right away. "But what would you think about seven?"

I took out my phone and opened a text to my mother (who, of my parents, was less likely to reply). "Ill be home late," I wrote. "Probably around 7." I showed it to Stephen before I hit send.

"You're missing an apostrophe," he told me, and frowned. "And T9 makes it so easy. There's no excuse for lazy texting."

"It's not really T9 any more," I said. But I went back and added the apostrophe. "Are you happy now?" I asked him.

"I am," he said.

At four fifteen, more than an hour later, my phone beeped. It was the special beep that meant one of my parents was contacting me. Most of the time, when this happened, the contact was in fact a random silly picture from the Internet (from my dad) or an equally random "thinking of you, you're beautiful"-type message (from my mom).

I was tempted to ignore it, but I had kind of been conversing with my mother. And even if she was telling me I needed to be home in ten minutes, I figured it was better to know (at least then I could try to bargain) than to ignore it and have even tighter restrictions imposed later.

I unlocked the screen and found a text that, followed by a winky face, read, "Ok c u then huny."

"What's that?" Stephen said.

I turned the screen off without showing it to him. "My mom," I told him. "She said seven's good."

"Okay," Stephen said, and rolled off the side of the bed to the floor. "Let's go."

Outside, he took his keys out of his pocket and went to the wagon, to my surprise; I'd thought we'd be walking. So I assumed, instead, that we were going to the college. I'd never been on a Monday before. "Do you think anyone's in the darkroom already?" I asked.

"Oh," he said.

"Oh?" I repeated.

"That, er, wasn't," said Stephen. He hesitated for a moment. "Will you go somewhere with me?"

"Where?" I asked immediately, though I wasn't really going to refuse. We were already driving.

"A while ago, you asked me for an event," he said. "And I almost had one, I really did. I'm just not the event kind of person any more, though." He paused. "But can I buy you a smoothie?"

"Is there any actual reason for me to stay until seven?" I asked.

He shook his head. "I just wanted to see you, I guess."
I didn't say anything. I wasn't disappointed, really; I hadn't expected anything. I suppose it was just that it felt so anticlimactic.

"Can I, though?" Stephen said.

"All right," I said, and I remembered suddenly that Stephen had said once that he liked small things better. To him, maybe something as simple as a smoothie actually did mean more. "All right," I said again.

We sat across from each other at a little table in the back of a coffee shop, almost hidden from view, and Stephen leaned forward across the table, his glass cupped in his hands. "Try some of this," he said.

I shook my head. His smoothie—I'd watched it being made—consisted of six different types of fruit and vegetable juice, plus frozen blueberries and chunks of banana.

"I know you feel safe with orange and peach," he said, "but what if this is the best drink you've never tasted?"

"I somehow doubt it is," I told him, then sighed. It was always very hard to say no to him. "But if you really want me to."

He brightened, more than I'd expected, and nudged the glass toward me. I took a long swallow, then looked back up. "It's not awful," I admitted.

"See?" he said. "Most things aren't awful, really, once you try."

I nodded. It was something I'd known for years, but knowing didn't make me any less afraid. I wasn't sure why, or how, but Stephen managed to make me feel okay. In some ways, he made me even more scared than I already was. But mostly I was glad he was there, making me change.

He pulled the glass back toward him, and for a while

we just sat there; he watched me, and I watched him. His mouth was on the same part of the straw where my mouth had been. I wondered if he realized that, and if it felt different after me.

He reached across the table and turned my hand over. His fingers were cold from the glass, and slightly damp from condensation.

A small part of me wondered if this was going to be the moment, but the larger part knew that it wasn't. And that, I realized, was okay. I didn't mind waiting for whatever Stephen was waiting for. As long as he was there, it didn't matter.

Friday after school I asked Stephen if he could drive me by the PhotoMat. "Oh, no," he said. "I hope this doesn't mean you're giving up."

I looked at him strangely.

"What," he asked, "could a girl like you possibly want at the PhotoMat?"

"Film," I told him.

He blinked, but he turned down the right street. "Do you want me to go in with you?" he asked when we got there, his hand on the keys.

"No," I said. "I'll just be a minute."

A little bell above the door rang as I entered; otherwise, the PhotoMat was quiet—apparently, nothing was being printed. I was the only customer. I found a hanging rack of disposable cameras near the door, and, after a fair amount of searching, a small wicker basket of unboxed film, sold by the individual roll, near the register. Everything else was digital. I picked through the basket and bought the only roll that wasn't C-41.

Outside, I saw that Stephen had gotten out of the wagon to wait for me, leaning back against the hood with one foot up on the bumper. "Hey," he said, and pushed forward. I held up my little bag of film, and his hand wrapped around my opposite wrist. He spun me around and kept moving forward, and my back hit the building wall. For a split second, I was able to remember that film was fragile and I must not drop it.

Then he kissed me.

It was different from before, harder; his entire body pressed up against mine. His hand left my wrist and crawled up my arm to my shoulder, then to the back of my neck, and I felt his fingers sliding into my hair.

I wasn't sure what to do with my hands. I think I wound up holding onto a fistful of fabric from the side of his shirt.

His lips were not, as I'd expected, situated squarely on mine, but slightly parted, centered more over my lower lip than the upper one. I let my mouth open and felt him exhale against me; then he sucked my lip in, just a little, between his teeth, and I gasped and almost started coughing. His hand dropped abruptly from my shoulder to my waist, then moved back up again.

The tip of his tongue traced along the outsides of my lips, and then—very briefly—the insides. Then he moved his head to the side, and I took a long, shuddering breath that I hadn't realized I needed. His left arm dropped again, and encircled my waist almost completely, pulling me in and, a bit, holding me up as well. He kissed the side of my jaw, right above the pulse point, in that little triangular intersection below the ear. I felt him linger for, perhaps, just slightly too long.

Finally he pulled back and looked at me. "Well," he said. "That was interesting, no?"

I looked up at him, unblinking. I was still holding the film. "That," I said, "to say the least."

A car whizzed by on the other side of the wagon and I turned my head, suddenly feeling very self-conscious. How many other cars had there been?

"Yes," Stephen said; he seemed to realize what I was thinking. "There is that. But it's not as though we were doing anything really inappropriate. You could've had your legs around my waist. Or"—he paused, then thought better of it—"I could be very graphic.

"However," he went on, "regardless of the increased traffic, you will note that I did choose to park on the side not next to the dumpster."

"Always the romantic," I said.

"Oh, no," he told me. "That was just being practical."

I introduced Stephen to my parents the Monday after. Not as the boy I'd made out with by the side of the PhotoMat—but, having now done that, it felt appropriate, somehow, for my parents to be informed. Not of the making out, maybe, but at least of his existence.

Stephen brought me straight home after school, but it was the first time he'd come inside. I knew better than to have him in my bedroom alone; we waited, awkwardly, in the living room. After a while, I started to lose my nerve. I'd had Stephen sit on the end of the sofa where Lasse liked to sit when he visited, and made him cross his leg like Lasse always did, but he kept uncrossing it, because no one but us was there yet, and because it felt unnatural, he said. I guess Lasse liked to take up more room.

Trying to, even subconsciously, remind my parents of Lasse when they first saw Stephen was a gamble, probably one that was too big to take, but I did it anyway because I knew that, even if nothing else, my dad wouldn't want to kill Lasse on sight. And I couldn't think of any safer way to present Stephen.

Dad came in first; I could tell from the sounds after the door opening: he hung his keys on the hook like he always did, and put his jacket in the closet. Next he'd cross the dining room to empty his lunch pail in the kitchen. If he happened to glance to the side at the right moment, he'd see Stephen and me through the open door and do a double take. If he didn't, he'd probably start making dinner right away, and I'd have to do something to get his attention. Although, I thought, perhaps I preferred that scenario. Perhaps I'd prefer to have Mom be the one to initially encounter Stephen.

Dad passed the dining room door and did a double take. He came into the room, lunch pail dangling limply from his hand. "Emily?" he said.

"Dad, this is Stephen." I tried to smile.

"Mr. Reed." Stephen wiped his hand against his jeans and stood up to shake hands with my dad. When he sat back down, I knew, he'd be sitting like Stephen again and not like Lasse. But maybe five seconds had been enough.

Dad hesitated. I imagined his train of thought: first, not wanting to have anything approaching a cordial greeting with this boy who'd been alone in his house, almost touching his daughter. Then debating whether he should attempt to crush Stephen's hand in the guise of a handshake. And— finally—giving in.

I stood up, too, slightly behind Stephen. "Stephen and I are in photography together," I told Dad, hoping it might soften him.

"I thought you said that was just a classmate," Dad said.

"I never said 'just,' " I replied, which under the circumstances was probably the wrong thing to say, but which was also true.

Dad frowned, although more at me than at Stephen.

The front door burst open and Tammy came in, singing a contemporary pop song, somewhat off-key, at the top of her lungs (and followed, with significantly less volume, by Mom). The chorus ended; Tammy paused, then shouted, "Hello?"

A moment later, her head appeared in the doorway. She spotted Stephen and came straight over. "Who're you?" she asked him, immediately following with her own introduction: "I'm Tammy."

"This is Stephen," Dad answered, before either of us could. "Emily's... friend from school."

"Why are you here?" Tammy said.

Dad and Stephen and I all looked at each other. "Er," I said after an almost unbearably long moment. "I wanted him to meet you."

"Oh," Tammy said. Sometimes she was easily pleased. She pushed Dad backward into the chair opposite Stephen and me, then climbed up next to him, taking his lunch pail.

Mom came in and Stephen shook hands with her, too. "Mom, Stephen," I said. "Stephen, my mom."

Mom nodded like she'd expected this, or maybe she'd just heard the interaction with Tammy. She leaned against the chair next to Tammy and Dad, a small smile on her face, while Stephen slid back onto the couch by me.

"Dad's eaten the fruit leather *again*," Tammy announced, having spent the past minute or so inspecting all the empty containers in Dad's lunch pail. She looked at Stephen. "If you had a fruit leather machine at your work, would you bring some home for me?"

Stephen, put in the awkward position of having to either disappoint my sister or side against my dad, hesitated. I didn't envy him. "I guess I don't see why not," he said finally, and Tammy beamed.

It was, of course, the right answer, though Tammy would have liked him anyway. I knew it wasn't because of Stephen himself, or even his hypothetical generosity; it was just that he fit her (small, but set) criteria: he was a teenage boy. Tammy had been looking for another one of them ever since Lasse'd moved out, years earlier.

Unfortunately, I couldn't say the same of my father. I think the only thing keeping Dad from demanding Stephen declare his intentions or, possibly, challenging him to a duel, was shock. (To be honest, I doubt he'd even noticed about the fruit leather.)

So Tammy carried on asking Stephen questions of the sort that only interest ten- to twelve-year-olds, and we all let her. My parents watched intently. I was fairly sure they understood that this wasn't just my photography classmate I'd brought home, but after a while, I moved my right hand from my lap to his, to make very sure that what we hadn't said verbally, our body language did. Stephen immediately, but very casually, moved his arm over and laced his fingers through mine.

My parents were very good. A muscle in Dad's neck pulsed, but other than that, they didn't even appear to draw in their breath.

Tammy asked Stephen if he was going to stay for dinner, and he excused himself politely. "Oh, no," he said. "My parents'll be expecting me."

Tammy turned to me. "Are you staying?" she said.

"What?" I blinked. "Of course I am."

"Oh," said Tammy.

"In fact, I should probably be going now," Stephen said, and stood. "It was nice to meet you all," he told them, then turned to me; I'd stood up, too. "I'll see you tomorrow, okay?" I nodded.

We waited in silence—even Tammy—until the door shut behind Stephen. "Well," my dad said. Now that Stephen was gone, and now that he'd had ten or so minutes to get past his surprise, I expected him to rapidly demand a series of answers—how long had I known this boy; where had we met; was he willing to provide multiple references and submit to a full background check? He didn't, though. Instead, he sighed. "Is he good to you?" he said quietly.

"Yes," I said.

"Well," said Dad, "I suppose you'd say that even if he wasn't."

I wasn't sure how to respond.

"I think he seems nice, honey," Mom said. Behind Dad's back, she winked at me. I was suddenly horrified, remembering the text she'd sent me a week earlier, with the winking emoji, when I'd asked to stay later than usual at Stephen's.

And then, I also remembered, in rapid succession, the fact that Mom woke up every day without an alarm clock, and never drank coffee, and was usually at her most alert in the early morning; she couldn't have missed the fact that I now left for school twenty minutes later than I used to, or that the vehicle that collected me each morning was the same one that transported me to and from photography. She must have already known about Stephen—even if she didn't know exactly who, she must've at least known there was someone.

Dad sighed again. "I suppose I'll have to trust you on this," he said. "You're a bit less... reckless than your brother, I'll give you that, so..."

"Honey?" Mom prompted again, still smiling unnervingly at me. She seemed quite pleased; I half expected her to whip out a box of condoms.

"He'd better not make me regret this," Dad said, sternly but at the same time almost sulkily. Then, abruptly, he stood. "I need to get the pork chops started," he said, and turned toward the kitchen.

That night, Tammy interrupted me in my reading. "So." She hung down over the edge of her bed, looking at me. "That guy," she said, conversationally, or in an eleven-year-old attempt at conversationality. I should've known she'd be interested.

I sighed. "Stephen."

"Do you, like..." She paused—"make out with him?"

I looked back at her. "Yes," I said.

"Ew!" she shrieked. Immediately her head disappeared as she pulled herself back onto the top bunk, out of view. "Ugh!" she shouted through the mattress. "Why would you *say* that?"

"You asked," I called back.

"Yeah, but I didn't think you'd actually tell me," she retorted.

I went back to my book.

A few minutes passed in silence and then the bed frame creaked. This time, Tammy stood in a crouch on the ladder at my feet, peering in through the space between my bed and hers. She only ever used the ladder when she really wanted to talk to me. I put my finger in my book to mark the spot. "Yes?" I asked her.

"Have you," she said, then stopped, dropping her voice to almost a whisper, though the door was shut. "Have you seen his…" She hesitated again. "You know?"

I hadn't—in fact, I'd only even made out with Stephen the one time, and that had been in a public place and, necessarily, rather brief—but Tammy didn't need (or, I figured, really want) to know either way. I gave her what I hoped was a very superior, this-question-is-ridiculous, look. "What do you think?" I asked.

"Oh," she said, and sagged a bit on the rungs—in relief. "Oh. Well, obviously." She went back up to her bunk and, curiosity apparently satisfied, didn't ask me anything else.

I wondered if there would come a point when her "obviously" became wrong. Actually, I didn't really wonder if. More appropriate, probably, was when.

Sylvia's next lecture ended unexpectedly early, and we drove around for what felt like hours—Stephen had already made it clear how he felt about parks—before finally winding up back at his house. His parents were both there, but we pretended they weren't; we sat in the dark in molded plastic deck chairs on the little paved patio behind his garage, out of their line of sight from the living room window. Stephen kept leaning over to kiss me, then leaning back. The too-narrow edges of the chairs' arms dug into our sides. We should've just moved closer, but maybe it still felt more comfortable to be sitting a foot and a half apart.

Stephen leaned toward me again and I felt his breath against my neck. "I never thought I'd get to this," he said.

I turned my face closer to his, brought my hand up to cradle the back of his head. The tips of my fingers slipped under the bottom of his hat, and for a moment he stiffened.

Then he relaxed against me, his mouth against mine.

The chairs' plastic bodies bent unusually and wobbled as we tilted closer; their legs, threatening to buckle, scraped across the concrete.

"Did I ever tell you you're pretty?" Stephen said.

He never had.

"I'm not telling you now," he said. "Just to be clear. We could say nonsense things to each other all night if we wanted to, right? I'm just asking because—I can tell you if you want me to. But I figured there are things you already know. That I've conveyed without words."

I wouldn't have minded being told I was pretty. But I knew what he meant. Sometimes words make things less. "Like you wouldn't just write 'wish you were here' on a postcard."

"Or, if you did, it'd mean so much more than that. Like a coded way…"

"Yes," I said. I drew his face back toward mine. "Like that."

"It's my birthday Wednesday," Stephen said, which was news to me. While I was still trying to take this in, he added, "My parents are taking me for dinner. Will you come?"

"I… your parents didn't seem very fond of me when we met," I said.

"Your parents didn't seem very fond of me, either, when I met them," Stephen said dismissively. "Well, your dad, anyway. But it's fine. They worry too much."

"I don't know," I said. "I mean, it's kind of a special thing, your eighteenth birthday. Or your child's eighteenth birthday. Maybe they want to do something special, just them and you. Should I really be there?"

"It's the kind of thing a girlfriend would do," Stephen said.

"Oh." I bit my lip. "Am I—well, am I your girlfriend?"

"If I stuck my tongue in your mouth," he asked, "would that answer your question?"

"Actually," I said, "no." Twenty years earlier, it might have, but it was so hard to know what things were, now.

(The previous weekend, for example, Lasse had surprised us all by failing to bring Melinda, the woman he lived with, to Easter dinner. "You and Melinda haven't broken up, have you?" my mother asked him finally. She had always been very fond of Melinda.

"What?" Lasse had said. "No. Of course not." He gave her a befuddled look. "Friends don't break up.")

"Fair enough," Stephen said. "It is just a word. But I have been thinking of you as such. It's something I suppose I should've discussed with you, though, isn't it?" He took my hand, stopped walking to turn sideways and face me. "So. If it suits you?"

I smiled, and sort of shrugged. As a way to stave off potential disappointment, I hadn't until that point allowed myself to believe that I actually was Stephen's girlfriend, but I had considered the possibility that I could be. "Yeah," I said. "Okay."

"Good," he said. "Now, that settled, would you mind if we go somewhere and I stick my tongue in your mouth?"

"Well." I rolled my eyes and borrowed one of his phrases. "When you put it that way."

He leaned in and kissed me then, quick—a closed-lipped peck of the kind that my dad sometimes gave my mom before leaving the house in the morning. His fingers were still wrapped through mine.

It was nice. It was comfortable. It was, I think, the kind

of kiss that happens only when you know someone very well. Nothing desperate; nothing hurried; nothing to prove. It seemed strange, in a way, that we had already progressed to such a point. But at the same time, it made sense. I didn't feel like anything had changed, going from being Stephen's friend to being his girlfriend. Kissing him didn't feel like a big deal. It just seemed like we were following a natural progression.

"So," he said after a while. "I guess I should probably ask. When's your birthday?"

"You don't know?" I said. I hadn't known his, but then, I hadn't looked up his student records in the counseling office, either.

"Of course I know," he told me. "August twenty-eighth."

"Yes," I said. "So…"

"Ah," he said. "I had to ask. Because if you hadn't remembered that I know, you might've misinterpreted my silence and thought I wasn't taking an interest."

"It's just a day," I mumbled. "You don't have to take an interest."

"Of course I take an interest," Stephen said. "It's you."

"Every time I've almost convinced myself you are utterly unromantic," I told him, "you go and say something like that."

"I'm really not," he said. "But if it makes you happy, go ahead and pretend that I am."

"I might actually kind of like it that you're not," I told him.

He smiled. "That," he said, "is what I like about you. So. Again. Wednesday?"

"All right," I agreed.

"Good. I'll pick you up," he told me. "Six thirty." He paused. "Please don't get me anything," he said. "I don't really like things."

It was a relief that he said it, not because I didn't want to get him anything, but because I wouldn't have known what to get. It was very true that he didn't like things. Maybe it was just a mark of how few people's bedrooms I'd ever been in, but Stephen had, by a large margin, far less stuff than anyone I'd ever met.

"Can I at least get you a card?" I said, because it would've felt weird not to do anything. "If I'm really going to dinner with your parents, they might think it's a bit rude of me."

Stephen sighed. "If you must."

In the end, I didn't even get him a card; I made it. Monday night, after he dropped me off, I walked back to the college. In the empty darkroom, I sat cross-legged on the floor under the safelight and went through all the film he'd given me. I didn't want the image of the underside, looking up—he already had that—but I found the water tower in the background of another frame. I blew it up and printed it on one side of a sheet; folded in half, the other side would be the card back. I had to put it in a manila envelope, the only size I could find big enough to fit.

Inside I wrote, "We're ready when you are." That's all.

I was tempted to give it to him right away, but remembered that the point of the card—or at least part of the point of it—was to not look bad in front of his parents. "Happy birthday," I said that morning when I got in the wagon.

In response, he just shook his head. "Eighteen," he said faintly. "Wow."

"Excited?" I asked. I wondered if his evening, once I was returned home, would be filled with legally-purchased porn and a box of cigars. (The remaining 364 days of the year, being old enough to vote isn't as enticing.)

"I dunno," he said. "I didn't really plan for this."

"Stephen," I said, "you barely plan for anything."

"You're right, I don't," he said, then took a deep breath. He reached over from the gearshift and squeezed my hand. "We'll have a good day, won't we?"

We were both tense and nervous that afternoon. Stephen drove me to the library, but left almost immediately after walking me in.

Sometimes he did just drop me off, but usually he stayed; it seemed like he genuinely liked the place, regardless of whether I was there or not. He was the only person I'd ever met—library employees included—who seemed to know, with complete confidence, how to work the microfilm machine. When I finally asked him why he'd learned to do it, he'd just shrugged. "So I can look things up," he'd said.

More often, though, he'd sit at one of the tables, folded into a hard, high-backed, chair, reading something from the nonfiction section—610s. Even at the library, we kept up the rule about not discussing what we liked to read, but after two and a half years of shelving, I'd gotten a pretty good idea of what was kept where.

That day, though, I probably wouldn't have had a clue, I was so distracted. I probably misshelved half the books on my truck. It was a relief when my mother showed up to collect me, but the relief was only momentary.

At home, I sat on the edge of my bed, digging my fingertips into the side of the mattress, and continued to be tense and nervous and distracted. Every few minutes, I started biting what was left of my fingernails, then, as I realized what I was doing, yanking them out again. Then I'd forget, and my hand would drift back.

I didn't understand why I was so worried. I saw Stephen

all the time. It wasn't as if we were going on a date; even as inexperienced as I was, I knew that it's not typically considered a date—not even a double—if your parents accompany you.

I suppose it was his parents I was worried about. I couldn't get past the way they'd stared at Stephen and me when we'd first met, the disapproving looks on their faces. I wanted them to like me, and, despite Stephen's reassurances, I was pretty sure they didn't. Knowing that I would soon have to eat in front of them only made matters worse.

Stephen picked me up by himself, which was a relief. "You look nice," he said, once we were both in the wagon and settled.

Earlier, I'd twisted my hair into a sort of updo and changed into a dress, dark blue and printed with gigantic flowers. I'd be a bit afraid if I saw flowers that size in real life, but it was one of the only ones I owned. I didn't say anything.

Stephen hesitated, then said, "I'm saying that because I want you to know I appreciate that you made an effort. For my parents?"

"What?" I said, turning my head sharply toward him.

"Because you know I think you look nice all the time," he said.

I didn't know whether to feel flattered or insulted. In the end I went with flattered. I'm pretty sure that's what he'd been going for.

Stephen's parents were waiting in the dining room when we arrived. They didn't look overjoyed to see me, but they weren't as cold as they'd been before. Maybe it was their son's birthday and they wanted to be pleasant for him. Maybe it was just that they'd had time to get used to the idea of me; it'd been nearly a month, after all.

We drove to the restaurant together, Dr. and Mr. Stuart in the front, Stephen and me in back. It was very quiet.

Midway, Stephen's watch beeped.

In front of him, Mr. Stuart sighed. "Stephen," Dr. Stuart said after a moment, without looking back, "I wish you wouldn't do that without water."

"Can we not, Mum?" Stephen said. "Today?"

Dr. Stuart sighed, too.

Inside the restaurant, I started to feel uncomfortable again. Everything on the menu seemed unfamiliar and far beyond my level of sophistication (and, based on the ingredients lists, as if it would be large enough to cover the entire table).

A lot of people think that because my dad is a nutritionist, I'll have eaten a lot of different and exotic foods. I haven't. I eat a lot of healthy foods, but not a great variety. In fact, unless it's something my parents can prepare at home, odds are I've never tried it. Dad is rational enough about most things, but for some reason he believes that his degree conferred on him some sort of magical insight into all restaurant kitchens, and he finds them all—every one—appalling.

Suffice it to say that I had a vague idea of what braising was, and an even vaguer idea of what endives were, but no idea what braised endive might even resemble, much less how one would go about eating such a thing.

Stephen and I were sitting diagonally to each other (his mother's idea), which probably made things even harder. After a while, he got up, came around, and knelt by my side, resting his crossed forearms against the edge of the table, the way servers sometimes do when you're a young child or they're annoying. "I'll get spaghetti," he said quietly. "Will that make you feel better? Everyone always says not to order long noodles in front of a date, because they're the messiest possible thing you can eat."

"I think ribs would be worse," I said without thinking.

"I can see how you might be right," Stephen said. "Sadly, not on the menu. So, what do you say?"

"Do you even like spaghetti?" I asked. I realized I'd never seen Stephen consume anything other than ham and cheese sandwiches and juice. And pills. I guess there were also a lot of pills.

"Well," he said, drawing it out. I figured that meant no. "They have a pretty decent-sounding pastrami on rye on the lunch menu, with, I think, provolone and mâche—though I'd be tempted to go all out on the pepper and use watercress instead." He paused. "But I'm under strict instruction not to order anything even resembling a sandwich this evening. What about you?"

"I don't even know where to look," I admitted.

Stephen ran his finger halfway down one of the columns. "This sounds excellent," he said, tapping once; I recognized the words spinach and Yukon gold and Gouda. "Gnocchi," he added, which was a good thing because, while I theoretically knew what gnocchi was, I had no idea how to pronounce it. "Actually, this sounds really excellent," he said.

"Why don't you?" I asked.

He shook his head. "No, I'm already promised to spaghetti," he told me.

"I hope you're not ordering it just to, I don't know, prove you can eat it in front of me," I said. "If you are, that's a stupid reason. I'm still... it won't affect me at all if you make a mess. And it's your birthday," I reminded him. "If you want gnocchi, that's what you should have."

"All right," he said. "It's probably easier, any rate." He scanned the menu briefly, and tapped another item. "Then you should have this. And I'm going to have a bit of it as well."

"Oh," I said. "I see what this is."

"Yes, well." He flashed a grin. "But you can't not admit it's been helpful."

"Fine," I told him.

"Settled, then?" he asked. He reached up and gave the outside of my hand a quick squeeze.

I swallowed. "Go back to your seat," I said.

Stephen's parents—his mother, especially—treated me like I was a bit of an afterthought, but I was happy nonetheless. They didn't ask any of the questions I'd expected—what I wanted to do after finishing high school (which, for me, was still more than a year away); what plans I had for the summer; what Stephen and I were going to do after he graduated and, in all likelihood (because he would've been wasted on Hayworth), went off to college. In fact, they didn't ask any questions at all.

Stephen talked about a project he and Kyle were working on for history. Stephen's father told a funny story about an interaction with one of his clients (whom he did a very good job of making anonymous. Years of practice, I guess). Stephen's mom didn't talk about her job. It would've all been medical; maybe they didn't consider that polite table-time conversation.

I had given Stephen the envelope with the card on the way into the restaurant, and he put it by the side of his plate without opening it. Halfway through the meal, he did. I watched him, sliding the card out carefully, partway in his lap, hiding it behind the envelope so no one else could see the front. He opened it, then looked up at me, and I knew I'd done the right thing.

He smiled, without showing his teeth, but the corners of his eyes crinkled up. It was the kind of smile, I'd realized, that meant he was really happy. That everything that had happened was exactly what he wanted.

He didn't smile that way very often. I was glad I'd made him do it.

The next day, before school, he handed me an unlined index card, folded in half. "Thank you," it said on the outside, in his horrible handwriting, though I could see he'd made an effort to be legible. Inside: "Thank you." (Again.) "I'm not ready yet. But I will be."

"Do you want to go to a party?" Stephen said.

"What?" I asked. It was Thursday, early—well, the middle of the afternoon.

"At Bonham's," he said, as if this made complete logical sense. "Tomorrow."

"What?" I said again.

Maybe it did make sense to Stephen. For me, it was a bit beyond that. I had never been to a high school party before, unless you counted the one Lasse had had when our parents went out of town for their twentieth anniversary. He'd been sixteen—old enough to take care of himself, but probably too old to be left in a house for a weekend on his own. I suspect my parents' reasoning was that if he had his ten-year-old sister there to take care of (they sent Tammy, who was only five and needed a lot more taking care of, to stay with an aunt), having a party would be a no-go.

Lasse solved that problem simply by barricading the stairs, confining me to the ground floor and keeping all his guests in the basement. So, even though it had been in my house, I wasn't actually at that party. (But I could hear it when I lay down and pressed my ear against the heating vents.)

It had been seven years ago, too. I didn't know anything about parties now. I knew that Jared Randall, indisputably, threw the best ones, and that he'd been allowed to sit at the cool senior table in the lunchroom since midway through his freshman year because of it, but I only knew these things through hearsay. Well, I'd seen him at the senior table, but as to why...

Actually it should have been fairly obvious. He had a pair of those neon green glasses that must be almost impossible to see through because, instead of lenses, they just had a series of horizontal bars running through the frames. Anyone who wears shutter shades to school has obviously got something going on.

Based on what little I knew of Bonham, I imagined his parties wouldn't be very far behind Jared's.

"Bonham's my oldest friend," Stephen said, which, though he'd sort of alluded to it before, very much did not fit with what I knew of Bonham. "He always invites me, for old times' sake, I guess. We don't have to stay long. But I always try to put in an appearance. For old times' sake there, too, I guess."

I wasn't entirely sure my parents would let me go to a high school party on a Friday night—or, for that matter, go anywhere with Stephen at night at all. But they did.

It occurred to me that, perhaps, they trusted me. Even Lasse, despite everything he'd gotten up to in high school, had managed to become a functional—even successful—adult. He wasn't unemployed, imprisoned, or paying child support—which, considering what my parents had thought they had to look forward to when Lasse was my age, was pretty impressive.

So perhaps his influence was finally starting to work in my favor. Or perhaps my parents didn't think I was cool enough to wind up anywhere really out of control. Or perhaps, at the very least, they were testing me. This was my one chance; if I messed up, I wouldn't get another. Maybe Dad was actually waiting for me to mess up. Or for Stephen to. Maybe he'd have liked that.

Whatever their reasons, they said yes.

Stephen parked half a block away from where he said Bonham lived. I wouldn't have been able to pick out the house if he hadn't known; it was just a normal single-story in a normal neighborhood. There was no swarm of teenage cars around, no loud music or flashing lights, no drunk girls out in the yard puking or screaming. Maybe we were too early.

Stephen texted Bonham while we walked, and he met us in the foyer. There were shoes all around the perimeter of the room; Stephen slipped his off and I did the same. Bonham (wearing moccasins) clapped Stephen on the back with one hand, a masculine almost-hug. "All right, mate?" he said, which I am absolutely one hundred percent sure Stephen must have taught him.

"All right," Stephen said back.

Bonham looked at me. "Emily, right?" he said, which surprised me, but which I guess Stephen must have also told him. "Hey."

"Hi," I said. I tried to smile.

Bonham nodded. He leaned back toward Stephen again, and his voice dropped a little bit. "Hey," he said, "do you, uh…"

"No," Stephen said flatly.

Bonham straightened up again and rolled his shoulders back, like nothing had happened. It was a move I'd often seen him do, at assemblies and in the halls. It made his entire upper body seem bigger, but I don't think he did it to be cocky or to draw attention. It was just something he did, maybe even to relax, the way someone else might shrug or take a deep breath and let it out again. "We're all in through here," he said, and a moment later disappeared.

I looked up at Stephen. He put his hand on the small of my back and guided me down the hall into the living room. I didn't know what to think; it wasn't wild or raucous at all. There were maybe fifteen people scattered around, mostly seniors. Kyle and Shelly were in the opposite corner, and Stephen steered me toward them. Kyle was sitting in what must have been a very old and sunken chair, and Shelly was on the armrest. They were drinking from the same bottle, some kind of cider that I could smell even from a distance.

"Hey," Shelly said brightly, as we got closer. Kyle sat up slightly and gave Stephen one of those elaborate handshakes.

I smiled at them. Stephen leaned over my shoulder, his free hand still on my back. "You know Emily."

"Of course," Shelly said, in an overly friendly way that made it clear she in fact did not. She smiled, though. She had the most beautiful teeth.

Kyle nodded, then sank back into the chair.

We stood and listened to Shelly talk about her plans for the summer, which, despite the summer being nearly two months away, were incredibly detailed—as one might expect from the senior class secretary, I suppose.

Stephen's left hand moved around to the outside of my hip and rested there; his right one found the opposite. He wasn't quite hugging me; it felt (stupidly, I know) more like we were in a couple's figure skating routine and he was about to perform a lift. After a while, he leaned into me, just a little.

After another while, which was probably only a few minutes, I leaned back into him a little, too.

Kyle got up in the middle of Shelly's monologue to get another bottle. He had to practically dig himself out of the chair to stand; he did this by bracing his left hand on the end of the chair's arm, his right on Shelly's knee. I couldn't tell if it was sexually charged or not. Shelly didn't react at all, which made it even harder to interpret.

"Bonham just kissed me, FYI," he said when he came back.

He handed the bottle to Shelly, who took a sip and rolled her eyes. "Lock up your sons," she said. Her eyes darted to me for a moment, then past me to Stephen. "I'd keep an eye on him if I were you, Emma."

"And on yourself," Kyle added. "Bonham tends to get a bit ambisexual when he's drunk."

"Bonham tends to be 'a bit ambisexual' all the time," Stephen said, his breath warm on my ear. "He just uses being 'drunk' "—somehow I knew that that was in quote marks, too, and not just because Bonham had been completely sober when I'd seen him fifteen minutes ago—"as an excuse to let the socially constructed persona slide a little."

Then he leaned forward and said, louder, "Stop rolling your eyes, Shelly. You're the one who started it. He was immensely pleased with that, by the way," he added, whispering again. "I think he was just waiting for someone to suggest it. He does still have somewhat of an image to maintain."

Shelly frowned up at us. "What d'you keep whispering to her about, Stephen?" she demanded.

I could feel Stephen turn his head slightly away from mine, and hear him smiling when he spoke. "Nothing much," he said. "The symptoms of acid reflux, if you must know. And other things ending with X."

Kyle grinned, and Shelly's nostrils flared. I got the impression that Stephen didn't like her very much, though I'd never gotten that impression before. Perhaps closer to the truth was that Shelly didn't like Bonham very much, and, when forced to choose between the two, Stephen took Bonham's side instead.

"Right," Shelly said, the vowel long and drawn out. She handed the bottle back to Kyle and resituated herself.

"Anyway," said Stephen, stretching out his vowels just as far, "we'd probably better go. Emily and I are, uh, actually working on a project at the college library, which I believe closes at nine. So."

This was the first I'd heard of any such thing, but I tried to look unsurprised. Kyle grinned again. Shelly rolled her eyes, but in a sympathetic way this time. "Parents," she said to me.

"Yeah." Stephen made a big show of looking at his watch. "Yeah, that better be it for us."

"Well, good to see you, man," Kyle said, even though they'd probably just seen each other at school.

"Yeah, and have a super fun weekend," Shelly told us.

"Be safe," Kyle said.

"Always," said Stephen. He leaned back toward my ear again. "Ready?" he breathed.

I nodded, just enough for him to feel it. "Um, bye," I said to Kyle and Shelly. "Nice to meet you both."

Stephen took one hand off my hip just long enough to wave, then turned me back toward the exit. We made a slight detour to the kitchen. Bonham was there, alone, with an incredible three-dimensional pyramid of Solo cups. Stephen patted him on the back of his arm, and Bonham just managed not to destroy the whole structure, then turned. "Oh, no," he said when he saw Stephen. "Not already?"

Stephen just sort of shrugged, and Bonham frowned. "You should stay," he said. "I'd really like it if you'd stay. We didn't even—"

"It's okay," Stephen said.

Bonham shrugged, too, but when he finished, his shoulders weren't as high up as they had been. He hugged Stephen—well, mostly just his neck—and nodded at me. "All right," he said. "Next time."

Stephen patted his arm again, and we went back to the foyer. There were a few more pair of shoes, but really not that many.

"I want to clarify," Stephen said as we walked back to the wagon. "Despite what you may have just been led to think, Bonham really isn't a slut. He's just a person. And he just likes people, and he doesn't care what body parts they're attached to. He actually tried coming out, but people still believe what they want to believe. You know, 'oh, that's just Bonham, he's crazy.' Which, he kind of is, but it isn't just that.

"And he's not some deviant predator, either," he added. "He only kisses Kyle because it pisses off Shelly. Kyle's not bothered, and it's pretty much the only thing anyone's ever found that pisses off Shelly."

"Are they a couple?" I asked. "Shelly and Kyle? I thought you said once... But I couldn't quite tell."

"No?" He seemed almost disappointed. "Yeah, I can't tell, either.

"Sorry if you were wanting to stay longer," he told me. "That's about all I can take. I mean, yes, they're my friends. And I know it's not a rager or whatever, and it's not like he's invited half the school, but it's really not my scene." He sighed. "I'm an introvert, and much of the time I'm still quite shy, and oftentimes at parties people seem to think the opposite, and I don't enjoy having a lot of people talking to me or looking at me, or even worrying that they're going to talk to me or look at me. I've something of the impression that you feel similarly."

"Similarly enough," I agreed.

"Also, Shelly can talk your ear off when she gets going, especially if she's first gotten a bit tipsy," he said. "I swear, she could discourse for hours just on the subject of watching grass grow."

"Actually, grass growing is fairly complicated," I told him. "All the photosynthesis and stuff. There's probably enough involved, scientifically speaking, for a pretty lengthy speech."

"Of course," said Stephen. "But you know what I mean."

"I know what you mean," I said. When I say Shelly was discussing the minutiae of her summer plans, I mean she was actually telling us what she had planned down to the minute. "Are you friends?" I asked. "You and Shelly?"

"Yes," said Stephen. He seemed surprised. "I mean, I think we are. Why?"

"I just kind of got the impression earlier, after Kyle said…"

"Oh," Stephen said. "About Bonham? Well, obviously. Bonham's my oldest friend, obviously I've got to take his side, especially when she starts getting all snippy and borderline homophobic."

"Are Shelly and Bonham friends?" I asked.

Stephen shrugged. "As long as he's not hitting on or, uh, actually engaging in relations with, Kyle, which is to say ninety-nine percent of the time, or, well, maybe ninety-five percent of the time, yes."

"So she doesn't mind with anyone else, just not Kyle?" Stephen nodded.

"Then they probably are some kind of a couple," I said.

"Oh, I know they're some kind of couple," he agreed. "I just don't know what kind."

I figured that was fair enough. I still wasn't quite sure what kind of couple Stephen and I were, either. We'd decided I was his girlfriend, which I assumed also meant he was my boyfriend, but there were still a lot of things that could mean. I wondered, suddenly, if it was odd that after two months of informal dating, or whatever it had been, it was only now that I was meeting Stephen's friends. But of course, Stephen hadn't met mine, either.

I decided I didn't want to think—or ask—about that. At least then I wouldn't get any answers about our relationship that I didn't want to hear.

So I asked Stephen about him and Bonham instead. I asked very awkwardly. "So, uh. You and Bonham..."

We had reached the wagon, and Stephen was more focused on getting the key in the ignition than anything. "Yeah?" he replied.

"You've really never kissed or anything after that one time?"

"Bonham? No," he said. "I'm not his type. He told me in seventh grade." He put the wagon into gear, then paused before pulling forward, considering. "Actually, if the circumstances were different, I think that I might in fact be exactly his type. But he's always seen me as too much of a friend-slash-brother, almost, to have any kind of romantic or sexual feelings, so…

"You know we've been friends since we were six," he said. "That's like… more than ten years. Two thirds of my life. You remember Skate City?" he asked unexpectedly.

I did. It had closed in elementary school, but the building owners had never taken the sign down; it was still there, an enormous, peeling pink roller skate above an otherwise unremarkable-looking warehouse.

"In third and fourth grade, we wore the same size shoes, and we used to go there and rent one pair of skates between us. But instead of switching back and forth, taking turns, we'd each just wear one. Bonham wore the left skate and I wore the right. It was sort of like skateboarding, I guess, only instead of the actual board, just a skate on."

"That was allowed?" I said, incredulous.

"Oh, no," he told me. "Can you imagine the liability, if one of us had gotten our bare foot run over? No, they always kicked us out. But it always took them a while to notice. And they kept letting us come back. I always thought it was more fun that way," he said. "Maybe they could tell.

"Bonham always had those little bubblegum cigarettes— not the kind they make now with the paper around them, just little powdery pink tubes—and after we got pulled off the floor and banned for the day, we'd sit on the bench out front, waiting for our parents to pick us up, smoking bubblegum and elbowing each other and laughing."

There was a sort of faraway sound to his voice. I wished I could see him in the dark. "Maybe," he said, "if they hadn't closed the skating rink, we'd still be that close." Then he sighed. "But our shoe sizes probably would've changed anyway."

We stopped at an intersection and he looked over at me; I could see him, just barely, in the glow from the traffic light. "You're thinking right now, aren't you, that it was Bonham's idea? It was mine," he said. "They were always mine. Bonham's always been a leader—I mean, look at him. But I think he was only a leader at first because I gave him things to do. Things I'd never have done on my own. But, you know, when you have a guy like Bonham standing next to you..."

"I'm sorry I'm not..." I said. "Like that."

Bonham, I knew, would've already climbed the water tower half a dozen times. Bonham would've happily ridden in a helicopter over one of those constantly-oozing volcanoes in Hawaii; he would've hung out the door in a rope harness and let his fingers skim through the air just inches above the molten surface. Bonham would do all the things on Stephen's not-list.

But Stephen shook his head. "Don't be," he said. "You are what you are, right? There's nothing wrong with that." He paused, and rubbed at his hat for a moment. "Anyway," he said, "I just sort of meant... Not a lot of people will even do something like that. Obviously it's not why we're friends, or why we're still friends, but it's sort of like... unless something really horrible happens, you can't have that kind of history, that kind of past relationship, and not still have something." He swallowed. "Right?"

"Right," I told him. I understood.

The following Monday, Stephen caught me at my locker as I was leaving for lunch. "Can I speak to you a moment?" he said.

"Sure." I shrugged, even though I was excited. I hardly ever saw Stephen at school. Our schedules were so different that even our paths through the halls, between classes, didn't intersect. "I can walk with you if you want," I told him. "I don't want you to be late."

"No, it's my lunch now, too," he said.

"What?" I'd spent the past two months, give or take, believing that we hardly ever saw each other at school because (among other things) when Stephen had looked at my schedule the first time, he'd determined we had different lunch periods and left it at that. "We have the same lunch?" I asked. "Why didn't you ever say anything?"

"I didn't want to overwhelm you," he said. "Or inundate you. And I know you have other friends. I didn't want... I mean, we can't be together all the time."

That was fair enough. To be honest, though—while I don't want to sound entirely like the friendless loner who needed Stephen to rescue her—I didn't have anyone else.

Mari had a different lunch schedule, so I usually ate with Jess, but we hadn't really been friends since eighth grade, maybe even before. Especially since starting high school, she had become more and more interested in the clarinet, and less and less interested in everything else, including me. At lunch, she would sit buried in sheet music, fingers moving as though playing notes on an invisible instrument.

We'd continued eating together, I think, because neither of us had anyone else to sit with, but my presence (or lack of) at the lunch table was barely on her radar. In other words, it was quite welcome to be informed that—assuming he didn't mind the additional time with me—I could start spending lunch periods with Stephen.

"No one will miss me," I told him. "I don't mind sitting with you."

"Are you sure?" he said.

I nodded.

"Actually, there's something I should tell you first."

"What?" I said, because something about that sounded rather not good.

Stephen swallowed. "If people have been looking at you strangely, it's because of me."

A part of me wanted to say "what?" again, but not in a questioning way, in a "that's preposterous" way. But another part remembered that Jared Randall had said yo to me in the hallway between second and third period that morning. It was kind of hard to tell because of his glasses, and I couldn't think of any possible reason he'd be talking to me—but just in case, I tried to smile back (though not with so much of a smile that I'd feel like an idiot if it turned out he was addressing someone else). As soon as he'd passed, I looked over my shoulder for the real recipient of the yo, but there was no one there. For the next three and a half minutes, I felt very odd. I was not the kind of girl Jared Randall lowered his shutter shades marginally and said yo to. I wasn't the kind of girl he even noticed.

Then we had a pop quiz and I forgot.

So there was that. But I still couldn't think what Stephen could've done that would cause people to look strangely and Jared Randall to greet me during passing time. "That's awfully..." I started.

"Big-headed? I know." Stephen leaned up against the locker next to mine and took a breath. "No one's ever really seen us together before," he said.

"You've been driving me to and from school every day for the past two months," I said.

"Yeah, they probably just thought we were neighbors," he said dismissively. "And beyond that..."

He'd spoken to me in the halls, I realized, a few times only, and those had been fleeting. We didn't hang out before or after school, just came and went. We had the same lunch period and had never once spent it together.

A couple, under normal circumstances, would be rushing through the halls to spend a minute or two together between classes, cuddling up somewhere during lunch. Stephen would carry my books before and after school, and sometimes, when it was cold, I'd turn up to class wearing his jacket. It still hadn't been that long that we'd been an actual couple, but it occurred to me that even "just friends" tended to spend more time together than we, observably, did.

"So, what happened?" I asked him. "What changed?"

"I guess someone at Bonham's."

"Oh," I said. There hadn't been that many people there, but I guess it only takes one. And I guessed it had been rather obvious. We'd come in together and left together, stood together the whole time, and Stephen, in fact, had stood most of the time with his hands around my waist. Normally I wouldn't have expected to be important enough for the high school rumor mill, but apparently he was. I felt suddenly annoyed. "So is that why you're here now?" I asked. "Cat's finally out of the bag?"

"No." Stephen pushed his hat back partway, then pulled it down again. He looked over his shoulder.

"You're embarrassed of me," I said flatly.

"No," Stephen said again, and he looked stricken. "Of course not. Fuck's sake, Emily, of course I'm not embarrassed of you. If anything, you should be embarrassed of me. Look," he said. "I just want to"—he sighed, scrubbed the ball of his hand against his forehead—"to apologize. There's not really a gentle way—I don't really know how to say this." Then he said it anyway. "There are a lot of people here who believe I'm on drugs."

Suddenly Jared Randall made a lot of sense. Jared Randall was not yo-ing at me, Emily; he was establishing contact with someone who could potentially be able to score him some acid.

"People are going to start to wonder," Stephen said. "So I understand completely if you want to, say, stage a very public break-up."

"But," I said, "I—you're not."

He smiled, a bit sadly. "I do not now," he said, "never have, and never will take recreational drugs."

I noticed he only said recreational. But I also knew it wasn't the right time to press.

"I would like very much to eat lunch with you," I said.

"Really?" he asked. "Really, I wouldn't feel bad."

I knew this was a lie, but didn't comment on that, either. "Really," I told him. "Where do you sit?"

"Okay," Stephen said. He reached over and touched my hand. We were inside, hiding from the clouds starting to roll in; Stephen lay back with his knees bent and lower legs hanging off the end of the bed, and I sat cross-legged next to him. I'd found a loose thread on the comforter, where the quilting was coming undone, and was slowly pulling it further free. "I've got one," he told me.

Eventually I'd figured out that when he said this, it meant he'd come up with something that wasn't on the list of thirty-six invasive questions but that he still thought was interesting and that, with enough discussion, might make me want to sleep with him.

"All right," I said.

"If you'd been a boy, what would your parents have named you?"

I was surprised. This didn't seem very interesting. Or, even if the name was interesting (and mine wasn't), it didn't seem like something that offered much room for discussion.

"Nathan," I said. "Nathan Patrick."

"Huh," said Stephen. "Your parents must have really liked Patrick."

"What?"

"Emily Patricia," he said. I should've known he'd know. It was on my student record.

"Well," I said. "I think they actually liked Nathan better." There'd been plans to name Tammy that, too.

"Just didn't like the girl version?" Stephen suggested, since obviously neither Nathan, nor any of its derivatives, was part of my name.

"What is the girl version?" I asked.

"Oh," he said after thinking a moment. "Well. It's Emily, I suppose."

"The girl version of Nathan is not Emily," I said. "What would you have been, as a girl? Stephanie?"

"Nope." Stephen shook his head. "No girl name. My parents didn't have one. Mum's a radiologist, remember? Scanning's her thing. They knew I was a boy right away."

"Oh," I said. My parents had wanted to be surprised.

"Here's what I wonder," Stephen said. "What do you think you'd be like if you had a different name? If your parents had named you, say, Nathanya Patricia? Or even Patricia Emily instead. Even if you were Emma instead. Biologically, you'd still be the same, right? You'd still have the same DNA; you'd still have started with all the same cells. But would having had a different name actually change you?"

"I don't know," I said. I'd never been called anything other than Emily. I'd gotten the occasional Em or Emmy, even, as Stephen had suggested, Emma from time to time, but none with any regularity. I'd never introduced myself using any of those. I'd never thought of any of them as my name.

There was a cheerleader a year younger than me named Emma Champlain. I couldn't imagine myself ever being a cheerleader.

And there had been a girl in Lasse's class named Patricia, who went by Pat (I knew from Lasse's yearbook). She wore half-moon glasses and was captain of the debate team. I couldn't imagine myself ever doing debate, either. I knew that wasn't what Stephen meant, but it was still unsettling to think of myself living the life of either of those girls. "I guess," I said. "What about you?"

"Yeah." He stretched forward, and then put his hands behind his neck. His brow furrowed. "Sometimes I wonder what my life would've been like if I'd been named Trevor."

"Trevor?" I repeated. Of all possible names.

Stephen took one hand out and waved it at me dismissively. "Shush," he said. "And no, before you ask. It was never a consideration."

"Why that, then?" I asked.

"I don't know," he told me. "It's just something I thought of. Maybe because it seemed so different. I mean, I could conceivably be a David, or a Paul, without changing that much, don't you think? But Trevor… Maybe I'd be obsessed with turtles to the exclusion of all else. Or maybe I'd talk like a gangster and dress like a chav, but without actually knowing what a chav is, because this isn't England and I didn't expand my vocabulary that way.

"Isn't it interesting, though?" he said. "I'd have started

out the same person. My parents would've raised me the same—to the point, at least, that they realized Trevor had different wants and needs to Stephen. And I really think he would've—I would've. Because we don't live in isolation." He turned to face me then. "People treat you differently based upon your name. Even if it's as subtle a difference as between Emma and Emily. And ultimately, I think that matters a lot. To you. You change."

"So are we talking nature versus nurture here?" I asked. We'd spent a lot of time in biology last year on the debate, and I was pleased I'd been able to come up with it; often the things Stephen talked about quickly went far beyond my comprehension—or, if not exactly that, at least beyond my ability to meaningfully contribute.

"In a way, I suppose, yes," he said. "But I'm not talking about two genetically identical individuals raised in different environments. I'm talking about—hypothetically—two genetically identical individuals raised in identical environments, and the only difference is in what they're called. How different would they be? How different would I be, Trevor? Would you still be friends with me?"

I shook my head—not because I wouldn't have been friends with him, but because I just couldn't picture Stephen as a Trevor. It was incomprehensible.

"It's also interesting to think about our perception of names," he said. "You're having trouble thinking of me as Trevor, am I right?" I nodded. "Even if you haven't thought of it consciously yet, subconsciously you're thinking of Trevor Solomon, and you're trying to associate me with him, and it's not working, and that's why, or at least part of the reason."

I had, briefly, been thinking of Trevor Solomon. He was a year younger than me, and one of Jared Randall's friends.

I'd never actually seen Trevor wearing shutter shades, but that didn't mean he didn't have any. I couldn't imagine Stephen even trying a pair on. Even just for fun.

"Okay," I said. "So probably, then, when you hear what someone's name is, even before you meet them, maybe, you start to decide what they might be like."

"Oh, definitely," said Stephen. "And maybe eventually it even becomes a self-fulfilling prophecy. That's part of why I think people sometimes give their kids really standard names. I mean, my parents had to have known I was going to be Stephen S. all through elementary school. Just like your parents had to have known you were going to be Emily M."

"Actually, I was Emily M.R.," I said. "To avoid confusion with Emily Milne." And she wasn't even the only other one. Emily was the most popular baby name in the United States the year I was born, and for several years on either side, too.

"When you have so many people in the category, it's harder to assign reliable characteristics," Stephen said. "And when you have a standard name—like Stephen, like Emily—people don't have expectations. You can slide by. But there are some names you just can't get away from."

"Yeah," I said. "Lasse, remember?"

"Oh, right," Stephen said. "Although, that's almost so unusual that there wouldn't be any expectations, either."

I shook my head. "No expectations, maybe, but if your name's so weird that no one's ever heard it, you're going to get made fun of."

"I thought you said he was cool," Stephen said.

"Yeah," I said. "He was. Is. I guess either you get made fun of, or you get everyone to think you're cool. Or, in Lasse's case, you get everyone to think you're cool but still sometimes kinda get made fun of, too."

Stephen was silent for a minute. Then he said, "I guess that answers my other question, then."

"What?" I said. I hated when people alluded to something they'd been planning to say and then decided not to say it.

"You not being able to think of me as a Trevor," he said. "I was going to ask, what if instead, you imagined me still having a different name, but one you'd never heard of? Or knew anyone called it, at least. Like Étienne."

I stared at him. This had to be even less feasible than Trevor.

He spelled it for me. "It's the French version of Stephen," he added, as if this would make it normal.

"I think you would've gotten beat up a lot," I said honestly. "And then, maybe about fourth grade, you would've decided to try going by Ethan, which would've only gotten you beaten up more."

Stephen looked hurt. "Really?" he said. "That's what you think?"

"Well, if it makes you feel any better," I said, "I also think that getting beat up on a weekly basis all through elementary school would've probably made you a profoundly different person from who you are today, even with all other things remaining constant."

"Better," Stephen said. Then, "Let's try an experiment. I want you to call me Étienne for a week."

"I am *not* calling you Étienne," I said.

"Come on," he said. "It's not like we use our names that much, anyway. Why not?"

"Why?" I asked.

"Fine," he sighed.

"I'm not calling you Steve, either," I added.

"Thank fuck for that," he said. He looked over at me and

smiled, then turned his head back toward the ceiling. "Trevor would've had his hands in your pants by now," he said.

"I take it this is chav Trevor we're talking about," I said drily, "not turtle Trevor."

"Of course," said Stephen. "You haven't got a carapace; turtle Trevor's not interested."

"Hm," I said.

"It's not you," he told me, "it's him. Chav Trevor, on the other hand…"

"It's probably also not me, with him," I said.

"Possibly," Stephen agreed. "However, presented with the same scenario, I still think he would've."

"Well," I said. "He might've tried."

Thursday, I opened the door and found a tiny bunch of flowers on my seat. They were miniature daisies—not the kind that grow tall in gardens, but the ones that come up in patches in less well-kept lawns, white with a pinkish tinge toward the middle, not even an inch from one petal tip to the other. The stems were tied together with a little piece of green plastic curling ribbon, the kind you use for wrapping gifts.

"What's this?" I asked Stephen.

"It's May Day," he said. "In pagan times, according to my mum, the first of May was the beginning of summer, and was celebrated by, among other things, ringing people's doorbells and sprinting away, leaving only a basket of flowers for them to find. I didn't know that you'd fully appreciate my ringing the bell, so…" He gestured toward the seat.

"I'm fairly sure that in pagan times, they didn't have doorbells," I said.

"Well, perhaps the ritual has evolved," he said. "Please accept the flowers and get in."

I sighed and picked up the little bouquet. It was small enough I was able to do so with just my forefinger and thumb. "Thank you for the flowers, Stephen; they're beautiful."

"They're from the park by Hill School," he said. "I got up early to pick them for you."

"Thank you," I said again, more sincere.

When we got to school, Stephen reached into the side pocket of his door and took out a slightly crumpled paper cup, then a bottle of water. He put the cup in the holder on the dash and filled it halfway, then nodded at the flowers. "They'll die if you leave them in your locker all day," he said. "Here."

I put them in the cup, and it seemed to make him happier.

"That's the bad thing about cut flowers," he said as we walked in. "It's so nice to receive them. They're so beautiful at first. But eventually they start to wilt, and eventually you have to throw them away, and that's how you remember them, all limp and faded and rotting. And you can't help but wonder, is that what's going to happen to us? To me? And you start to wish you'd never gotten them in the first place, because then you could still pretend that everything would be all right. Flowers are a visual reminder of decay."

"Then why did you give me a visual reminder of decay?" I asked.

"I don't know," he said. "I didn't think of it like that until a minute ago. I just wanted to do something nice for you."

"It's okay," I said. "I didn't think of it that way, either. It is nice." No one had ever given me flowers before. Even if they were just tiny flowers plucked haphazardly from the grass in the park by Hill School.

"Remember when I asked if you wanted to go hiking?" Stephen said that afternoon.

"Wow," I said. I remembered. But it seemed so long ago. "And you said it was still too cold?" he went on.

I nodded.

"I'm pretty sure it's warm enough now. It's been calendar spring"—he grinned, presumably because it was so similar to the phrasing I'd used—"for more than a month."

"It has," I said.

"So…?"

"You want to go hiking?" I asked. When he had first asked me, at the end of February, it hadn't seemed that unusual. But that was because I hardly knew anything about him then. Now, wanting to go on a hike didn't really fit with the Stephen I knew.

"Not *hiking* hiking," he said. "Not with, like, a tent and those weird climbing poles. I meant more like walking hiking. You can do it in regular shoes. It could be a photographic expedition."

I knew then that I would agree—not just because there were only three weeks left before our final class and I was still missing many of my required photos, but also because I simply liked the phrase. The idea of going on a photographic expedition with Stephen—it was just a little bit magical.

"Saturday?" he asked.

I was immediately disappointed. Unless you counted that very first day (which I didn't, because at that point I think he was just throwing things out randomly, hoping I'd bite), Stephen had never before asked me to do anything with him on a weekend. And this was the one weekend I couldn't.

"I can't," I said. "It's Tammy's birthday. She probably won't speak to me all summer if I'm not there. Actually, my mom probably won't, either, if I'm not there to help." Mom had been regretting, for the past several years, telling Tammy that she could invite a number of sleepover guests equal to the age she was turning. (I regretted it, too.)

"Can't argue with that," he said. "Next Saturday, then?" I was surprised. Aside from the photography class (which I didn't count, either, because it was ongoing), that—a week and a half—was the furthest out we'd ever planned anything.

"Really?" I said, and he nodded. "Okay."

"Okay," he repeated. "Also, do you want to go to prom?"

That startled me even more. Prom was even further away—a full three weeks, in fact. So much for Stephen never making plans. Also, it was prom. "Do *you* want to go to prom?" I asked.

Stephen shrugged. "To be clear," he said after a moment, "I'm not asking you to go to the prom with me. I'm just asking if you, completely independent of me, have any interest in attending."

"Oh," I said.

"So you do want to go," he inferred.

"I don't know," I said. "In a way—I mean, it's prom. But also, not really. I guess… I don't really think I'd actually enjoy it. I don't know," I said again. "Maybe it'd be different with a date. But I definitely don't want to go if you aren't."

"I'll go if you want to," Stephen said. "But I don't want you to go just because you think I want to. I was just asking to gauge interest."

"Oh," I said again.

"I feel similarly to you," he said. "It doesn't really sound appealing, but it's senior prom—I feel like it's something I should attend. Or at the very least put in an appearance."

"Maybe we could just go for a little while," I said.

"Or pretend we were going to go, but not," he suggested. "Or 'change our minds' at the last minute."

"Or we could just go for pictures, and skip the actual dance," I said.

"Oh," said Stephen. "I'd probably wear a white tux for that. Even the trousers. You down?"

I laughed. "We're probably not going, are we?" I said.

"No, probably not," he agreed. "You won't be too disappointed, will you?"

"No."

"Even so, let me know if you change your mind."

"I highly doubt that prom will become appealing enough in the next three weeks to make me change my mind," I said.

"Probably not," he said again. "We can do something else instead. We will," he told me.

"Okay," I told him.

"Possibly also involving the white tux," he added. "What do you think—graduation, maybe? Or would that be too much?"

"Possibly a little much," I said.

"I suppose you're probably right. But we'll cross that bridge when we come to it," he said. "So, back to Saturday. Any place particular you'd like to go?"

There wasn't, of course. We decided we'd cross that bridge—of deciding—when we came to it, too.

Stephen found me in the hallway between sixth and seventh periods. "Hey," I said. "What are you doing?" It was so unusual to see him then.

He frowned for a moment, then leaned closer. "I'm sorry," he said. "I can't hear you."

"What are you doing?" I shouted, adding to the noise in the hall. Then I thought better of it and added, "Is everything okay?"

"No, I just wanted to see you," Stephen shouted back. "I missed you at lunch." This was plausible, I supposed. With graduation getting closer, Shelly was starting to go into panic mode more and more often; there'd been an emergency lunchtime meeting that day.

"But you're going—" I started, then stopped, and repeated myself at a higher volume. "You're going to see me in an hour and a half, anyway."

"But I wanted to see you now," he replied.

For a second, something passed over his face, and I wanted to ask him again if everything was okay. Then his watch beeped. He looked away, swallowed his pills.

"Stephen," I said.

He didn't turn. He hadn't heard me.

"Stephen," I said again, and put my hand on his arm.

He turned this time, smiling brightly. "Are we still on for the weekend?" he said.

"Of course," I told him. He'd asked me half a dozen times over the past week if we were. I couldn't figure out why. I leaned forward, and held onto the front of his shirt with both hands, and kissed him. He put one hand up on the back of my neck. "I'm in if you're in," I said.

He pulled back a bit, then tilted forward so his forehead rested against mine. "Don't worry about that," he said. "I'll be there."

Stephen asked if I wanted to drive, but I told him he could. He'd picked a route from a local nature walks pamphlet my mom had. (Another short-lived phase.) The gist of its description, he said, was that it was only three miles and relatively easy—easy enough to be managed by people who sucked at this—but also far enough off the beaten path that we wouldn't constantly be interrupted by other people who'd also chosen to try that route that day. There was no one else parked at the trailhead, which was a good sign.

We'd both brought cameras—that was kind of the point, or at least it was the point on which it'd been sold to me—but only Stephen had his out. He kept stopping and setting up a photo, then catching himself and telling me to take it instead.

"It doesn't really matter if you're not in it," I finally said, after we had paused for him to swap out a 135-200 zoom for a 50. He was down on his knees at the edge of the path, accosting one of those impossibly neon green, almost translucent, caterpillars—or at least he had been until he remembered.

"All right," he said. I'd meant for him to take the photo himself, but instead he passed the camera to me, then got down very close to the caterpillar and put his hand directly in its path. "Use the yellow filter," he said while he waited for it to crawl onto him. "And put the zoom back on."

"What?" I said.

"It'll be good," he told me. "I promise."

He stood up and turned his hand over as the caterpillar crawled around, but didn't come closer to help. "Lower your F-stop all the way," he said. "And you'll need to adjust your exposure time to compensate."

He held his hands out, and as the caterpillar made its way along the ridges of his knuckles, he talked me through the whole process. "Keep me in the frame, for Sylvia," he said, "but focus on the caterpillar, not my face. Get in as close as you can without going out of focus."

I shuffled forward until the caterpillar started to distort. Behind it, Stephen's face was still recognizably his, but mostly a blur. I could see through the lens that he'd turned his head to one side, dropped his right arm down. He rotated his left arm again, and for a moment, the poor caterpillar (probably hopelessly confused by then) balanced on end atop his index finger. I pressed the shutter.

Stephen turned his hand palm-up and let the caterpillar crawl across to his right hand, lifted again. He got down on his knees and I took a second shot as it passed from one hand to the other. His fingers curled up slightly, holding it in a little cradle.

The caterpillar reached his thumbnail, and Stephen looked up at me. "Okay?" he said.

I nodded.

"How did you know all that?" I asked, after he'd nudged the caterpillar into the grass and we'd started walking again. Sylvia had talked about it in class, I knew, but how had he remembered?

He shrugged. "I pay attention," he said. "And of course, you do, too—ask me about all the processing stuff that you can rattle off in your sleep now, and I wouldn't have a clue. We just listen to different things." He paused. "Did you think I wouldn't really try?" he asked. "I have to. I want to do my part well for you. I mean, if I just take a lot of uniformly blurry pictures with no contrast, that doesn't give you a lot to work with, does it?"

"I guess not," I told him.

"It's just technical," he said. "Once you figure out how the camera works, it's easy enough to manipulate to get it how you want."

But it wasn't all technical, I knew. Every time I developed a roll of Stephen's film, I was startled by how good it was. He had the right kind of eye. Even if I'd known, on my own, how to set up the photo I'd just taken, I never would've thought of it. I never would've thought to take a photo of the underside of the water tower, either, but it was beautiful. I just didn't see things the same way Stephen did. I told him as much.

"Composition, you mean?" Again, he shrugged. "I think black and white photography is really just two things: angles and light. Light, mostly. Shadows and contrast and the difference between one area and another, between something dark and something pale.

"Of course, it would make things easier if we didn't have to see in color," he said. "I mean, I understand that color is nice, but sometimes I think the world would be so much prettier monochromatic."

"I get that," I said.

"Black and white is so much simpler. You're just left with the light. Doing different things, finding different ways to work with the light you're given. What you're given."

The way he said it, it did seem simple.

Later I took another picture, at the edge of a viewpoint atop a small valley. Stephen was looking away from the frame, into the photo. It wouldn't have worked at all as a portrait, but I wanted it for a landscape. I liked that he wasn't looking.

After I took the photo, I went and stood next to him. He put his arm around my shoulders and leaned his head against mine. We stood there for a long time—minutes—without speaking, even though it wasn't that spectacular a view. It wasn't really much of a view at all.

I wondered which of us would break the silence. I didn't want it to be me. But I didn't want it to be Stephen, either. In a perfect world, we could have stayed there forever—in a not-very-special place, doing a not-very special thing. At the very least, we could've been interrupted by something beyond our control, like a bear suddenly lumbering up the hill or an overly jovial hiker rounding the bend, so that neither of us would've had to bear the burden of being the one who said, "Let's go."

"We should probably," Stephen finally said.

Just before we reached the end of the trail loop, the pine trees on one side opened up into a wide, flat meadow. The young grasses were still green, and not quite knee-high, studded with hundreds, perhaps thousands, of delicate, long-stemmed blue and white flowers. "Oh, no," Stephen said, looking over the field. I looked at him with some concern, wondering if I was about to discover a previously unmentioned allergy of his. "I suppose we'll have to stop," he said.

"What?" I asked.

"You're a girl," he said, as if it was obvious. "Look at it. Isn't this every teenage girl's dream photograph? Lying in a field of flowers, with your hair spread out in an arc around you?"

"Apparently not every girl," I said flatly. "And my hair doesn't arc."

But he insisted. "Sometimes I like clichés," he told me.

"Stephen," I protested as we waded through the field toward a small boulder, just big enough for him to stand on, "this is absurd." It might have looked better, I told him, if I was wearing something diaphanous, and wasn't wearing ratty tennis shoes, and if the loose short tendrils along my hairline weren't plastered to my forehead with sweat. He didn't agree.

Eventually, I made him promise that if he could take such an obvious photo of me, I got to take one of him, too. After he climbed back off the rock, I sat up again, and he let me pull him down. He lay on his side next to me, his right knee hooked over mine. His left arm was under my neck. I bent my arm up at the elbow; our fingers just barely touched.

"Wait a second more," he said. "And look up."

"You're not," I said. "It's film. Nobody uses film to take a selfie."

In response, Stephen grinned and stuck the camera up in the air as far as his arm would extend, and depressed the shutter. He was looking at me; I was staring at the camera, wide-eyed. If it turned out to be in focus—and if both our faces were actually in the frame—it would be a ridiculous picture.

"If you get one, then I get one," I reminded him.

"Here?" he said, and passed the camera over. I wrapped the strap around my wrist and held it up shakily. He leaned in after a moment and kissed me. He closed his eyes. I did, too.

I let the camera come back down and rest on top of my ribcage; Stephen unwrapped the strap and moved it out of the way, then rolled back with his hand still on my shoulder, pulling me with him. I wound up at a forty-five degree angle, half on top of him and half on the ground. It wasn't the most comfortable position in the world, but it worked.

"Huh," he said after a while. "I can't decide if it would be more clichéd to actually fuck here or to just lie in the grass and look at clouds with you."

I looked up. There weren't any clouds, really. "I don't think fucking is ever really clichéd," I said. "If we called it making love, then it might be."

"Point," he agreed.

"That said, sex is not on the table." Some people might think it was romantic, but I didn't really relish the idea of losing my virginity while simultaneously getting weird places on my body marked with grass stains.

"I don't see any tables," Stephen said. But I knew he knew what I meant. And I knew that it was okay.

I shifted again and he turned toward me. His knees bent up and his arms encircled my shoulders; his lips almost brushed my neck. "This is very nice, too," he said. "Thank you."

"Thank you?" I repeated.

"I never expected any of this," he said quietly. "Not any of it."

After a while, he tilted his face up to kiss me, then let go. I stood up and put the camera back around my neck.

Stephen hadn't moved at all, still on his side, wrapped around where I'd been. His right hand splayed in the grass below his left elbow, fingers bent just slightly around a wide blade of grass. He looked, somehow, very vulnerable, which I figured was a calculated look, but was still compelling.

On a whim, I stepped past his feet, stood on my toes, and took a picture.

It wasn't supposed to be the final picture. But Stephen had heard either the click of the shutter or the little whirr of the film advance lever being pulled across, and was already starting to sit up. Maybe I would've had time to press the shutter down a second time, if I'd been very fast, if I hadn't even minutely adjusted the focus. But he was already moving; it would've been blurry anyway.

I sighed, and Stephen smiled and got to his feet. He put his arm around my shoulders and we walked to the wagon quietly. Then he handed me the keys and I drove us back home.

"I think we should sleep together," said Stephen.

"No surprise there," I said, without thinking.

I could feel him laughing. We were in his room, Monday

afternoon. I was lying on top of him—my head tucked under his chin, with his arms crossed atop my back and hands tucked into my pants pockets—so it wasn't the only thing I could feel. "I really like that about you," he said. "Once you get past being nervous and always censoring yourself, you really tell it like it is."

"Mm," I said.

He took one hand out of my pocket and brought it up to my chin, tilting my face toward his and then pushing my hair back out of the way. "Come up here," he said.

I slid up a little to face him properly. He ran his thumb down one of the tendons at the side of my neck and smiled, the corners of his eyes crinkling up. His thumb traced back up, and around the outline of my earlobe. "How 'bout your hand?" he said.

"How about I just kiss you?" I asked.

His smile twitched. "Okay," he said. "That sounds really good."

It wasn't that I didn't want to have sex with Stephen. I was just scared.

Mari was as inexperienced as I was, if not more, and I'd never had a female role model. Of course I had my mom, and our relationship was, I think, pretty good for a teenager and parent, but it still wasn't such that I ever wanted to ask her about sex. I could have asked Lasse, maybe, but he didn't really have the feminine perspective. If he'd brought Melinda to Easter like everyone expected him to, maybe I would've asked her. But maybe not.

I didn't know what it was I wanted to hear, either. I wasn't scared of sex, per se. I didn't believe I was ruining myself by not waiting for marriage; I had no worries of being branded a slut. What I was scared of was doing it wrong.

Prior to Stephen, I'd considered sex, vaguely, as something other people—primarily fictional people—did. It didn't seem unnatural—for them. But when I thought about it myself, it did. I knew, technically, how it worked, but the idea of actually doing such a thing was completely foreign to me. I was convinced I had to be missing something. Maybe some sort of adapter.

Fiction, it must be said, is not always the best teacher. And my sex education otherwise was rather lacking. At school, it had consisted of a horrifying video about menstruation in fifth grade and an equally horrifying two-week-long STD unit in eighth.

And at home, I'd gotten the talk when I was really young—too young, really, to make any use of it, or even, probably, to understand it all. I had just turned ten; it would be more than two years before I even started my period. I certainly hadn't asked to be talked to, or done anything that might have suggested I needed it. I assume Lasse must've somehow provoked our mother, but I've never known what he did. Although perhaps it's better Mom didn't say.

I remember parts of the evening very well, but none of the useful parts.

Mom came into my room with a condom and a banana, and we sat next to each other on the bed. It was very awkward—more awkward, even, than you might expect. She struggled, first, to open the wrapper, and then, once that was completed, she struggled again to properly sheath the banana. "It's been a long time since I did this," she told me finally. "Since before Daddy got fixed."

I shuddered, and after Mom finished enclothing it, I stared at the banana in repulsed fascination. There was a tiny, pointed bubble of air left at the end ("for the semen to go,"

Mom explained; I would've rather she hadn't) and the whole thing appeared to be rather sticky and gross. "Is it supposed to look like that?" I asked her. "All… gloopy?" If I had come upon this condom on its own, I would've guessed it had already been used.

"Yes, honey, that's for lubrication," Mom said. "It helps the penis go into the vagina more smoothly."

I flinched. I flinched every time she said penis.

"You wouldn't want something like those powdery dry doctor gloves pushing into you, would you?" she asked.

Frankly, at ten, I didn't want anything pushing into me.

"I'm showing you this because I want you to be safe," Mom said, brandishing the banana. "It's very important that you use protection. Even if you're having sex with another girl," she added. "Obviously in that case, you don't have to worry about getting pregnant, but you still need to take precautions before you go mixing your fluids around. I assume you're having sex with boys—"

"Mom!" I shrieked, horrified.

"In the future," she amended. "Far, far in the future." (This was mollifying, but only slightly.) "When that time comes, unless you're in a committed relationship and trying to have a baby, you need to use birth control. If you want to go on the pill, just tell me, but keep in mind that condoms protect you from disease, too."

If I haven't made it abundantly clear, I thought the condom itself looked rather diseased, but by that point I had decided the best course of action was to say as little as possible, nod often, and hope Mom finished quickly. I nodded.

"Good," Mom said. She leaned over and set the banana on the floor. "I know the traditional mother thing," she said, "is to say that losing your virginity is a special act that should be shared with someone you love, and that every subsequent time you have sex should be special and shared with someone you love. And it can be. But it can also be a very pleasurable thing that's done purely for the sake of pleasure.

"I'm telling you this not because I want you to be promiscuous, but because I don't want you to build up sex in your head as this sacred, important act. The current way of thinking, equating physical and emotional—it isn't realistic, and it attaches a huge importance and a huge amount of anxiety to something that should be as natural as, say, learning to walk. Do you understand? You don't have to love your partner, Emily."

She reached over and put her hand on my knee, looking me straight in the eye. I don't know if I'd ever seen her so serious before. "If you do love him, that's okay. But you don't have to. What's important is that when you do have sex, you do it with someone who respects you, and that you respect yourself. That's the most important thing, honey— that you respect yourself, in everything you're doing, but in sex especially. Don't let anybody push you into doing something you don't want to. There isn't a set time, or place, or anything, so don't worry. When it's right, you'll know. It'll feel comfortable.

"Not physically," she clarified. "Physically, your first time won't be very comfortable at all, unless he has a very small penis." She paused, considering. "No, that'd have to be an incredibly small penis. I don't think that's possible."

She turned serious again. "Your first time will probably hurt, but it improves after that. What I mean is that emotionally, you should feel comfortable. You don't have to wait forever, but don't let anybody push you into doing something you don't want," she said again. "Okay?"

I nodded.

"Okay," she said, and smiled. "You can ask me anything, honey. Do you have any questions?"

"No," I managed. This was not wholly true, but I was ten. I didn't want to have questions. And I think I was probably also a bit in shock.

"Okay," Mom said again. She leaned over and kissed me on the forehead. "Have a good night, honey," she said, then picked up the banana and left the room, peeling off the condom as she went.

After she closed the door, I lay back on my covers and tried to erase her words, and the mental pictures they'd brought, from my brain. Mostly I'd failed.

I looked down at Stephen and wondered what his sex talk had been like. Hopefully it had been at a more appropriate age. Also, hopefully he actually knew how to put on a condom. The image of what it was supposed to look like, once in position, was burned in my brain forever, but I had very little idea of how to get it there.

I also wondered if Stephen's downstairs was possibly as big as the banana my mom had chosen. If it was, no matter how much lubricant came with the condom, there was no way it was going anywhere inside me. I still sometimes had trouble with tampons.

Stephen put his hands on my arms and rubbed, up and down, up and down. "What's wrong?" he asked. "You're worried."

I nodded. He was still hard. I wondered if I should move off him; my proximity probably wasn't helping things.

He tilted his head up a bit, just far enough to touch the tip of his nose to mine. "It's okay," he said. "We don't have to if you don't want—"

"I do want to," I told him. "I just… don't know how."

Stephen let go with one hand and beckoned me forward; I leaned down until my ear was close to his mouth. "My understanding of the matter," he said, "is my penis gets hard and we put it in your vagina." He paused, and I could feel as well as hear him breathe out. "But beyond that, I don't really know, either. It's okay," he said again. "We'll figure it out. I don't want you to worry, at all. It doesn't have to be perfect. I certainly don't expect it to be perfect. It doesn't even have to be good, at first. Okay?"

I remembered what Mom had said about being comfortable, about not letting anyone push me into doing something I didn't want. But it wasn't that; he wasn't pushing. He was just reminding me, like he always did, that the things I thought I was scared of—the things holding me back—were things that really didn't matter at all. "Okay," I said.

He moved his hand up between my shoulder blades and rubbed my back. "I hope you aren't expecting it to be perfect," he added. "Obviously I'll do my best, but I strongly suspect my performance may leave something to be desired."

"Your best is all I can ask for," I said. Then I hesitated again. "I'm also slightly worried that my best—I'm also slightly worried it won't fit."

I felt Stephen shaking his head. "Now you're just flattering me," he said. Then, more serious, "It'll fit. And if for some reason it doesn't, we'll figure something else out instead. But really, Emily, when you hear guys saying they're eleven inches—no one is eleven inches. Well, *I'm* not eleven inches." He paused. "There is also the possibility that it won't be big enough."

I was pretty sure that wouldn't be a problem. I was pretty sure Stephen was aware of this, too; I had, after all, just suggested it might be too large. "Are you fishing?" I said.

"Possibly." He smiled a tiny bit and glanced away. "It's—look, every guy on the planet is self-conscious about the size of his dick," he admitted. "Probably especially guys who've never done anything with it before."

"I'm sure it'll be fine," I told him. "And it's not like I'd know the difference, either, anyway."

"Really?" he said, smiling more now. "Really, wow. That's what's supposed to make me feel better?"

"Does it really matter, though," I asked, "how big or how small it is, I mean, as long as it actually works?"

"Of course it works!" Stephen said, pretending to be affronted.

"Then it shouldn't matter," I said, "relatively, how yours compares to… anyone else's. Because I'm not going to compare it to anyone else's. The only person I'm planning on having sex with is you."

The side of Stephen's mouth turned up a bit, this time for real; I think he was happy with that. Then, very suddenly, he frowned. "Penis," he said.

"What?" I asked (trying not to flinch).

"Penis," he said again, very clearly. "Say it."

"I—what?" I asked again.

"I've never heard you say it," he said. "We've been talking about this for, I don't know, weeks, maybe months, and you've never. Why won't you say it?"

"I…" I said. "I just… My mom gave me the talk when I was ten," I told him.

He actually pulled back slightly. He looked as revolted as I had felt.

"I couldn't eat a banana for almost two years," I said.

"Oh"—he closed his eyes, grimaced—"ugh."

"It kind of just left a bad taste in my mouth—"

"No pun intended."

I rolled my eyes. "It just feels weird."

"All right," Stephen said. "Fair enough." He paused. "Are there any words you do use?"

"Just euphemisms," I said. Lots and lots of euphemisms.

"Well, we can work on that," Stephen said. "Speaking of, the mental image of you condomizing a banana, age ten, has kind of…" He nodded downward. "It's not, shall we say, quite as pressing a concern any more."

"Sorry," I said. Then, "Actually it wasn't me. I mean, I didn't ever do it. My mom did. Very unskillfully," I added.

"Ugh," he said again. "Not better." He closed his eyes and turned his head away. "Let's make a rule," he said when he turned toward me again. "No talking about our parents with anything sexual in the same conversation, ever again. Yes?"

"Seems like a reasonable rule," I said.

"I think it seems like an excellent rule," Stephen said.

"Yeah, that's probably a better word," I agreed.

"While we're on this topic," he asked, "anything else you'd like to mention? Any other caveats?"

I looked away, bit my lip, then looked back again. "The hat," I said. Stephen looked startled. "I know," I said, before he could respond. "I know you never take it off, but I don't think—I can't have sex for the first time if you have a hat on. I just can't."

He looked at me for a moment, quiet. "Okay," he said.

"Okay?" I repeated. I don't know why I was surprised, but I was.

He nodded. "In the greater scheme of things," he said, "I think I can manage a while not wearing a hat if it means, well."

"Well." I smiled at him. "You're not so bad at the euphemisms, yourself."

He smiled back. "I do my best," he said.

Thursday afternoon, I printed contacts of the two rolls of film I'd developed during the previous class. A lot of the shots appeared to have come out well—even (and just as Stephen had said) the caterpillar. I wanted to run out into the hall and show or at least tell him, but I knew he wouldn't be surprised. I had been the hands on the camera, but he'd told me what to do, and he knew what he was doing.

I resisted printing off enlargements, and put the contact prints on a shelf to dry, then spun myself back out into the hallway and the light and Stephen.

"Hey," he said, and stood up. We walked to the wagon and he drove me home; then, instead of pulling up in front of the house, he shifted back into second and drove around the block again. He put the engine in neutral at the last stop sign and looked somewhere just in front of me. "Can you come over tonight?" he said.

I said okay.

He was back to pick me up at five forty, just like we were going to photography. I didn't figure we were going to photography, though. And we weren't.

At Stephen's house, the driveway was conspicuously empty for that time of day. I looked over at him. "Where are your parents?" I asked.

"Out," he said.

He asked if I'd had dinner yet and I told him I had. "Good," he said. He got a glass of water from the sink and drank half, then offered it to me.

"I'm okay," I said.

"You can have your own. Glass," he said.

"Really, it's okay," I told him.

He took the glass with him into his room and put it on the corner of the nightstand. Then he came back down to the foot of the bed and stood next to me.

"It looks like some of the photos are going to come out," I said. "From the weekend."

Stephen nodded. "Are you excited?"

"I…" I said. I was, in a way. But excited wasn't really the right word for it.

"Magic," he said, softly.

"Yeah," I agreed.

Stephen sighed. "Can I," he said, then stopped, held his eyes shut for a moment.

"Stephen," I said.

He sat down heavily and I sat next to him. I put my hand on his knee. I wasn't sure what was going on, but it seemed like the right thing to do.

Stephen looked at my hand, and then he looked up at me. He blinked once. Then, very deliberately, he took off his hat.

My breath caught in my throat.

"Is this a bad time?" he said.

"No." I swallowed. "It's—it's good."

"Okay." He stood up and leaned forward to shut the door, then slipped out of his shoes, balancing against the dresser as he stood on one foot, then the other. I watched him without moving. Then he turned toward me—he didn't even have to take another step over; we were already that close. I leaned back and sort of crab-walked up the bed, and he followed.

He put his hand around my ear, thumb in front, palm below, and fingers reaching up behind, weaving into my hair. "Smile," he said. "Show me your teeth."

I did, and he smiled back, but just the corners of his mouth smiled. He pressed his forehead against mine. Finally I reached up and kissed him.

"Wait," I said after a minute, and he pulled back, just far enough for me to sit up partway and pull my sweater over my head.

I was wearing a T-shirt underneath, but still he hesitated slightly. "Okay?" he asked.

"Yes," I told him. "I want this," I said.

I don't remember the rest of our clothes coming off. Or my shoes. Stephen did the condom, which was a relief. I didn't really look. There was a part of me that still didn't want to see, didn't want to know.

I had felt it, and as much as I wanted it—both mentally and physically—inside of me, I was still terrified that it wouldn't fit. The further we went, the more convinced I was; even his middle finger felt dangerously over-large.

Then that conviction faded. I understood that it would indeed fit—but only after my insides were split apart the way a log with a tiny crack can be opened with a wedge and a sledgehammer. It was the most incredible pain I'd ever felt. All I wanted to do was get away. I focused on trying not to make any noise or look too agonized.

Stephen kept asking if I was okay, if he should stop. I kept telling him to keep going.

After a while—I don't know how long it took, just that it was far too long—he stopped moving suddenly. For a moment it seemed that even his breathing ceased. Inside it didn't feel any different (possibly because of the condom) but I figured it meant he was done. I managed to unclench my fingers from his shoulders and rubbed his upper back as he collapsed on top of me.

For a moment or two—or maybe twenty or thirty—he stayed there, his skin pressed close against mine, warm and slick and slightly sticky. Then his fingers brushed my arm again, and he pulled out and sort of slid away.

I felt better immediately, which was a shock. I also felt like I should kiss him again, or—something.

I turned my head toward him; he was on his side, watching me already. He still seemed slightly out of breath. "Yeah?" he whispered.

"Yeah," I whispered back.

After a while, I reached over and put my hand in the middle of his chest. He didn't say anything, but smiled a little. He raised his right hand up and rested his fingers on mine. The tips curled around the outside edge of my pointer, and we stayed that way.

At seven, his watch beeped from the nightstand. He leaned over to shut it off, then sat up halfway, but no further. There must have been pills there, too; he swallowed them with his back to me, with some of the water. I'd never seen him swallow with water before.

I'd tucked my hand up under my chin while I waited, and he didn't reach for it when he lay back down. "I have to tell you something," he said.

For a moment, I had the horrible fear that, now that we'd had sex, I'd exceeded my usefulness and Stephen was going to break up with me.

What he actually said was much worse.

When he spoke, his voice was dull. "I have an inoperable brain tumor," he said.

I stared at him. I wanted very badly for him to be joking, but I knew it was far too terrible a thing to joke about. And, I knew, it made sense. It made perfect, sudden sense. All of it: the burning desire to do everything, now. The small pharmacy he carried around, parceled out so carefully throughout the day. Even, perhaps, the way he sometimes seemed to inexplicably lose his balance.

I felt like all of my insides were being compressed into a tiny pinpoint of horror, pinched so tight that I could no longer keep my legs or back straight. If I hadn't been lying down, I would've doubled over. As it was, it was all I could do to keep from curling completely into a ball.

Stephen did not look at me. I couldn't stop staring at him.

"I should have told you," he said at last, and then he finally did look. "But I wanted you to like me first."

"I..." I said. I managed to reach one arm out, and touched his shoulder. "Stephen. I would've liked you anyway."

"Would you?" he asked, but he didn't sound belligerent, just sad. "All right," he relented, "maybe you would have. But I never would've known. Imagine this: going up to someone and saying, 'Hi, I'm Stephen. I'm about to die.'" He nodded, mock-knowingly. "'Brain cancer.' Now, unless they're an absolute asshole, in which case you're better off not knowing them anyway, that person is probably going to be quite a bit kinder to you than otherwise."

I didn't know what to say to that, because it was probably true.

"I'm sorry," he said. "I really, probably, shouldn't have talked to you at all. You probably would've been better off, too."

He started to cry, silently at first, the tears running down his face. Then he lost control and gasped and started to shake. I rolled over and wrapped my arm around him as tight as I could. He turned his face into my hair, and I could feel the tears seeping through, and he clung to my arm with both hands. "I don't—" he kept choking out. "I can't—I—"

I didn't say anything; if I had, I would've started crying, too. I just held on.

It stopped as swiftly as it had started. Stephen sniffed, and let go with one hand to swipe across his eyes and over the tear tracks on his cheeks. "I'm sorry," he said again.

"Don't apologize," I said.

"I can't believe I did this," he said faintly.

"What?" I looked up at him.

"All of it," he said. He took a breath. "Fuck. All this... I shouldn't even be alive right now. I was diagnosed two years ago." He said that like it was a really big deal. "The odds are awful. I wouldn't have bet on me. No one would've bet on me. Not even the worst gambler."

I hadn't forgotten the word inoperable, but I still hoped he was exaggerating. There were other ways to cure cancer, and people survived all the time. What kind could possibly be so awful that the odds of still being alive two years after diagnosis were unbettable?

"I won't bore you with the details," he said. "Suffice it to say that, as it turns out, I didn't beat the odds, just held them off for a while. I don't know if you know this about cancer, but typically when it comes back, it's much more aggressive than before. And I've had a progression." He took another breath. "It's not going away this time. Well, it never went *away*. It's not going to stop this time.

"I'd done so well," he said. "I was"—he coughed, and took another breath—"I was stable for so long. Everyone's trying to be optimistic, hoping it'll continue, but I can feel it. I can feel that it's grown. Growing. Best-case scenario—best—I might have four months."

I gasped. I couldn't help it. Of course I knew that people died from cancer, too, but not people I knew. And Stephen was only eighteen. I couldn't bring myself to believe it. "Surely there's something they can do," I started.

Above me, I felt him shaking his head. "Diffuse intrinsic pontine glioma," he said. "I don't expect you to recognize it—if you did, it would mean you know far more about cancer than anyone not intimately acquainted with it ought. But it's what I have. It has one of the worst survival rates there is."

He sighed. "It starts in the pons and spreads out through the rest of the brainstem, growing in and out of the regular cells as it pleases. It's not a tidy self-contained lump in an accessible place, so they can't excise it. The blood-brain barrier means it doesn't respond well—or, really, at all—to chemotherapy. Radiation can kill enough of the cells to halt their growth, and sometimes even shrink a bit, but it's a temporary fix. It doesn't kill all of them, and eventually they wake up and start growing again.

"There's nothing really to do for me now. I can't have more radiation; it'll wreck the rest of me. I'll probably be put on a clinical trial, but that's not really for my benefit; it's more what doesn't work for me might help them figure out what will work on future people. The rest is just palliative. Actually, it's almost always just been palliative."

"What's palliative?" I whispered. I was embarrassed to ask it, and even more scared to hear what he said.

"It's trying to make me more comfortable until I die."

"Stephen," I said. "Please."

"I'm going to die," he repeated. "It's not a matter of fighting harder, or finding a newer, better treatment. And it's not like, say, breast cancer, or leukemia, where it comes and goes, sometimes, again and again. With this, it comes, and I go, and that's it. I've always been terminal, Emily. It was always only a matter of time. And now mine's up."

I swallowed hard. And then I pushed myself up and looked at him. Everything he'd said had been so emotionless, so—almost—hollow. He hadn't moved, just stared at the ceiling. We were holding onto each other, and his skin was still warm, but in those moments, I felt I might have been holding a person carved from stone.

"Can I ask you something?" he said. "I know it's impossible to pretend nothing's changed, but could you please just... not tell anyone? Given the choice, I wouldn't have picked being thought a junkie, either, but it serves its purpose. I just want to be as normal as I can for as long as I can. I can't be the kid who gets sad looks in the hall."

"All right," I told him. I understood what he meant, to some degree.

"Thanks," he said.

He still wasn't looking at me; pointedly, he'd actually turned his head. "You can say whatever else you want. Make something up. Whatever."

"What?" I said.

He swallowed hard. "I understand if you want to break up with me."

I reflected that it was not the first time he'd suggested this. I was just as flabbergasted as I'd been before—more so, in fact. Then, it had made some amount of sense, if I'd had a social reputation I wanted to preserve. Now, I couldn't think of any reason. "I'm not breaking up with you," I told him.

"I'm dying," he said. "Soon it'll start to become very obvious. I won't be able to..." He paused, shook his head. "You don't want that."

It wasn't ideal, certainly. But it wasn't a deal-breaker. "I want you as long as I can," I said, borrowing his words from earlier. "I'm not going to break up with you just because you have cancer."

"And," he said, "are you sure you're also not *not* going to break up with me because I have cancer?"

"Look at me," I said, and waited until—finally—he did. "I just had sex with you." (And, I thought, but didn't say, it was excruciating.) "Obviously I care. And we're still—I'm still lying here in bed with you, naked." I leaned in close and looked right at him. "I'm with you, all right?" I said. "Cancer has nothing to do with it."

"All right," he said at last. His voice sounded shaky.

As much as I wanted to cry, I knew I couldn't. I had to show him, somehow, that it would be all right, that in at least one facet of our lives, cancer didn't matter, that I was still Emily, and he was still Stephen. "Would it help you understand," I said, "if I stuck my tongue in your mouth?"

He smiled a little bit, which was more than I'd expected. "Under normal circumstances, I'm sure I'd say yes." He glanced down the lengths of our bodies, then let out a long breath. "This all got really serious really fast," he said. "Give me a couple minutes, and I'll try to act like a proper boyfriend again." He paused. "We should probably put our clothes back on."

It didn't seem entirely necessary to me, but I figured it would give him the time he seemed to need. I nodded; he swung his legs off the side and sat up, and for a long time he stayed there, palms braced against the edge of the mattress, head hanging.

When we were dressed again he pulled up the sheet and the bedspread, smoothed out the wrinkles. He sat back in the same place he'd been, facing the wall with the desk and the closet. I reached over and took his hand, and he pulled it onto his lap, wrapped both his hands around mine.

"I'm sorry," he said. "I didn't even ask. How was it?"

"Yeah," I said, trying to sound positive and probably failing.

"Honestly," he said. He let go with one hand and reached up to smooth my hair, carefully tucking the escaped little pieces back under my headband. His own hair was almost completely hidden again. He'd put his hat back on, too.

"I… it hurt really bad," I said quietly.

He winced. "I'm sorry."

"It wasn't your fault," I said.

"It was," he replied.

"Well, I mean it would've hurt with anyone. You didn't do anything wrong." I hesitated. "Did it hurt for you, too?"

"What?" Stephen looked surprised. "No, of course not. Not that."

"Oh," I said. "You just looked like you were maybe in pain. Sort of." Or at least he had the few times I'd opened my eyes.

He shook his head, and for a second he grinned. "That's probably because I was trying so hard not to come in the first fifteen seconds. You probably wish I had, though, with how much it hurt. The faster done."

I thought this was incredibly perceptive of him. I nodded, though I felt slightly guilty. To be honest, I felt a bit guilty about the whole thing. I had wanted very much to enjoy it—not just for my sake, but for Stephen's as well. I knew he'd wanted me to enjoy it as much as he had. He had tried very hard.

"Are you okay now?" he asked. "Do you need anything?"

"No," I said, then added quickly. "I mean, I don't need anything. I feel, actually, completely fine."

"Good," he said. He seemed relieved, too. "Next time, tell me to stop."

"It'll be better next time," I said. "I just have to... acclimate."

"Okay," he said seriously. "But tell me."

I nodded.

It was finally starting to get dark out. I'd always thought of sex as a thing that happened at night; I wondered if it was weird that we'd done it while it was still light outside. Even with the curtains on both windows drawn, the dimmest we'd gotten was a moderate twilight. And I figured that any future opportunity we might have would be even earlier in the day. "Where are your parents, really?" I asked again.

Stephen bit back a smile; I could tell. "I don't know," he admitted. "Out. I told them I—we—needed some time. I'm sure they assumed I wanted to tell you about—well." He twitched the corner of his lip upward a bit, and somehow I knew he was gesturing toward the cells that weren't supposed to be growing in his brain. "But I doubt they thought it would be post-coital."

"Did you really plan it?" I asked.

"Not like that, no," he said. "It's not exactly a subject you'd consider for pillow talk. Sorry," he said again.

I shook my head. It was true, it had been rather jarring. But I wished he'd stop apologizing.

"I figured it'd be one or the other," he said, "not both. Whatever seemed right. I mean, it was my original plan to tell you, but then it occurred to me that there was something more pleasant we could do instead. Mum and Dad would've understood if they came home and I just said I hadn't been

171

able to tell you. And I guess I kind of thought if we didn't, we might not have another chance. And then as it happened, it came out anyway. I hope it wasn't too awful."

I could hardly think of anything more awful, but I knew that wasn't what he meant. "No," I said.

Stephen smiled, but it was the kind of smile, this time, that you only give when you know you can't do anything else. "It's been a bit of a rough day for you," he said.

It had.

"Most of the time I don't talk about it," he said. "Never, really. I ignore it the best I can. That might be a bit different now that it's progressing, but I'm not going to let it become me. I'll do the best I can." He paused, tilted his head and looked at me. "Can I kiss you?"

"Of course," I told him. "Of course you can."

It was a little kiss, soft and gentle and even a bit scared. Stephen moved one hand up my arm, but that was as far as it went. Only our dry lips touched, no teeth, no tongues. It didn't even last very long.

Somehow it meant more than all the others.

I realized that I'd always thought Stephen had been so open and honest with me, and I hadn't really been mistaken: he had been, except with that one thing. It was a huge secret to keep, but I understood why he had. And now he'd told me—not all the details, but enough that I knew—and I was still there. Even if I hadn't known there was anything missing before, I knew it was different now. It was the first kiss with nothing hidden between us. It felt good.

"I'm glad you told me," I said when we pulled apart, my eyes still lowered.

Stephen didn't respond, but his hand squeezed mine a little tighter.

"Thank you," I said.

I glanced over at him; he was looking down, too, but he looked up when I said that. "Thank you," he told me. "You don't know what this means."

"I don't want this to matter," I said. "I mean, it does, now, but…"

"I know what you mean," Stephen said.

I nodded. "I liked you anyway," I said. "I like you anyway."

Stephen told me things would start to move very quickly, but I was still surprised by how rapidly it all progressed. He gave me a timeline: diagnosed a week before the end of sophomore year (at a very early stage, he said, thanks to a combination of headaches and his mother being a doctor and a hypochondriac). Six weeks of radiation therapy that summer. Stable for a year and a half—all of junior year and most of senior. That was a long time—a really long time—to be stable with DIPG, he said. He hadn't expected to even get to senior year, much less have a shot at graduation.

He'd gone for an MRI the previous Sunday, but it was only to confirm what he'd already felt. When I asked him when he'd known, for sure, that the tumor had started to grow again, he shook his head. "It's been a while," he admitted. "But it's not the kind of thing you want to believe. So I talked myself out of it, again and again. Told myself I was tired, or nervous, or even dehydrated. That I was starting to build up too much tolerance and needed to switch to a different pill. The moment I really knew, though, had to admit there was no other explanation? That was last Thursday, in the hall. When I couldn't hear you."

I remembered that. I'd thought the hall had just been too loud.

"It's one of the symptoms," Stephen said. "Hearing loss. One of the many symptoms."

I didn't ask him to tell me the rest.

Tuesday he asked me to stay over instead of going home before photography, as I usually did. "I want you to talk to my mom," he said. "Actually," he amended, "I should probably ask you first. Will you go with me?"

"What?" I said. "Go with you where?"

We were sitting at the dining room table; Stephen had been eating a sandwich, but he stopped then, and picked up a pen from the top of an adjacent pile of papers, clicking it, slowly and unevenly, back and forth. "I have a consultation on Thursday," he said. "With all the doctors. Well, some of them will just be teleconferencing, since they're not actually trying to save me now, but more or less. My parents will be there too, but..." he paused, and stopped clicking at last. "I don't want to go alone."

I didn't even have to ask where it was, or whether I'd have to miss class to attend. "Okay," I told him.

"Now you can't say I never take you anywhere interesting," he said, but quickly sobered. "Mum won't think it's right. But I'm the one dying. And it's not as though you're going to make any medical decisions. I just want..." He trailed off.

I reached over and took his hand. I understood.

Stephen's parents arrived home one after another, shortly before five forty-five. "Mum," Stephen said, not letting her get past the dining room or take her jacket off, "about Thursday."

Immediately she frowned. "Stephen, we understand how you feel, but darling, it's important. You can't put this off again."

I glanced sideways at Stephen. He hadn't mentioned postponing anything.

"No," he said. "I'll go. But I want Emily to be there."

His parents exchanged looks, and then his mother gave me a sad little smile and said, "I'm sorry, Stephen. But Emily isn't a family member or a medical professional. You know—"

"No," Stephen said again. "I'm eighteen now."

"Yes, but Emily doesn't have the background," Dr. Stuart said. "It might be better—" She paused, pursed her lips. "I'm not trying to exclude you," she told me, "but I just don't think this idea… it might be a bit much."

I didn't realize until later that what she'd said was actually true. That every time we made eye contact, and she frowned—however fleetingly—it wasn't because she didn't like me. It was because she felt bad—because she didn't want to see any of the pain she'd felt inflicted on me. She wasn't trying to force me away for any selfish reasons of her own; it was simply that she knew her son's life was a horror show that was only getting worse. She was only trying to protect me.

At the time, this didn't occur to me. The only thing that occurred to me was that while, yes, it might very well be a bit much, what she was proposing was the exact opposite of what Stephen wanted. But even if I'd understood her motivation, I think I still would've disagreed. "It's okay," I told her. "I'll manage."

"The doctors might not—" she started.

Stephen cut her off. "I don't care. It's important," he said. "To me. I know you can find a way, Mum." He hesitated; she didn't respond. "Nobody wants me to play my card," he said.

She glanced away abruptly; Mr. Stuart moved half a step closer to his wife. They exchanged looks again, and finally, Dr. Stuart nodded.

Later, against my better judgment, I asked Stephen what that unspoken card was.

He put on the parking brake and the emergency flashers, even though we were at a stop sign, and in the semi-dark, he looked hard at me. "You're included in that nobody," he said. "You understand that."

I nodded.

"We all know it already, but it's so much worse to hear it out loud. Are you sure you want to?"

I nodded again, and he looked away. He flicked the flashers off again, and turned the blinker on. "The worst card there is." His voice was awfully flat. "I am a dying boy," he said.

Stephen signed me out himself at the beginning of lunch, simply writing "appointment" in the reason for absence column for us both. I hadn't known he could do that, but the secretary didn't seem to think anything was odd. I wondered if it was some kind of special privilege, but knew better than to ask.

"Please don't say anything," Stephen said as we walked out to the parking lot; the consultation, as he called it, was supposed to start at one. (That, I could tell, annoyed him, because he'd have to start things off by swallowing a pocketful of pills in front of everyone.)

I was surprised. "I wouldn't even know anything to say," I told him.

"No, not that," he said. "I meant—here."

"Oh." I swallowed. He'd asked me already, but even if he hadn't, I wouldn't have thought of saying anything, anyway.

"I really don't want them to know," he said. "Not that it's not obvious. But it's not too directly obvious. Enough people have seen me dry-swallowing pills on the one o'clock schedule, I'm sure they all think I'm on drugs by now. And I say let them. It spares me the false pity, anyway."

"So does anyone…" I said. For a moment I felt very unsettled, almost terrified, with the realization that I could be the only person Stephen cared about enough, or, perhaps, felt close to enough, to trust with the truth. It wasn't as romantic as it sounds.

Stephen sighed. "Aside from my parents, obviously? When I said I didn't want anyone to know, I really meant anyone. There's Grandpa, and now you. You two are the only ones I've told myself."

He paused. "My aunt and uncle also know. I didn't want to tell them, and I think Dad would've actually agreed, but Mum insisted it'd be too hard to explain otherwise. I don't know if she meant my current state or after I…" He didn't finish that thought, and I didn't blame him. "They've never mentioned anything, which I appreciate, but I can tell she told them because they act different around me now. Not like you'd act around somebody you think is an addict," he clarified. "The way you'd act with somebody fragile you're scared is going to break."

"What about your cousins?" I asked.

"No, they're too little," he said. "They wouldn't understand. In a few years, they probably won't even remember me. Maybe their parents'll tell them I went to live on a farm, like Hoover."

He stared at me for a moment, almost as if daring me to respond. Of course I didn't. Oddly enough, it was that comment, I think, that made me realize how much Stephen hated the idea of pity.

"So really, no one else knows?" I said.

He sighed again. "No. Mum also insisted on telling the

school nurse, and then *she* insisted it was big enough that we had to tell the principal, too, so that someone in a position of authority would know what was going on in case I, I don't know, died in the middle of class. Really." He rolled his eyes. "On the bright side, he did waive my PE requirement. Saved me four and a half months of dodgeball last year. But—" he hesitated, "I did still have to take health, which was almost worse—everyone whispering and surreptitiously glancing at me during the drug unit, and when Mr. Andreason told us about the addiction hotline, he addressed the entire lecture to me."

I thought about that, about how quiet Stephen had kept, and what it had gotten him in exchange. I supposed it did make sense that he'd rather have people look at him with thinly-veiled contempt during the drug unit, and know it was all misplaced, than have them look at him with pity during the cancer one and know they were correct.

But I still didn't think I could've borne it. I was his girlfriend, and even I had eventually come to the conclusion that there was some sort of addiction at play. I hadn't thought he was lying when he said he'd had a headache for a year and a half, but perhaps, I'd thought, he'd self-medicated himself a bit too well, to the point that he didn't need the pills just for his head any more. I'd seen him checking his watch, sometimes, every thirty seconds; I'd seen the swallows that were more like gasps. I'd seen his hands shake. And I was his girlfriend—I was supposed to know him better than anyone. It must've been so hard.

"You won't actually... die in the middle of class?" I said.

"No." He almost scoffed. "It doesn't work that way. Mine is more of a long decline—steady at first, then exponential. If I keel over in class, it won't be because of this. By the time

I get to where it could actually kill me, there's no way I'd be making it in to school any more."

We were at the wagon; he reached over and jerked the door open. He unlocked mine from the inside without popping the handle, and I knew better than to say anything.

Two years earlier, when Stephen had gone through diagnosis and treatment, he'd had to fly out of state to see specialists several times—that's how rare his cancer was. But once they'd hammered out a plan, he'd switched back to the regional hospital. He wasn't undergoing surgery, and radiation and pills could be delivered just as well there as in a highly-specialized cancer center. Even so, his hospital was an hour away; the one in town, while fairly state-of-the-art in what it could do, was simply too small to deal with people like Stephen.

The same was essentially true now. Of course, any clinical trial he might take part in would be headquartered elsewhere, but at this point, no one really thought it was necessary, or prudent, to shuttle him back and forth across the country. He had a team at the regional hospital, but most of his original doctors wouldn't be at the consultation, attending remotely only. I thought, but didn't say, that the fact that Stephen was still important enough for highly specialized doctors from far-off, famous hospitals to take time out of their schedules for a phone conference about him was pretty significant.

I wasn't sure if it was a good or a bad thing.

Despite Stephen's preparations, and even with the physical absence of those dialing in, I was surprised by how many people were there. I'd imagined we'd be in an exam room; Stephen might get to sit on the paper-covered table while the rest of us—me, his mother, another doctor or maybe two—crowded around a speakerphone.

Instead, we sat at a long, highly-polished table in a small conference room. In addition to an assortment of doctors and nurses, both Stephen's parents were there. His father was in street clothes. His mother was wearing a lab coat; we were in the same hospital where she worked. Neuroimaging wasn't her specialty—she was just there as a parent—but she had nonetheless taken it upon herself to personally vet Stephen's entire team.

The conference video came on, and the doctors exchanged pleasantries. Stephen sat quiet. He didn't tell any of the doctors it was good to see them again, and no one asked how he'd been. Understandably. Finally, someone on the other end cleared their throat, and everyone quieted.

"Well," Stephen said after a moment, "to begin with, why is Dr. Banks here? No offense, Dr. Banks," he added. "But I'm not getting any more radiation."

Dr. Banks didn't answer, just smiled faintly at Stephen and nodded. I liked the look of him. He was easily the oldest person in the room, completely bald except for two tufts of hair above his ears, as thick and erratic as Einstein's. He looked like the kind of man who cried at home—quietly, except, perhaps, for occasional loud bursts of nose-blowing—after a patient died.

It was Dr. Edwards, Stephen's primary oncologist, who responded. "No," she agreed. "But because Dr. Banks is so familiar with you, I asked him to sit in on this preliminary meeting."

I liked that she'd said simply "you." Not "your case" or "your situation" or even "your cancer." I had a feeling Stephen appreciated it, too.

"Oh," Stephen said.

Dr. Edwards opened the file in front of her, and made a

show of straightening the papers in their stack. "Well," she said, "as the recent scan has shown, the tumor appears to have resumed progression. I estimate that at this stage..."

I didn't really follow most of what was being said. To be fair, I'd had less than a week to become knowledgeable about—or even interested in—brain tumors. Mostly I just watched Stephen. He didn't say much. He held my hand under the table, and sometimes his fingers tightened, but his face, always, remained impassive.

Until one of the video-conferencing specialists (I couldn't tell them apart) said something wrong. Stephen's jaw hardened. "That's not acceptable," he said, cutting off the man in the middle of what I assume was an explanation.

Around the table, everyone looked surprised.

Stephen sighed. "It's just—that doesn't really promise a very high quality of life, does it?" he said. "I'd have to basically live in the hospital."

"Well," Dr. Edwards started, then hesitated.

"Go on, say it," Stephen said. "That you're thinking I'm not likely to have a very high quality of life, regardless."

Stephen's mother attempted to bite back a gasp and didn't quite manage it.

"I know it's an important, promising trial," Stephen said to one of the doctors in the video frame. "I know I've been incredibly lucky—inasmuch as anyone with DIPG can be lucky—and I know that now I'm being selfish. I know we're supposed to do the clinical trials when we progress, because what doesn't work on me..." He trailed off, rolling his free hand in circles—it was almost sarcastic. We all knew what he meant.

"And you're already getting my whole brain to poke at, after I die," he added. "But this—I just can't bring myself.

Maybe if there was something less invasive, maybe if there was even the smallest chance I thought it might help me, maybe then I'd do the decent, selfless thing and try. But the way I see it, I'd check into the hospital tomorrow, and I'd never leave. Driving home today would basically be the last time I ever do anything."

"Well," said Dr. Edwards, "that's not entirely true. There are lots of things you can do in the hospital. You've been here before; you know that."

"I am not," Stephen said tersely, "talking about watching satellite re-runs. Or being wheeled around the courtyard in a chair."

"We do also have the art cart," said Dr. Edwards.

"I do also have right-side ataxia," Stephen replied.

"That's a bit of an oversimplification," said Dr. Edwards.

Stephen shrugged, with just his left shoulder. "Even so. It's a bit of a stretch to imagine me doing painting." He paused. "I don't know why we're even arguing about this. It's already decided: I won't do it. If you find something else, ask me again, but I don't have a lot of time left, and I don't want to lose any of it. I don't want to spend the end of my life in and out of consciousness in a hospital bed, getting fed experimental concoctions that make me feel even more miserable than I already am. Okay?"

I could tell the doctors in the video were disappointed. "We don't have a lot of opportunities like this, Stephen," one of them said. "And—I'll be blunt—there's not a lot of time for you to change your mind."

"You don't say," said Stephen.

"Well," said the doctor, "there's always the chance…"

"No," Stephen interrupted, "there's not. Not at this stage."

"Well," the doctor began again.

"Please," Stephen said. "Don't fuck with me. It's a high-grade tumor, and it's not getting any smaller. I get that you want us to be optimistic, but I'm the one dying here. Don't I deserve to know what's true?"

The doctor on the other end sighed. "Yes," he said. "I'm sorry. The five-year survival rate, for previous participants in the trial, remains negligible. Well, we haven't even gotten to five years, so." He paused. "You're something of an outlier, with your age, so I don't want to estimate..."

Stephen shook his head. "Four months," he said. "You know I've read it all. I got lucky for a long time, but my life expectancy, from this point forward, is at best four months."

Dr. Stuart made another small sound. Mr. Stuart scratched his ear uncomfortably, looked away. A few of the less senior staffers shifted in their chairs.

"What?" Stephen said. "Don't look at me like that. We've said it before. You know it, and I know it's true. Four months is being optimistic. And I have a life to get on living in the interim, as long as I can." He leaned forward and looked squarely into the conference camera. "I swear," he said, "I will not die a vegetable."

"All right," the doctor said. "I won't pretend I'm not disappointed, but no one's going to force you to do anything you don't want. If you do change your mind, however..." He sighed, heavily. "You may find that the time which you have, practically, to 'get on with living' is less than you think. I'm not trying to be discouraging. I'm just speaking from experience."

"I know it's not much," Stephen said quietly. "That's why I can't..."

The doctor nodded. "There I can't fault you. I wish I could've come to you today with a miracle cure, but you're right that at this point we're still mostly just eliminating therapies that won't work. It likely wouldn't even prolong things much."

"Stephen," his mother said, and I knew she was clinging to the word "much." When someone you know is dying in four months, "much" becomes a lifetime. Every additional moment becomes more.

Stephen shook his head. "I'm going to die, Mum," he said. "I'm sorry. It's inevitable. And it's not a trade I'm willing to make—the possibility of a few extra weeks, unrecognizable in a hospital bed, in exchange for actually living. It's not just the time I'm after. Some things," he said, and looked away from her, away from all of us, "some things aren't worth the time."

For months I had been asking Stephen what he liked, because that was the question he, too, persisted in asking me. Usually he put me off or gave some facetious answer like blueberries or (a bit later) getting head. But once, he'd frowned and twisted his mouth to one side in thought. "Living," he'd said finally. "Not being alive; that's different. Living."

It wasn't until then, I realized, that I fully understood what he'd meant.

The talk turned to palliative care. Stephen was already on a veritable cocktail of maintenance meds; I hadn't been entirely wrong when I'd suspected he did need pills for more than just a headache.

"How are you feeling right now?" one of the doctors, at the far end of the table, asked. Dr. Svann, her nametag said.

"No worse than usual," Stephen told her. "All things considered."

"And your energy level?"

"Good enough," Stephen said.

"Do you find this is consistent throughout the day?" Dr. Svann asked.

"Do you mean—you're not asking if I don't get tired," Stephen said. "Everyone gets tired."

"I suppose I meant irregularly so," Dr. Svann told him. "And both your energy and other symptoms, in general. For example, do you find that the medications you're currently taking are effective for the full required duration, or do you start to... deteriorate, say, an hour before the next one is due?"

"Or," Dr. Edwards added, "some patients find their headaches are more severe, often accompanied by nausea, immediately on waking in the morning. Have you experienced that?"

"I thought that was natural," Stephen mumbled. Clearly not a morning person.

None of the doctors seemed to know quite how to respond to that. "We can consider shunting if the hydrocephalus gets to be too much," Dr. Edwards said after an awkward moment.

"No." Stephen shook his head firmly. "I don't think I need anything else right now," he said.

"You must have questions," Stephen said when we were back in the wagon, heading home. "Questions," he added, "for which you quite possibly don't want to hear the answers."

This was true. After a while, I'd started to feel sort of relieved that I didn't understand most of what they were talking about.

"It was probably a lot for you to take in," he said. "I probably should've prepared you more."

"Yeah," I said, although I meant it more in response to it

being a lot to take in than that he hadn't adequately prepared me. I'm not sure it's possible to prepare for terminal cancer.

"Thanks for going, though," he said.

"Of course," I told him. I wanted to thank him for inviting me, but I couldn't think of a way of phrasing it that wouldn't have sounded incredibly awkward. But it meant a lot that he'd wanted me there.

"Do you want to go to prom?" he asked after a while.

It was two days away. "I don't have a dress," I said.

Even though I think what they wear to prom is more important to some girls than their actual dates, Stephen simply shrugged this off. "I don't mind what you wear," he said. "Obviously I haven't got the white tux, either. But I'll take you, if you want to go."

"Not really," I admitted. "But I'll go with you, if you want to."

"No," Stephen said. He didn't even have to think about it. He tapped his fingers along the top of the steering wheel; he still could. "If Bonham would actually date someone for once, he'd be prom king." He glanced at me sideways. "If I told everyone what was really wrong with me…"

I just smiled at him. I was starting to understand a lot more. "I thought Bonham had a girlfriend," I said.

"Does he?" Stephen's tone suggested he wasn't really convinced but would humor me anyway. "Well, I wouldn't know."

"I thought you were friends," I said.

"We are," he told me. "But I don't keep track of his comings and goings any more. You'd need an app for that."

"Oh," I said. I could see how that might be true. But it also made me sad. What did it mean when one of your—allegedly—closest friends was so busy, so distant, that you didn't have any idea what he was doing?

"Do you want to meet my grandpa?" Stephen asked.

"What?" I said. It was kind of a strange juxtaposition.

"My grandpa Art. I'd like to see him," he said. "We could go Saturday. In Waldburg."

"Oh," I said. "Um, okay."

Which is how Stephen and I wound up going to a retirement home instead of our respective senior and junior proms.

I was afraid to meet Art. Not as afraid as I'd been of meeting Stephen's mom and dad—but, in a way, because of having met them, more so. I hadn't expected his parents to so plainly disapprove of me. I understood now that it was less me they disapproved of and more Stephen, and the fact that Stephen had allowed a person like me to exist. Still, it was hard. What if his grandfather, once introduced, felt the same way?

I needn't have worried. From the moment he spotted Stephen, a thread of sadness ran through Art's every expression, but he only seemed pleased by my presence. I figured he knew, or at least suspected, that I knew already.

Stephen hugged his grandfather hello—Art hugged like he'd been very strong once—and then they shook hands. "Well, this is a surprise," Art said, stepping back to look at Stephen. "You making it clear over here to see me. Still driving around in that old wagon?"

Stephen reached back and propelled me forward, into Art's line of sight. "Yes," he said. "And this is the girl I drive around."

Art shook my hand, too, and smiled. He and Stephen had the same smile. The one that, on Stephen, I hardly ever saw—the one Stephen only ever showed when he was really happy. Art smiled almost all the time.

I had been prepared for infirmity, for a tortured visit in

a sterile, hospital-like room—a preview, almost, of the end Stephen was desperate not to have. But the center where Art lived was nice, a lot more "minimally-assisted living" than "nursing home." The bathroom had a bar next to the toilet and a walk-in door to facilitate access to the tub, but other than an ordinary pill minder on Art's dresser, there was nothing else present to suggest a medical facility. It even smelled good.

We took lunch to Art's room and sat around a little table in the breakfast nook. Art propped the patio door open with one of his shoes, and sunlight streamed over us.

At one o'clock, Stephen's watch beeped. He took his pills, and the three of us all acted like nothing was out of the ordinary.

Later we moved out to the courtyard. Art and I sat in wrought-iron chairs with Stephen in the grass at our feet. He crossed his ankles and wrapped his arms around his knees, gazing up at his grandfather like a little boy would.

I kept having to fight back the urge to cry.

A little after three thirty, Stephen excused himself to the bathroom. As soon as he was gone, Art turned to me. "It's back, isn't it?" he said quietly.

I nodded.

His face crumpled a little bit.

"How did you know?" I asked.

He shook his head. "It's not the visit," he said. "Stephen visits me all the time. But I can see that something's changed."

Stephen came back, and Art just looked at me and smiled.

We stayed much longer than we'd thought we would; Art made hash browns for dinner and Stephen took his seven o'clock pills. Art told all the stories Stephen had promised he would, and then some. After a while, I realized they were lingering, neither of them wanting to admit the reason why. Art hugged me goodbye, finally, but then he hugged Stephen again, too.

Twenty minutes into the drive home, Stephen pulled over, into a gravel viewpoint at the side of the road. I looked through the windshield, and then out both my window and his, but there was nothing to see in the dark. I looked over at Stephen. "Can you drive?" he said.

"Okay," I agreed.

Neither of us moved.

"I probably shouldn't be, any more," he admitted. "Not that it would be such a terrible tragedy if I were to go off the road." He paused. "But I'd hate to drag you into it."

There was nothing, really, to say to that. I got out and walked around to Stephen's side. After a moment, I opened the door. He pivoted around on the seat to face me, but didn't step down. "Can you?" he said finally.

I moved closer; he put his arm around my neck, and I sort of dragged him out of the cab and into the gravel. We switched sides and, with him using my body as a crutch, managed to get around to the passenger door again.

He slumped against the wagon and I stood next to him, arm around his waist, leaning against his side. "It's not always like this. It comes and goes," he said. He put his good hand up and petted my hair.

"I know," I told him, even though I did not know. But I believed him. It was all we had.

I opened the passenger door and put him in, which took some doing. When I stepped back, he put his hand on my wrist. "Wait," he said; I looked up at him. "Would you kiss me?" he asked.

I leaned in, just for a second.

His hand moved from my wrist to my back, and he pulled me closer, pressing my body against his. The edge of the doorframe dug into my shins, and I put one knee up on the floor, my thigh against Stephen's calf.

"Did you plan this?" I asked him, which was really a less direct way of asking whether he was faking, even though he was still barely moving his right hand.

Stephen shook his head. The tip of his nose brushed against mine. "I told you," he said, "it comes and it goes."

He kissed the side of my neck.

"I thought you were above making out in cars," I managed.

He lifted his lips, fractionally, from my skin. "That was the back seat."

"Come up here," he said after a while.

The wagon was bigger than a lot of vehicles, but there still wasn't really room for both of us in the passenger seat. I wound up wedged between Stephen and the console, trying not to fall off or impale myself on the gearshift. "It's okay," he said, and moved me on top of him.

I bent my knees around his legs; he reached over and pulled the keys out of the ignition, flicked the lights off. After a while I undid his jeans and he went still for a moment. "We're probably pushing the cliché just a little bit here," he said finally. "I just remembered it's prom night."

"I remember," I said.

He sighed.

"On prom night, I believe the cliché traditionally takes place in a hotel," I said.

"Does it?" he asked.

"It does."

I still had my hand around him, held lightly, not moving. "Okay," he said quietly.

I leaned forward and kissed him, hard. "And you're eighteen years old," I said, when we broke apart to breathe. "You deserve a few clichés."

His right side came back after a while. He got my zipper undone, even managed to push the waistband down a bit, but the way we were sitting prohibited anything further. "I'd reciprocate," he said, although he was struggling a bit for breath by then, "but in this configuration, I don't think we'll be able to. Women's jeans just aren't designed for access the way men's are. I suppose there is something to be said for wearing dresses."

He twisted one hand in my hair, and the other clutched at my thigh. His head tipped back. "Shit," he said. He took several shallow breaths, then looked back at me. "I'm going to come." He sounded almost alarmed, like he hadn't previously thought of this prospect. His eyes were wide, maybe a bit scared. "I don't have a sock."

I did the only thing I could, at the time, think of. I pushed off him, dropped to the floor, and replaced my hand with my mouth. I didn't have time to think about whether I would gag or what it tasted like. I didn't even have time to move—or to have to move—before he came. I swallowed. (It wasn't like there was anywhere to spit.)

I felt him sink into the seat again; his fingers relaxed and his hand moved forward to cradle the side of my face. It was shaky, but I knew it was from the orgasm this time, not the cancer. "You didn't have to do that," he said.

"It saved the mess," I told him, then smiled, in case he couldn't tell I was joking. "It's all right. I wanted to," I said.

"Why?" he asked.

I hesitated. I didn't really know how to articulate what I meant. "Didn't you like it?" I said.

"Of course I did, yes. But you—I didn't do anything."

"Life's not always one for one," I said. "I like it, enough, just that you're happy."

"All right," he said finally. He put himself back together, and I fixed the front of my jeans, too, then crawled back up. I sat sideways, my legs diagonally across his, almost in his lap but not quite. He wrapped his arm around my shoulders and I tucked myself in against him. It wasn't very comfortable—certainly not for me, and probably not for him, either—but we stayed that way for a while, just the same.

Out in the dark, we couldn't see anything, not even the stars. "It'd be nice to spend the night with you," Stephen said.

"It would," I said.

He laughed a little.

"I meant it'd be nice to spend the night with you, too," I said.

"I know," he told me. He paused. "It's always nice with you. There are moments, sometimes, when I even forget…"

"I wish I could do—more than that," I said.

"We all wish a lot of things," Stephen said. It was very dispassionate, a simple statement of fact, much like you might say that today is Saturday or dinosaurs are extinct, without any emotional attachment, nor any suggestion that you could have even the slightest ability to cause such a thing to change.

"I—" I started.

"You do enough," he said. "You do more than enough." In the dark, his hand brushed my face, skittering across my cheek to my nose, then down. His thumb traced back and forth along my lower lip.

I thought about suggesting a move to the back seat, then. But I didn't say anything.

Stephen moved his thumb to the side and kissed me, light and long and sweet. "We should probably get home," he said. "Before we fall asleep."

"Right," I said. I wasn't tired, but I understood he must be.

He fell asleep on the way back. In his seat, he curled slightly toward me, head resting on his shoulder. Under the low dashboard light, he looked soft and indistinct. He looked like nothing was wrong.

I drove him all the way home. His eyes were puffy when he woke, and his blinks came slow. "Come on," I said gently. "We're here." He was walking okay, as I led him into the house; if he stumbled, it was only because he wasn't quite awake yet.

We went in through the garage and kitchen, like always. Dr. Stuart's car was gone; she must have been on call. But the light in the dining room was on and Mr. Stuart sat at the table. He wasn't waiting up (it wasn't even that late), but had an array of papers spread before him and the end of a pen in his teeth. He looked at Stephen, and then at me. It must have been immediately obvious which one of us had been sleeping.

"I'm going to bed," Stephen announced. He turned and kissed me—it was the first time we'd kissed, or even touched much, in front of either of his parents—then walked past his father and disappeared down the hall.

A long moment passed. Then Mr. Stuart cleared his throat; his chair scraped back and he stood. "Come on," he said. "I'll drive you home."

We didn't talk in the car, except for my giving directions. Mr. Stuart stopped in front of my house and I turned to thank him, then released my seatbelt and unlatched the door.

"Emily," Mr. Stuart said, and I turned back. He cleared his throat again. "Stephen loves driving," he said. "And he's a good driver. I know he wouldn't fall asleep if he wasn't already… not driving."

I nodded. I had an idea what he was getting at.

"You know he'll only get worse," Mr. Stuart said quietly.

"I know," I said. "I understand."

"I figured you did," Mr. Stuart said. He sighed. "Thank you for bringing him home."

"Of course," I said.

He sighed again; he seemed at a loss. "How's my dad?"

"He's good," I said.

"Did Stephen tell him?" he asked.

"No," I said. "But he knew. He could tell anyway."

"Right," he said.

I felt like I should say something, but I didn't have any idea what to say. "I should probably go," I told him finally. "Thanks for the ride, again."

He waved a hand dismissively. "Have a good night, Emily," he said. Just like his son, he waited until I was all the way inside before he drove away.

Stephen came with me to the photography final, though he didn't have to. Sylvia had told him and Robin the previous week that they were welcome to show work too, even though they weren't getting a grade.

Over the previous three months, I'd printed a number of Stephen's shots that he could easily have put out with the rest of ours, but he'd only shrugged when I'd mentioned it. "Do what you want," he'd told me.

And I'd been too pressed for time, finishing my own prints, to pick any.

He may not have been showing any himself, but Stephen was in all ten of my photos. It was strange looking at them, laid out on our table in their matching black mattes. Seeing them all together, I realized something I hadn't noticed before: that Stephen wasn't looking at the camera—at me—in a single one. Not even the portrait.

In my favorite photo, his head wasn't visible at all. He had surprised me, a few days after the photographic expedition with the flowers, by simply handing me a waiting camera when we got to his house after school. He himself picked up a small, round mirror, perhaps eight inches in diameter, broken free of its frame.

In the empty field behind his house, he stood near the top of the hill, half above the horizon and half below it, and held the mirror in front of his face, reflecting the sky behind me. The hardest part was keeping my own reflection out of the camera's view.

I'd taken a close-up, which I'd briefly considered for the portrait, but with an illusion instead of an actual face, I wasn't sure Sylvia would approve. Instead, I'd used a wider, almost landscape-style shot, as one of my four "open" images.

In the end, I was glad I'd chosen it. The full body, rather than just shoulders, spoke more.

It had been an odd enough experience taking the photos that day, looking at Stephen and seeing that part of him no longer appeared to be there. In the print, that unsettling sensation was even stronger. The edges of the mirror were just barely visible, if you got a close look. But mostly it looked like a boy's abandoned body, hands cradling the empty place where his head used to be.

As we'd walked back down the hill, I'd asked Stephen why he'd done it. I'd expected him to cite some online example, maybe even an obscure article in a photo book, but he hadn't. "That's how I feel sometimes," he'd said. "Well, no. Not exactly. But sometimes I think that would be better."

Two days later, while the negatives on their half-finished roll still rested, dark, inside the camera, he'd told me he had a brain tumor.

I looked over at Stephen, at his fingers tracing shakily along the tops of chairs as we passed, and I thought I knew what his "better" meant.

In the classroom, it was mostly quiet; those people who did talk used low voices. We all moved slowly from table to table, silently judging everyone else's work against our own. Some of the photos were very good. Some were just okay.

We stopped at the desk where Robin usually sat. He'd put out six pictures, all of his children. Only one of them looked posed. They were nice.

From across the room, Robin saw us looking and hurried over. He told us his daughters' names, pointing to them in every frame. He seemed so proud. "This one's going over the mantel," he said, and for a moment, I was scared he'd point to the posed one, but he didn't.

Stephen smiled. "I think it's really good," he said.

"Oh," said Robin. "Well." He looked down. "I suppose for an old man like me, it's not that bad." He wasn't really that old. But he was, I realized for the first time, easily old enough to be my dad. Or Stephen's. "I'll let you two be," he said, and smiled, then wandered off in the direction we'd come.

Stephen leaned up against the desk again and ran his finger along the edge of one of Robin's mattes. "Do you want kids?" he said.

"Uh…" I replied.

"Oh, no, not like that," he said. "I'm not asking you to

immortalize me. Not that that's really even an option for me any more. I just meant—in theory."

"I don't know," I said. In middle school, like everyone else, I'd tried on potential baby names with the last names of boys I thought were cute, but it had always been just a game to me. Since then, I'd become even more practical where children were concerned. They weren't bad, but I had no delusions of giving birth to a perfect infant; having been old enough when Tammy was born to remember her as a baby, I knew what they were actually like. I suppose it's different when a child is your own, rather than the usurper of your semi-spoiled five-year-old throne, but it can't be that different. And then, of course, there's all the stuff that comes after the baby stops being a baby.

I'd never thought about it a great deal, but when I did, I wasn't entirely sure I wanted (or, to be fair, didn't want) one of my own. "I don't know," I said again. "Do you?"

Stephen looked back down at the picture of Robin's three girls. "I don't know, either," he said. "I never really thought about it until it was too late."

"I always sort of figured I'd do what my partner wanted," I said. "I mean, not totally—that sounds awful, doesn't it?—but I don't think I'd be absolutely distraught if I couldn't be a parent, and I also don't think I'd hate my life if I did become one. And there are some people, I guess, who it's really important to, and I wouldn't want—if everything else was perfect, but we couldn't agree on that one thing, you know, I'd hate for that to ruin it."

"Yeah," Stephen said. He glanced around to see if anyone was within hearing distance, and apparently decided they weren't. "Ever since I was diagnosed, sometimes I get these twinges where I wish I was a dad—you know, something to remember me by—but mostly, I think that's about right. I could go either way. I'd be happy either way." He paused. "Of course, that's all hypothetical. I'll never be a dad. Even if you got pregnant tonight, I wouldn't live long enough to even feel it kick."

I swallowed.

"But even if I could," he said, "I wouldn't—I'd never leave you with such a horrible thing. What a reminder. That's the other thing I sometimes think. Imagine what this is like for my parents. I don't think—I don't think I'd want to have kids if I knew there was the chance of pain like this."

"I know," I said. I'd thought that, too. "Although, now aren't you getting into better to have loved and lost than never to have loved at all?"

"I suppose," he agreed. "I suppose you have to weigh the potential costs and benefits. But—" he sighed, and finally turned away from Robin's pictures, "you can't really do cost-benefit analyses on people."

He leaned over and tapped the side of his head gently against mine, sighed. I turned toward him and he put his hand on the small of my back, then stepped sideways and slid in close behind me, his other hand resting on my hip, too. "Let's look some more," he said.

There was speculation among some members of the class, but Sylvia didn't tell us who had gotten As or who had "won." I knew I would emerge with a passing grade that would grant me credit, and beyond that—as far as grades were concerned—I didn't really care. I had done what I'd wanted to do—learned to develop film and make prints—but I still didn't feel like I was really finished.

Stephen and I stayed after everyone else left, and Sylvia, with characteristic bluntness, gave me permission to keep using the darkroom throughout the summer. "I'll email you the new door code," she said dismissively, when I asked if she'd approve me for by-the-hour rental. "The rental rate is beyond inflated. I'm just happy to have somebody who wants to be in there."

Then she looked past me to Stephen. "I saw some of the prints Emily was working on earlier," she said. "They weren't here tonight. Yours, I presume?"

Stephen twitched the side of his lip in a half smile.

"You've done some nice work," she said. "Both of you." She looked at Stephen again. "Will you continue, also? I'd be pleased if you did."

Stephen coughed a little, and looked away. "Unfortunately," he said, "I don't think I'll have that option."

"Ah," Sylvia said. She stood up, and gathered the rest of her things together. "Well, if circumstances do change." She paused. "Best of luck with your endeavors."

"Thank you," Stephen said.

At the door to the classroom, Sylvia flicked off the lights, and we turned one way while she went the other. We got to the wagon, and Stephen reached into the back seat and handed me a manila envelope. I opened it and realized he'd given me back the same card I'd made for his birthday. "What's this?" I said, stopping with the image of the tower still half inside.

"I'm ready," he said. "Finally. Are you still down?"

I looked at him and swallowed. I knew I should say no. People with motor difficulties shouldn't climb step ladders, much less water towers closer to a hundred feet high. At the same time, I knew I couldn't say no. That was probably what he expected me to say, but it would've been so crushing. For both of us.

"Okay," I said quietly.

"I was thinking next week. Next Tuesday. We should have some free time then."

"Are you sure?" I said.

He looked at me and nodded, slow, serious. "Yes."

Friday he wasn't in a good mood. Partly it was because of the hospital visit—he'd missed class that morning, for a meeting with Dr. Edwards—and partly, I think, he was just having a bad day. I could tell he was trying not to take it out on me, but—I could still tell.

Since the initial diagnosis, Stephen had come to hate hospitals. And he had to go in a lot—not just for the regular check-ups and meetings, but also for MRIs. He'd agreed to have one a month, even though no one, he said, had MRIs that often. They were more to appease his mother than for any diagnostic use. Stephen himself never looked at the images, but his mother liked knowing, and, he said, it was the least he could do for her. "I'm still her son," he'd told me. "And it's not like they had another kid as a contingency plan."

"I don't think it works like that," I said, because I wasn't sure what else to say.

"No," he said flatly. "Of course it doesn't."

He'd made us each half a ham and cheese sandwich, but he wasn't eating.

He sighed. "When I said four months, a while ago," he said, "I wasn't really being realistic. It was more for her." He paused. "And my dad. And you."

By that time, I'd done my share of research, and I understood that this was probably true, but I still didn't really understand, overall. It was all so hard to take in—probably in large part because I didn't want to. I didn't want to admit to myself that anything was wrong, that any of these things were going to happen. Everyone wants to believe that they'll be the lucky one.

"But, realistically," he said, "four months is not all good days. Four months is the time it takes for the cancer to compromise enough of my brain that it literally cannot keep my body alive any more. It gets ugly," he said. "Hemiparesis. Ataxia. The inability to do tandem gait, although I haven't done that in years." He let out a breath. "Hearing loss. Double vision. Inability to control movements in, or properly close, the eyes. Trouble chewing. Trouble swallowing. Loss of sense of taste. Speech. Essentially all facial functions. Edema and hydrocephalus. Increasingly severe headaches. Nausea. Vomiting. Fatigue. Eventually, total loss of muscle control. Heart. Lungs. Everything." He listed them all off flatly, emotionlessly. It was impressive, in an awful way.

I swallowed. "So eventually," I said, "you're going to lose the ability to breathe on your own?" I couldn't stop myself.

"Oh, no," Stephen said. "I won't let that happen."

In my experience, when you had cancer, you didn't get to let things happen. They happened to you, whether you wanted them or not. But at that point, my experience with cancer consisted solely of what had come through Stephen, and he'd been dealing with it a lot longer than I had. It was reasonable to assume that he knew things I didn't. There were ways of managing, hadn't he said?

"They say I'll still be conscious for it all, though," he added. "So at least there's that." He sounded like it was the most terrible thing he could imagine.

I didn't blame him. I had always thought drowning would be the worst way to die. Now I wasn't so sure.

"I'm sorry," he said.

"Please don't apologize to me," I told him.

He sighed again, shook his head. "Sometimes I'm cynical," he said.

We drove up the hill to the water tower the following Tuesday, early evening. It looked just as deserted as it had before—perhaps even more so now that spring was in full bloom and the weeds and vegetation had sprung up, thick and uncut. In fact, judging by the amount of greenery poking through the gravel, it didn't look like anyone else had even been there since our previous visit, two and a half months earlier.

We stood side by side in the gravel and looked at the tower rising up above. Stephen's right hand quivered slightly, and I told myself it was just nerves—an emotional, not physical, incapacity; he was, after all, still afraid of heights. Even so, I couldn't help feeling like I should be strapping him into some sort of harness. The catwalk around the base of the tank looked very, very far up.

"Well," Stephen said finally, and moved to open the door of the wagon, to boost himself onto the roof, "no use standing around."

"Are you sure?" I blurted. "I—are you sure you're okay?"

"I'm not going to fall," he said. He climbed onto the running board, then looked back down at me. "However, if I do fall, you should probably walk home, so it looks like I came up here by myself."

"Stephen," I said, very sternly.

He looked at me again. "I'm not going to fall," he repeated. "It's a ladder, an ordinary, fixed, metal ladder. It doesn't work like that. I might not always be able to move my body, but my body also doesn't move beyond my control. All right, my hand does sometimes shake, but I don't get seizures. If worse comes to worst, all I have to do is stay in the same place." He paused. "Please, Emily. This might be the last chance I—I might not be able to do this again. I need to be able to do this," he said.

He didn't say why, and I didn't ask him to explain. I understood: this was something—perhaps the only thing—that Stephen could be in charge of: climbing to the top of an almost-derelict water tower, even though he was terrified of doing so. It was his way, perhaps, of proving to himself that he was still alive, that he still had agency. That he still had a life that was worth anything, at all.

I stepped over to him, in the V between the wagon's open door and its body, and touched my fingers, very briefly, to his wrist. "Go on," I said.

He went first, slowly but deliberately, without looking down. I was probably more scared than he was, tense and full of adrenaline, ready to reach out and snatch at him if he came tumbling past—although realistically, by the time I even got on the ladder, he was probably far enough up that any attempt to catch him if he fell probably would've done us both more harm than good.

But he didn't fall. He didn't even have to pause for breath. Maybe it was the repetitive, straightforward motion; maybe he'd just made up his mind to be able to do it—to force himself to be able to do it—without needing to stop. Maybe it was simply one of his good days. He still had a lot of pretty good days, then.

At the top, he pulled himself onto the platform and stood, holding onto the railing with both hands, while he waited for me. His eyes, I saw, were pressed closed.

I climbed up next to him and placed my hand on his arm, slowly, carefully. "Are you going to look?" I said.

"I don't think I can," he whispered back.

I moved my hand down and laid my fingers along the top of his, though I didn't expect him to let go of the bar, and he didn't. "Shuffle a bit to your left," I told him, and guided him away from the gap in the rail.

I kept the bulk of the tank between us and view from the city, just in case. Looking away, there wasn't much to see. There was the pumphouse, and then a long plateau mostly covered in greenish-grey brush. An abandoned fence stretched partway across and then ended abruptly. In the distance, there was a slightly greener and more orderly-looking field that was probably some kind of crop.

But we weren't there for the view.

"You did it," I told him. "The water tower. You're up here."

He opened his eyes, slowly, toward my voice, and I saw that he was focusing solely on me, ignoring the open air around and below us.

"Hey," I said.

"Hey," he said back. He smiled a little bit.

I leaned back against the warm metal of the tank and pulled him toward me. Slowly, reluctantly, he let go of the railing. He clung to my arm with his left hand; his right came up over my ear, the tips of his fingers reaching into my hair. He ducked his head down and rested his forehead against mine. I put both my arms around him, tight.

When his breathing levelled out, I kissed him. Our lips were already so close, I couldn't not. He leaned hard into me, then broke away and tucked his head in against the side of my neck. It was where he often kissed me, but he didn't then. "It's things like this," he said.

I wanted to ask what—things like this that what?—but at the same time, I realized I kind of already knew.

We didn't stay long. It wasn't that Stephen had wanted to do anything up there—he'd just wanted to go up, to do it. It was a process, not a result. And once the process was done, there was no real reason to linger.

Back at the bottom, we sat side by side on the roof of the wagon. "Thank you," Stephen said, looking up at the tower. It was simultaneously harder and easier to look at now, from the ground. I was horrified by the fact that we'd actually been up there.

"Just please don't ask me to do it again," I said.

"No," he agreed, with what sounded like relief. He was quiet for a minute. "Even before," he said, "I never thought I'd be able to do that."

"I'd never have dreamed of it," I told him.

He laughed a bit, and reached over and took my hand. "You should," he said. "You've got plenty of time to dream."

"You're doing pretty well still," I said. He had, after all, just climbed up and down a water tower. Without any safety equipment whatsoever. That seemed pretty impressive.

"Still," he said quietly. His thumb ran back and forth across my knuckles. "Sometimes I feel guilty. There are people, I know, who keep fighting, to the very last second. Who try everything they've got, and then. It's what my mum would do. She'd find a way to irradiate me at home, if she thought there was even the slightest chance it'd help. Or if I'd agree to it. Some people would say that I'm giving up, taking the easy way out. Sometimes I think maybe..."

"You're not," I said firmly. "You made a choice, right? You're not giving up. Don't ever let anyone tell you you're giving up."

"No," he said. "I know." He paused again, pushed his hat up off his forehead, then pulled it back down again. "There isn't—there's nothing easy about this. And there are different ways of fighting, I think. It's not just about exhausting all conceivable options. It's about weighing the options and deciding what's best. I have this time, and I don't—I can't waste any of it."

He sighed and leaned back, tilting his face up toward the sky. "Remember when we talked about books?" he asked.

"Yeah," I said. It seemed like so long ago.

"In cancer stories," he said, still looking up, "there's always a hot guy in a motorcycle jacket who comes along and makes the sick character's dying days wonderful. But I figured out a long time ago that there's not going to be a hot guy in a motorcycle jacket for me, so I'd have to make life wonderful for myself." He looked over at me, smiled. "Even if you haven't got the right bike or the right clothes, I'm glad you're part of it." Then he looked away and bit his lower lip, shaking his head. "That sounded incredibly cheesy, didn't it?"

"Well," I said.

"What I mean is, it's not nearly—it's not any fun to climb a water tower by yourself."

"That's what I figured."

"Thank you," he said again.

I just shrugged.

To that point, Stephen had never had a really bad day at school. And he'd certainly never had a bad enough day that it had affected—or even been enough to bring about the notice of—anyone else. At the time, I hadn't known to take any precautions. Later, I told him he could always come and get me, though I knew he probably never would.

Fourth period Thursday, I was in history when someone came in, handed the teacher a note, and stepped back out again before I looked up. "Emily," Mr. Fredericks said, and nodded at me, then the door.

Kyle was in the hall, waiting. "Hey, Emily," he said. "Have you seen Stephen?"

"Um," I said. Obviously, that morning, I had seen Stephen. Equally obviously, he wasn't with me now. I gave Kyle kind of a bewildered look. "He should be in math?"

"Oh. Yeah." Kyle shoved his hands in his pockets and started to slump away.

"Is that it?" I said. "Really? You went to the trouble of looking up my schedule just to ask me where Stephen was? Wouldn't it have been easier to just look up his?"

Kyle looked like he was a little embarrassed, and also a little sorry to have to be the one to tell me, to finally clue me in to what everyone else had known for ages. "Yeah," he said, looking at his feet, "I know Stephen's schedule. He's not in math."

"Excuse me," I said. I'd left my backpack and all my things in the classroom, but at that moment, I didn't care. I walked straight past Kyle without hesitation.

To his credit, he didn't try to stop me, or say anything about all efforts being futile. Then again, he didn't come with me, either.

I let myself out of the side door and kept walking. Stephen was exactly where I expected to find him: in the back of the wagon, slumped so that his head came up only as far as the hollow between the neck rest and seatback. His eyes were closed, but so tightly that I knew he was awake. I got in and sat next to him. "Are you okay?" I said, even though it was obvious that he wasn't.

Stephen mumbled something vague and indecipherable.

I reached over and took his hand, and he let me. It was

completely limp. "Do you have—maybe you could take an extra pill?" I suggested.

"No," he managed. "I can't go off schedule. It'll mess up everything."

I didn't argue. It seemed reasonable enough. I brought my right hand over and wrapped it around both of ours, and rubbed the back of his hand with my thumb. "Is there anything you want me to do?"

"No," he said. He was quiet for a long time, then took a deep breath. "Go back to class. I'm fine. I mean, this happens sometimes. It's normal. I'll be fine in a bit."

I had no plans to go back to class, and I really didn't think this was normal, even for him, but Stephen didn't need to know that. "Kyle was looking for you," I said. "Do you want me to tell him you're...?"

"No," Stephen ground out. "Fuck. Fourth period already?"

"Yes," I told him.

"We're supposed to be having a meeting about what to do for graduation," he said. He was back to almost mumbling again. "Fuck. Graduation. I don't even know if I'll make it that far."

"Don't say that," I said. "It's only two weeks away."

Stephen didn't respond.

His condition at the moment was a bit unnerving, but I was hoping it was a fluke. And that aside, I didn't think he was already doing so poorly that he wouldn't still be alive for graduation. But, while it had gone unspoken between us, I think we both knew that if he couldn't still do it on his own, unobtrusively, he wouldn't walk at all.

After a while, he opened his eyes and squinted up at me. "I need to lie down," he said.

I moved forward, leaning against the back of the console,

so he could stretch across all three of the seats on his side, legs curled up beneath him. He closed his eyes again and pressed his forehead into the vinyl. His left arm hung over the edge of the bench.

A minute passed and then he reached under the seat, withdrawing a folded brown paper bag—small, unprinted, the kind you might use to pack a lunch in, or wrap around a bottle of alcohol. He managed to open it—one-handed, without looking; he must have done it before—and positioned it upright on the floor, and I realized that its intended purpose, in this case, was a barf bag.

I didn't know what to do.

Stephen reached out again, toward me this time, and his hand brushed my knee. I leaned down, and held on. This hand—his good hand, even, not the one I'd had before—felt weak, too, and clammy. "Can you drive?" he said.

I got the keys out of the pocket of his jeans, and spent a few moments debating the relative merits of putting Stephen in a seatbelt, but in the end, I decided it wasn't worth making him any more uncomfortable than he already was. I climbed over the console and drove him home, slowly, carefully, shifting as smoothly as I could. By the time we got there, his head had slipped halfway off the seat and tears were starting to leak from his eyes. I parked in the gravel and cut the engine. "We're here," I told him softly.

Stephen took a long, slow breath, and then another and another, gathering himself. Then, somewhat to my surprise—though he didn't seem to be having much trouble moving, just with the pain—he got up, got out, and shuffled, almost blindly, into the house.

Inside, he stopped at the bathroom and shut the door. I stood in the hallway, listening to him retching and, alternately, choking, and hating myself because there was nothing I could do. After a while, the toilet flushed and then the sink ran for some time. When he came out, he still looked awful, though not quite so much so. His face was wet and he smelled like toothpaste. "I'm just going to go lie down," he whispered. He listed a little toward the wall. "You don't have to stay."

But I went in with him, and when he sank, almost spineless, onto the bed, I took his shoes off and crawled up by his side. He fell asleep almost immediately, and I could've left then. I probably should have. But I stayed.

At one o'clock, his watch beeped, and for a few moments he seemed confused. He went for the nightstand first, fumbling for the watch until he realized he was still wearing it, and then, once that was silenced, fumbling again for the pills. "In your pocket," I finally said. "It's afternoon."

For a second, he stiffened. Then he got the afternoon pills out of his pocket and swallowed. And then he turned over to face me. He looked a little less in pain; more, perhaps, aggrieved. "I wish you weren't seeing this," he said.

"I know," I told him. "But I am."

He reached across the small gap between us and rested his hand on my forearm. "Sometimes it hurts so bad, I start to get dizzy," he said. "And I start to see things that... aren't right. Not double vision; that's different. Just from the headache. The colors get brighter. Everything seems louder." He paused. "And then sometimes it gets so bad—even worse than that—that all I want to do is throw up."

"Does it help?" I asked him.

"It helps a little," he said. "Doesn't everyone feel better after they throw up?"

I sort of shrugged, as much as one can shrug while lying down.

"This is the first time it's been this bad," he admitted, "since before. Before I started the radiation." He paused. "That means the tumor's back, maybe, to almost the size it was before treatment. I don't know how much longer it'll be."

"Don't think about that right now," I said.

"I have to think about it," he protested. "I have to plan."

"Does it still hurt?" I asked.

He nodded, reluctantly, and I swallowed. "Does sleeping help?"

He nodded again.

"Then go back to sleep," I said. "You can think about it later."

"Okay," Stephen mumbled. He tucked his chin down into his chest, and brought his knees up almost as high: the fetal position, I realized. Then he lifted his head again and looked at me. "But you should go back," he said. "Please. I'll be all right now. I just need to sleep it off."

"Promise?" I said.

His hand swept down my arm and his fingers brushed against mine. "Normally I wouldn't," he said. "Make a promise. But today I will. Yes."

"Okay," I agreed. I closed my fingers around his, linking them together. "Do you want me to stay until you fall asleep?"

"It's all right," he said. "I'll see you tomorrow morning, okay? Dad'll pick up the wagon."

"Okay," I said again.

He disentangled his fingers from mine, and tucked his head back down. I slid off the bed, and stood for a moment in the doorway, watching him, wondering if he would really be all right, if I would really see him the next morning like he'd said I would. I supposed there was nothing to do but hope.

That night, after the wagon was gone—his parents came by a little after eight—my phone rang. For a moment, I thought it might be Stephen, but it was Mari. I felt bad for being disappointed.

"Hey," she said, and then, without waiting for me to respond, "my uncle says they still need youth leaders for summer parks and rec. I already have the café, obviously, but that's mostly nights and weekends, so if you put in an application by the end of next week, I will, too, and Tío says he'll put us in the same spot. We get paid to teach all the kids soccer and stuff, and last summer all the rec staff got free passes to the pool. So?" she said. "Sounds pretty awesome, right?" And then, finally, "Emily?"

"I…" I said. It suddenly occurred to me that Stephen had probably never had a summer job. And never would. And that if I spent my summer—Stephen's *last* summer—herding grade schoolers around a park with Mari, I'd barely see him at all. "I don't know. This isn't…"

"Is something wrong?" Mari said, in that way she had of making everything sound like she couldn't believe whatever it was, but it was also the most important thing in the world.

"No," I said. "And it does sound cool, I just—"

"You sound upset," Mari said. We were both silent for a moment; then she sucked in her breath. "Did Stephen do something? Did he cheat on you? The rat bastard, I should've known. Emily, you—"

"No," I said, very firmly. "He—everything's—our relationship," I settled on, "is fine."

"But you sound…" Mari said, almost meekly. "I almost thought you were going to cry."

"My throat hurts," I told her.

"Oh," she said. "But that'll be gone in no time. So, this summer, parks and rec? You in?"

"I don't know if I can," I said, and then, to distract her, added, "maybe you should ask Chase." I could almost feel her blushing through the phone.

"Well, maybe," she said, which was a big step for Mari. Aside from me, Chase was probably Mari's best friend. She was terrified to ask him to do anything, though, in case he thought it was a date, even though she would have loved to go on a date with him. As far as I could tell, Chase wouldn't have minded going on a date with her, either, but Mari was not optimistic—or even very willing to entertain the possibility.

"But, I still feel like I never see you any more," she said. "First, our stupid schedules for lunch, and then you didn't come out for spring soccer. I almost feel like, if we were sleeping together, would I get to see you more?"

"Mari," I gasped.

"So are you sleeping together?" she asked. "You and the rat bastard?"

"He didn't do anything wrong," I protested.

"I know," she agreed. "I believe you. I'm just a bit jealous."

It was awful, I realized, that even with all the effort he'd made toward misdirection and disguise, anyone could look at Stephen and be jealous. "Don't be," I told Mari. "We'll hang out, I promise."

"Whatever," she said. "I mean, don't worry about it. I'm sure I'd be the same if Chase suddenly started acting interested in me."

"Chase is interested in you," I said.

"Whatever," Mari said again. "But are you sure you're okay? I want you to know, if he does do anything, you always have me."

"I've got you, too," I told her.

"Thanks, babe," she said. She hesitated. "But, so, about Chase. I thought he was maybe going to do some, like, landscaping thing, but do you really think I should ask him?"

"Mm," I said. Mari immediately went on. One of the things I liked about her was that most of the time when we talked, I didn't really have to converse so much as just listen. We—or rather, she—went in circles for fifteen minutes, and when we hung up, she was no closer to making a decision about Chase than she'd ever been.

Things between Mari and Chase may have been a convoluted mess, but I found myself wishing my relationship with Stephen could be so simple. Mari didn't have to worry about Chase dying. She didn't have to face the reality that in a few months, the person she cared about more than, perhaps, anyone else in the world would be gone.

I realized that Mari's explanation for it was wrong, but she had been right about one thing: I was starting to cry. My chin trembled, and I kept swallowing, even though there was nothing to swallow. I tried to close my eyes, but when I did, all I could see was Stephen in the back of the wagon that afternoon, stretched limp across the seats, his head and arm hanging over the edge like he didn't even have the energy to pull them back up. And his eyes, pressed so tightly closed that he was crying, too, without even realizing it.

I put my phone down on the end table and curled up against the arm of the couch. It was a relief that I'd taken my call in the basement—I'd done it so Tammy wouldn't eavesdrop, but now, it also meant that none of my family would be close enough to hear me cry.

Nevertheless, after a while my mother appeared on the stairs, probably on her way to turn the lights out before bed. Her face fell when she saw me. I was scared she'd ask questions, but she just scooped me into her lap, even though I was far too big for her lap, and held me. "Oh, honey," was all she said. "Oh, honey."

Eventually there were no tears left to cry. I hiccupped, and Mom kissed me on the top of the head. "It'll be all right," she said.

I nodded, even though I knew that it wouldn't.

"I'm here if you want to talk," she said. "Daddy, too."

I nodded again. I wished, so much, that I could.

"I'll let you come up on your own," she said finally. I scooted a bit onto the sofa arm, and she wriggled away. "Turn the lights off when you leave, okay?"

"Okay," I said.

"Good night, honey," she told me, and gave me one last pat on the leg.

I didn't want her to go. I didn't want Stephen to go, either. I probably could've gotten my mom to sit with me longer, but other things—more important things—there's just nothing for.

At lunchtime, I'd find Stephen at his locker, and we'd walk out to the parking lot. We'd sit in the back of the wagon, and he'd try to gag down ham and cheese sandwiches (he refused to give them up) and pomegranate juice (or, sometimes, sugar-free grape or blueberry juice—always something high in antioxidants) with varying degrees of success. Sometimes I'd wind up eating more of the sandwich than he did. Even cold, they were always really good, each one in an entirely different, unexpected way. Almost invariably, I'd take a first bite and give him a thumbs up.

Then Stephen would tell me what I was eating. "It's honey ham and Emmantel on whole wheat toast with a barley start," he said once; that was one of his less adventurous combinations. "With red oak and a bit of raspberry jam."

I hadn't gotten to the jam part yet. I gave him another thumbs up when I did.

"Is it really good?" he said, a bit wistfully. He wasn't partaking that day; the toast, even barely toasted, was too rough on his throat. Instead he had a blueberry concoction that he called juice but looked to me more like a semi-solid. Every few mouthfuls, he'd gag a little bit on that, too, but pretended he wasn't. I pretended not to notice.

"It's really good," I told him. "The raspberry really adds to it."

"I thought it might," he said.

"It's almost an entirely different sandwich."

"Good," he said. "Thanks." Then, "I wish I could taste it."

"Maybe you could try it again later," I suggested, "just without toasting the bread."

Stephen shrugged. "It doesn't matter," he said.

"It's really good," I told him again.

"I know," he said. "Theoretically, I know." He paused, and forced down another mouthful of the blueberry stuff. "I could've been a serious foodie. I had the palate. Now I can barely swallow anything, much less actually taste it."

"What?" I said, because this was something of a shock. Not the swallowing. The other part.

"Some people lose their sense of taste during radiation," he said simply. "Some people later get it back. I didn't. It could've been worse, I suppose. I can still discern a little. And nothing tastes really awful to me. But every sandwich I've made since then tastes the same, no matter what I put on it. I only know what works in theory. When I said I wanted to eat a really good ham and cheese sandwich, I didn't mean I just wanted to eat it. I meant I actually, physically, wanted to recognize what I was eating."

"I had no idea," I said. I kind of stared at him.

"I keep hoping it'll come back," Stephen said, "but it never has." He shrugged. "Well." The way he said it was very final.

He leaned back into the seat and slid down a little, draped his free arm up around me. He took another slug of blueberry juice.

Outside, Bonham walked by, then doubled back to slam his fist against the wagon's hood, ducking his head down and grinning through the windshield. He nodded at Stephen. For a second, Stephen seemed startled—not, I think, so much by the manner of Bonham's greeting but by the fact that he'd bothered to do anything at all—but then he grinned and nodded, too. Bonham kept walking.

I looked at Stephen. He was looking at Bonham, walking away. "Damn," he said.

"What?" I asked.

"Sometimes I wish I could say something," he said. Then, almost immediately, he shook his head. "But it's better this way."

I sort of understood, or thought I did. Yes, he may have been Stephen's oldest friend, but at the same time, Bonham was—well, he was Bonham. He wasn't supposed to do serious things. He wasn't supposed to know—or even want to know—about something like this. He was supposed to be perfect and happy and protected. Stephen didn't want to be a burden.

And Bonham didn't ask. He was probably just as aware as Stephen and I were that he had a role to play, and asking about such things wasn't part of it.

"He's not bad," Stephen said. "I know he'd be able to… deal with it. When other people are around, he keeps up appearances, you know, the whole Bonham Show. And, in a way, supporting cast in the Stephen Show. He plays along. Sometimes I'm not so sure, but sometimes I think he has to know something's up. Sometimes, so long as no one else's there, he'll just come up and ask me if I'm okay."

"What do you say?"

Stephen blew out a long breath. "All all right, mate," he said. "Just like that. But at the same time," he added, "sometimes I wonder if he's not faking it just as much as me."

"How so?" I said.

"He's not perfect," Stephen said simply. "I don't begrudge him anything, but—that's not something a lot of people know. That he's really not perfect, I mean. And that he's more than just a caricature of himself. Or at least at some point he was." He paused, rubbed his hat up and down on his head. "I don't know," he said. "I don't… I remember the look on your face when we went to his dad's, before spring break. You were shocked."

"It was so… mellow," I said.

Stephen shrugged. "To the outside observer, yeah, he does seem more the kegger and ketamine type. And even then, you saw…"

"You mean when he asked?"

He nodded, once. "He always asks me," he said. "It's the done thing to do. But he's never seemed even the slightest bit disappointed when I've said no." He paused, looking down at his lap, running his thumb around the rim of the blueberry bottle. "The reality is, he's seen what I'm like, and he doesn't want what I've got.

"Every school should have at least one really obvious junkie," he said, his voice hard. "It's the best form of drug prevention there is. Bonham doesn't even smoke weed any more because of me. He must think it was my gateway drug."

I thought about how hard it must be to have all your friends think you were an addict, the bad example that they should avoid. By that time, it was pretty clear that there were rumors about Stephen—by that time, to be honest, there were probably rumors about me, too—but I don't think anyone had ever said anything directly to him. No one had ever directly suggested he get help. That probably made things easier for him, not having to refuse, but I wondered how it felt—having something so obviously wrong, and none of the people who were supposed to be your friends ever doing a thing.

Maybe their way of helping Stephen was simply not ostracizing him, not intervening or accusing him right out. I suppose there were ways the situation could've been much worse. It made me feel somewhat better to know that Bonham, at least, had the decency to pretend whatever it was he was pretending. I wasn't entirely sure what Stephen had meant, but it seemed to make him happy.

Kyle, on the other hand, I couldn't quite get a read on. I knew he and Stephen were friends, but maybe they still weren't close enough for Kyle to feel he should speak up. Or maybe he just didn't care.

"How did you wind up on student council?" I asked, rather abruptly, though I'd always wondered.

Stephen just shrugged. "Habit," he said. "I mean, it's been seven years."

"Before that, then," I said, rolling my eyes. "Before it became habit. Originally."

"Oh," he said. "Actually, that was Bonham's fault. Well, kind of. At the start of sixth grade, my parents were worried I wasn't adjusting to middle school well enough, and I tried to distract them by talking about Bonham, which in retrospect was an awful idea and had the opposite effect of what I'd intended, because then, you know, they wound up comparing me to the most socially adept person in the class.

"Then I made the further mistake of mentioning that Bonham was running for student council, and obviously I wasn't going to join the football team, but they decided being a class officer was something I could reasonably do. Dad picked treasurer because no one else was running for it yet. I probably gave an okay speech, and people knew I was in top level maths, but really they mostly voted for me because I was Bonham's friend."

He paused, thinking for a while. "That's probably the same reason people voted for Kyle, too. He's good at it, obviously, but he was new in sixth grade. It probably took him all of two hours to figure out Bonham was the running mate he'd need."

"And you?" I said.

"No, I would've rather not had the votes by association. It made my parents happy, but I never really wanted it." He shrugged. "I just sort of rode along. We've had the same class officers—all four of us—since sixth grade. Shelly says we're the first class to have done that in years and years. Decades. I tried to resign at the start of junior year," he added. "They wouldn't let me. This year, I didn't actually run."

"What?" I said. "You didn't?"

He shook his head. "People thought I was giving up, for a variety of reasons, none of them correct. I really just thought it would be too inconvenient—too inconsiderate—to make the senior class have to elect a new treasurer midway through the year. So I never filled out any of the paperwork, and I didn't give a speech, or campaign at all. But my name was on all Kyle's posters, anyway. His whole thing was 'you've trusted us for six years, trust us for one more.' Even the dude who takes opiates between sixth and seventh period."

"That wasn't—" I said.

"That part was implied, then," he said. "Somebody actually ran against me, but they must not have tried very hard at all, because Shelly said I won by a lot. It says a lot about my peers, don't you think, that even when given a different option, they still picked someone they believed to be a drug addict to be in charge of the senior class fund? And I don't mean it says they're tolerant."

"Maybe they don't all think..." I said, "as much as you think they do."

He shook his head again. "You've seen," he said. "Even Kyle thinks I am. Anyway. That's how I wound up on student council."

"Did you ever enjoy it?" I asked.

"No." He shrugged. "We're kids. Even now, class treasurer is mostly just a nominal position. I always just thought of it as another class. Why do you ask?"

"I don't know," I admitted. "I guess it just seemed so unlike you."

"Mm," said Stephen. "We're not really joiners, are we, you and I?"

It wasn't entirely true—we'd done a few things, after all—but I knew what he meant. The things we did weren't the kind of things other kids our age were lining up for. "I guess not," I said.

"You should start doing things," Stephen said after a moment. "What ever happened to spring soccer? You mentioned that once."

"Yeah," I said, "but Mari didn't invite me."

He frowned. "You know, you can still do things even if no one invites you to them."

"I know," I said. "But…"

Stephen sighed. "We'll keep working on that," he said. And then, "What are you going to do next year?"

I knew that what he was really asking was what was I going to do after he was gone, and I shook my head. "Right now, I'm doing this," I said. "And I'll figure out next year when I get there. Right now, this is what I want."

He didn't protest; he just said all right. Then he looked at his watch. "We should probably head back," he said. "The bell's going to ring soon."

He walked me to the building, and then we went our separate ways. After school, when we met, he started the conversation again as if we hadn't let off at all. "I applied to State," he said. "In the fall. Mostly I did it for Mum, but also, that was before I'd progressed; there was still a little bit of a chance then. It'd been more than a year, I mean."

He paused. "Up until a certain point, with every day that passes your remaining time decreases; with every day that passes, that's one day less that you have left to live.

"But then you get to that point, and you start to think that, with every day that passes, your chances are going up. Like, if I was going to die, I would've done it already. Like maybe I was the zero point one percent, because somebody has to be, you know?"

I nodded; I knew. Because that was what I—still—kept hoping for, too.

"I probably could've gotten into fancier schools," he said. "I could've gotten scholarships. And not just because of the cancer essay. But I didn't apply for any. What's the point of me taking somebody else's place, or winning money that somebody else could actually use? Just to prove a point? But it's not even really proving a point if it's just an apology or a token thing because I'm dying.

"When I was at the pediatric hospital," he said, and hesitated slightly, "some of the kids talked about, I guess, cancer perks. There was a girl who was homecoming queen. And her dream was to graduate from high school, so they had a special ceremony for her in January and gave her a diploma. That I don't mind; it's not doing anybody any harm. She didn't entirely earn it, but it's not like she lived long enough to put it to any use.

"And there was another girl a couple years older than me who won pretty much all her local scholarships. Which, good for her, because she actually got better, and graduated, and she's in college now. But at the same time, would she have won all those if she'd been healthy? I know there are a lot of people who think, sort of, 'you have cancer, you deserve to be compensated,' which I can understand, because getting childhood cancer is a really shit hand. But I still feel like, 'yeah, I have cancer, please keep treating me the same.' No one ever does, though."

"Stephen," I started, and he shook his head.

"Shit," he said. "I hope I don't sound like I'm being too high-minded. It's really, a lot of it, just self-interest. Maybe

I'm too old; maybe by the time I was diagnosed, I'd already become too cynical." He sighed. "But every time I hear about cancer perks—that will never, never make up for what we've lost—all I can think about is pity. Getting some sort of prize doesn't make the fact that I'm dying go away," he said. "Nobody can make my greatest dream come true, because that's, well, it's obvious."

"Stephen," I said on Friday, "I have to ask you something. You're not going to like it," I added, before he could say anything or even nod.

He sighed.

"My parents," I said. "They need to know. They don't understand."

Now that the school year was drawing to a close, it was becoming more and more of a problem. My parents—and Mari—wanted me to have a summer job, which, under any other circumstances, I would've considered completely reasonable, even exciting, perhaps. The current circumstances, though, were that I didn't want to lose any more of what little time I had remaining with Stephen.

But I couldn't tell my parents this.

My parents, I'm sure, believed Stephen would spend the summer working. And, due probably in large part to his enrollment in a community college art class, they also believed he was college-bound. My mother had even gone so far as to counsel me on the practicalities of a long-distance relationship. I couldn't really explain that that sort of thing wasn't a concern. I couldn't tell them that if Stephen was even still alive at the start of the coming school year, it would be cause for a major celebration. All I could do was repeatedly refuse, for what my parents deemed woefully insufficient reasons.

My dad thought I was being negligent and willful. I could tell that he was starting to believe his original stance on the character of adolescent males, and whether I should be allowed in their presence, was the correct one. "How long have you even known this boy?" he had asked the previous night at dinner. We weren't even talking about summer.

Stephen wasn't aware of my job situation. I doubt it had occurred to him that a healthy teenager like me would be expected to work. Even if it had, I was fairly sure he expected I'd be spending most of my time in his company, anyway. Until my parents had started suggesting otherwise, it was what I'd expected, too.

I wondered later, though, if Stephen did know. He didn't try to argue with me, or ask for clarification. He just sighed again. "All right," he said. He sounded very resigned. "But not Tammy." He made me promise.

That night, while Tammy was brushing her teeth, I went into my parents' room. I stood at the foot of their bed, looking up at them; I felt vaguely like a small child wait-ing—hoping—to be comforted. "Stephen has cancer," I said without preamble. "He has a progressive brain tumor that's non-operable. He's been given, at best, three and a half months to live."

My mother gaped at me. Her blinks were very rapid. My father looked numb.

I had wondered, briefly, if they would think I was lying. But their reactions looked about the way I'd felt when Stephen had first told me. Like they were just as aware as I'd been that you didn't make this kind of thing up. "Oh, honey," Mom finally said.

I looked at them and my chin trembled. "I'm not going to get a job this summer," I said.

I didn't usually win arguments in our family, even when I had Lasse on my side, but I knew I'd won that one.

"Honey," my mom said again, and started to reach out for me.

"No," I said, and turned away. "Don't. Please." She'd already seen my crying once that week, so I don't know why it mattered then, but somehow, it did. Maybe there was only so much of Stephen that I felt able to share at a time. Or that I wanted to.

Back in our room, Tammy had left the overhead light on for me, but her reading lamp was off and she was already making the sound Lasse and I said was snoring but she insisted was just "breathing loudly." Whatever the sound really was, it meant she was asleep. I turned off the light and crept into my bunk below her, legs hugged to my chest, and shook.

Tuesday evening, Stephen picked me up like we were still going to class. It was the first day of the college's summer term, although neither of us were enrolled. My parents knew, and I'm sure his did, too, but none of them said anything to stop us.

There was still the darkroom, though. Stephen drove to the college, and we walked halfway down the hall, then stopped. The fluorescent lights made him look worse than he was, and suddenly I realized I didn't want to be there. "Let's go," I said, and he nodded.

We walked to the wagon and made out in the back seat. Outside it was still light, but the parking lot was mostly empty, and neither of us wanted to leave. "Well," Stephen said, sitting up after a while, "done that."

I reached under my shirt and twisted my bra back into position.

We both looked over at each other.

"I suppose I *can* see the appeal," he said.

"Thanks," I told him, meaning to be sarcastic.

"You are," he replied, formally, "very sincerely welcome."

The next day, he was worse again. Not to the level he'd been the day he missed the meeting with Kyle, but not good, either. After school, I was the one who drove home. He handed me the keys right away.

I think part of the problem was that he'd suddenly realized he was three days away from graduating. The seniors had spent half the morning in a pre-graduation assembly; it really was coming soon. I don't think Stephen had ever actually planned on attending—or, on being able to attend. Now it would look pretty odd if he just didn't show up. Now, instead of a lofty, unrealistic aspiration, graduation had become something he had to do.

I'm not saying all of Stephen's problems were psychosomatic. In fact, I think that in a lot of cases, he was able to manage himself, physically, better, because he had so much mental control. But with something like graduation, the stress must have been too much. His arm wouldn't stay still, nor go where he wanted it. His right eye kept twitching. "Don't look at me," he finally said, in disgust.

I wanted to tell him that I didn't care what he looked like, but I had a feeling he wouldn't receive it well. Besides, it wasn't my thoughts he was worried about. So I pointedly looked away until he spoke again.

"I'm scared," he said, and I realized it was the first time he had admitted such a thing. "What if I can't—what if I just can't do it?"

"You'll be able to," I told him. "You'll manage."

"But what if I can't?" he said again.

I realized it wasn't the possibility of not being able to do it, for his own sake, that bothered him. It was the fact that, if he couldn't, his infirmity would be exposed in front of such a large portion of the community. I imagined people clapping for him as he crossed the stage in the same way they do when athletes who've gotten hurt in a game finally stand up and limp to the sidelines. He would hate that.

He would hate to have any attention drawn at all. And—at least for the course of the actual ceremony—I couldn't think of anything to do that wouldn't draw attention, except to cross our fingers and hope for the best.

"I know you can be that strong," I said, and I hoped it was true.

Stephen didn't respond to that. "I should've dropped out," he said. "Nobody would've questioned it." (This I knew was true.) "Or—they offered to give me an early diploma. Two different times, actually. But it would've been an honorary thing, a cancer perk. I didn't want that." He paused. "I never thought I'd actually graduate with my class. And now that I actually am, I kind of wish I hadn't managed it."

"It'll be okay," I told him. I didn't know what else to say.

"You'll be there, won't you?" he asked.

"Of course I will," I said. "Why would you think I wouldn't go?"

He shrugged, looking away from me. "I dunno."

At times like this, I had learned, it was better to just let him sit.

After a while, he looked at me again. "I hate that I need you," he said. "Not you, specifically. I hate that I need anyone, for things like this. When you're eighteen, yeah, you're an adult, but no one really expects you to be independent; you're supposed to need help with some things, but not with, like—like walking. I'm supposed to need guidance sorting my student loans, not coordinating a pill minder."

Stephen, I knew, didn't even have a pill minder. He took so many medications, they wouldn't have fit.

"I don't know what to tell you," I told him. I didn't know how to solve his problems. And, even though I knew he didn't expect me to, I hated that.

Stephen sighed. "I'm sorry," he said. "I'm being a bit of a shit."

"Not really," I said.

"Well, I'm not being very constructive, either," he replied. "That's what a therapist would say."

"Have you ever—" I said, "not that I think you need—but have you ever actually talked to anyone about… not just the medical side of it?"

Stephen frowned for a moment. "I did," he said. "That was part of my initial treatment, the radiation. Not that the counselor was part of the radiation. But when I had the radiation, there was a man I spoke to. He spoke to my parents, too. It was part of the process, to help me come to terms with my confusion, and anger, and grief." He said these words, though, as if he didn't really believe in them.

"I don't know how useful it was because at the time, I was so sick mostly all I could do was lay on the sofa in his office, shivering, and try not to throw up. Once I finished the round, that kind of fell by the wayside. Maybe it was an oversight, but I was in remission, so to speak, and obviously I wasn't going to drive back and forth twice a week. We probably could have found somebody local, but I guess no one really thought I was going to make it long enough to matter.

"And Mum made me go to an AYA support group once. Once only," he clarified. "It's good for some people, I'm sure, but I thought it was awful. There were people there who'd made it—survived—which I guess was nice, but there were so many others who were still going through, and didn't know, and were just sort of hoping... Seeing the torture they were all going through, and not just physical...

"I think it actually made it easier for me, knowing right away that I wouldn't survive. It's final. Finite. You can grasp it. I never had to get on the see-saw of wondering what are my odds. I think being told you have a thirty, or sixty, or even ninety percent chance of living must be a terrible emotional roulette. Whereas, when you know that regardless, it's only a matter of time, I never really had to get my hopes up. I've always thought of it as a practical issue. Fact: I will deteriorate. Fact: I will die. No ifs, ands, or buts about it."

"So..." I said, and he sighed.

"The reason I'm upset now is that I didn't prepare for this. Graduating wasn't part of the plan. Shit, the entire senior year wasn't part of the plan; I've hugely outlived my expectations. So of course it's something I want to do, but I couldn't ever allow myself to even hope. And now that it's a reality, I'm entirely unprepared, and I'm terrified of messing everything up."

"Okay," I said. Frankly, I was surprised that Stephen had recognized, and acknowledged, this. "What's the worst thing that could happen?"

"That I could do something—or fail to do something—and everyone will realize that I'm going to die," he answered, "and why, and how. I don't want people to know. I don't want it to be special." He sighed. "*I* don't want to be special." He shook his head. "Do you think I should speak to someone?"

"I think that's something only you can know," I told him. "But if you really want my opinion, I think you're doing pretty well, given the circumstances." It hadn't occurred to me before that it might be easier to know, absolutely, that you were going to die than to have a future that was entirely up in the air. Unpleasant as it was, Stephen's certainty meant that, in a way, he had actually been able to plan. The problem now was that he hadn't planned this far.

"Current crisis aside," he said, "yeah, I think so, too. I mean, psychosocially, I think I'm okay. Obviously a brain tumor's not what I would have chosen—and I think a lot of people would think I'm crazy if they knew what I have chosen—but I've made my peace, as it were. I mean all things considered, I'm not unhappy. I'm living the life I wanted." He paused, catching my eye. "That sounded bad."

"A bit," I agreed.

"What I mean, I suppose, is that I'm still here. Like that trial—I'd much rather live for six weeks, out here, really living, than be kept alive for six months in hospital. And I actually got to make that choice. Most people who get what I have, they're little kids. They don't even know. DIPG, on average, you get it between age five and nine."

He shook his head. "I can't decide if that makes it more or less awful. Less, because you're seven years old, you can't really comprehend what's happening to you. You haven't lived as long and you don't know as much, so maybe you aren't as aware of all the things you're missing now and that, later in life, you're going to miss. You aren't as aware of what it'll be like for the people you leave behind. You get your wish trip to wherever—somewhere superficially fun—and you're happy with it." He paused. "But more because, I mean, you're seven. Think of all the life you could've lived.

"There's so much," he said, "that I did get to do. Ride a bike. Learn to drive. Roller skate. Climb the fucking water tower." He shook his head. "Three days from now, graduation. And you."

"I love that I'm included on the list of things you got to do," I said, dryly.

"Oh." The corners of Stephen's mouth went up a bit, though I could tell he was trying to keep them down. "I was thinking more in a general sense, but when you put it that way, I suppose there is that, too."

Saturday morning, Dad dropped me off at the Stuarts'. We went by four houses with balloons and streamers out front on the way there. There were no visible decorations at Stephen's, even though I knew it was a bigger deal for his family than, perhaps, anyone else graduating that day. It would indisputably be the last major accomplishment of Stephen's life, maybe of his parents' lives as well.

Maybe they thought it would be bad luck to start celebrating before it was actually finished. I know I was, in spite of myself, scared.

Stephen was in the bathroom when I got there. It was the fifth time already that day, he later said, that's how nervous he was.

Stephen's grandfather, Art, was at the house, too, with a walker he hadn't had before. He came over to greet me while I waited for Stephen, leaving it abandoned by his chair. I squinted at it, frowning, and after a moment he noticed and rushed back over to retrieve it.

"It's not mine," he told me, when he came back. "I borrowed it. I know how much they make you walk at these things." He glanced over his shoulder before speaking again, his voice low. "It's for Stephen," he said. "Just in case. But we can't let him know that."

"No," I agreed. "Of course not."

Art looked down at his hands, knotted together atop the walker's crossbar. "It isn't right," he said, and shook his head. "You hear a lot of talk about how hard it is to lose a child, and I don't argue with that. But you don't hear as much about how hard it is for a grandparent. You think about how awful it is to lose someone so young when you're fifty, forty-five; imagine how much worse it must feel when you're almost eighty. Look at me," he said. "I'm old. It's time for me to die. It shouldn't be time for Stephen."

"No," I said thickly. I blinked.

Stephen appeared in the doorway, and Art and I both turned toward him. "Ready?" I asked, with forced cheer. He looked like he wanted to turn and run back down the hall again.

The evening before, I'd taken Lasse's old cap and gown out of the hope chest in my parents' room and ironed them. Not for Stephen—he had his own, which his mother, unable to be anything but optimistic, had purchased in the fall—but for myself.

I was relying on the seniors' assembly area at school being barely-organized chaos, and I was right. It was. None of the adults had time for head counts or matching faces with names, and I wasn't worried about Stephen's classmates. They, I figured, would all be too worried about themselves to be bothered by the fact—or even, frankly, notice—that I wasn't supposed to be there.

No one said anything until just before the ceremony started, when we lined up to walk to the entrance. Stephen's partner, Kelsey Stornoway, frowned at me. "Don't worry," I told her. "I'll go back to my spot when we get to the doors. We just want to walk down the hall together."

"Are you sure?" Kelsey said.

"It'll be fine," I told her.

She looked from me to Stephen, at the rigid expression on his face, at his fingers, vice-like on my arm. "All right, whatever," she said. "I just don't want to look bad."

Stephen stiffened even more.

"Don't worry," I said again, ostensibly to Kelsey, though really I meant it for him.

When we got to the doors, I unzipped my gown, very casually rolled it up, and stuffed it into my shoulder bag. Kelsey was at the other set of doors, and, as predicted, no one else seemed to notice.

I kissed Stephen on the cheek and he squared his shoulders. The teacher at the door leaned forward to shake Stephen's hand, as he was doing with every student, and I took the opportunity to duck around him and slip into the seat Tammy was saving. It was the worst seat in the room—on the outside edge of the aisle, very back row on an unsloped floor. But it also happened to be the seat that was closest to the door.

I'd sent Tammy in to secure it two and a half hours earlier, bribing her with the promise that, as long as she kept it on silent, she could play with my phone for the entire ceremony. Tammy was at an age where she either questioned everything or shrugged and agreed with absolutely no show of interest. I was lucky. She was apparently familiar with the advice of not looking a gift horse in the mouth, and the promise of uninterrupted smartphone time was enough to keep her questions entirely at bay. The only thing she'd asked me—repeatedly, over the past several days—was whether my phone was charging.

Stephen was lucky, too, that a lot of the girls in his class seemed to think the processional should take place at approximately the same pace they would use when walking down the aisle at a wedding, or slower. We hadn't tested it, but I had an idea that for such a long stretch, without stopping and without assistance, that glacial pace would be about all he could manage.

He was also lucky that Kelsey didn't want him to carry her down the aisle. I don't think they were supposed to, but there were always a few pairs that did. It wasn't like the superintendent of schools was going to run out and stop them in the middle of things.

I sat up on my knees and watched Stephen and Kelsey. They met at the head of the middle aisle, and she tucked her hand in the crook of his elbow, beaming. Halfway along, they shifted slightly. Stephen hesitated for a moment, and Kelsey's free hand disappeared from her side.

But they made it to the front of the room, and Stephen made it around the stage to his chair behind it. Before the rows ahead of him filled in, I could see him, leaning forward slightly, both hands tight on the back of the chair in front of his.

If anyone was comparing the names of students graduating with honors diplomas to the scholarship recipients the principal read out, Stephen would've been conspicuously absent from the second list. But I doubt anyone but me was paying such close attention.

And if Stephen moved across the stage a little slower than everyone else, if he shook the principal's hand for a moment longer, if the principal braced his arm with both hands and Stephen hung on a little tighter, no one seemed to notice that, either.

And people clapped—not just polite, disinterested audience applause, but in the student section as well. It was nothing like when Bonham's name was called, when the entire room's response was so immediate and raucous that even Tammy, who was slumped halfway to the floor next to me, with earbuds in, jumped. But then, no one expected a response like Bonham's. That said, I knew that if Stephen had told people he had cancer, his would've been even bigger.

The hardest part was at the very end. All four of the class officers were called up to lead the turning of the tassels. They were seated alphabetically, so Stephen was furthest back to begin with. Kyle and Bonham and Shelly all got to the stage ages before he did.

Kyle adjusted the microphone. Twice. They all shifted a bit. A couple of whispers drifted up from the audience. Finally Bonham glanced over his shoulder and said, "Stephen, mate, what're you doing back there?"

I don't think he meant for all of us to hear, but the microphone picked it up, and we did.

Shelly looked horrified. "He's in the middle of the row," she hissed. "Be quiet." Of course, we all heard that, too.

Bonham stood frozen for a moment. Then he leaned past Shelly and said, very directly, "I'm not going to have to come back there and carry you, am I?" Bonham had been one of the people who'd carried his partner in, to no one's surprise. In fact, he'd probably been the one who'd suggested it.

The audience let out a collective sigh of relief. I realized Bonham had made it okay, made it out like it was a pre-planned joke. A poorly-executed one, yes, but still, just that. A joke. People laughed, gently.

Stephen made it onto the stage. He stood on Kyle's other

side, leaning against the podium. Bonham reached across and bumped his fist.

Kyle cleared his throat. "All right," he said. "Okay. By the power vested in me, I now pronounce you…" He paused, and a few people—those who recognized it, I guess—tittered. "Nah," he said. "Just turn your tassels."

I watched the caps swirl into the air, lit up by the flashes of hundreds of camera phones. I watched Stephen watching them fly, his face upturned, his cap still firmly on his head.

"Congratulations!" Shelly screamed. "We did it!"

The superintendent made his way onstage, ready to give closing remarks. Shelly and Kyle collected their caps and exited to the left. Bonham crossed behind the podium and, without warning, picked Stephen up, cradling him, bridal-style, like he weighed nothing.

"Fuck, put me down!" Stephen said, laughing. And that came through the microphone, too, just as clearly as everything else had.

Stephen was one of the last graduates to exit; the PA had already stopped blasting the last bars of the recessional by the time he made it to me. Art had joined him somewhere along the way, surely as a precaution, but, though they were moving slowly, they weren't touching. I stood up to hug Stephen. "You made it," I said in his ear, as he leaned against me.

"Mm," he said.

Art nodded, then drifted away, encouraged by the press of the rest of the audience coming up the aisle behind him.

Stephen leaned in a little closer. "Kelsey had to hold me up," he murmured.

I rubbed his back. I hadn't been going to say anything, but I had wondered. "But you made it," I told him again. "It's okay. You're done."

237

After a while we pivoted around, and Stephen sat down in my chair. Tammy looked up. "Oh, good job, Stephen," she said, then held up the phone. "Here, take a picture with me." She put her face right up next to Stephen's; the tassel hung down between them. "Smiles or silly faces?" Stephen said.

"Smiling," Tammy decided, and Stephen smiled just enough.

I sat next to him, half on the edge of the chair, half on his knee; he put his arm around my waist to keep me from falling. Tammy looked at us coolly. Then she tapped a few times on the phone and slid back down her seat.

We waited until the gym had almost entirely emptied out. Outside, there were still a lot of people; the graduates were expected, informally, to stick around and be congratulated by their teachers and each other. I wondered if anyone would congratulate Stephen.

"Can I go now?" Tammy asked, as we stood by the doors, looking for anyone we knew. "If you let me keep your phone, I can just text Dad to get me," she said craftily.

"Fine," I told her.

"Thanks, Tammy," Stephen said.

"TTYL," Tammy replied, as if she was already texting. She darted across the courtyard, clutching her prize, and disappeared behind an enormous concrete planter with a small, poorly-sculpted shrub in it.

Stephen and I went the other way. We detoured to shake hands with Kyle, who practically had a receiving line. Shelly, next to him, put her hands on Stephen's biceps and leaned forward for a second. It was kind of a hug. I guess.

Kelsey passed by, carrying a huge plastic-wrapped bouquet of flowers. I wondered if she'd noticed that my name had never been called in the ceremony, that I'd never walked across the stage. I wondered, too, if she'd stood next to Stephen for long enough to realize something was really wrong, or if she just thought he'd taken too much of whatever he'd taken. She nodded at us, but didn't stop or say anything. I figured it was probably still the latter.

We found Stephen's family in the grass area to the side of the main doors, huddled together under a little tree. Stephen's mother had a single program tucked under her arm. None of them had cameras.

I think we all wanted to leave, Stephen especially. He was tired, and not just physically; the mere thought of graduation had caused him a lot of stress, and even now that it was over, he'd be a while recovering.

"Well," Stephen's mother said with false brightness. I wondered how hard this occasion must be for his parents. Bittersweet, certainly. But they were like Stephen, making the most of the time they had, pretending there was nothing awful lurking around the corner. Back home, I knew, Dr. Stuart had made a cake.

After a while, Mrs. Chalmers, the senior class advisor, picked her way across the lawn to congratulate Stephen. She didn't ask him about college, even though asking about college was a big part of her job. Stephen said she never had.

Stephen's lab partner, Terry, came by, and slapped Stephen lightly on the arm with the flat part of his cap. Terry was going to Yale.

Stephen's dad shifted from one foot to the other. We all, in turn, swallowed.

Twenty or thirty feet away, I watched Bonham appear at the edge of the crowd. He made his way in our general direction, slowly, stopping every few feet. Everyone knew

Bonham. I wondered what would happen when he got to us; I still wasn't sure of his relationship with Stephen. Every time I thought I'd put my finger on it, something else happened and I got confused again.

Bonham hugged a girl standing a few feet away from us. She squealed a little bit and pressed close to him; her smile was bigger than it had been since we'd been out there. Her friend, or maybe her sister, took a picture, and she darted forward to look at it, still clinging to Bonham with one hand, then nodded.

(Later, because she'd tagged Bonham, and Bonham showed up in Stephen's feed, I saw her post online. "me and @bonhamvice at #grad," she'd written, followed by two mortarboard emojis, a parade of various other happy icons, and an even longer list of tags. I wasn't surprised to see that Bonham had his own hashtag, too.)

Bonham hadn't checked the photo. He was looking past her, at Stephen.

He greeted Stephen's parents first, then Art, who he called Grandpa Stuart, and who he gave a one-armed hug. Then he looked at Stephen and grinned. "Most likely to drop the F-bomb at graduation, man, I knew I should've nominated you."

Stephen smiled, shook his head. Gently, he let go of me and he and Bonham pulled each other in. Bonham hugged him for a long time, holding him close, their heads next to each other. I realized for the first time that they were the same height. Bonham just seemed so much bigger.

From where I stood, I could hear what Bonham said, but not Stephen's replies. "I'm really, really happy you're here," Bonham told him. "No, I really am. I love you, man," he said. "I love you."

Stephen had already traded the graduation cap for his traditional stocking hat, and Bonham reached up and scrubbed the back of his head with it. "Stay golden," he said when they finally pulled apart.

Stephen looked at him. Bonham's arm was still around his neck, and he seemed, for the first time that day, almost relaxed. "Stay pyrite," he said.

Bonham grinned—probably at my reaction more than anything. "Studies have shown," he told me, his phrasing revealing it was a practiced response, "that to the untrained eye, pyrite is often more attractive than gold. And it's a perfectly good mineral with plenty of uses, in and of itself. It's only when you get past the surface, look really deeply, that you start to see the comparative lower value. Most people don't look that far."

I wasn't sure what to say. I'll admit that I'd always been a little afraid of Bonham. It wasn't that I felt threatened, but he was, in a way, intimidating. I didn't think—scratch that; I *knew* I wasn't cool enough to be around him. And now, the first time we'd ever really spoken, I had to deal with this. "I still wouldn't say it's the most... flattering," I said, doubtful, cutting my eyes toward Stephen. I wondered which one of them had come up with this attributive.

"I don't mind," Bonham said. "Glitter works out well for me. I've always been pyrite." He paused. "Stephen's always been gold. Kyle wanted me for vice because he knew if I ran against him, I'd have won. It's true." He said it without any pretense of modesty. "But if people actually paid attention, Stephen could've beat even me like nothing."

Stephen looked completely mortified.

Bonham looked from me to Stephen and back. "You drew a good one," he said. "Fuck what anybody else says."

Stephen now looked not only mortified, but also moderately surprised. "Wow," he said after a moment. "Please don't kiss me in front of everyone."

Bonham laughed, and I almost wondered if this was a conversation they'd had before, too. "I told you years ago," he said. "You're not my type." Then he squeezed Stephen in against his chest once more, and thumped him on the arm, before finally letting go. "I'll see you, mate," he said. "Okay?"

Stephen managed to nod, and then he just stood there, watching Bonham leave. I thought he looked almost wistful. Maybe he knew, watching his oldest friend walk away, that that "I'll see you" was a lie, even if Bonham didn't realize it. But Stephen knew—they probably wouldn't ever see each other again.

Bonham disappeared into another group of people who, minutes later, would probably also gleefully upload hashtagged-Bonham pictures to their various social media platforms, and Stephen turned back to face the rest of us. "I think I'm ready to go now," he said.

I still had four days of school left, and Monday morning, Stephen picked me up, just as he'd always done. I'd told him not to bother, but he'd insisted. "I always get up at seven anyway," he'd said. And I wondered if maybe he was scared that if he stopped, if we no longer had the structure of our routine to keep us together, I'd disappear.

He was waiting for me after school, too. With all the other seniors gone, the student parking lot was a lot thinner than it'd been a week ago. "You really didn't have to," I said.

He shrugged, handed me the keys. "Nothing better to do. Well, Bonham did invite me to go jump off a cliff into the river," he allowed, "but I figured it's better for a person in my position not to flirt too closely with death."

I couldn't tell if he was being serious or not. Or, if he was, to what extent.

"What did you do?" I asked.

He held up a thick, colorless medical journal. I frowned; I'd thought he couldn't possibly have had a less entertaining day than I'd had. He shrugged. "Before my eyes go," he said.

I sighed and shifted into gear.

"Hey, Emily," he said, later.

"Yeah?" I asked.

"You remember at that first meeting?" he said. "When I said four months?"

I turned toward him on the bed, curling to my side. "I remember," I told him. "And then you said later..." I stopped and let it hang. We both knew what he'd said later. We both knew it was neither necessary nor desirable to hear it again.

"Down to three now."

I swallowed.

"I want you to know—" he said. "You know I won't wait that long."

"I know," I said, then started. "Wait, what do you mean, wait?"

Stephen took a long breath. "I don't want to die," he said. "And I don't think of it as suicide. I think of it as seeing what's inevitable and taking some control over my life, not just lying there and letting cancer call every last shot.

"Maybe it's selfish of me," he said. "No, I know it's selfish of me. But I think it's even more selfish of other people to keep me alive against my will, just because, out of some twisted sense of morality, they think I need to be. Look at it this way. If I was a cat..."

"You're not a cat," I said, but I already knew what he meant.

"No," he said. "I'm not. But if I was a cat, at a certain point, not too far in the future, I'd be put down, to spare me the pain and suffering. It would be—what's the word?—inhumane not to. So why aren't humans given any of that same consideration? If you took me to the vet, they would tell you it'd be cruel to continue keeping me alive.

"Alive," he repeated, like the word just eluded him. "Is it really worth it—is it really even anything—when all I'm capable of is lying there registering my own misery? It's not worth it to me.

"I'm not saying what's right for me is right for everybody," he said. "It's not. But I can't just wait and let it take me. I mean, DIPG is not some quiet, peaceful death. Before it kills, it tortures its prey. And I said I wouldn't die a vegetable, and I won't. If I thought there was any possible chance… but there isn't. I don't want to do it," he said. "But I have to.

"I already have my DNR," he said. "Just in case. That's what I'm more scared of than anything, waiting too long and not being able to. This way, maybe I lose a week; maybe I lose a month. But maybe I won't lose much at all. And I'll get to go knowing I didn't give in. To me, that's the braver thing—doing it on my own terms. But if I start to fail… There's no reason to keep me alive, to keep trying to bring me back, if there's no expectation of life to bring me back to. I don't want that." He turned, finally, to face me, started to reach over, then stopped. "I don't want that, for anyone who cares about me. I mean—" he said. He brought his hand up over his eyes and then back down again.

"Stephen," I said finally. I should've said it long ago. "Stephen. You don't have to convince me."

"What will you do?" I asked him, later.

"I have," he said, very matter-of-factly, "a very large quantity of barbiturates at my disposal. I was so sick during radiation. So sick I couldn't sleep. Benzos didn't help. Allegedly." He swallowed. "I've been reading medical journals since I was thirteen—one of the side effects of having a parent who's a devout medical professional. I always thought I'd become a doctor, too. So I already knew how to die with cancer, maybe a full year, even, before I got it. I probably read too much." He swallowed again. "Barbiturates, though. That's how it's done. Even someone with as high a tolerance as I have to most things can still overdose eventually."

"How—" I said. "Aren't you…"

"Of course I'm not supposed to," Stephen said. "And it's really just… kind of incredible that I'm not supposed to. I mean, I get that people think—but it's my life. It should be my death, too. Once they told me what it was, and what the outlook was, there was never any doubt in my mind." He paused, sighed. "It's not ideal, but I'm sure I won't be the first person to do it like this. And I'll make it clean. And"—he sighed again—"well, nobody's really going to investigate the death of a kid they know had a brain tumor. Are they?"

On the last day of school, Stephen picked me up at precisely twelve thirty-five. He was supposed to be at the hospital at two, which was going to be a close shave, but he'd said he'd rather be late, or get a speeding ticket, or both, than have to go, yet again, on his own.

He was scheduled, that day, for another meeting with Dr. Edwards. I knew that Mr. Stuart was often tied up, sitting in court or doing a visit with one of his clients, but I'd expected Stephen's mother would be there. She wasn't. The palliative nurse and one of Dr. Edwards' interns were the only other people present. Neither of them spoke the entire time.

Stephen flopped into a chair across from the doctor without saying hello, and I sat, a bit tentatively, next to him.

"Well," Dr. Edwards said, "I thought we'd start by going over the results of your last scan." She leaned toward the computer mounted on the wall, and Stephen stopped her. "No," he said, "That's for my mum. She looks at them, I don't."

Dr. Edwards looked confused. Then, perhaps remembering that Stephen's mother was a radiologist, she said, "I can explain the images to you, as well. Your mother won't have seen these yet. Don't you want to know the progress of your tumor?"

"Do you think I don't know its progress?" Stephen asked her. "Do you think I can't feel it?"

"Well," Dr. Edwards said.

"I thought we'd established this already," Stephen said. "The MRIs are no longer diagnostic. I am submitting to them solely in an attempt to preserve my mother's sanity a little further. It doesn't do anybody except her any good to know what they say. You can tell me, if you must, but I don't want to see anything."

"Well," Dr. Edwards said again, and reluctantly minimized the window, "I'd only noticed that the tumor appears to have progressed to a size such that it might be causing you discomfort."

"It's always caused me discomfort," Stephen replied.

Dr. Edwards sighed. "I know you don't enjoy this," she said, "but if you think that I take any personal pleasure from pointing out your situation, you're mistaken."

"Well, I'm acutely aware of my situation, thank you," Stephen said.

"And so am I. And I'm still your doctor, and I'm still the head of your team, even if you're no longer enrolled in curative therapy. I still want to see you do the best you can for as long as you can."

"Fine," Stephen said. "If you have some miracle wonder drug that can keep me functional and make me numb, by all means, talk to Dr. Svann. But I don't know what else you expect me to do. I mean, you still won't even give me a straight diagnosis."

"Stephen," Dr. Edwards said heavily, "you've made it quite clear that you already know."

"I do know," said Stephen. "But I'd still like to hear it. Just"—for a moment I thought he might break down—"just in case."

Dr. Edwards looked down, straightened the folder in front of her, nudging it one way, then the other, until its alignment with the edge of the table was exact. Then—nothing else to do—she sat up and looked Stephen straight in the eye. "I've been in contact with your oncologist from Children's, and his opinion, as well as mine, is that given current medical knowledge, the state of your tumor, and the rate of its progression over the last few months, it is reasonable now to suspect you will fit into the general results paradigm for patients with progressed DIPG, despite your age and earlier success. We would give you," she said, "an optimistic prognosis of eight to ten weeks to live. This would entirely likely remain the same, regardless of any changes to treatment." She looked down again. "I'm sorry, Stephen," she said.

"Don't be," he said finally. "It's what I figured, anyway."

But hearing it from a doctor—and, in Stephen's case, *finally* hearing it, unexpurgated, from a doctor—made it so much more real.

"Are you entirely sure you don't want to try any further curative therapies?" Dr. Edwards asked. "Occasionally, even young patients with high-grade gliomas have shown some response to temozolomide. It might not be too late."

"You've just told me changes to my treatment won't make any difference," Stephen said.

Dr. Edwards at least had the decency to look somewhat abashed.

"I'm not going to change my mind."

"All right," Dr. Edwards said. She asked Stephen a few more questions, and in return, he asked her a few more, too. Watching their back-and-forth, I could see why Stephen had decided he didn't like hospitals, but he certainly didn't make things easy for the doctor, either. Finally they came to an accord, or at least a temporary truce. Dr. Edwards didn't seem entirely satisfied, but she let us go.

"They all think I'm being uncooperative," Stephen said as we walked back down the hall. "But all these things they're proposing take time, which I think we all know I don't have.

"Although that said," he went on, "when I think about ye olde philosophical question, would you rather live forever or die tomorrow, even if I was completely healthy, I'd pick tomorrow. You?"

"Tomorrow, too," I said. "I think living forever would be awful."

"A lot of people disagree," said Stephen, apparently playing the devil's advocate.

"I know," I said. "And I'm sure they all have their reasons, and I'm sure some of them are even very good, but I think anything infinite would wind up being unbearable, really."

"I think so, too," he said. "I always thought of it as a choice between two terrible outcomes."

"I think they're supposed to be," I said. "It's not much of a question if you get to choose between one thing that's awesome and another that obviously sucks."

"No," said Stephen. "Unless—the trick is to find things that some people think are one way, and other people disagree."

"Would you rather remember everything or not be able to remember anything?" I asked after a moment.

"Nothing," he said. "And I don't even have that much I want to forget. But remembering everything? You'd go mad after a while. But I tend to like more practical ones. Like, would you rather be forced to wake up at five a.m. every day for the rest of your life or, say, spend the rest of your life working graveyard shifts and only see the sun once or twice a year?"

"Ugh," I said, and chewed on my lip. "Five, I guess. At least I could take naps. Would you rather be deaf, or blind?"

Stephen didn't answer right away, and I realized, a moment too late, that I'd just named two things that would, or at least could, eventually happen to him. But then he forced a smile. "Actually, that's another easy one," he said. "It's easy for people to just not say anything, or to quietly cry. But it's a lot harder to hide your face when you're that sad. Selfish, maybe, but I'd rather go blind."

I knew, horribly, what he meant—because I'd always tried my hardest never to cry in front of Stephen. There wasn't a lot I could really do to help him, but at least I could give him that. I reached over and took his hand.

He didn't ask me what I'd choose.

That night I lay in bed, staring at the bottom of Tammy's mattress above me, thinking about what my summer was going to be like. "It's going to be different now," Stephen had said on the drive home. It was.

Sometimes still, he was completely normal, as if nothing had changed, nothing was wrong. But sometimes it was hard to be around him. I felt like the worst person in the world, because he was in so much pain, because he was losing—not even gradually but at a rapid rate—the ability to do even the simplest things.

We had stopped, on the way back, at a co-op in the city that was far enough away to not have a hospital view; Stephen said they stocked one of the special, extra-healthful, kinds of juice he was supposed to drink. It was sunny, and there was a cluster of small, slightly wobbly, metal tables out front. We sat, the keys resting equidistant between us on the tabletop.

I had orange juice, as usual, and Stephen had... something else. He fiddled with the bottle for a minute before setting it down; after another moment, he reached out with his left hand and pushed it a bit closer to me. He was always trying to get me to try his weird drinks, and I was always telling him no. I nudged it back toward him. "That's okay," I said, and took a sip of my own.

"No," he said quietly, and looked at the table. "It's not that. Can you open it for me?"

After that, something unspoken passed between us. Whenever he handed me things, whenever he looked at me oddly or winced or twitched his fingers in a way that wasn't involuntary, I knew I'd try, very hard, to figure out what he wanted me to do without making him say. It was bad enough, silently acquiescing to the fact that he was no longer really able to drive. But being eighteen and having to ask someone else to open a twist-top bottle of juice for you isn't an experience anyone should have to repeat.

That said, for a while, the ataxia—the hemiparesis—whatever he called it—seemed to come and go. Eventually I realized it was always there; what changed was Stephen's ability to control it.

The first Tuesday after the end of school, we were sitting on his living room couch. I had my feet up on the cushions, and Stephen was leaning against the armrest, reading something complex. I had a headache, but I didn't want him to know.

He turned a page and looked up. "What's wrong?" he said after a moment.

I shook my head. "I'm fine," I told him.

I guess the fact that I wasn't doing anything made it kind of obvious. "No, really," he said; he put the magazine aside and moved closer to me, "what's wrong? Tell me."

"It's nothing, really," I said, and looked away. I felt horribly embarrassed. "I just have a slight headache. It's fine."

Stephen sighed, and I turned back to face him. He looked very serious. "The fact that I also have a headache," he said, "should not make yours any less. Mine is not somehow better than yours."

"I know," I said, "but I still feel like I shouldn't be complaining when you... I feel like, comparatively, I'm whining over nothing. Or at the very least, that you'll feel like I am."

He sighed, again. "Please," he said, "don't feel that way. There's no rule that says only the person who's damaged the most counts. There's not a fixed amount of pain in the world. In fact, speaking relatively, I might be in less pain than you are right now, because I've had two years to get used to this and you've had—what?—an hour? You'd think it wouldn't affect me as much by now."

"I don't think it works exactly that way," I said.

"Maybe," he said. "Maybe not. Regardless, mine doesn't make yours any less legitimate. Okay?"

"All right," I said.

"Do you need some naproxen, or anything?" he asked.

"Oh." I was slightly startled. "No, I took an acetaminophen already," I told him.

"Oh," he said, "right." He slumped a little bit. "I guess that is more along the lines of what a normal person would need."

I sighed. I still didn't know the names—trade or chemical—or dosages of any of the medication Stephen was taking. We'd never discussed it. (But I doubted that if he was even on naproxen, he possessed any in an amount that was low enough to be appropriate for me.) "I wish you'd tell me things," I said, though I didn't mean *tell*, necessarily. (I didn't want to know all the drugs.) I just wished he'd let me in a little more. He'd still never let his guard down.

His head whipped over toward mine. "I tell you so much," he said. "I tell you almost—nearly—everything."

"I don't even know what your real voice sounds like," I said. I don't know why I thought of that.

"What?" he asked, obviously confused. Then, realizing, "This," he said. "This is my real voice now."

And I knew it probably was. I'd noticed him struggling a little to speak a few times, but the accent was always still there. I figured if it was really put on, he wouldn't have bothered. Or he wouldn't have been able to even try bothering.

He looked at me for a long moment, sad. "What do you want to know?" he said.

"I—" I started. "I just want to understand."

He sighed, then shifted on the couch. "Let's play Red Light, Green Light."

"What?" I said.

"You remember the rules," he said. "When I say red light, you can't move, or speak, either. When I say green light, you can. But to make it more realistic, we'll also do yellow light, when you're allowed to move and speak, but only very slowly."

"Stephen," I started.

"Yellow light," he said. "Starting now." Then he went back to his magazine. "By the way," he added, "I think you have an itch on your ear."

Of course, as soon as he said it, I did.

I wasn't entirely sure this was a productive (or even very realistic) game. I was pretty sure Stephen was aware of that, too. But I also knew that refusing to play the ataxia version of Red Light, Green Light would be kind of like saying to him, point blank, that I didn't care how he felt, that I didn't care what the cancer was doing to his body. It was awkward and unwieldy—it felt like a test more than anything, although I don't know why he still felt the need to test me—but I couldn't just ignore it.

I moved my hand, exceedingly slowly, toward my ear, finally reached it, and, with the same rate of speed, scratched.

"No, your other ear," Stephen said. I gave an exaggerated sigh. My arm was halfway across my face when he said, "Red light."

I stopped moving.

Stephen turned another page.

My arm started to ache.

This wasn't realistic at all. Stephen's limbs didn't get stuck in active positions. But red light also meant I wasn't able to talk, so I couldn't protest.

"Green light," he said finally.

I rushed my hand across to my ear, touched the lobe

cursorily (the itch had long since gone) and quickly dropped it to my lap, before he could change his mind and leave it stranded somewhere again.

"I'm going to—yellow light—get some water," he said, folding the magazine open and standing up. "Do you want any? Red light," he added, just as I was starting to answer. He stood there for several moments, arms folded, looking at me expectantly. "Emily?"

I couldn't answer.

"Whatever," he said finally. "Let me know if you change your mind." He walked around the corner to the kitchen, and I heard him opening the cupboard, taking out a glass, turning on the tap. "Last chance!" he called. "Yellow light!" And then, immediately, "Red light!" again.

He came back in, and I tried to convey a frown without moving any of the muscles in my face.

He sat in the chair opposite me, holding the glass in one hand, then hovering it a few inches over the coffee table. "Oh, hey," he said. "Could you hand me one of those coasters? They're right next to you," he clarified, when I didn't respond. He rolled his eyes. "Really, Emily," he said, and started to stand up. "Yell—" Then he paused, considering, and didn't finish.

I was furious.

"Green light," he decided, and I lunged toward the coasters, just before he reached them himself. Stephen recoiled a bit, in pretended shock. "There," he said, as I handed him one. "That wasn't so hard, was it? I don't know why you're being so sullen. Yellow light."

He reached across me and set the glass and coaster down together on the end table, then laid his hand along my jaw and turned my face toward his. I moved my hand up to his arm. He kissed me, slowly, and I responded at an even more glacial pace.

"Red light," he breathed against my lips.

He moved to the side of my neck, then my ear. "It's worse in real life, because then, only I can tell when the lights change. Nobody else knows what the fuck's going on.

"You don't seem like you're enjoying this," he said. The fingers of his right hand tapped, briefly, against my shoulder. "Maybe I should've added that, too," he considered. "Another facet of yellow light—when you mean to do, or maybe not do, one thing, and your body winds up doing another." He pulled back and looked at me. "Green light, I guess."

He kissed me again before I could say anything. "This is horrible," it would've been.

He fell sideways, pulling me along, and I let him. I fit in between his legs. "Change in the rules," he told me. "Your left side isn't affected any more. Right arm and leg still are, but on yellow, now, you've got to make everything a bit shaky. So," he said after a pause, "since today you're apparently being non-verbal, let's also play that game where you trace a letter on my hand and I try to guess what it is without watching. Yellow light."

I did my best to draw a capital R. I should've picked something easier. A couple times, Stephen, with his free hand, nudged mine out of line even further. "Really?" I asked.

"That's what it's like," he whispered, then announced, "I have no idea what that is. Try another."

He gave me a green light, then switched back to red when I was halfway through the O.

"C?" he guessed.

I gritted my teeth.

"Green light," he said again.

"It was O."

Stephen raised his eyebrows. "All right," he said. "Do one more. Maybe you want to try using your other hand?"

So I tried my left. Even I couldn't have identified the letter I made.

"Poor show, Em," Stephen said, and moved his hands to the small of my back.

"Is it really that bad?" I said.

"Not all the time," he admitted. "But when it is…"

"I feel bad asking this," I said, "but can we be done?"

"I'm kind of surprised you did it," he said in response, which I guessed was a yes. "If it makes you feel any better, I didn't like it any more than you did."

It didn't really make me feel any better, though.

"For the most part," he said, "the more energy I have, the better I feel, the more I can sort of… control it. Of course there are little glitches sometimes, but for the most part…" He hesitated. "I get tired more now. It's an effort now. Just to walk without limping."

"Does it hurt?" I said.

"That part? No. It's mostly numb. Or maybe that tingly red feeling you get right after you realize your foot's fallen asleep. It's not the same thing—it's not asleep. I don't know how to explain it," he said.

"It means a lot to me that you made the effort," I said.

"Yeah," he said, rolling his eyes. "You hated the effort."

"Well," I admitted.

"I hate it, too," Stephen said. He turned his head so his jaw rested along my forehead.

"At least you're still standing," I said.

"I'm lying down."

I just shook my head.

By Thursday, less than two weeks after graduation, Stephen was sick of his house. "At least last time," he said, "there were lasers to distract me." I figured he was alluding to the radiation, and didn't comment.

He wasn't well enough to go out on his own (not that he'd have wanted to, anyway). In the morning, he'd begged to come with me to the college, and after lunch, he begged me to take him somewhere—anywhere—again. "It's not that I'm really bored," he said. "Although, you know, I am now completely caught up on JAYAO. They only started publishing in 2011, so it's not like I had that many back issues to get through, but it's not an insignificant achievement."

"Congratulations, then," I told him, even though I wasn't entirely sure what JAYAO might be.

"Thank you," he said. "Unfortunately, it means I now have to find something else to do with my time, and that was really good for shutting me up and making me forget how, sort of, trapped I am. Well, not exactly trapped, but just being here, sometimes it gets so…"

"Cabin fever," I said.

"That," he said. "And guilt."

I looked up, surprised. "It's better when you're here," he said. "Or Dad. I know he's not quite okay, but he's never really shown his feelings, even before all this. But when I'm alone, with Mum, she keeps looking at me and then having to leave the room."

"I—she'll be all right," I told him, hoping it was true. "She wouldn't be a mother if she wasn't a little bit…"

He sighed. "I know, but… I don't know. I just can't be here right now," he said. "All right? Just for a while."

We went back to the wagon, drove with the windows down. I thought about places we could go, but didn't suggest any. Eventually I just drove home.

We came through the gate and an instant later, Tammy, barefoot and clad only in a bathing suit, streaked across the yard in front of us. She reached the end of the house and threw herself around the corner head-first.

"What the…" Stephen's eyes went wide.

I didn't blink. "She's set up the slip'n slide," I said. It happened every July.

Lasse had made the first one, years ago. And, predictably coming from Lasse, it was massive, taking up the entire width of the side yard between our house and the neighbors' fence. It was impossible to climb up the plastic, hence the sprinting across the front yard—anyone using it had to go all the way around to the other side yard to get back up again. Initially, we'd tried to shortcut through the house, but after one day of tracking in enough debris that, my mother claimed, it looked like a herd of javelinas had rampaged through our home, the direct route was forbidden.

I explained to Stephen and he nodded slowly. We walked over and looked down the slope. Tammy ran past us, then whizzed down again. "Is it safe?" Stephen said, watching her.

I shrugged. "She's twelve," I said, "and it's a water slide. She'd keep doing it even if it wasn't. She's still trying to break Lasse's record." Lasse claimed that the summer he was seventeen, he'd managed to run the entire course eleven times in fifteen minutes, though none of us had actually been there to see it. Tammy claimed that if she managed to best this, Lasse had promised to buy her a tablet. She was out there all the time.

Tammy came up again as, somewhere in the backyard, the kitchen timer, barely audible, sounded. Her shoulders slumped, but she brightened again when she saw us. (I wouldn't have been surprised if she'd failed to notice we were there before.) "Hi, Stephen," she said, still slightly out of breath. She looked him over quickly and, apparently determining he wasn't dressed for water, asked, "Are you here to play yearbook?"

At the high school, yearbooks didn't come out until the following autumn, but in middle school, they were distributed on the last day of school. A week earlier, Tammy had gotten her first one ever. She, of course, had already been through it several times, but we hadn't had a chance yet to look together. Yearbooks were a bit of a tradition for us, I suppose—even Lasse occasionally looked—but I don't know why Tammy thought Stephen would want to participate.

Stephen looked between Tammy and me. "How do you play yearbook?" he said.

Tammy gave me a horrible glare, as if my only task in life had been to explain the particularities of playing yearbook to Stephen—a task in which I'd obviously failed. She sidestepped us and plunged down the slide again, probably in punishment.

I explained yearbook to Stephen. He laughed.

Tammy appeared again, and frowned at both of us.

"All right," Stephen said. "I'll play."

Tammy looked taken aback. (Frankly, I was a bit, too.) "Really?" she said.

"Sure." Stephen shrugged. "I don't mind yearbooks."

Tammy spun on her heel and ran for the front door. "Change your clothes!" I yelled after her. Tammy knew enough to wipe her feet when she went in, thus avoiding the worst of the javelina mess, but I wouldn't have put it past her to expect to join us still in her sopping wet one-piece.

When she found us—in the basement, where it was slightly cooler—she was wearing another, albeit dry, bathing suit and her laughably huge PE shorts. She'd even changed her headband, though it was barely visible under her hair, damp and frizzing out all around it.

Most of Tammy's attire, in fact, was not visible, as she carried not only her own yearbook but also all of mine and all of Lasse's, in a stack that reached nearly from her waist to her chin.

Stephen looked at me and raised his eyebrows. I shrugged back at him. He was the one who'd agreed to it, after all.

Tammy thumped the yearbooks down on the coffee table and wedged herself in between Stephen and me. "Let's start with mine," she said, and opened the book to the sixth graders. "Here's my class. So, who do you think is pretty?"

Stephen balked. "I'm, er, not sure how comfortable I feel evaluating the attractiveness of eleven-year-olds," he said.

"We're mostly twelve now," Tammy said, then sighed. "Well, can you at least do the boys?"

"How about you and Emily do them, and I'll tell you if I agree?" he suggested.

Tammy thought about this for a moment and decided it was acceptable. "All right," she said, and turned the book ever so slightly toward me.

"Boys first, or girls?" I said.

"Boys," Tammy answered, as if this was the most obvious thing in the world.

"One person per page, or both pages combined?" I asked.

Tammy looked at me sternly. "Every page, Emily."

It had been some time since we'd looked at a middle

school yearbook—Tammy generally preferred judging people who were much older than her—and at the time, I'd been in middle school, or fresh out of it, myself. I understood what Stephen meant about feeling weird picking out pictures of hot eleven-year-olds. I tried to find someone Tammy and her peers—or, at the very least, a television producer casting for a pre-teen audience—would think was cute, and pretended my own preferences had nothing to do with it.

"Okay," I said. "Ready."

Tammy looked at me expectantly, then back at the book. I pointed to a child in the fifth row.

"Oh, *no*," she said, aghast. "Emily, he's only like four feet tall."

"The photos only show them from the shoulders up," I said defensively.

Stephen looked over Tammy's head and grinned at me.

"Well, obviously Stephen agrees with mine," Tammy said, though she hadn't identified anyone. "I don't even need to ask. Right?"

"Right," Stephen said quickly.

We managed to make it through the rest of the book without any further mishaps. On any question involving girls (except when Tammy asked me to pick the meanest ones), I tried very hard to remember and avoid anyone she had mentioned she didn't like. Stephen didn't contribute much, other than to (usually) agree with Tammy, and once, unexpectedly, to tell us that he liked a boy's ears.

At last, Tammy exhausted the book. I noticed she didn't do all the categories we usually used, like best couple or most likely to be in a movie or even most likely to become a crazy cat lady. Maybe in middle school, kids weren't old enough to have such distinct traits and personalities. Maybe she just didn't know. Or maybe she did know, and it wasn't as fun picking people when you already knew their answers.

She eyed the stack of yearbooks on the table, and nudged them with her toe. "Are you in here?" she asked Stephen.

"What?" Stephen said. "Of course I am."

Tammy pulled out the volume from the previous school year. She put her feet up on the cushions and balanced the book on her knees, leaning close as she pored over the pages, scanning every face. "I never noticed you before," she said when she got to Stephen.

To be honest, I hadn't either. I looked from the photo to Stephen, and back again. He was wearing the same hat, an indiscriminate shirt. He didn't look that different, really. A little older now; not that much more tired. He would've been stable when the photo was taken, at the beginning of junior year, but only a little over a month out of radiation. He was smiling faintly, but still didn't look like he felt all that well.

Tammy moved her thumb across photo-Stephen's shoulders. "Did you get picked for anything?"

Stephen laughed, hollowly. "Most likely to OD and die."

I was surprised. Tammy just looked confused. "Why would you do that?" she asked.

Stephen didn't answer.

Tammy flipped through a few more pages, passing the end of Stephen's class and proceeding well into mine. "I think him," she said at last, tapping her finger on Jared Randall. He was smiling widely, but his eyes, in the picture, were barely open. "He won't OD, but he might have to get his stomach pumped. Like, for alcohol poisoning."

Stephen and I exchanged looks over her head.

Tammy gave Stephen a long once-over, lingering on his arms. "You don't even have track marks," she said.

I was stunned. "How do you even know about track marks?" I asked her.

She turned to me and rolled her eyes. "I've seen TV." Then she flipped back to the start of Stephen's class section and pursed her lips. "Most likely to become a teen mom."

"Tammy!" I said. That was pushing it, even for her. The yearbook designations were supposed to have at least some modicum of decency. (Apparently some people liked the idea of being a crazy cat lady.) Although, compared to what Stephen had just suggested for himself, I supposed being a teen mom wasn't half bad.

"What?" she said. Then she huffed a sigh. "Fine. Most likely to be a teen dad?"

I frowned in her direction, though at least she was being equal opportunity.

"I'll check you on that," Stephen said.

"Seriously?" I said, more to Stephen than to Tammy.

"Yes," Tammy answered. She straightened the book in her lap. "Dad would approve," she said, righteously, decisively. "Stephen is showing us who we should avoid."

I sighed. Stephen shrugged.

This round, Tammy didn't pick a person on every page. I hoped it was because she didn't think there were that many teen parents (although, realistically, there probably were). The first person she identified, Stephen sort of shrugged at; he didn't know.

The second person made him laugh. "Not him, not a chance," he told Tammy. "He just looks like that."

Tammy wasn't put off. The third person she picked, Stephen swallowed. "Er," he said, "yeah. He does."

"What?" Tammy demanded. "Yeah he does, what?"

"Yeah, he has a kid," Stephen said.

"*He has a kid*," Tammy repeated, making her voice sound like a cross between the robot narrator of a haunted house and a valley girl with severe laryngitis. "Whoa." She turned to face Stephen. "Did he have it here?"

"It doesn't look like he's holding anything," Stephen said.

"No. Guh." Tammy rolled her eyes. "I mean was it born yet?"

"No," Stephen said. "It was just a while ago."

"That doesn't mean anything, Emily," Tammy told me, as if she suspected I would use this information to challenge the veracity of her identification. "Anyway, it's more important to be able to tell beforehand. By the time you have the actual baby, it's too late to stay away. And," she added, "this is super old. That picture's from almost two years ago. He could have, like, seven hundred baby mamas by now. I know how it works."

"I'm pretty sure he just has the one," Stephen said, grinning.

"Augustus the Second had over three hundred illegitimate children," Tammy informed us. "Also he threw foxes in a slingshot."

"What?" Stephen asked.

"He was the king of Poland like three hundred years ago," Tammy said (which made more sense. Some). "We learned about him in history. Scott Tyler did his famous figures report on him. Probably just because of the tons of kids and the foxes."

"Ah," said Stephen.

"Did I show you him?" Tammy asked. "Scott?" She tossed my yearbook back on the table and retrieved her own again. "He's kind of nice-looking," she said when she'd found the right page, "but also kind of an ass."

Stephen laughed.

"Anyway," Tammy said. She shut the book and leaned forward. "I'm going back outside."

"Okay," I said. "Good luck."

"See you later," Stephen said.

Tammy climbed, inelegantly, over the coffee table, and disappeared up the stairs.

Stephen moved closer to me. "She's pretty good," he said.

I nodded. Not just about Kale Hamilton—whose ex-girlfriend had recently had a kid—but also Jared Randall. He probably wouldn't actually get alcohol poisoning—surely he was too practiced for that—but he might very well be the supplier when someone else did. Then I shook my head. "I can't believe she knows about intravenous drug use," I said.

Stephen smiled a bit. "Good thing I haven't had my blood drawn in a while." He pulled last year's yearbook back out of the pile and reopened it to his class. "Most likely to OD and die," he murmured, then turned to look at me. "Most likely to fake cry and post virtual flowers and loving remarks on social media when they find out I've died."

I swallowed. I would've rather picked prospective teen mothers. "That depends," I said. "I mean, do they still think you've OD'd?"

"I am going to OD," Stephen said.

I swallowed again. "Yes," I said, "but not…"

He let out a breath. "Not like that," he agreed.

I turned a couple of pages, but knew I wouldn't pick anyone. Besides, half the class would probably end up doing that.

"Okay, most likely to actually cry," Stephen said.

I stopped, and looked up at him. I didn't need the yearbook for that. "Bonham," I said, and Stephen looked away.

"You know he will," I said. "You should tell him. He's your best friend."

"You're my best friend."

"Aside from me," I said.

I was prepared for him to protest that aside from me, his best friend was probably Kyle (which may have been true—well, maybe at one point). But Bonham was Stephen's oldest friend. Bonham was the one who would really care.

But he didn't protest. He just looked down at his hands in his lap, palms turned up, fingers folded in slightly. "I can't," he said. "I can't let him—I don't want him to think of me like this." His left hand curled slowly into a fist. On his right hand, only the ring finger and pinky moved. "I don't want him to look back and feel bad," he said.

I failed to see how allowing your oldest friend to remember you as a drug addict, which he was currently doing, was preferable, but in a way, it made sense. Maybe it was Stephen's form of denial—pretending that if no one knew what exactly was wrong, they would somehow also not notice that anything was even amiss. Years down the road, when Bonham thought back on Stephen, he would remember him as an older version of his healthy, wild, ten-year-old self, not as a slowly dying teenager.

But of course that was a fantasy.

"I just want things to be good for him," Stephen said. He sighed again. "Let's talk of lighter things."

After a while we went back outside. "Stephen!" Tammy shrieked, rushing by. "Are you going to try it?"

We watched her disappear around the corner, and then Stephen shrugged. "What the hell," he said. He kicked off his shoes and socks and we stood at the beginning of the tarp, waiting for Tammy to come back up.

She seemed pleased to find us waiting there. She didn't care at all when Stephen said he wouldn't try for the record, and was only slightly disappointed that he wouldn't go head-first. "It's the best way," she told him, "but if you absolutely won't, you should like tuck your knees up to your chest and try to spin."

Personally, I thought this sounded even more dangerous than Tammy's running dives, with a high likelihood of careening off the side of the house or the neighbors' rather splintery-looking fence, but Stephen seemed to think it sounded all right.

"And get under that for a while," Tammy said, indicating the dripping plastic hoop at the top of the slide. "It goes faster if you're wet already."

Stephen nodded. "Should I have my shirt off?" he asked.

Tammy shuddered and violently shook her head, which I thought was funny, considering she'd just been educating us on who all the best-looking boys in her school were.

She went down first, spinning, to demonstrate what he was supposed to do. I stood at the top and watched Stephen follow; he tipped over halfway down—though that was to be expected—and wound up sliding backward, and head-first, anyway. At the bottom, where the tarp widened, he sank completely under the surface of the pool, then emerged, shaking his head and grinning. He pulled his hat off and wrung it out.

"Your hat," Tammy squealed, splashing back in and squeezing it, too. "I didn't even notice!" I hadn't either. I was so used to seeing it on him it hadn't even occurred to me that it was something he might want to take off before going down a slip'n slide.

Stephen said something I couldn't hear.

They stood side by side, calf-deep in the water, and looked back up, shouting for me to slide down, too. In the background, the timer went off again. We all ignored it.

Another day, maybe I would have gone down. But that day, I didn't. I went through the house and met them in the backyard. Stephen was sitting in one of the chairs by the sliding glass door, a small puddle growing around him. I could tell just by looking that he was too tired to even attempt the slide again, and Tammy wouldn't let him back inside; who would believe her, she asked, if she claimed that the javelina mess that was sure to result had actually been caused by Stephen? That was true enough, I guess.

We went back to Stephen's instead; he said he'd been away long enough. Inside, I sat in the chair by the door while he changed clothes with his back to me. He put on another hat. It was blue, but otherwise almost exactly the same as the old one.

He sat on the bed facing me, and we both moved forward until our knees touched. "I was thinking," he said. "The yearbooks. It's funny—everyone does that, just maybe not in so obvious a way. Sometimes you're right, sometimes you're wrong. I mean, look at Kale Hamilton. But also, I mean, your brother doesn't really have sleeve tattoos, does he?"

"No," I agreed. He didn't.

"It's weird how long it takes us to know people before we stop treating them like they're exactly what they look like," he said. "Even though almost none of us actually are."

This was true, too. I had no idea how Tammy had guessed Kale Hamilton. He did look, perhaps, slightly too smug in his class photo, but I'm sure it was just a fluke.

Of course, I doubted Stephen really cared one way or the other about Kale Hamilton. I knew what he was really getting at. I moved over to the bed and scooted next to him. "I'm sorry," I said.

He shook his head. "It's better this way. It's weird, though. I thought everyone'd gotten used to me. But, you know. The summer between sophomore and junior, I lost a lot of weight. Couldn't keep anything down. And a lot of hair. So when I came back, I was wearing a hat all the time, and I guess only skaters do that. And of course they're all stoners, right? It wasn't so bad at first, but it built up. It's not like nobody's ever seen the pills. But I actually do think it was the hat that clinched it. A fucking hat," he said.

"I could've gotten rid of it after a while. I mean, obviously my hair's grown back. But by then it had become a security blanket, kind of. Like, if I wear this hat, if I obscure the only obvious visible evidence, no one will know the truth and we can all pretend it's okay.

"There are other signs, but that felt like something I could—I needed to—protect. When people see someone who's lost weight, or seems tired all the time, or has bags under their eyes—even all those in combination—their first thought's not usually that we're sick. But when someone suddenly turns up with a shaved head, unless they're on the swim team or in, like, Hitler Youth, everybody just goes straight to cancer."

"I didn't know you even had—" I started. It made sense that the hat was incidental to the cancer, but I'd never thought of it that way. Yes, he did always wear it, but from the few occasions I'd seen it off, I also knew that there was nothing wrong with his hair. He had it. And it didn't look like post-chemo regrowth. "I thought you didn't have chemotherapy."

"You're right," he said. "And generally it is the chemo that makes your hair fall out. But if you're having targeted radiation on your neck and head, that doesn't work wonders, either."

He reached up and pulled the blue hat off, held it in his lap. "It feels, honestly, strange now. Not just physically. Now, I know, with everything else, it marks me more and more as a cancer patient, but taking it off—it's like taking my last remaining defense and saying, 'No, that thing you thought you had...' Have you ever done something you thought was really awesome—special or unique or creative or whatever—and then looked back a few years later and realized it was really bad?"

I nodded. (Middle school diaries, hello.)

"It's sort of like that. Factually, I already know; I know I should get rid of this horrible thing, even if just for practical reasons. Eighty-eight degrees out and here I am in a wool blend cap," he added under his breath. "But if I don't actually take it off, I don't have to look at it, and I can still pretend I don't know, or that maybe I'm just being too hard on myself. Maybe it's not that bad. Maybe not quite everybody would laugh."

He paused. "I guess it's not that good an analogy. It really is just a security blanket, infantile as that seems. The harder part is defining what I think it's still protecting me from."

He twisted the hat around in his hands, then shook his head once and put it back on. "What do you see when you look at me?" he said. "Skater? Stoner? Junkie? Cancer kid?"

"I just see you," I said.

"That's nice of you to say," he said. "I guess it means you know me. Unfortunately most people can't do it that way. People like to put people in boxes. *I* like to put people in boxes. It's convenient and orderly and it makes sense."

"But why should you have to be one of those things?" I asked.

"I'm not saying I think it's good," Stephen said. "I'm just saying those are usually what the choices are. Very clearly defined. No one gets to be undetermined. Which I guess is probably part of the reason it was so easy to steer people into not thinking I have cancer, because cancer's an absolute box on its own, not something people think of as floating around and affixing to a person who's already some other thing. If it's not A, it must be B. Certainly can't be both."

"I didn't know," I said. I thought, suddenly, of how I'd felt when Stephen had first told me about the tumor. It had made sense, in retrospect, but it had also felt like being struck with an unexpected blow. It wasn't anything I had even momentarily suspected. I was supposed to be close to him. I was supposed to notice things like that—even if he didn't want me to.

"Really?" Stephen said. "I think you did, after a while. You knew something was wrong, anyway. And not just in the way everybody knows, with the drugs… you knew it was something beyond that, even if you didn't know what." He sighed. "I certainly couldn't blame you, anyway. Cancer isn't the kind of thing anybody wants to notice. Or, if they do notice, they want to convince themselves they're wrong. I wish I still could."

He flopped backward onto the bed and I lay there with him.

Eventually, Dr. Stuart came in and invited me to join them for dinner. She seemed to actually want me to stay. I wondered if I had become her buffer, in a way. She knew that I knew, just as much as—perhaps even more than—she did. But I was still, in a way, an outsider. She had to act normal

271

in front of me. If I was there, she couldn't collapse. If I was there, she couldn't cry.

Dinner was quiet, and Stephen barely ate. When he walked back to his room, he leaned against the wall slightly. It was almost seven o'clock; I told myself that was why.

We lay on the bed and finished a crossword—several crosswords—by which I mean I held the pen and read the clues and positions of any existing letters, and Stephen told me the answers to fill in. We did a lot of crosswords that summer. Stephen was good at them, I'd discovered, but his handwriting, even before the progression started, was too terrible for practical use.

After a while, his answers got slower. The light under his parents' door went out.

I tucked the clip of the pen around the page we were on and put the book down. "I should go," I said. It was long past nine thirty, though Stephen didn't really have a curfew any more—but we both knew he wasn't going to drive me any-where. I'd take the wagon myself, and then I'd bring it back in the morning when I came. It was simple.

Stephen looked over at me. "Why don't you stay," he said. It was a statement, not a question.

I took off my shoes and socks, and then my shorts, folded and put them on the chair. He turned the light off; I lay under the sheet next to him, and he moved my arm over his shoulders, pulling us closer. In the dark I held him, spooning our bodies together. His fingers wove through mine.

At one o'clock his watch beeped and, eyes still closed, he rolled away, retrieving the pills from the nightstand and swallowing them in one motion, smooth and automatic. And then he rolled back into me, as automatic as if we'd been doing that for months, too.

The next Tuesday, we went to the hospital again. Dr. Svann—it was Dr. Svann's meeting this time—talked a lot. Stephen didn't say much, except to say he was fine. "And how are you emotionally?" Dr. Svann finally asked.

"The same," Stephen said.

"You know it's never too late to add a social worker to the team," Dr. Svann told him.

"That won't be necessary," Stephen said.

She gave him a long look. "We just want to help you," she said. "To make this as easy, as comfortable, as possible. Emotionally as well as physically."

"I understand," Stephen said. "In terms of all of this—I understand. I've accepted what's happening. I don't need to speak to anybody. It's all right." He paused. "Well, it's not all right. That's not the right thing to say. But it's as all right as it'll ever be."

Dr. Svann let him go, and we drove home. "Did you mean that?" I said. "Everything's all right? Or were you just saying that so she wouldn't…"

I wasn't sure what I thought Dr. Svann might actually do, but Stephen seemed to know what I meant. "I think she'd actually be less concerned if I screamed and cried all over the place" he said. "And I know my parents have spoken to someone. But yeah. I meant what I said."

He looked at me, hesitated, like he wanted to ask something, but wasn't sure he wanted to hear my response. "I won't presume so much about my significance as to suggest that you'd need grief counseling," he said, "but I should still probably ask. How are you?"

I looked back at him. "I'm happy if you are," I said.

Thursday evening Mom sent me to pick Tammy up from bowling, one in her vast array of summer recreation activities. Even though she was off at rec more often than not, I was feeling a bit guilty about almost never being home for her, so I went. I parked three blocks away from the rec center because I still didn't like parking downtown, and because I knew Tammy wouldn't mind. It gave her more time to narrate her bowling escapades, which she was doing animatedly. I tried not to be distracted.

Bonham drove by. Because it was Bonham, I knew what his car looked like. Tammy and I caught him at the light, and he looked over at us. Then he performed an illegal turn and parked in the lot opposite, rolled down his window, and waved me over.

Tammy stopped talking about bowling and glanced, with a very poor attempt at surreptitiousness, over her shoulder, then up at me. She looked pleased—she must have recognized him from the yearbook—until I handed her the keys and told her to go wait in the car. I figured there was very little overlap between anything Bonham wanted to talk to me about and anything that could be fit for Tammy's ears.

He reached over and turned off the stereo as I sat down. "How is he?" he said. No beating around.

I swallowed and looked up at Bonham. I wasn't really sure how to answer that.

He waited a moment, then turned the stereo back up again. It was some kind of slowed-down, dark house music, with vaguely liturgical vocals, without real words. It wasn't what I would've guessed for Bonham. (Especially summer Bonham.) But it didn't not fit him.

His entire back seat was a sub cabinet. That did fit him pretty well.

"I know it's not what everyone thinks it is," he said. His voice was low, cutting under the sound. "I'm not asking you to tell me what's really wrong, just like I won't ask Stephen. We both pretend I don't know, and that's okay. I get it," he said. "He has his reasons."

I nodded. It was hard to look at Bonham, then; Bonham wasn't a person who was ever supposed to look sad. I made myself do it. Bonham was Stephen's friend. He deserved to be looked at, at least. And he deserved to have honesty, as much as I could give to him. "Okay," I said.

"He's my best friend," Bonham said. "I know people don't think—Stephen thinks I have so many friends that individual ones don't matter. Like I've exceeded a certain number, and no relationship I have now is really real. And sometimes that's true," he admitted. "But mostly it's not. Stephen matters as much to me as I do to him. More, maybe, because of how long he's been training himself out of me. But all the things he thinks I did just for show—I always wanted him there."

I remembered, suddenly, Bonham at graduation, hugging Stephen, saying I love you. Saying it again. At the time, I'd thought they were just words he was throwing away. People like Bonham could afford to throw away words like that.

But I realized then that the opposite, perhaps, was what was really true. Everyone Bonham knew assumed they were far out in his periphery, an insignificant, easily replaceable body. People loved Bonham the way they loved pictures in magazines. And the people he loved thought he didn't care.

"He's my best friend," he said again. "I'm glad he has you, to do the things he won't let me. But he's still my best friend. I just want to know—is he going to be okay?"

I swallowed.

"Is he going to die?" Bonham said.

I looked at the car door, at the pocket at the bottom of the car door. I blinked. Bonham was even more direct than Stephen.

"I see," he said carefully. "How long?"

I kept looking at the pocket in the door. It was so clean. Grey molded plastic, a faint texture to it. Straight until the end, where it belled out to the shape of a cup holder. There was nothing inside.

"Oh," said Bonham. He choked a bit. "If I could hold him," he said, "if I could hold him in my arms, and never have another person light up when they look at me, never have another girl text all her friends, 'today I got smiled at by *Bonham*,' never so much as be recognized ever again, if that was what it meant, if I could just pull him in to me and hold him there and give him everything I have, and make him okay, fuck, you know I'd do it."

I looked over at him and quickly looked away again.

"Fuck," he said again, "I get it. He doesn't want to see me cry. No one's supposed to see me cry."

I gave him a moment.

"Do you think he'd let me see him?" he said, and he sounded normal again.

The truth was that I didn't know if he would. And, it depended. "You should go as soon as you can," I said. "Like tomorrow. Today, maybe."

He looked stunned. Like I'd slapped him in the face. I think he'd known even before I got in the car that Stephen was very unwell, perhaps even dying, but being told the time frame you have to get your last visit in is so very short—I don't think it's something anyone expects. It's certainly not what anyone wants to hear.

"It's not as bad as that," I said quickly. "It'll be longer than that. But, already—he doesn't want to tell you—he won't tell you—because he doesn't want you to remember him like this. And as it gets worse... he won't want you to see him like—you know." I looked away again.

"I know," Bonham said.

Whatever we were listening to ended and, after a moment's pause, started again.

"I always throw myself into everything as hard as I can, until I can't feel any more," he said. "Stephen taught me that. Not the part about not feeling, but the rest. The important part." He paused. "But there's nowhere you can throw yourself with this."

"No," I said. "There's not."

He reached forward and turned the volume up, until I could feel the bass coming in behind me, could feel the different, synthetic, frequencies higher up. He rested his head against the back of the seat and closed his eyes.

He didn't move. He didn't cry.

The song ended and restarted yet again. "Please don't tell him I talked to you," Bonham said, without opening his eyes.

"Okay," I said.

He didn't say anything else. He put one hand up over his forehead and held it there, the base of his palm over the bridge of his nose, his fingers in his hair. His shoulders twitched, once, twice, a third time.

I opened the door, and quietly shut it behind me, and walked away.

"Bonham was here earlier," Stephen said the next day, without preamble.

I nodded. "Did you tell him?" I asked, when he didn't say anything else.

"Did *you* tell him?" Stephen replied. "He just showed up."

I shook my head. "You know I wouldn't do that," I said.

He sighed, and his head dropped. "He's not stupid," he said heavily, more to himself than to me. "He probably just figured it out on his own." He paused, looked up at me, sighed again. "Like Tammy said, I don't have any track marks."

"I didn't want to see him," he said after a while, then reconsidered. "I did. I just didn't want him to see me."

"What did you do?" I asked.

"We just talked about when we were kids," Stephen said after a minute. "Stupid stuff. Bonham's good like that."

I'd thought he might be.

"Is he going to be all right?" Stephen said.

I nodded, because what else could I do? "He'll be fine."

"I used to be able to take care of him," Stephen said quietly.

"He'll be fine," I said again. "We'll all be."

Monday we went back to the hospital. Again. Stephen was wearing a hat, the same one he always wore. I'd considered, earlier, suggesting he not wear it on hospital visits, although in light of the previous week's discussion, it seemed a bit beside the point. Still, out in the real world, he just looked like someone wearing a hat. (Maybe a junkie, maybe not.) But there, in a hospital—even in an outpatient area—a stocking cap gave the pretty clear impression that here was someone who had lost his hair to chemo.

It was time for his next MRI, and we were waiting for the scan. A boy came through one of the doors down the hall and started toward us. He was past his early teens, but still looked a few years younger than Stephen, with a shaved head and a checkerboard-print hooded sweatshirt (hood down). He started across the lobby toward the elevators, then stopped and came over. "Hey, man," he said to Stephen, "I've seen you before. I'm Ryan."

Stephen didn't respond at all, which admittedly was quite rude, but which also, by that point, was pretty typical hospital behavior for Stephen.

Ryan didn't seem offended, though, or even put off. "So what's happening with you?"

"Cancer," Stephen said flatly. The giant directional sign on the wall above our heads made it obvious enough.

Ryan sat down in the empty chair on Stephen's other side, which was somewhat surprising. "Yeah, man," he said. "But at least you're here, right?"

Stephen had gone back to not responding.

"Okay, let me tell you this," Ryan said. "It's crazy. I'm fourteen, right, just got my braces off and I go in to the dentist to see if my wisdom teeth're coming in. And they set me up and the hygienist goes out to take the X-ray, and then she's gone forever, like, ages. I finally had to spit the thing out myself, even though they always say not to.

"So finally she comes back, and she's got this cute, bouncy ponytail and she's wearing these scrubs with little dancing teddy bears all over them, and she's got this real almost scared look on her face. And she says, 'Sorry to take so long. I've been going all around the waiting room, trying to find one of your parents. The receptionist finally told me you came in by yourself. Is that true?'

"And I said yeah, because my mom dropped me off, and then I was gonna take the bus home, and she looked more worried and swallowed and—this is the dental hygienist, right—she goes, 'I don't mean to be an alarmist, and it's probably just a blip on the lens, but it does show up from all the angles, and I've looked at a lot of these, and I feel I'd be remiss if I didn't say something.' But, you know, the way she says it, you can tell she's checked and double-checked and it's not just, like, some lint on the screen. And then she pulls up one of my X-rays and points to this spot in the corner, like above and behind my jaw, and tells me, 'there's something weird here.'

"And then she says, 'I think you need to have this looked at by someone more experienced than I am,' and I say, 'like the dentist?' and she says, 'no, like a neurosurgeon.'

"So I tell my mom, and, you know, of course she freaks, and drags me in to the GP, and he's like, 'yeah, yeah, a dental hygienist? It's probably nothing but I'll book you for an MRI just to make you feel better.' So the next week I go in for an MRI, and then the guy comes out and he's like, 'so, yeah, it does look like you have a tumor.' And he was really surprised to have caught it so early—like, I hadn't even shown any symptoms yet. And everyone was like, 'you better fucking thank that dentist.' And I was like, 'it was the hygienist, man.'

"So they start me a round of chemo, for safety, and then like two weeks later they just went in and cut it out." He leaned forward and showed us a scar near the base of his head. It was tiny. In a few more months, his hair would grow out and cover it completely. No one would even know it was there.

"So, like, it gets better, man," he said. "I mean, it was, like, almost the size of a walnut, and now it's *gone*. I just came out of my second check—officially cancer-free for two months."

"What kind was it?" Stephen said suddenly. I think he surprised both of us.

"Pilocytic astrocytoma," Ryan said. "Sorta near the back of my sinuses, I guess. You?"

"DIPG," Stephen said, which definitely surprised me. It was the first time I'd ever heard him tell anyone. I guess he figured he and Ryan didn't know each other or know anyone else who knew each other; they didn't live in the same city; they'd probably never see each other again. It was probably easier to tell him than not to.

Ryan's expression didn't change. "Eh?" he said.

"Diffuse intrinsic pontine glioma," said Stephen.

Then Ryan sucked in his breath. I still don't think he knew what it was, but he must have recognized one of the words. Glioma, probably, if that's what he'd had. Or maybe he was just smart enough to know the definitions of diffuse and intrinsic in common English and put them together. "That sounds like shit, man," he said.

"It is shit," said Stephen.

Ryan didn't say anything for a moment. Then he leaned forward, looking past Stephen to me. "What about you?"

I blinked.

"She's just being a supportive girlfriend," Stephen said. He put his hand on my knee. His fingers on my inner thigh, where Ryan couldn't see, dug in so hard it hurt.

For a second, Ryan looked startled. Then his face softened, and he looked—almost—wistful. "That's really cool," he said. "I wish Amy was here."

Stephen didn't respond. "Girlfriend?" I asked, to be polite.

"No, my hygienist," Ryan said. "I fucking love her, man. I sent her flowers. I got so many, and I was like, look, I'm a dude. What am I gonna do with flowers? But I sent her some. Not mine, I mean. I got her her own. Like, I actually bought her flowers and had them delivered. Four times. I fucking love her.

"Look," he said, "I know this is crazy because she's the reason I'm not dead—well, I probably wouldn't be dead, but, like, she's the reason I'm already okay now, and, like, theoretically, I could've died, you know? But I'd die for her. I'd fucking die for her. That's how you know you really love someone, right?"

Stephen closed his eyes and let his head fall back against the wall, which I guess shows what he thought about that.

Ryan was too caught up to notice. "She came and visited me once, a couple days after surgery, and held my hand." There was something dreamy in his voice. It was incredibly sad, in a way.

And I knew how he felt; sometimes I thought I would rather die instead of Stephen. But of course Stephen would never allow it. If someone had magically removed his cancer, held it equidistant between our heads, and said, 'Okay, one of you gets it, the other one lives,' I know he would've said, without even blinking, to put it back in. It was comforting that I knew that, knew it with such certainty. Even so, I wished I didn't. I wished like anything that it wasn't true. If I could've taken what he had, I would have.

I wondered how Amy felt. It wasn't surprising that she'd come to see Ryan in the hospital. People did things like that when they found out someone had cancer. But I didn't think that would be an appropriate thing to say. "That's nice," I told him, noncommittal.

"Yeah," Ryan sighed. "It really makes you think. I mean, shit, yeah, I had to go through all this, but it makes you think, you know, what about all the stuff that never would've happened?" He punched Stephen in the arm. "You know? I'm telling you, man, yeah, a lot of it fucking sucks, but it's not all bad. It gets better."

Stephen took a deep breath and opened his eyes. Then a nurse down the hall stuck her head out a door and called, "Stephen?" She waved at him with a clipboard.

Stephen stood up sharply and walked away without saying anything.

Ryan watched him for a few moments, then moved over into the empty chair he'd left. "Is he..." he said, his voice low. "I mean, I didn't mean to, like... He didn't even say goodbye."

"He hates hospitals," I said. I didn't want to be awful to Ryan, because he hadn't meant to be. And it was true that Stephen wouldn't have been in a brilliant mood even without his conversation. But I couldn't help it. "Right now, he also hates you a little bit." Because—I will not lie—at that moment, I hated Ryan a little bit, too.

Ryan looked—there's no other word for this—shocked. "Is it because I'm..." he said finally, then trailed off before he finished. "I've seen him before," he said. "And he always looks so... you know. I thought maybe a success story, first-hand, would cheer him up. It does get better."

"He isn't getting better," I said.

"Shit," said Ryan. "Is it—I mean, I didn't mean he looks, you know, sick, I meant, like, depressed. Is he really that bad?"

"Compared to other people with what he's got, he's

actually done very well," I said. I was impressed, and a bit unsettled, by how composed I sounded. But, I realized, it was composed almost to the point of being robotic. Maybe, it occurred to me then, that was how people dealt with terrible things: by simply turning off all their emotions, going full-on into cyborg mode.

Ryan looked confused.

"You don't know what DIPG is, do you?" I said.

He shrugged. I was surprised, but I shouldn't have been. Most people don't know what DIPG is, and I expect that, but I guess I expected more from someone who'd had a brain tumor himself. Then again, DIPG is really rare, and it isn't anything like what Ryan had had. There wouldn't have been any reason to suspect it, or to tell him about it. And he'd been in the cancer world for such a short time that it was absurd to expect he'd have encountered it on his own.

He swallowed. "Well, he said glioma, right? That's what I had. So it can't be that different, really."

He looked like he really wanted me to tell him he was right. I didn't. "You said yours was the size of a walnut?" I asked.

He nodded. "Yeah. And that's pretty big, for growing inside your brain, I mean. So—"

"His is like a duck egg," I said. "With silly string. It's everywhere through his brainstem, and it's in everything. They can't kill it, and they can't cut it out. The best they can do is try to make him comfortable until he…" Stephen said it all the time, but even with someone who'd been cured (or perhaps because he had been) it just felt wrong to say "dies."

"He isn't going to get better," I said again. "You don't get better with DIPG."

Ryan didn't say anything, just stared—which was legitimately astounding. Even if his treatment had been as in-and-out as he'd described, it was unbelievable that he'd never before encountered anyone who wasn't expected to make it. Who already hadn't made it.

"Shit," he said finally. "Fuck."

"Pretty much," I said.

He swallowed. "I should probably go," he said, looking away. "I'm supposed to meet, um, a friend, and the bus—if I miss this one, it only comes, like, once an hour." He paused, then looked up at me suddenly. His eyes were so wide. "But don't tell him I said that, okay? Tell him my mom picked me up."

"Okay," I said, not because that was what I'd actually tell Stephen, but because it was what this kid needed to hear. Normally I might not have been so sympathetic, but, I realized, Ryan *had* been through a lot. There had been a moment, however fleeting, when he'd thought he might die. There had been a time—times—when he was terrified.

He stood up, and looked at me, hesitated. I thought he looked like he wanted to say something else—to ask me to tell Stephen good luck, maybe, or to apologize. I thought about telling him good luck with Amy, even though it sounded more like hero worship, or a delayed version of the adrenaline rush that makes people think they've fallen in love with the fireman who rescued them from a burning building. But I didn't, and he didn't say anything, either. He looked down, and scuffed the toe of his shoe against the carpet. "Bye," he said, and then walked away.

I wondered what it was like to know, the way Ryan knew, that you had survived cancer. I wondered if he would spend the rest of his life being a cancer survivor, if it would define him the way Stephen was so set against being defined, or if he would find other things, other pieces to make up his life, until eventually having had a brain tumor as a fourteen-year-old would just become a footnote in his past. I wondered if he'd even had cancer long enough for it to really sink in.

I wondered how long he would tell his story. (It was, admittedly, pretty good.) And I wondered, foolishly, if he would ever get anywhere with his dental hygienist. Maybe, in the end, cancer really would work out for him. He wouldn't mind people knowing. He wouldn't mind being a bit defined, because it would be only one thing of the many that made up who he was. It was so different when you weren't dying. It was different when you'd lived.

Stephen came back after a few more minutes and sank into the chair next to me. "Okay?" I asked him. "Ready?" Usually he wanted to leave the moment he was released. Sometimes he didn't even come over to get me, just nodded in my direction as he strode past on his way to the elevators.

He took a while to gather himself, and didn't answer. We were still walking through the hallway downstairs when he gave me the keys; he never drove any more, but I think he still liked to pretend he was going to. I put them in my pocket and took his hand. Then I let go again and put my arm around his waist. He melted a little bit against me.

We were halfway home before either of us said anything. Stephen's watch beeped; one o'clock. He took out his handful of pills and swallowed them, one at a time. I remembered when he'd taken them all at once. But of course, there were also more now.

He swallowed again, and looked over at me. "Fucking kid," he said at last, and his voice cracked. "Pilocytic astrocytoma. He got the best kind."

I spent as much time as I could with Stephen, at the same time trying not to keep him from spending as much time with his parents as they could. After all, they'd known him a lot longer than I had. Still, I wound up spending more time at Stephen's house that summer than I did at my own. Nights, too.

Some days he couldn't do much. He'd suck on ice cubes and, from time to time, convulse. I'd lay next to him and we'd do crosswords, even as he struggled with speech.

A cane appeared in the living room one day, and later, a walking frame. Stephen tried his hardest never to use them. (And, I knew, he'd stop getting out of bed entirely before he'd ever succumb to a wheelchair.) He wouldn't take them out of the house, and in his room, where we were most of the time, space was so tight they would've been more hindrance than help, anyway. Usually, he could get by bracing himself against the walls and various pieces of furniture. And he never seemed to mind holding my hand.

Other days, he still seemed almost normal. Then, we spent a lot of time at the college. There weren't as many students in the summer, and they were less motivated—or else our timing was just good; there was hardly ever anybody in the darkroom when we went in.

Unless he did it all in secret, Stephen never developed a single roll of film. He never made a print. While I was in the darkroom, he'd sit for hours in the hall, reading medical journals—still, even when he had to hold them six inches away from his face.

But often, when we were the only ones there, he'd come into the enlarger room and talk to me while I made prints.

He was never very loud, under any circumstances, but his voice always got quieter in the dark.

I couldn't tell you all the things we talked about. Stephen talked about science, sometimes—real, smart science that I mostly didn't understand. It wasn't just because I was a year younger and hadn't had that class yet; it wasn't the kind of science that you learn in high school at all. I hadn't realized at first, and then I kind of had, but assumed it was mostly just medical jargon he'd osmosed as a result of having cancer—but it was more than that. He was, really, a lot smarter than me. He really could have become a doctor.

When I worked on the dry side, he would sit in the enlarger berth next to me, leaning against the partition. He never seemed to pay much attention to what my hands were doing. Sometimes I'd show him what I was working on, but he never offered any advice or criticism.

On the wet side, though, he'd always watch, with child-like fascination, even when he could barely manage to stand without bracing his weight against the gutter. He made me develop all my prints facing up. Every time I processed a new one, his eyes would widen, watching the image fill itself in, and he'd smile, a little—the smile where the corners of his eyes wrinkled—but at the same time, he'd also look slightly sad. "It's still like magic," he said once, and it occurred to me then that he had been the one who'd originally used that word.

"Magic?" I repeated.

"Sometimes I think it's the only real magic left," he said, still watching the sheet.

"What about magic yet to be invented?" I asked, though I didn't really believe in such a thing.

Stephen shrugged. "You're talking about a cure, aren't you?" he said and leaned forward over the print. I couldn't tell if he was just taking a closer look or really needed the support. "Maybe that day will come. But not for me." He didn't sound sad about it, or even resigned. If I hadn't known better, I would've said he sounded almost optimistic. "There's no magic in the world, now," he said, "that can help me."

We were quiet after that; the timer, ticking by its seconds, seemed impossibly loud. It was a relief when I could seize the print by the tongs and move it over. It didn't make any more sound than there already was, but at least it was something to do. Some movement.

"Sorry," Stephen said after a while, and I told him, yet again, not to apologize.

Another time, he came up behind me while I was at the enlarger. He put his hands on my shoulders and I turned around, and he kissed me for so long—I forgot about counting, and I forgot about the lamp—I turned an entire sheet of paper black with light. That was a better day.

The worst day in the darkroom, I was there without Stephen. He'd been there with me that morning, but we left together for my library shift. I always felt slightly bad dragging him along, and asked him if he wanted me to take him home instead, but he shook his head. "Something you want to look up?" I asked him, only half joking. He just shrugged.

As part of the summer reading program, the library had toddler storytimes on Wednesday afternoons, which consisted less of stories and more of very loud singing, clapping, and stomping around in the children's area. When I couldn't find Stephen in any of his usual places after I finished shelving, I'd worried the noise might have bothered him so much he'd had to leave. But then on my way out to the wagon, I saw him, leaning against the wall on the children's side, watching as the toddlers jumped into the air and landed first on one foot, then the other.

I stood next to him and put my hand on his arm, but he didn't turn. "Look at them," he said. "I wish…"

"Changing your mind about having kids?" I asked.

"Oh, no," he replied. "I guess, just, sometimes I wish I was still that young."

One of the first things he'd told me, I remembered, was that he had to do things now because a time would come when he wasn't able. He'd talked about children, and all the things they could do that older people couldn't. And I knew that when he said he wished he was still that young, he didn't mean in terms of age, he meant ability.

He turned away from them, finally. "It's all right," he said. I nodded. He rested his hand on my arm as we walked out to the wagon. We didn't look back at the toddlers.

I went home that evening after dropping him off; I was trying not to entirely avoid my family. My parents weren't there yet, but Tammy was, sitting cross-legged in the middle of the living room, surrounded by yearbooks. I shut the door as quietly as I could and managed to tiptoe by her. I wasn't in the mood for yearbooking.

She must have known I was there, though; after a while she came back to our room. She was holding one of the books—my freshman year, I could tell from the cover. "Come here," she said; then, when I didn't immediately stand, she came over and sat next to me on the bed.

She turned to one of the pages of candids near the back, which, like ninety-eight percent of all yearbook photos, weren't really candid. I knew right away which picture she wanted me to see, even before she pointed to it. "Yeah, that's Bonham," I told her. He was, as always, immediately recognizable, but I didn't know who he was with. With Bonham, it could've been anyone. And it might actually have been a candid, I realized; even as early as sophomore year, people were taking surreptitious pictures of Bonham. They might not have been looking at—or even aware of—the camera. They might even have really been laughing. It was hard to tell, with the sunglasses.

Tammy kept staring at the photo, a slight frown on her face. "And?" she said.

"I don't really know him," I said. "I don't know what you want me to tell you."

"No," she said, and I expected her to argue this—I'd been sitting in a parked car with Bonham less than a week ago—but she didn't. "Not that. Not him." She looked up at me, frowning still, then back down, and moved her finger to the other boy. "That's *Stephen*."

I was about to tell her that of course it wasn't. Then I realized she was right.

It must've been taken at the start of their sophomore year, before the tumor started, before he started to get sick. I couldn't remember who or what I'd been paying attention to my freshman year, but obviously it hadn't been Stephen. I wouldn't have recognized him. I *hadn't* recognized him.

Bonham had his arm around Stephen's neck, and it looked like he was reaching up to do it. Maybe that just meant Bonham had gotten taller since then—a reasonable enough assumption—but Stephen also looked like he could've played football. Or, almost. His shoulders weren't as wide as Bonham's, but they were wider than they were now. He wore sunglasses, and no hat. He looked, for the first time I'd seen him, like someone it made sense for Bonham to be friends with. He looked like he was actually alive.

There weren't any current pictures of Stephen in the Stuarts' house. There weren't any from several years ago, either. Nothing, I realized, past perhaps fifth or sixth grade. If I'd ever thought about it, I'd assumed they'd gotten a digital camera, and never gotten around to ordering prints. But it occurred to me then that perhaps the lack of more recent photos was intentional. Maybe it was too hard to see them— pictures from recently before. Pictures where Stephen still looked like what he was supposed to look like.

Tammy turned her face up toward mine. "Is something wrong?" she said, then swallowed when I didn't respond. "Sorry." She reached over and squeezed the side of my hand. Her fingers were soft and warm, and so small. I wondered how much she understood, how much she'd put together. I wondered if she knew what she was apologizing for, or if she was just saying it because she knew she should say something, and knew nothing else to say. For a moment, she rested her head against my arm. "You know I love you, always," she said. "Right?"

"I know," I mumbled. I told her I loved her, too.

"You don't have to say that," she said. "I didn't mean to make you sad."

"I was sad already," I said.

She lifted her head again and looked at me. "I kind of figured you were." She slid the yearbook off my lap and brought the pages closed, then stood, clutching the book to her chest. "I won't show you any more." She took a step backward, then another, hesitated. "Are you going back to Stephen's?" she asked, and tripped a few more steps toward the door. "Tell him I said hey."

"Okay," I said. "I'll tell him."

I wondered what was wrong with me that I hadn't

recognized Stephen, who I'd seen every inch of, while Tammy had been so confident in her ID. It didn't occur to me until later that Tammy obsessed over the yearbooks; she'd probably checked against Stephen's sophomore class photo, maybe even his pictures from middle school. But it still hurt. Even beyond not recognizing him, the simple realization of how much, physically, had changed—not because I'd missed it, but because of how hard it must have been for Stephen. I'd never realized how much the cancer had, literally, taken out of him.

I wished, briefly, that I'd known him before—not because I thought he'd been a better person, but because he'd so clearly been different. I knew who he was now, of course. But I had no idea about the person he'd been before. About the person he'd meant to be.

I knew Stephen would say it wasn't my fault; I hadn't known him then, and why should I have? It made sense that I wouldn't recognize all the ways he'd changed. And when I thought about it, I didn't really feel guilty. Just awful. Beyond that, even. Lost, maybe.

I wondered how many pictures there were, over the years, of Stephen and Bonham like that. I thought of all the photos of him Sylvia had made me take—ten pictures with him intentionally placed in the camera's way, and not one where he was looking. Maybe, I told myself, he and Bonham hadn't really been looking at the yearbook photographer's camera, either. Maybe not looking had always been his thing.

I didn't go back to Stephen's that night; instead I returned to the college. In the darkroom, I pulled my contact sheets out of their box and flipped through the pages under the safelight. I'd printed many of them by now, but there were a few I never had.

When I got to the roll I was looking for, my hands shook slightly taking the negatives out. I knew the print I was about to make would be good only to me. It was an image from months ago, on the hike, when we'd stopped just before the end in that field of tiny flowers. Less than a week before he'd told me he was dying.

There was a series of four negatives; I'd cut them in a strip together—first the one Stephen had taken of me, then the two of us together, and then the almost-accidental one I'd gotten of him, lying still, not even facing the camera. It was the last one I wanted.

I'd printed the others already, but always passed over the last; Stephen's eyes, I knew, were closed. And eyes were important. It was eyes, Sylvia had stressed, that made the picture. Although I don't think it would've been a better photo if Stephen had been looking; it wasn't just his eyes. There was no movement in the image, no life. To anyone but me, it would've been nothing other than a missed click of the shutter.

But when I thought about it, I realized that perhaps it also meant something that I'd taken a picture of Stephen still, quiet, where his eyes could have been open, but weren't. I couldn't get past it now.

I moved around the darkroom quietly, almost on instinct, and as with the first contact print I'd made, I ran the exposed sheet through each bath face-down, transferring it from tub to tub with the front carefully turned away. This time—this print—the magic wasn't something I wanted to see.

When the final wash was finished, I had to force myself to turn it over. And it was terrible, as terrible as I'd known it would be—even more haunting than the one with the mirror, albeit in a different way. Stephen looked, I realized, the way I felt, eyes closed against reality, holding onto something that was no longer there. His lips were slightly parted, his empty hands reaching out. And—something I'd forgotten, and hadn't noticed in the negative—you could still clearly see the depression in the grass where I had been.

But, in the world of magic and photography, the hole could just as easily have belonged to the person he used to be.

I knew I could never show it to anyone, much less to Stephen. I could barely stand to look at it myself.

I slumped against the tray table and slowly slid to the floor, the print clutched in my hands. It was dark there, even with the soft red glow of the safelight, and silent but for the low hum of the air pump that kept the water in the final bath circulating, and the sound of that water quietly bubbling. It should have been calming, peaceful, almost womb-like in its comfort. And I sat there on the ground, the wet print dripping onto my knees and down my legs, and cried until I couldn't cry any more.

The next morning when I went over, Stephen was up and dressed, sitting at the dining table alone. He stood up, one hand still on the back of the chair, and kissed me. "How are you?" I asked.

"I missed you," he said. Then he told me, like always, that he was fine.

In waiting rooms, time passed slowly. I didn't like leaving Stephen alone, but we'd already been there longer than expected, for a second visit tacked on at the last minute. The earlier, original, chat with Dr. Svann had gone off without a hitch, but she wanted blood work done as well—something about drug interactions. After a while, Stephen asked me if I could get him some water. I'd seen a dispenser built into the wall opposite the elevators, and I knew that even if there was a line, it wouldn't take long.

When I came back, a woman was with Stephen. After a moment, I realized it was his mother. His two appointments were nothing but routine, really, and I was surprised to see her—until I recognized the white coat she wore and the clipboard on the chair beside her, and remembered that she worked in the hospital. This wasn't her department, but Stephen wasn't usually there, either, so she wouldn't have known to avoid it. She must have just seen him while passing through.

Stephen was sitting, as he often did in waiting rooms, stiff and rigid, staring straight ahead, but he'd wrapped his good arm around her shoulders as she clung to him. I couldn't see Dr. Stuart's face, buried against his chest. But I could hear her.

From TV, I think, people often expect hospitals to be loud and frenetically busy. Maybe in emergency rooms, they are. But most of the time, hospitals are silent. The waiting room was, aside from the sound of Stephen's mother crying. I could hear her perfectly. "My baby," she kept saying, in between broken gasps. "My baby."

It must have been so hard. I couldn't imagine the horror of seeing your child in a hospital waiting room and knowing that, even after years of med school, interning, residency, and actual practice, there was nothing you could do for him. That there was nothing anyone could do for him.

A long, shrill beep cut through the silence; it was Dr. Stuart's pager going off. She pulled back from Stephen and stood; she ran both hands along her temples and blew her nose on one of the industrial tissues from the box on the end table.

"Mum," Stephen said, looking up at her.

She smiled, tight-lipped. It was the same smile Stephen sometimes gave me when we both knew we were pretending to be braver than we felt. Dr. Stuart put the tissue in her pocket, then reached down and touched the top of Stephen's hat, right over where his hairline would be. She didn't say anything to him. She exited, thankfully, through a different hallway than I was in.

"You saw," Stephen said flatly, when I sat back down.

I nodded.

"My goal," he said after a minute, "not that you really make goals when you have DIPG—but my goal was to make it to eighteen. My parents will always think of me as their child, because that's what parents do, but at least I won't actually, technically, be a child. Adults die. It happens. But children aren't ever supposed to."

I didn't know what to say. He reached over and took my hand. It was with some relief that I let go when the phlebotomist finally appeared and called his name.

"Stephen," I said, "there's something I always wondered. From the beginning. Why were you so intent on knowing me?"

He didn't answer for a while; when he did, I was surprised. "Remember when we talked about books?"

"I do," I said, "but that was later. I mean, you'd already started following me around."

"Well, you let me follow you," he said, then sighed. "It's not because of the books. It's related to what I said. The books we read—even though we can't relate to them, we want to read about people who're special, people whose lives are different, because that's how we want to be. But I got it—I got to be special, and I'd give anything... I just want to be normal." He swallowed. "You said I was normal. The first day. You weren't even thinking, and that's how I knew you meant it. You said I was a normal, decent-looking boy. And it's stupid, I know, but for some reason it stuck."

He stopped, swallowed again. "I wanted it so badly, Emily. And—I don't know—maybe I thought if I could be normal to you… I mean, no one else knew. Who knows what they did think—what they *do* think—but at least they don't know. But you didn't even think anything yet, and I thought, 'here is someone who I can be normal with.' "

I reached over and cupped his face in my hand.

"I don't know if you remember this," he said, "but I told you very early on—or at the very least I implied it—that it had nothing to do with you. I didn't pick you because I liked you. I didn't even really care about you. I just picked you because of what you didn't know. Because of what you thought, and didn't think, about me. I'm sorry—I mean, I'm really sorry. It's different now, obviously, and I didn't mean…

"Honestly, I didn't even think I'd make it this long. As optimistic as I was at the time, I didn't really believe. I didn't think I'd mean enough that it'd matter to you when I was gone. I didn't think I'd matter enough that you'd care."

"Of course I'll care," I said, appalled. "How could you think I wouldn't care?"

"Ever since—well." He shook his head. "I don't think in terms of years or even months any more. I think in weeks and days. And weeks and days don't matter as much, even if you move as fast as I was trying to. I figured you'd move on and forget. Or forget and move on. However it goes."

"I'll still care, though," I said. "Even if it had been… less than a month. I'd still care."

"I know," he said, "now. But I still wish you wouldn't. I still wish I hadn't done it. And I know I can say that and say that and it won't change anything, and I know that even if I could go back and change it, knowing what I know now, it would be so incredibly difficult to give you up, but I still wish I hadn't done it. I did a terrible thing to you. I don't mean dying—nothing I can do about that. I mean letting you get close to me when I knew I was going to die. I should've left you alone," he said. "You probably never would've thought about me again, if I hadn't gotten in your way."

"But you did, and I'm glad you did."

He shrugged.

"Look," I said. "The books, again. You also said, sort of, that my life was a book where nothing had happened. I get that that's what you wanted—to be uninteresting, to be ordinary. To be a book that no one wanted to read. But I wanted to be the girl in the story. And you made me that girl. You made me special."

Because I may have only been a pawn when he'd started the process of making his life awesome, but regardless, I'd been pulled along with him. Whether he'd done it intentionally or not, he'd made my life awesome, as well.

"Maybe," he said. "But at what cost?" I knew he didn't mean the cost to him. He was talking about the reason I got to be special. That the whole reason either of us had done anything at all was that he was running out of time. That I was weeks, maybe days, away from being the girl whose boyfriend died.

"Everything has its costs," I told him. "Would I have rather stayed ordinary if it meant you didn't have to die? Of course I would; it's not worth anything even close to that. But it wasn't a one-to-one trade. Look, I can't qualify it, or quantify it, or whatever, but there are all these things…" I swallowed. "I never really did anything," I said, "until you."

"All right," Stephen said finally. "All right." He brought his hand up and laid it on top of mine. For a moment, his shoulders shook. He kissed the end of my thumb.

"You know," I told him, a while later, "when I asked that, I was expecting you to say something silly, maybe a bit cute, like, 'I liked your hair.' Something ordinary." I paused, considering. "Maybe something a bit more severe, or opportunistic, but still perceptive, like that I seemed lonely. But this…"

"No," Stephen said drily, "I don't suppose anyone would have expected this. And," he added, then reached over and patted my head, "I do like your hair."

"Well, I'm glad there's one of us," I said.

"Sometimes," he said, "I don't believe you like *me* at all. No," he went on, stopping me before I could protest, "I know, but sometimes I tell myself, 'no, Emily must be a cancer hallucination.' It's not supposed to affect my mental faculties, but some of the medications I take… And I'll tell myself, 'there's no way, no way, bro, you could have pulled this off. She isn't real. Maybe I'm in the coma already.' And then I roll over and you're here."

"Of course I'm here," I told him. "Of course I'm real."

"Yeah, but that's also what an hallucination would say," he said. He smiled. "But I think if I was hallucinating that bad, I wouldn't still feel like this." The smile got sadder.

"I promise I'm real," I said.

"I know," he whispered.

I sat up and took his shirt off. He was so thin. There was a dark bruise on his left forearm, purplish-green and slowly fading, and another, only slightly smaller, just above his wrist. For whatever reason, he'd never had a PICC line put in, and his veins, by then, were terrible. The phlebotomist on Monday had gotten the needle in eventually, he said, but only after four failed tries, each involving a good amount of vein-chasing. I'd kept cringing as he told me about it. Whereas, "I don't really notice it much any more," he'd said.

I put my mouth over the bruise by his elbow and he inhaled shakily. I kissed his shoulder, and then the inside of his collarbone. He brought his arm up and held me there, for just a moment.

"All right?" I said.

"All right," he told me.

I think sex is probably better when both partners can contribute physically. But it's still not bad, even when they can't.

After, I slipped to one side, but kept my head on Stephen's chest, listening to his breathing—fast, heavy at first; then, gradually, it slowed and evened. Or, at least, it evened as much as it ever did. "Emily," Stephen sighed, "you don't deserve to have a boyfriend who's dying."

I looked up just a bit.

"Nobody deserves to have a boyfriend who's dying," he clarified. "But especially not you."

"Especially not me?" I asked. "What makes me so special?"

"You're someone I care about," he said.

I put my head back down, and found his hand.

"I'm going to go to sleep," he told me after a while. "If you don't mind."

"Of course I don't mind," I said.

"You don't have to stay," he added.

"I want to," I told him. And he put his arm around my shoulders, and I put my left knee over his, and I stayed with him while he slept.

Saturday was worse. He woke up frowning, just after five. The headache got better, a bit, after he threw up, but the whole ordeal put a damper on the day. I think he would've been happier to stay in bed.

We got up and joined his parents for breakfast, which, for Stephen, was more a show of pushing food around than actually eating any. At nine, Mr. Stuart left to go golfing—reluctantly; Stephen had insisted. "It's important that they not isolate themselves," he'd told me once. "They need to keep doing their regular activities."

I wondered what Stephen would say if confronted with my schedule. Before I'd left the previous Wednesday, I'd told my supervisor at the library that I needed to take some time off, and I hadn't spent the night at home in more than a week. By then, Stephen had become pretty much the full extent of my activities.

Dr. Stuart didn't seem to have any activities, either. Even when Stephen suggested she work in the garden while he watched her (which was basically what we did, too, with film), she seemed reluctant. "Mum," he said finally, and I could tell even before he said it that he was annoyed, "sometimes I think you want me to be ill."

Dr. Stuart looked stunned. Her mouth opened and closed, but no words came out. "Of course I don't want you to be ill," she said finally. "But, darling, you are."

"Can't we still be normal, though?" Stephen said. "Even when I can't, can't you?"

"It's not that," his mother said. "It's *not* normal. *You're* not normal." She paused and closed her eyes briefly, reached her hand down, pressing her fingers hard against the countertop. "No," she corrected. "You're too normal." Her voice was very even; at the same time, she sounded almost desperate. "You aren't—darling—you just aren't being realistic. You aren't responding, emotionally—I'm worried you aren't accepting—"

"No," Stephen said. "I'm not. Would you?"

"That's not the point, Stephen," she said, and it occurred to me for the first time that, as a doctor, she would have seen this before. Cancer. Brain tumors. Dying. Not in anyone as close as her own son, but still. She'd been there. "Every consultation we've been in, every appointment, you sit there impassive and you tell them, over and over, you feel fine. Everything is all right. You'll deal with it. It makes me worry—do you really understand? You've never asked for anything," she said, and her voice started to break. "You've never asked *me*.

"That I could understand," she said. "I'm your mother, and I know you're independent. But you've never even seemed upset. Never angry. You've barely shown a single emotion through this whole thing. And you've never told a single person what was wrong without our insisting. You—you're still pretending. To a certain point, I could understand, but it just isn't—you can't do this any more. I don't want to admit it, either, Stephen, but you have to be prepared. You have to stop lying to yourself."

"You think I'm pretending?" Stephen said, very quietly. "That I'm in denial? You think I'm not very acutely aware of what I have and what I have left? You think I don't think about this every single day?

"If I haven't seemed upset, haven't begged you to stop the pain, if I've kept you out of appointments and tried to be the smallest burden I possibly can, I've done that all for your sake, Mum. So you wouldn't have to think all the time about my going to die. I'm going to die," he said again. "I know it. And I've accepted it. I've done everything I'm supposed to and everything I need to and there's nothing else we can do. Being upset doesn't do any good. I remember *you* saying that. I don't know what you want me to do."

"I just—you've never even cried," his mother said.

Stephen had looked away from her, but his head whipped back then; it was the fastest I'd seen him move in a while. He stared at her for a long moment, then shook his head. "Give me an onion, then," he said. His jaw was tight, and his eyes were narrow. "Give me a fucking onion, if that's what you want."

I felt so awkward standing there, with Dr. Stuart trying not to crumble, Stephen staring her down. I wanted to cry, too. I knew what she'd said wasn't true—I'd seen Stephen cry, even if only a few times; he said there was no point in it. I'd assumed his mother had seen, too—and, probably, more than I had. I didn't want to know what it meant that she hadn't.

"Are you really okay?" I asked him, later, back in his room (no onions produced). "The truth?"

"The truth?" He sighed. "Maybe sometimes I do pretend. Or did. But not nearly so much now. And never in a way that's unhealthy. I've always known what would happen in the end; it was made clear to me very early on. Sure, of course it's a coping mechanism; sixteen-year-olds aren't supposed to die. I'm two years older now, but still. Sometimes it's better to act like—to actually tell yourself—everything's all right.

"We all do it. It's not just cancer or dying. And it's not just me. Everyone likes to believe horrible things don't exist."

That night at dinner, Stephen told his mother he didn't want to do the monthly MRIs any more. "They upset you," he said. "I know they do. And you can already tell what's happening."

I expected her to argue, but she didn't. Maybe, in a way, it was a relief.

Of course, he still had to go for the regular check-ins with Dr. Svann. Well, I say he had to go. But by that point, I'm pretty sure that even if he wouldn't consciously admit it, he wanted to.

"Stephen," she said when we arrived. "And Emily." She was always so cordial. She stood up partway, then hesitated and sat again. Stephen and I sat across from her. "How are you?" she asked.

"I'm fine," Stephen said curtly. "How was my blood?"

"It's fine, Stephen," Dr. Svann said. "Really, though. Do you need anything?"

Stephen took a long breath and let it out again.

"I know you're trying to be brave," Dr. Svann said. "You don't have to be brave. My job is to make you comfortable, until the end."

"What if I don't just want to be comfortable until the end?" Stephen said. "What if I want to—to end comfortably?"

Dr. Svann didn't say anything.

"I hate this," Stephen said. He pushed his hat up his forehead, then dragged it back down again. "I'm barely even human any more. There should be some kind of... dignity."

"I'm sorry, Stephen," Dr. Svann said quietly. "That isn't how it works."

Stephen sighed again. "All right," he said. "I—I have been having trouble sleeping." This, I knew, was—unless he was very good at pretending to be asleep—untrue; if anything, he slept more now than he ever had. "It's not that I'm not tired," he said. "I am. I fall asleep all the time now during the day. But at night, when I'm actually supposed to be sleeping… Having to wake up at one o'clock doesn't help, either. I just lie there, for ages, waiting. Do you think I could get—" He paused, sighed heavily. "Do you think there's anything?"

Dr. Svann tapped her pen back and forth on the tabletop for a moment. "Have we tried you on diphenhydramine?" she asked.

"OTC?" Stephen replied. "On me? You know that'd be like giving a single tablet of aspirin to a walrus and then doing open-heart. Last time, you had to give me secobarbital." He made it sound like he hated suggesting it.

"I'm well aware, Stephen," Dr. Svann said. "But it's not… optimal."

"What about morphine?" the nurse suggested. It was the first thing I remembered him ever saying.

"I already have morphine," Stephen said.

Dr. Svann tapped her pen some more, scrolling up and down her chart. "All right," she finally said. "All right. Seco, again. I'll write you a prescription for a week's worth."

"A week, really?" said Stephen. "That's encouraging, thanks. I mean, you really think I'll last that long?"

Dr. Svann sighed. "It's not a matter of how long I think you will or won't," she said. "But considering what you already take, and what you've taken in the past, these pills may have no effect at all. Or you might react very badly. We know you've demonstrated corticosteroid hypersensitivities, and these things—allergies, intolerances—tend to develop over time. So, one a night, no more. I'm writing for only a week," she told him, "simply on a trial basis. If after that time, you find they're helping, I'll extend the prescription for another. If they aren't, then we'll find something else to try."

Stephen mumbled that that was fine.

"Is everything else still holding up?" Dr. Svann asked. "You're still able to swallow all the capsules?"

"Mum got me a thing to crush them up," Stephen said quietly. "But I haven't needed it yet."

"We can always consider a different delivery method," Dr. Svann said.

Casually, Stephen turned his wrist over, exposing the lingering bruises up the inside of his arm.

"Or smaller capsules," she amended.

"I think I'll be fine," Stephen said.

"I'll email the prescription over when we finish," Dr. Svann said. She hesitated. "This is never an easy topic to broach. But your directives. I know you have them on file, both here and locally. Keep in mind that you can always—"

"I know," said Stephen. "If I change my mind, nothing's set in stone."

Dr. Svann let out a small breath. "I take it, then, that everything remains current?"

"Completely," Stephen said.

Dr. Svann nodded. She ran a finger over her tablet, then looked across to Stephen again. "Unless there's anything else you want to address," she said, "I suppose we're ready to wrap this up."

Stephen shook his head; of course he did. He stood, and Dr. Svann did, too. She reached across the table and shook his hand. "Good luck," she told him.

At the time, I thought it was kind of an odd way to end the meeting. Later I realized that what she was actually saying was goodbye.

I drove home, and waited in the lot while Stephen picked up his prescriptions; he always went in by himself. He'd said, once, that he had so many controlled substances it was better not to bring anyone with him, but I think it was just one of those sad things that he simply found too hard to share. Even when he'd still felt relatively well, refilling prescriptions for almost a dozen different medications in the same day must have been a hell of a reminder of how ill he was, really.

Back home, in his room, he shuffled through the little bags, lining up all the bottles along his desk—all except one. He pivoted to the right and opened his nightstand drawer, which I'd never seen open before. It was lined with bottles, eight or nine of them—more, even, than the desk had—and all with the same word on their side. Secobarbital, straight. It didn't even have a trade name.

Stephen looked up at me as he tossed the last one in. "I'll get rid of the old bottles," he said, "don't worry. They're past date by now. But of course they'll still work." He swallowed, and then looked away. "It takes a lot more," he said quietly, "than you can get here in one prescription. I've been saving a long time."

Friday while Stephen was sleeping, I went home for lunch. Tammy was there, too; my parents came home at the same time and we all ate together. Tammy kept wiggling in her chair and smiling at me; she was, I think, somehow under the impression that only she was aware of my "sneaking out."

Of course Mom and Dad knew the truth, but they never said anything. I knew it was because if Tammy realized our parents knew where I really was, she'd have wanted an explanation. No one wanted to explain to Tammy that I was allowed to sleep over at Stephen's every night because he was about to die. I didn't even want to acknowledge it.

I pretended, instead, that our parents were exceptionally

tolerant, forward-thinking. Mom actually might have been. Dad wasn't; I assumed he must have convinced himself Stephen was too terminal to pose any threat to my virtue, or whatever else it was that concerned him.

I don't know what Stephen's parents thought. I guess they probably felt they weren't in a position where they wanted to deny their son anything. Anything, at least, of the few remaining things he could still have.

When I got back, early afternoon, he met me in the kitchen, bleary-eyed. He asked if I'd eaten, and I said I had. When I asked him the same thing, he said no. "I could make you a sandwich," I said. He still told me what to put on, but he hadn't made one himself in weeks.

He shook his head and leaned against the fridge. "Solids don't really do it for me any more."

I didn't know what to say.

After a moment, he reached out toward me with one hand. "Would you kiss me?" he said; I nodded. "On the counter."

So I sat on the counter, and wrapped my legs around his waist. For a moment he leaned his head against my shoulder, then looked back up. "Kiss me hard," he said. "If you could make me bleed—in a non-biting way—that'd be fantastic."

I looked at him.

"Sometimes I just want to feel pain," he said, "and know, absolutely, that it's absolutely unrelated."

I kissed him as hard as I could. He barely responded.

I woke up with my face pressed in between his shoulder blades, his arms held tight under mine. On the bedside table, his watch was beeping. Stephen had reached backward, awkwardly, and was shaking my arm. "Emily," he was saying. "Em. You've got to let go."

"I wish you were here," I whispered.

"I know," he said back. "I know. I do, too."

His watch began to beep with intensified volume. I released him, and he slipped over to the bed's other side, away from me. He stopped the watch. He—slowly, painfully—swallowed his ground-up pills.

He turned back over, propping himself up on one arm to look at me. "Thank you," he said. "For all this."

"Stephen," I said.

He smiled. It didn't quite wrinkle his eyes.

Later, he turned over in my arms, facing me. "You know, I was thinking. Early detection of cancer is so important. Which is why I'm going to show you how to do a breast self-exam."

"Really," I said, as flatly as I could.

"That's pretty much the only cancer-related pick-up line I know," he admitted. "And I very much doubt anyone has ever used it with success."

"All right, then," I said.

"All right?" he repeated. He sounded surprised. But I wasn't about to tell him no. He seemed almost normal then. Almost. "Take off your top," he said after a moment, assertive. "And you'll need to put your arm up above your head."

I did, but I let him do my bra. He seemed to enjoy doing that, when he could.

He ran a hand slowly over each of my breasts, the ends of his fingers moving rapidly up and down, almost as if he was typing. It was ticklish at first, then faintly arousing. But mostly it just felt a bit strange.

"How do you even know how to do this?" I asked partway through. "You don't have breasts."

"I've told you, I read a lot," he said. "Also, one clinic I went to, early on, used to play horrible informational videos in their waiting room. The breast exam was the only one I could ever stand to look at. Although I do know how to do a testicular exam as well. We can explore that later if you'd like."

I didn't dignify that with a response.

"Seriously, though," Stephen said. "You do know this?"

"Theoretically," I said. I felt awful. When your boyfriend is dying of cancer, it's beyond irresponsible not to be checking yourself for it.

Momentarily, Stephen's fingers stopped. "You have to," he said sternly. "Once a month. Please."

"Okay," I said. And I knew that now, I really would.

"What I'm doing," he told me, "is essentially the same as what they'd do if you went to a doctor. Just like this. But the doctor's only annual. You have to check more regularly, and if you know your own body, you're the one best equipped anyway to detect irregularities."

"Okay," I said again.

After a while he reached the middle of my chest, having completed both breasts. I hadn't thought he'd actually finish. "I think you're safe," he said, and his hand rested briefly on my solar plexus.

But then it moved back up, not the typewriter movement this time. "Under normal circumstances," he said, voice low, "a medical professional wouldn't use their tongue. But," he said, and shifted next to me, "I think we can make an exception in this case, don't you?"

"Yes," I agreed. "Yes, I think we can."

It was the saddest thing, maybe, I've ever done. It was sad, and that's all. There's nothing beautiful about dying.

"Hey, Emily?" Stephen said. He looked over at me in the semi-dark.

"Yeah?" I said back.

"Remember Trevor?" he asked.

I nodded; I remembered. Chav Trevor, the hypothetical, alternate reality version of Stephen, who might've managed to get a hand in my pants, so long ago. It had seemed an almost insurmountable achievement then.

"All those things I said…" he started. "I really meant—I only ever thought it up because I always wondered, just a little, if I'd've been called Trevor, things would've been different, and maybe I wouldn't have… this."

I moved toward him and put my hand on his arm.

"It's easy to wonder, of course," he said. "And of course I'll never know. But—do you think things would've been better?"

"I think it's impossible to know," I told him. "Unless we went back in time, and your parents gave you a different name. And it could've still happened, anyway. And then you wouldn't be Stephen."

"Do you ever wish you could go back?" he said. "Do you ever wonder, what would've happened if you'd ignored me, or told me no, or even, you know, just decided to buy Tammy a candy bar from the vending machine?"

"No," I told him.

"But what if you could go back? Even further than that, if you wanted. Before all this—you wouldn't have to do all this. You'd go, wouldn't you? You'd trade? You can't say this is what you'd choose."

"But I would," I said. "I wouldn't lose you."

He took a long breath, drawing in his energy. I hardly noticed him breathing any more, not because it wasn't noticeable, but because I'd so quickly gotten used to it. It was only when he inhaled, so deep, like that, that I remembered anything was wrong—that breaths weren't supposed to be apneic, or even audible; that you weren't supposed to fight to inhale; that it wasn't supposed to hurt.

"I'm going to ask you something," he said finally, "and I want you to promise. All right? When I used to ask you what you wanted—when you find it, when you figure out what it is you want—I want you to take what you've got, and go with it. It's yours now," he said. "It's all yours."

"All right," I said. "I promise."

He swallowed.

"Is there anything—" I said, and he shook his head.

On the nightstand by his head was a glass of water, a spoon, little envelopes containing the pulverized pills that were all, now, he could manage to swallow. I guessed he knew which ones they were.

He put his hand up on mine, and we lay there for a while. I waited for him to close his eyes first, but he never did. "Emily," he said finally, and I could hear him gathering his breath again.

"Yeah?"

"Please," he said. "Can you sleep at home tonight?"

"Are you sure?" I asked. But I knew already what he was going to say.

"I'm sure," he said, and his voice, in that moment, was perfect.

"All right," I told him.

And that was all.

CPSIA information can be obtained at www.ICGtesting.com
Printed in the USA
LVOW08*1442010716

494929LV00009B/54/P